Dead on Dartmoor

a&b

Dead on Dartmoor

STEPHANIE AUSTIN

Allison & Busby Limited
11 Wardour Mews
London W1F 8AN
allisonandbusby.com

First published in Great Britain by Allison & Busby in 2019.
This paperback edition published by Allison & Busby in 2020.

A CIP catalogue record for this book is available from
the British Library.

10 9 8 7 6 5 4 3 2 1

ISBN 978-0-7490-2452-9

Typeset in 10.5/15.5 pt Sabon LT Pro by
Allison & Busby Ltd.

The paper used for this Allison & Busby publication
has been produced from trees that have been legally sourced
from well-managed and credibly certified forests.

Printed and bound by
CPI Group (UK) Ltd, Croydon, CR0 4YY

For Dad, who would have loved this

AUTHOR'S NOTE

The town of Ashburton is real, and people living there will recognise streets, shops, pubs, cafes and other places of good cheer mentioned in this book, but there are a few foggy areas around the town where fact and my imagination merge, places that will not be found on any map. For taking these liberties, I apologise.

CHAPTER ONE

A week before the murder, my van went up in flames.

It seemed fine in the morning, when I took the dogs out. I only had three to walk that day and I collected them in the van as usual, before their owners left for work, and drove them to the woods beyond the edge of town where they could romp around unfettered.

They raced ahead of me in the cool shade beneath the trees, sniffing at trails left by night-time creatures, snuffling at prints in the soft, dark mud. As I followed, they dashed off through the undergrowth, bursting from beneath the shadows onto sunlit grass and sending strutting black crows flapping into the air. Here, in open pasture, I could launch balls for them to chase. I could see up the valley, fields sweeping upward to the moor, green grass fading to tawny yellow and the granite knuckle of a distant tor. It was going to be another fine day.

Later I deposited two of the dogs back at their homes, using spare keys to let myself in.

I don't have a spare key for EB, because his mum is always waiting for him at home. But as we approached her front door, I could see a scrawled note taped to the wood. *Juno*, it read, *Alan taken to hospital with chest pain. I've gone with him in ambulance. Can you hang on to EB until I get back? I will ring you. Sorry. Elaine x*

EB waited patiently by my feet as I read the message, his overarching eyebrows twitching in confusion. He didn't seem to mind getting back into the van. I let him sit on the front seat with me instead of putting him in the back behind the wire grille where the dogs normally ride. He leant the weight of his warm little body against mine and I turned back to Ashburton, meandering between hedgerows in full green flourish.

It had been a long, hot summer that seemed as if it would never end, sunshine and blue skies lasting through September. But the swallows had flown, and although the sunny weather continued, the green treetops were brushed with bronze and gold; the leaves were on the turn.

I was forced to brake suddenly. A woman was in the road, standing perfectly still, a few inches of floral nightdress hanging down beneath her long blue dressing gown. Her hair was a silver halo but flattened at the back of her skull, as if it had not been brushed since her head left the pillow that morning. I pulled on the handbrake and climbed out, shutting the door on the muzzle of a curious EB. Despite the noise of the van's approach she seemed oblivious of my presence, staring up at the flickering light through the trees above her, at the shifting shadows, and murmuring quietly to herself.

'Hello,' I called out. 'Are you all right?' She turned at the sound of my voice, not by twisting her head, but by a series of tiny, rocking steps, until she had manoeuvred herself around to face me. Her eyes were blue, her skin rose petals crushed into a thousand tiny wrinkles. She would have been pretty once.

'Can I help you?' I asked.

She scowled at me, didn't answer. A few hundred yards further along the road was Oakdene, a care home for patients with dementia, and I reckoned I was looking at an escapee. 'Only, if you're going for a walk,' I went on reasonably, 'I think you'll need your slippers.'

She gazed down at feet wrapped in woolly bedsocks and wriggled her toes experimentally before returning her gaze to my face. It was an untroubled gaze, full of childlike innocence, as if all care, all stress, had been gently washed away. She reached out. For a moment I thought she was going to slap me, but instead she grabbed a handful of my curls, squeezing lightly with her fingers. 'All curly,' she breathed in delight, 'all red.'

All curly, all red – she'd just about summed up my hair.

'You're not Samantha,' she told me, although she didn't sound sure.

'No, I'm Juno. What's your name?'

'Marianne,' she declared after a moment's thought. 'Are we going in the little bus?'

I glanced back at the van. It was yellow with black writing on the sides. I suppose it didn't look unlike a small bus, except for EB frowning at us from behind the steering wheel.

'Why don't we?'

She allowed me to lead her to the passenger door and sit her in the seat, despite being hampered by EB, who'd decided

11

that any friend of mine must be a friend of his. Fortunately, Marianne didn't seem to mind an enthusiastic face licking, and responded with cries of rapture and much patting. In spite of the two of them, I managed to get her seat belt done up and headed for Oakdene, hoping to God that was where Marianne had come from. If she hadn't, I didn't have a clue where to take her next, and somehow I had the feeling that she wouldn't know either.

Thankfully, the next bend revealed two ladies in blue uniforms peering anxiously into the hedgerows as they scurried along, as if hoping to find something hidden amongst the brambles and blackberries. I stopped, flashed my lights and tooted at them. At the sight of my passenger one cried out in relief. 'Oh, thank God! Judith!'

Judith? What happened to Marianne?

The woman approaching on my side began talking as I wound the window down. The name badge pinned to her ample bosom identified her as Barbara. She was a comfy, little body and was slightly out of breath. 'Thank you so much! Where did you find her?'

'Not far,' I answered as Judith-Marianne climbed out with the help of her colleague, who was younger and taller, her hair scraped back to reveal a large, pale forehead. 'Has she gone walkabout before?'

'All the time, bless her! She keeps trying to find her way to her old home . . . Oxford,' she added in a whisper.

I'm not sure how many miles away Oxford is, but it's a long way from Ashburton.

I watched her depart without a backward glance to me or EB, her arm linked companionably with that of the care assistant, the two of them chatting amiably. 'She seems happy enough.'

'Oh, she's a sweetheart,' Barbara informed me. 'Anyway, thank you so much . . . um . . .'

'Juno.'

'Juno,' she repeated. She hesitated a moment, brows drawn together in a worried frown, her lips compressed in a line. 'I wonder . . . our boss doesn't know she's got out again. We don't want to see her locked in her room. I wonder if . . .'

'Your secret's safe with me.' I didn't know the boss of Oakdene and I certainly wasn't about to go round there causing trouble.

'Thank you,' she breathed and then hurried off after Judith-Marianne and her colleague.

'Life is full of strange little happenings,' I informed a mystified EB, watching them go, and we set off once again towards the town.

I was half an hour late arriving at *Old Nick's* because I'd driven home on the way to check my answering machine for any message from Elaine. She might not have been able to contact me on my mobile: the signal is dodgy on Dartmoor, to say the least.

There was no message. I wondered if EB had been fed before we went walkies this morning, or whether he was still awaiting his breakfast, so I stopped at the baker's in West Street and bought him a jumbo sausage roll.

Old Nick's has only been open for two months. The shop belonged to an elderly client of mine, Mr Nikolai, who lived in the flat above. He was an antiques dealer. Unfortunately,

Nick was a bit criminal around the edges and got himself murdered as a consequence. Why he decided to leave the entire property to me is still a mystery. I suppose he felt I'd earned it; a feeling not shared by members of his family.

Whatever, it is no longer the shabby, run-down old junk shop it once was, but is now freshly painted in pale green, its windows glossy, and *Old Nick's*, picked out in gold, swinging on the sign above the door. Each time I draw up outside it I cannot resist a tiny stab of pride and offer up a silent prayer of gratitude to cousin Brian, my one remaining relative, who'd come up with the cash for the makeover.

Unfortunately, no amount of cash could magically transport *Old Nick's* from Shadow Lane to North Street or East Street, where it needed to be to bring in the required customers. The little town of Ashburton is one of the four stannary towns on Dartmoor, where locally mined tin used to be stamped and assayed, and the townspeople are proud of its history. It also had a reputation for drunkenness. Nowadays it's a real tourist trap, with more antique shops than taverns; but *Old Nick's* is obstinately stuck around the corner from the scene of all the action. The only other businesses in Shadow Lane are a launderette and an undertaker, so there's not a lot of footfall. Generally, people who don't own washing machines are not in the market for the art, crafts and antiques which we sell, and those who need the services of an undertaker have lost interest in buying things altogether. I've placed a hopeful cafe board at the corner of the lane, pointing the way for customers. *Old Nick's: Art, Crafts, Books, Antiques and Collectibles.*

Another problem is that when Nick died and left me the shop, I already had a business of my own. Not exactly thriving, but it kept body and soul together. *Juno Browne, Domestic Goddess – Housework, Gardening, Home Help, Domestic Care, House-sitting, Pet-sitting, Dog walking. No job too small.* The legend is still proudly proclaimed on the sides of my van. I don't want, and can't afford, to give my business up: I'm too attached to some of my clients, and until there's sufficient income from the shop I can't even consider it – and that day, I fear, is a long way off. The stuff I sell is mostly bric-a-brac and the profits so far amount to pocket money, whilst the overheads for the shop are draining money I rely on to live.

One sensible move I could make, apart from just selling the property and pocketing the cash, would be to give up the flat I currently rent from Adam and Kate and move myself into the empty rooms above the shop. But I can't bring myself to do that. I'm not of a nervous disposition, but I just don't fancy living in the room where Nick was murdered. Not yet, anyway, not unless I have to.

The lights were on inside the shop when I arrived, and I could see Pat arranging her display of craft items on one of the wide windowsills. She gave me a little wave. I let EB trot into the shop ahead of me. He pattered over to her and began an exhaustive inspection of her trainers. She and her sister and brother-in-law run a sanctuary for abandoned pets and farm animals and her shoes are covered in information of great interest to the canine mind.

I was surprised to see her, though. 'I thought Sophie was opening up today.'

'It was her turn,' Pat stooped to stroke EB as he snuffled around her shoelaces, 'but she got offered a shift at The Dartmoor Lodge so I said I'd swop with her. I don't mind.'

15

Sophie and Pat man the shop on alternate days, instead of paying me rent. They get free space to sell the lovely things they make, and I get the time to keep my business going. The downside is that I don't get any money.

I've divided the shop into several rental units, hoping to attract a variety of sellers under one roof. Sophie and Pat take up the front of the shop, with two other units behind theirs. My own unit is at the back, in what was once the old storeroom. A sign in the corridor points to it: *This way for bric-a-brac, antiques and collectibles* – an optimistic way of describing a few sticks of junk furniture and an assortment of cheap knick-knacks.

As yet, the only other unit that is taken, and the only one paying me rent, belongs to Gavin, who sailed past the window on his bike at that moment, clad in pointy helmet and full racing gear, like a Lycra-covered stick insect on wheels. I don't know why he dresses up as if he's riding in the Tour de France, he only lives five minutes' ride away. What, I ask, is wrong with cycle clips?

Pat rolled her eyes at the sight of him. 'He's driving Sophie up the wall,' she whispered.

Gavin would be chaining up his bike in the alleyway at the side of the building and would not appear for at least five minutes; even so, I whispered. 'Is he?'

'He's got . . . you know . . . a *thing* about her,' she mouthed. 'He won't leave her alone, always hovering, looking over her shoulder when she's working.'

Sophie didn't really like painting in the shop as customers tended to watch her working, which she found unsettling. She was prepared to put up with it if it might lead to a sale, but wasn't keen on people who hung around too long, stood too close, or chattered too much. She got all three with Gavin.

I could understand why she attracted him. Sophie was twenty-five but could pass for seventeen without make-up – and carried an air of childlike vulnerability. An orphaned seal pup abandoned on an ice floe could not melt your heart more easily than Sophie Child when she turned her big brown eyes on you. They even worked on me, for God's sake, so what chance did a poor sap like Gavin stand? Gavin, nineteen, but with all the emotional maturity of a twelve-year-old, was no match for her at all.

I looked down at the artwork that currently occupied Sophie's desk, the thick watercolour paper pinned at the corners. It was one of her hedgerow paintings: a drystone wall, its rough, mossy stones seen through a delicate tracery of wild flowers, some, as yet, white and unpainted.

Gavin appeared in the doorway, tall and bespectacled, carrying his silly helmet. EB let out a little yip and he scowled. I don't think Gavin liked dogs. 'Where's Sophie?' was his first question.

'Good morning, Gavin, and how are you?' I asked pleasantly.

'Isn't she coming in today?' Poor boy, his disappointment was obvious.

'She'll be in later. She's waitressing on breakfasts at The Dartmoor Lodge.'

'I don't know why she wants to bother with that,' he sneered loftily, 'wasting her talent.'

'She's gotta live, Gavin,' Pat told him flatly. 'We can't all go to the bank of Mum and Dad.'

He grunted, colouring slightly, and hurried through the

17

door at the back of the shop and up the stairs, to change. There was a bathroom on the landing, once part of Nick's flat, and we used his old kitchen for making refreshments.

'Now he'll be half an hour changing,' Pat complained, 'and then he'll come down with a cup of coffee, you'll see. Never offers to make one for anyone else.'

I couldn't hang around to find out; I had clients to get to. 'Look, Pat, I don't want to leave EB in the van, can I dump him with you? I can put him up in the kitchen if you'd rather.' But EB had already settled down by her chair and I handed her the slightly greasy paper bag containing his breakfast.

The Brownlows were a husband and wife team of GPs with three teenage children and a breezy, devil-may-care attitude to safety and hygiene in the home that I fervently hoped did not extend into their professional lives. I spent half of my allotted two hours washing dishes – the dishwasher was already full – before I could reach the kitchen surfaces I was paid to clean. But after I'd scraped brown gloop out of a gravy boat and cleared up spattered globules of pink icing after someone who'd made a cake, I attacked the waiting worktops and the floor, and left the kitchen looking sparkling; temporarily, at least. I just had time to call in on Maisie, check her agency carer had arrived to help her bathe and dress, change her bedclothes and stuff them in the laundry basket, before I headed out again. I did an hour's ironing for Simon the accountant who likes the collars of his shirts *just so*, and made it back to *Old Nick's* a little before midday.

Sophie had obviously arrived, her jacket and bag hanging on her chair; but there was no sign of her. Gavin was sitting at the table of his unit, hidden behind one of his graphic novels, and Pat was concentrating ferociously on counting stitches on her knitting needle. Neither of them spoke. There was, to say the least of it, an atmosphere.

EB skipped over to greet me, his claws clicking on the wooden floor.

'Where's Sophie?' I asked.

'Upstairs.' Pat directed a fierce glance at Gavin. 'Trying to rescue her painting.'

I flicked another look at Gavin, whose ears were suspiciously pink, and climbed the stairs to the kitchen. Sophie was by the sink, her painting laid out on one of the worktops, dabbing at it carefully with a sponge.

'What happened?'

'Bloody Gavin,' she responded, not looking up. 'He would bring me a cup of coffee. I told him I didn't want one. Then he put it down on my table and knocked it over with his sleeve.'

'Has he ruined it?'

'I'd already covered these with masking fluid,' she said, pointing at the white, unpainted stalks of cow parsley, 'so they were protected. But some of this background will need repainting.'

'Oh, Soph, it's taken you ages! What did you say to him?'

'Not much. I didn't need to.' She chuckled. 'Pat gave him a real ear-bashing.' She pushed her big red-framed specs up the bridge of her tiny nose. 'Well, you know what she's like.'

Pat was one of most generous and kind people I knew, but she seemed to have it in for Gavin. 'I hope she doesn't piss him off too much, I don't want him to leave. I need his rent money.'

'It's one of those days, I suppose.' Sophie blotted a tiny

flower with a corner of paper towel. 'I was supposed to be taking some stuff to that new arts centre near Dartmeet. I got it all packed up, ready to go.' She turned her dark eyes on me mournfully. 'But I'll have to cancel, I can't get there now.'

'Why not?'

'Mum's had to work and has taken the car.'

'I'll take you.' I heard the words come out of my mouth before I'd even thought about it.

Sophie continued to gaze at me soulfully. 'Don't you have to work this afternoon?'

'I said I'd help Ricky and Morris, but they won't mind. I can put some time in for them later. I'll give them a call.'

I'd kept Nick's old phone in his living room, sitting on the floor. Like the bedroom, it was empty, cleared of his furniture, walls painted, floorboards sanded down and varnished, new spotlights in the ceiling: just waiting to be rented by traders or to be moved into by me. Pat was of the opinion that the rooms were haunted; at least that's what she told Gavin to wind him up. I'm not sure I believe in ghosts, but I still couldn't walk into those rooms without thinking of Nick, hearing his chuckle, seeing his wicked blue eyes. My call made, I went back down into the shop.

'Gavin,' Pat called out when I appeared, 'what have you got to remember to tell Juno?'

He looked up from his reading, returning to the real world after a definite pause. 'What?'

'What happened yesterday?' Pat insisted.

'Oh . . . yes,' he responded, peering vaguely through his specs as if struggling to remember. 'Some woman came in, enquiring about a unit.'

'Great!' I was instantly cheered at the possibility of more rent. 'What does she do?'

He shrugged. 'I don't know. I told her she'd have to come back when you were here.'

'Well, did you take her number?'

'No . . . sorry,' he added, in the voice of someone who really couldn't give a shit and tried to return to his reading.

'Well, if she comes in again, or if anyone else comes in enquiring, will you be sure to take their details, please? I need to fill these units.'

'Oh? Yes, of course.'

'And by the way,' I added, addressing the room in general, 'I had eighteen pounds extra in my cash box last night. Someone must have taken a sale for me yesterday. Does anyone know what it was?'

'That was me.' Gavin was beginning to look sheepish. 'You sold a silver thing . . . a rounded knife, bone handle . . . um . . . bit like an apple corer.'

'That would have been the stilton scoop,' I told him, 'it would have been written on the label.' I was trying not to lecture him but failing miserably. 'That's why we all label everything, Gavin, so we can keep track of sales. Next time, please write the details in the book on the counter. That's what it's for.' It was a simple enough system if we all followed it. Poor Gavin; if I'd had any idea what terrible things were about to happen, I like to think I'd have been more patient with him, more understanding of his complete lack of interest, his callow lack of charm – but probably not.

* * *

21

Once we'd loaded Sophie's paintings, we put EB in the back of the van. He wanted to ride in the front, but dogs tend to make Sophie wheeze, although EB's mum would have pointed out indignantly that Miniature Schnauzers' coats never shed hair. But I made Sophie check she had her inhaler with her before we left, I know what she's like. We weren't taking any of her big hedgerow pictures, but some of her miniatures: charming studies of birds, bees, dragonflies and amphibians. We took boxes of these together with a portfolio containing prints of her larger works. She had, after a great deal of nagging from me, begun to paint pet portraits, but so far EB was her sole commission.

We took the road to Buckland. No sooner had we climbed the wooded hill towards the church and farmland opened out beneath a wide blue sky, than an irritating ping from my bag announced my mobile phone had returned to the land of the living, and a fuzzy buzzing noise told me that a call was coming in. 'I bet that's Elaine. Have a look, will you?'

By the time Sophie had dug the phone out of my bag, it had switched to voicemail. She listened as I pulled into a gateway to let a farm vehicle pass in the narrow road, a huge machine with spiky arms folded up in front of the cab like the claws of a praying mantis, something to do with hay cutting, probably: the long, dry spell meant that many farmers locally had managed a second cut.

'Alan's fine,' she reported, phone to her ear, as the deeply cut treads of the machine's giant tyres rolled past my window, bending my wing mirror out of position. 'He's had a stent fitted and he's staying in hospital for a couple of nights. Elaine's home and you can take EB back whenever you like.'

'Would you text her and say I'll be an hour or two?'

She nodded and got busy with her thumbs.

After we'd left Sophie at the collection of old stone farm buildings, which had been converted into the new gallery and arts centre, I took EB for another walk. At the end of the lane we sat on a drystone wall and gazed over fields of stubble scattered with golden rolls of hay. A second crop had been harvested here. In the distance, a machine was lifting the rolled bales into a pile, wrapping them in black plastic ready for silage, an activity we didn't usually see in September.

Back to the arts centre, where we waited for Sophie in the shiny new cafe and tested their crumbly apple cake. She appeared after another twenty minutes, grinning broadly and empty-handed except for her portfolio.

'They're taking all my paintings,' she announced happily, 'sale or return.'

I offered tea and cake in celebration but she declined, and we decided to get going. I put EB into the back of the van, but Sophie decided to hang on to her portfolio and we started off for home.

'This is going to deplete your stock at the shop,' I said, after we'd rattled over a cattle grid and turned onto the road that led home across the moor. The rough grass on either side was parched after the drying winds of summer, the leaves of stunted hawthorn bushes already withering and yellow. 'You're going to have to get busy with that paintbrush.'

'Actually,' she admitted after a sly, sideways glance at me, 'they asked for some local scenes.'

I groaned. 'Isn't that what I'm always telling you?' I took

my hand off the wheel to wave an arm at the rolling grandeur of the moor around us, a ragged granite tor like a ruined castle snagging the horizon. 'Local scenes sell!'

She ignored this completely and switched on the radio.

'Honestly, Soph, what's wrong with painting Buckland Church or Hound Tor?'

'Everybody does it!' she said dismissively. This was an argument we'd had before. 'Can you smell burning?'

'Don't change the subject. What about some paintings of Ashburton? I've got lovely photos of St Andrew's churchyard in the snow . . . Yes I can!' There was a definite whiff of burning and a blue haze was rapidly filling the cab. 'I'm going to pull over.' I'd barely made it to the verge before tiny bright flames began licking their way up from under the dashboard. Sophie dabbed at them ineffectually with her fingers.

'Out!' I ordered her, switching off the engine. 'Get out now!'

She already had the passenger door open, her portfolio clutched to her chest. Smoke was pouring from under the dashboard, hot and black. I had just the time to rescue my bag from the footwell. I held my breath and grabbed the vehicle's paperwork from the glove compartment. 'Ring the fire brigade!' I yelled, coughing. 'I'll get EB out of the back.'

CHAPTER TWO

I count that moment when I tried the handle on the back door of the van and it refused to turn as one of the worst of my life so far. It had never stuck before. I jiggled it. It wouldn't budge. I pressed down hard. Inside the van EB was barking, trying to tell me how wrong things were.

'It's OK, EB!' I called. But it wasn't. I yanked on the handle, bracing one foot on the adjoining door to give myself extra pulling power. The smoke from the engine was blowing back towards me, rolling over the roof of the van, stinging my eyes, making me cough. It must be filling up inside. I looked around me desperately for a stick, anything I could use for leverage. Behind me I could hear Sophie screaming down the phone.

There was a fist-sized lump of granite lying in the ditch and I picked it up, raised it in both hands and clobbered the handle with it. No good. I could hear EB scrabbling at the door with his claws, whimpering to be let out. I rushed to the front of the van. Could I get back inside and rip out the grille behind the driver's seat, get him out that way? But I couldn't get near it. Choking black smoke belched from the open doors; it would be impossible to see, let alone breathe. Orange flames were shooting up from under the bonnet, the air above quivering with heat, with a suffocating smell of boiling oil and melting plastic, of engine fluids sizzling, getting way too hot. How long before the fire brigade could get here? There was a retained service at Ashburton, but by the time they were mustered it would be too late for poor EB. There was a bang from the engine, the bonnet burst open, flames and sparks spiralling into the sky. Those sparks could set the dry countryside alight. I didn't care. All I cared about was EB.

I tried the stone again, raising it above my head. I could hear the terrible sounds of EB choking. *Don't let him burn*, I whispered to whatever god might be listening, *please, don't let him burn*. I brought the stone crashing down, feeling the shockwave up my arms. Sophie was running about in the road, screeching. I tried the rock again. Dimly I heard a voice ordering me to stand back. It barely registered before I was thrust aside and a fist with a lump hammer in it struck a mighty blow at the lock. The door burst open and smoke poured from inside as EB's inert little body was hauled out and carried to the side of the road. I followed, dazed.

A Cherokee Jeep was parked a few yards behind us, its doors wide open. Sophie must have flagged it down. Its driver was laying EB down on the grassy verge. An older man, in baggy tweed jacket and a flat cap, was approaching my blazing van with a car fire extinguisher.

'He's not dead?' I knelt down next to EB.

His rescuer was rubbing EB's furry chest. 'Come on, little fella,' he kept saying encouragingly. 'Come on.' But EB didn't move.

'EB, please!' I begged stupidly.

Sirens in the distance announced the fact that the fire brigade was coming. A few moments later it arrived, blue lights flashing, air brakes hissing as the engine drew to a halt. Suddenly the road was full of men in yellow helmets and big boots, and hoses unreeling; all too late for my van.

'Got a casualty, have we?' A young fireman squatted down by the roadside and then yelled over his shoulder. 'Ed! Bring out the MARS, will you?'

The MARS turned out to be a resuscitation machine about the size of a diver's air tank. The fireman fitted a plastic mask over EB's muzzle and turned on the oxygen. After a few heart-stopping moments, EB's head jerked, and he snuffled and coughed his way back to life.

'Oh, thank God!' I cried, as he raised his head. The fireman gave EB a few more deep breaths of oxygen before he removed the mask, by which time his patient was already trying to scrabble it off his nose with his front paws.

'He'll be fine,' he assured me, picking up his machine. I drew EB onto my lap and cuddled him hard, rubbing my face into his smoky-smelling fur.

'And the next!' the fireman called out cheerfully. It was only then I looked around for Sophie. She was sitting in a heap on the grass verge, white-faced and in serious danger of overdosing on her inhaler.

'Oh, Soph!' I hurried over, clutching EB in my arms like a baby. 'Are you all right?'

'The petrol tank won't explode, will it?' she gasped nervously as the van gave vent to a belch of black smoke.

'Contrary to what they'd have you believe in films,' the fireman replied a little severely, as he fitted the mask over her face, 'petrol tanks rarely explode.'

I looked around for our rescuer, but he was standing by his jeep, barking orders into his mobile phone. His companion, the old guy with the flat cap and fire extinguisher, hovered deferentially at his elbow, an air of subservience about him; the younger man was obviously the boss.

So I sat by the roadside, and watched the fire brigade's finest having a wonderful time hosing down the smoking, blackened hulk that had once been my van. Steam rose hissing and fizzing, and shiny rivulets of water ran off the tarmac into the grass.

'I hope you're insured!' one of the fire crew called to me jovially.

Of course I was insured: third party, fire and theft. Trouble was, my insurance company was not going to pay out megabucks for a clapped-out old Astra. It was worth next to nothing. The paint job on the sides had cost more than the vehicle; the paint job that was now just a leprous rash of blisters on scorched and buckled metal.

The fireman with the MARS machine, whose name, he told us, was Andy, had finished with Sophie.

'Will she need to go to hospital?'

'I'm all right,' she assured me wheezily. 'And I'm not going to sit around in casualty for hours just to be told to go home and rest.'

Andy gestured with his mask towards me.

28

'I don't need it.'

'I'll be the judge of that,' he insisted.

'Juno, you do look dreadful,' Sophie added solemnly.

It was only as I breathed in cool, clear oxygen that I realised how sore my chest and throat felt from inhaling scorching smoke. I began to cough. Andy told me to relax and breathe deeply. Whilst I sat there, breathing obediently, he went away and came back with a can with which he sprayed the pads of EB's feet. 'Floor of that van would have been hot,' he remarked in a mastery of understatement. 'This will cool his paws down.'

Sophie put an arm around my shoulders and gave me a hug. 'I'm so sorry about your van. What are you going to do?'

I couldn't answer. I didn't know. I didn't even know how I was going to get us home. The firemen had obviously done all they could. They were rolling up their hoses.

'Well, it could have been worse,' I coughed. 'If this had happened on the way there instead of on the way back, we might have lost all your lovely paintings as well.'

'We got EB out.' Sophie smiled, rubbing his head. 'That's the main thing.'

'Well, someone did.' EB was huddled in my lap, very subdued, very frightened. He licked my hand.

'Ah, ladies!' cried a cheerful voice and we all looked up. The tall figure of EB's saviour was standing in the road in front of us. 'Is everyone OK?'

'Thanks to you,' I told him. 'I can't thank you enough. I—'

He dismissed my thanks with a wave of his hand. 'Not at all,' he said, 'damsels in distress and all that!'

He squatted by us and stroked EB's head. 'How is the little

fellow?' This was the first time I had looked at him properly. He was younger than I'd thought, about my age. Beneath short blonde hair he had lively blue eyes and an engaging smile. He was pretty bloody gorgeous, as a matter of fact.

'Now, what's going to happen is this,' he began, as if he were an army officer addressing chaps about to go on a mission, 'I've phoned a break-down firm and they're sending out a lorry to haul away your van. Well, what's left of it,' he added, grinning. 'It can stay at your local garage until your insurance assessor arrives. Moss,' he indicated the old chap in the flat cap, 'will stand by here until the break-down lorry arrives.'

Moss did not look thrilled, but he was obviously under orders. 'Sir,' he muttered.

'Meantime,' our hero continued, 'I will drive you ladies home.'

'We live in Ashburton.'

'No trouble at all,' he assured me.

'Well, thank you, Mr . . .'

'Jamie.' He held out a large hand. 'Jamie Westershall.'

We shook hands and introduced ourselves. We all stood up. I was still carrying EB, who whimpered when I tried to put him down.

'I'm afraid I shall have to call in at home on the way,' Jamie warned us, as we clambered into the back of the jeep. 'I hope that's not inconvenient.'

The fire brigade were climbing back into their engine and slamming doors. As we pulled away, we left Moss standing gloomily in the road, next to the smouldering, blackened hulk that had once been my pride and joy.

'Um, how will Moss get home?' Sophie asked, turning back to look at him.

'Oh, I don't know,' Jamie responded breezily. 'He'll think of something.' He pulled out his phone as he drove along, obviously unconcerned about the rule of law. 'Danny!' he called loudly after a few seconds. 'James here. You still at Home Farm? About to pack up? Excellent! How did we do? All clear! No reactors at all? Well, that's fantastic news. Listen, you couldn't come up to the house when you're done, could you? I've got a little casualty I'd like you to run your eye over. You can? Splendid!' He disconnected. 'My vet,' he explained, thrusting his phone back into his pocket, 'he's just been checking the herd for TB.'

'You're a farmer?' Sophie asked.

'Well, we have several farms on the estate. I'm more of a farm manager, really.'

We were travelling with the woods of Holne Chase on our left. On the other side, the short grass and granite outcrops of open moorland spread to the horizon, black-faced sheep grazing amongst clumps of gorse still yellow with flowers. We passed a muddy track leading to a farm, and from then on were driving alongside a high stone wall enclosing cultivated woodland, majestic green crowns of mature oaks, beech and hornbeam rising above it. Suddenly the jeep swung between tall stone gateposts. I just glimpsed the legend carved into the stonework as we flashed by, a name I can't remember now without a shudder: Moorworthy House.

CHAPTER THREE

The vast Victorian mansion, at which we arrived after driving through acres of rolling parkland, loomed above us like the setting for a Gothic horror movie: tall chimneys, steeply pitching roofs, gargoyles glaring down from high parapets, balconies with stone balustrades – all haphazard somehow and confusing to the eye.

'Ghastly old pile, isn't it?' Jamie said cheerfully, as we gazed open-mouthed.

'Is this house yours?' Sophie breathed.

'Afraid so.' He grinned. 'I ought to pay someone to set fire to it. Anyway, come in, ladies!' We followed him through an arched doorway into a lofty hall. Oak-panelled walls bristled with antlers and the mounted heads of creatures with tusks and bared teeth. It wasn't exactly welcoming.

'Mrs Johnson!' Jamie called out, striding on ahead of us, his voice echoing around the hall. 'Mrs Johnson? Hello! Anyone at home?'

We trailed behind him, gawping around like tourists in a

stately home as portraits of ancient ancestors stared down at us with obvious disapproval. A wide staircase with heavily carved bannisters swept up to a landing overlooked by a tall stained-glass window letting in patterns of light in rose, green and gold. A brass candelabrum as wide as a wagon wheel hung down from above and a suit of armour lurked on the turn of the stairs.

'Is this place haunted, d'you think?' Sophie murmured.

'Well, if it isn't, it ought to be.'

Just like a ghost a woman materialised quietly from somewhere: dark-haired, smart but workmanlike in a navy skirt and cream blouse.

'Ah, Johnnie,' Jamie called to her affectionately, 'is my uncle or my sister at home?'

'Miss Emma is down at the stables, sir,' she responded quietly, 'but I believe Mr Sandy is in the library.'

'Ah, I'll go and roust the old devil out! These poor ladies,' he went on, indicating Sophie and me, 'have been in an accident. Van caught fire. I wonder if you could come up with some tea in the drawing room?'

'Of course, sir.' She turned to us with raised brows and a smile that didn't reach her eyes. 'Come with me.' I assumed she was a housekeeper or perhaps a secretary. I couldn't quite place her. 'Perhaps you'd like to visit the guest cloakroom first.' She spoke in a tone that didn't brook any argument. 'And when you've finished, the drawing room is over there.' She pointed down the hall, opening the door of the guest cloakroom for us and leaving us no option but to go inside.

I think the guest cloakroom was larger than my flat. Dark panelling gave way to rose-coloured marble, covering the

33

floor and walls and surrounding the washbasins that stood side by side, complete with oversized gold taps and heavily framed gilt mirrors.

I often feel like shrieking at my reflection, but this time it wasn't the mane of untameable red curls that was distressing. My face was black with sooty smudges except for two white tracks where tears had flowed from my red-rimmed eyes. It was no wonder Mrs Johnson didn't want me in the drawing room.

I passed EB over to Sophie whilst I filled the basin and washed my face with the fragrantly expensive hand soap provided. 'My God, I smell like a kipper!' I moaned as I splashed repeatedly.

'You did get well smoked.' Sophie was filling up the adjacent basin. I picked up a snowy-white towel from a pile folded in a basket and rubbed my face with it. It wasn't snowy any longer. Meanwhile EB was enjoying a long, gulping drink from the basin Sophie had filled.

'Poor little boy!' I took him back when he'd finished, his whiskery chops dripping, his eyebrows twitching anxiously.

I gazed at our reflections. Sophie and I are such contrasts. She, small and delicately boned with her neat, dark head: me, tall and – well, 'statuesque' is a word I have heard applied to myself. Standing next to Sophie always makes me feel like a bloody great Valkyrie. 'Am I fit for the drawing room?' I asked.

She made a face. 'Have you got a comb?'

'I can only get a comb through this lot when it's wet.'

She sighed. 'You'll have to do, then.'

We found our way back to the drawing room after

first opening the wrong door which revealed a long empty room with gilded mirrors and an acre of shiny floor: it could only have been a ballroom. 'Bloody hell!' Sophie squeaked in amazement.

The drawing room was large and chintzy with three sofas grouped around a carved marble fireplace wide enough to drive a horse and cart through, a scattering of occasional chairs, a grand piano and long windows opening out onto a wide terrace. Flower arrangements and silver photo frames stood on various tables, porcelain figurines adorned the mantelpiece, oil paintings depicting classical subjects hung on the walls and there was no sign of a television anywhere.

'Do you think we've fallen through a time warp?' Sophie asked. 'What decade are we in?'

'I think we're back in the Agatha Christies.'

I wandered out onto the terrace. A balustrade separated it from the garden, marked every few feet by a heavy stone urn filled with trailing flowers. In front of me a wide lawn stretched away into the distance. Beyond it I could make out the rocky outline of a distant tor, but I couldn't work out which one. We'd taken too many turns since leaving the main road; I had lost my bearings. I turned back to look at the house.

It didn't look so ugly from the back. Much of its granite walls were covered by an ancient wisteria, twisting stems as thick as ships' cables testament to its extreme age. It reached almost to the third-storey windows and must have been a hundred years old. I wished I could have seen it back in May, hanging with clusters of flowers, with dripping waterfalls of blue.

The soft click of the drawing-room door and the faint tinkle of teacups announced the arrival of Mrs Johnson with the tea. She set the tray down on a table by the fireplace.

'Mr Jamie asks you to excuse him for the present,' she said, as she straightened up, 'but he'll be with you before long.'

I put EB down gently on the hearthrug, where he seemed happy to lie. I was afraid Mrs Johnson might feel it necessary to hang around but, to my relief, she headed for the door.

'I think you have everything you need, ladies,' she pointed to the laden tray, 'but if there's anything else you require, just ring.' She indicated a bell push in the corner and went out.

'Do you find her slightly scary?' Sophie whispered when she'd gone.

'Definitely,' I nodded, surveying the silver teapot, dainty china cups and saucers, plate of biscuits and buttered tea-loaf that filled the tray. 'She's got a touch of the Mrs Danvers.'

I turned over a delicate tea plate to look at the maker's marks. 'This is Spode,' I told Sophie as I poured tea and passed her a cup, 'for God's sake don't break anything.' I slipped EB a biscuit. I'd already ruined his figure that morning with the flaky sausage roll, but I can testify to the reviving effect of a biscuit and, sure enough, he showed signs of perking up.

Sophie and I fell on the buttered tea-loaf like a pair of starving gannets. Left to ourselves, we would have demolished the lot, but we were forced to restrain our uncouth behaviour when the door opened again and a jocular voice drifted in from the hall.

'Now, now,' it said, 'I hear we have visitors, two lovely ladies.'

The man who came in, dressed in a dark blazer and yellow cravat, was in his sixties, his purple veined nose and raddled complexion evidence of considerable debauch. He sported a silver comb-over that ended in a tiny little flick above his left ear. He stopped and surveyed us from heavy-lidded eyes. 'How delightful!' He came forward to shake our hands, his own extended. 'No, please don't get up. I'm Jamie's wicked Uncle Sandy,' he informed us proudly, 'how do you do?' His hand was smooth and pale with manicured nails; not a farmer's hand, obviously. He dutifully patted EB, who disgraced himself by growling.

I was shocked, it was so unlike him. 'EB! Mind your manners!' But I didn't blame him: he sensed something about the man I couldn't put a name to, something vaguely unpleasant like the very faint odour of corruption.

He sat down on a sofa. 'Ebee?' he repeated, brows raised faintly.

'EB,' I corrected, 'his initials.'

'What do they stand for?'

'It's a secret, you have to guess.'

'Juno won't tell,' Sophie complained bitterly. 'I've been trying to guess it for the last two years.'

I changed the subject. 'This is a most interesting house.'

'Not mine, my dear,' he answered, puffing out his cheeks. 'It was my elder brother who was the squire. Jamie is the heir – not that I envy him – a crumbling pile of death duties and dry rot, that's what this place is.' He chuckled. 'I used to tell his father he should have sold the lot to the National Trust years ago, but he wouldn't listen. But Jamie's a sensible lad,' he added, laying a finger against his nose, 'he's marrying the money!'

I exchanged a glance with Sophie. Neither of us knew if this was a joke. Meanwhile, Uncle Sandy had begun leafing through the portfolio that Sophie had dropped onto the sofa. 'I say,' he remarked, studying the reproductions of her paintings, 'this is lovely work.' He glanced at me. 'Is this yours?'

I pointed at Sophie. 'Really?' He looked surprised. 'Did you do all these by yourself?'

I have to say that Sophie replied with admirable composure, used, as she is, to being taken for a minor.

'Well, well!' he exclaimed at the portrait of EB and pointed to him on the hearthrug. 'It's this little fella to the life!'

Just then, a young woman strode in from the terrace. For a moment I wondered if she might be the 'money' Jamie was marrying, but the resemblance to her brother was too strong.

'Emma!' Uncle Sandy hailed her breezily. 'How went the dressage?'

'Foul!' she flung back without looking at him, tossing a riding hat onto a chair as she passed. She headed for a table on which stood decanters and began to pour herself what I guessed was gin. A little early in the day, I thought. 'Digby behaved like a fucking brute!'

Ah! Perhaps we weren't in the Agatha Christies, after all.

Emma was stunning: slim with straight, gleaming blonde hair drawn back into an elegant chignon. She wore thigh-hugging breeches, a fitting black coat, and a white stock tight around her swan-like neck. She turned, glass in hand, and for the first time registered our presence. She stared at Sophie and me as if we'd come in on the sole of her riding boot. Her uncle hastily introduced us and explained why we were there. She neither spoke nor smiled, clearly resenting our presence. 'Look, Em, look at this,' he went on, showing her the photo of EB's portrait. 'It's that little fella there. Hasn't little Sophie captured him to the life?'

She glanced at it over his shoulder. 'It's quite a good likeness, I suppose,' she admitted grudgingly, then turned her back on all of us and stood, gin in hand, pacing in front of the windows, staring moodily out onto the terrace, as edgy and highly strung as a thoroughbred racehorse.

'Well, I wish Old Thunderer was still alive,' Sandy prattled on, oblivious of her bad manners. 'I'd have loved to have had his portrait.'

Before we could ask who 'Old Thunderer' was, Jamie came into the room accompanied by the vet, who got down on the hearthrug next to EB, listened to his heartbeat and pronounced him perfectly fit. 'He's got a few blisters on his paws,' he said to me, 'best not to walk him for a day or two.' No danger of that, I thought miserably, wondering how I was going to exercise the Tribe next morning with no van to pick them up in.

Shortly after this, we left, Uncle Sandy expressing the hope that he'd see us again, Emma ignoring us, pouring another gin and striding out onto the terrace. 'We've got a garden fete on next week,' he told us, 'why don't you girls come along? Bit of fun, eh?'

We lied through our teeth and promised him we'd think about it. As we followed Jamie back out to the waiting Cherokee, Sophie whispered, 'He's gorgeous isn't he, Jamie?'

'Yes, but it's no good looking at him,' I murmured, 'he's "marrying the money".'

'I wonder who she is.'

'And does the poor girl know she's the money?'

'She may not be *only* the money,' Sophie pointed out, in an effort to be generous. 'Anyway, it makes no difference,' she sighed. 'The only men who are interested in me are perverts.'

'There's Gavin,' I reminded her, and she gave me a dark look.

On the ride home I suggested that she sit in the front with Jamie so that EB and I had more room in the back. 'Your garden goes on for ever,' she observed as we drove through the grounds. 'That lawn must be a mile long.'

He grinned. 'It's a trick of perspective. You have to watch out for the ha-ha.'

'Ha-ha?'

'It's a sunken wall,' he explained. 'You can't see it until you're on the edge of it. By then it's too late. The Victorians were fond of putting them in gardens to help open up their views. They called them "ha-has" because they thought it was so bloody funny when people fell off 'em. Odd what some people find amusing.'

'They didn't have television in those days,' I pointed out.

Jamie laughed. He chatted on, happy to regale us with how extensive the Westershall estate was, how many hectares of land, how many farms it contained, mostly, it seemed, worked by tenants. The grounds of the house were edged on one side by thick woodland, the mature oaks and beeches that we had glimpsed earlier, a long ribbon of woodland walled off from the road. 'This will be a beautiful walk in a week or so,' I said, 'when the leaves have properly turned.'

'There is a footpath through a small section, but most

of the woods are fenced off, I'm afraid. Site of Special Scientific Interest,' Jamie explained. 'Rare bats – we can't have the public wandering about, disturbing them. I don't know much about bats, myself.' He gave a slight shudder. 'I stay well away. But the woods are full of old mine workings, disused shafts. That's another reason we can't have people wandering about – it's dangerous.'

We had driven through the gates by now and were back on the road, although still, Jamie assured us, surrounded by Westershall land. We hadn't gone far when he suddenly brought the jeep to an abrupt halt, cursing. 'Will you look at that!' he cried out in disgust. 'Will you bloody look at that?'

What we were being asked to bloody look at was a narrow track leading off into a farmer's field. The earthen trackway was strewn with rubbish – plastic packing material spilling out of broken cardboard boxes, scraps of paper flung into the hedge and scattered on the ground like dirty confetti. Further off, a torn sofa bursting with foam stuffing lay on its side amongst piles of shattered timber and oil drums. 'These damn fly-tippers!' Jamie slammed out of the car, ordering us to stay put while he went for a closer look. He came back, shaking his head. 'Does it happen a lot round here?' I asked. Things were often dumped on the tiny patch of waste ground at the end of my lane, usually just an old microwave or a shopping trolley, nothing on this scale.

'It's gets worse every year,' Jamie started up the car again. 'Bastards! They'd get what for if I caught them.'

'Don't the police do anything?'

He gave a grim laugh. 'We'll report it, of course. But there's so much of it going on. The police don't have the resources.' He was clearly angry and for a few minutes we travelled in silence.

'I wish they wouldn't wrap hay bales in black plastic,' Sophie remarked idly as we passed a pile of them stacked on the edge of a field. 'They look awful.'

'They're silage.' Jamie still sounded on edge. 'I suppose you're one of those people who want the countryside to look romantic.'

'People who buy my paintings do,' she answered honestly. 'They don't want rolls of black plastic. They want old-fashioned haystacks and wooden wagons piled high with rosy-cheeked children riding on top.'

'Tell me, would a combine harvester be allowed in one of your paintings?'

'Certainly not!'

'What about an old tractor,' he asked, 'a vintage John Deere, for example?'

Sophie considered for a moment. 'Only if it's rusty,' she decided.

Jamie threw his head back and laughed. They were getting on well, these two, I thought. And he was marrying the money; shame.

CHAPTER FOUR

'What sort of bleedin' time do you call this to turn up?' Ricky demanded acidly. 'You're a day and a half late.'

'My van caught fire and nearly cooked a dog.'

Just for a moment he hesitated, blue eyes narrowed, not sure if I was serious, then he grabbed my arm, pulled me inside, propelling me across the patterned marble floor of the hallway, past piles of cardboard boxes, towards the breakfast room.

'Maurice!' he bellowed up the stairs. 'Get your arse down here! You'll want to hear this! I'm putting the kettle on. Sit,' he pushed me down into a chair at the breakfast table, 'and don't say another word until Morris gets here!'

I did as I was told, sitting mutely, lusting after Morris's teapot collection proudly displayed on the Welsh dresser and wishing I had at least one of them for sale in my shop.

Ricky and Morris live in a lovely Georgian house, not on the scale of Moorworthy, but large enough to house them both and their stock of several thousand theatrical costumes.

They run a costume hire business. The cardboard boxes in the hallway were stuffed with World War I uniforms, which they were selling to a film company. They were always moaning about retiring, reducing their vast stock of costumes. At least in selling the uniforms they were making a start, and that was why I was supposed to have been with them the day before: I was meant to be helping with the packing.

Morris arrived, looking slightly flustered after hurrying down the stairs. He and Ricky are as much of a contrast as Sophie and me. Ricky is tall, with iron-grey curls and completely wasted, rugged good looks. Morris is short, fat and bald with little gold specs perched on his nose. They've been together since they met in the theatre as chorus boys.

'What's up?' he puffed.

I recounted my adventures whilst they fussed about making tea and Morris produced a chocolate cake he'd baked the day before.

'Moorworthy House? We've been there!' Ricky told me. 'We did a concert there a few years ago, didn't we, Maurice?' He and Morris performed as Sauce and Slander, a musical double act, usually to raise money for charity. 'We're going there again in a few weeks.'

Morris nodded. 'We are. But you should have phoned us, Juno,' he stared at me reproachfully over his specs, 'we could have popped down and picked you up. You needn't have walked all the way up this hill.'

I had meant to phone them the night before, just hadn't got around to it. Jamie had been wonderful, driving us first to Elaine's house, so that I could deliver EB, and waiting while I explained what had happened and made necessary enquiries about her brother. He was quite prepared to take me and Sophie to our respective homes, but we felt we'd troubled him enough and got him to drop us both back at the shop.

The lights were still on in *Old Nick's* and Pat was on her own, tidying up.

'Has Gavin gone?' I asked, although the answer was obvious.

She gave a grunt of disgust. 'He went half an hour ago.'

We told her about our exciting afternoon. She gasped and looked horrified in all the right places. 'What about you?' I asked her eventually. 'Any customers?'

She shook her head. 'None that bought anything, but that creepy bloke came in again.'

'What creepy bloke?' I asked.

'I don't think Juno will have come across him,' Sophie told Pat. 'I don't think he's been in here when she's been here.'

'What bloke?' I repeated. 'In what way creepy?'

'He only comes in when Gavin's here,' she went on. 'He never buys anything, just sort of hangs about, around Gavin.'

'Lurks,' Pat confirmed, nodding mysteriously. 'And he walks ever so quietly. You never know he's there until he's right behind you.'

'Is he some friend of Gavin's, then?'

'We're not sure,' Sophie went on. 'Gavin's really awkward when he's around. They talk in whispers. You can tell, whenever this man comes in, that Gavin wishes we weren't here.'

'He tried to get rid of me this afternoon,' Pat told us, voice hushed with drama. 'He said to me, "Why don't you

45

go upstairs and have a tea break, Pat? I can look after the shop." Well, I wasn't falling for that, I stayed right here. I wouldn't leave that pair alone down here. God knows what they might get up to!'

'But this creepy bloke has never tried to steal anything?'

Pat's eyes narrowed. 'No, but I don't trust him.'

'Haven't you asked Gavin who he is?'

'That's just it, he won't say,' Sophie explained. 'If you ask him, he changes the subject.'

'What does this man look like?'

She wrinkled her brow in a frown. 'Small and sort of ferrety.'

'Shifty,' Pat added.

I wasn't sure I'd be able to identify him from that description, but I was certain that he hadn't come into the shop when I'd been around. And it wasn't really any surprise to me that Gavin had weird friends. 'Oh, let's go home, girls,' I begged, 'it's been a long day.' And Pat dropped the pair of us off at home.

My flat occupies the upper half of a decrepit Victorian house and the bathroom lacks the facility of a proper shower, so I soaked for a long time in the old enamel bath, repeatedly washing the smell of smoke out of my hair. Then, wrapped in my dressing gown, I flopped down in my chair with a mug of tea. I knew I ought to concoct some kind of supper from whatever scraps were in the fridge, but after apple cake and tea-bread I wasn't that bothered. This was unusual for me as I have an appetite so healthy it glows. I'm not a great cook. My dietary needs are mostly taken care of by my landlords, Adam and Kate, who run a vegetarian cafe, *Sunflowers*, and are very generous with leftovers. Little plastic boxes and parcels wrapped in foil are often left on the table on the landing outside my door, like offerings for some gluttonous god, and I am rarely at a loss for a vegetable samosa or a helping of bean casserole. As I like a balanced diet, and Kate and Adam provide the healthy stuff, I get the unhealthy stuff from Ricky and Morris who are always stuffing me with cake. I don't put weight on. Ricky says this is because I have hollow legs, but really it's because I work too bloody hard. But that night I couldn't be bothered with food: I had more urgent things to think about.

The following morning, as every morning, I had to walk the Tribe. On a Friday, there were usually five of them. I wouldn't be taking EB; he'd be staying at home for a few days, resting his paws. Of the remaining four, two would be easy to fetch because they lived in Ashburton, within walking distance of the town; the other dogs I always collected in the van because they lived further off. I rang their owners and explained I couldn't pick them up in the morning and why. Then I sat with my diary and worked out what I could and couldn't do next day without transport. Thank God the weekend was coming up, but I needed a new vehicle by Monday. I couldn't afford to wait around for the insurers.

I spent a couple of dispiriting hours comparing prices of second-hand vans on the Internet and got so depressed I weakened and ate a banana. I knew I could always ask my cousin Brian out in South Korea for money, but he had already been so generous with funds for the shop, money I intended to repay, that I cringed at the idea of approaching him for more.

By the time I'd slogged up the hill to Ricky and Morris's place that afternoon, I'd already spent most of the morning with Maisie, unclogging the drain of the sink she swore she wasn't responsible for clogging. I went into town to do her shopping, her beastly terrier, Jacko, on the lead. I refuse to walk him with the Tribe because he's so badly behaved. As usual, he growled filthy language at any other dog we saw, lurching at anything within snapping distance.

I took him on a detour along a path that sweeps in a curve behind St Andrew's churchyard. On one side, ivy clings to ancient gravestones leaning at odd angles, their carved epitaphs worn smooth by age; on the other side of the path brightly painted play equipment stands in the recreation ground, together with the sweeping concrete lines of the new skateboard park. It's as if Ashburton's past is on one side of the path, its future on the other.

The lane led me to a small commercial estate where I was sure, a few days before, I'd noticed a van with a 'for sale' sign in its window. It was still parked there, a little white Peugeot Partner, with '£500 ono' written on a notice on the windscreen. It was an older model, but big enough for me to get the Tribe in the back, or carry stock about. It also had windows in the back doors, which the old van hadn't, and would give me a decent rearward view as well as allowing the dogs to see out. I scribbled down the seller's number so that I could phone him later.

'So is little EB all right?' Morris asked, cutting me a slice of chocolate cake.

'He's fine.' I'd rung Elaine that morning to enquire after both the invalids.

'What about you, Juno?' He blinked at me anxiously. 'Are you fine too?'

I'd had to trim off a few frazzled ends of singed hair but otherwise I was unscathed.

Ricky lit up a cigarette and strolled to the open door to aim his smoke into the garden. 'You know we'll run you anywhere, Princess, if you need a lift.'

'Thanks, but I've arranged to meet the man selling the Peugeot tomorrow morning so I'm hoping I'll be mobile again by Sunday.'

Morris flicked a sly glance at Ricky. 'You know, Juno, we've had an idea.'

'We have.' Ricky came back to the table and drummed his fingers on it in excitement. 'It's brilliant!'

I groaned. I'd heard their brilliant ideas before.

'We're going to rent a unit in your shop.' They were both grinning at me broadly, waiting for my reaction.

'No, you're not.'

Their faces fell.

'This is just an excuse to help me out,' I went on. 'It's very kind of you, but I'm not letting you do it.'

'But we've got lots of stock we want to get rid of,' Morris argued, 'vintage sixties and seventies stuff that we don't get much call for theatrically.'

'Its lovely stuff,' Ricky put in, 'all very saleable.'

'Then sell it on the Internet. You'll get more money.'

'Can't be arsed!' he said flatly. 'And let's face it, you've got sod all to sell at the moment, your bit of the shop is half-empty!'

This was true; the back room I occupied was practically

bare. What little stuff I had was spread out to make it look less empty. I didn't have much spare cash and didn't get time to go hunting for stock. As a result, I was spending far too many evenings in front of the laptop, trawling through auctions, hunting for stuff I could afford to buy online.

'You're not paying me rent,' I insisted.

'No, and nobody else is either,' Ricky retorted. 'You've let Beatrix Potter have her unit for nothing.'

'Sophie needs a chance to establish herself without all her money going out in rent,' I argued. 'She can barely afford to buy paintbrushes, as it is. And we've agreed to review the situation at Christmas. As for Pat, she sells her stuff to raise money for the animals. If I took money from her, I'd just be taking it from them.'

'Juno, love, it's not your responsibility to solve other people's problems,' Morris told me. Ricky nodded frantically.

This was rich, coming from them. They were always trying to solve my problems. Ricky pointed his fag-hand at me, his cigarette trailing smoke. 'You're always doing it, you silly cow, and it's what gets you into trouble.' He took a long drag as if to underline his point.

It was time to divert their minds from my failings. After all, selling the vintage clothes was a good idea and would help to fill some empty space. 'How about this?' I suggested. 'I'll put the clothes on my unit and sell them for you, just take a commission.'

It was a compromise that seemed to mollify them. After a few moments of slightly sulkily tossing the idea back and forth, they agreed. 'But you'll have to price everything,' I warned them, 'because I won't have a clue.'

Morris clapped his hands together like an excited child. 'We'll sort out the clothes this afternoon.'

'No,' I said firmly. 'I'm here to help you pack up those uniforms.'

'Well start packing, then.' Ricky rose and stubbed out his cigarette in the sink. 'The sooner we've got 'em finished, the sooner we can have some fun.'

CHAPTER FIVE

If Thursday was a weird day, what with Judith-Marianne and the van catching fire, Saturday contained elements of the surreal. It started off well. In the morning I took the white van for a test run. It had new tyres and a year's MOT, but it also had a few miles on the clock and I managed to buy it for £450. I was to become a White Van Woman. Perhaps an anonymous-looking vehicle wouldn't be such a bad thing. In the past, the advertising on my yellow van had made it easy for the wrong people to find me and nearly got me murdered. Anyway, I shook hands with the vendor and agreed to bring the money around to his house first thing next morning. White Van would be mine.

When I got to *Old Nick's*, I found a more expensive vehicle parked outside: a brand-new soft-top Mazda MX5, in powder blue with beige leather interior, was blocking most of the pavement. I squeezed past it, barely able to get in through the door. Inside, who should be in conversation with Sophie but Jamie's sister, the lovely Emma. I suppose her brother must have told her where to find us. She was wearing a summery dress, her pale gold hair loose about her smoothly tanned shoulders. She'd dazzled Gavin into an awed, slack-jawed stare.

'So can you do it?' she was demanding of Sophie, as I came in. 'You can work from photographs, I take it?'

Sophie was leafing through a thick sheaf of photos. 'Oh yes,' she replied, nodding, 'no problem at all.' She smiled and held out a photo for me to see. 'The Old Thunderer,' she explained. 'He's a Highland bull. Isn't he wonderful?'

'Hello, Emma.' I took the photo from Sophie. The Old Thunderer was certainly impressive, his massive head crowned with thick, curling brown hair and wide, wicked-looking horns. Beneath a long fringe one baleful eye glared at the camera.

'Does Jamie have a herd of these?' I asked. Highland cattle were often to be seen grazing on the moor, imported from Scotland because they were hardy enough to stand up to Dartmoor weather. I'd have preferred to see Ruby Reds or South Devon cattle, but I can hardly complain about imports when I'm a bit of an import myself.

'No, Thunderer was Sandy's, really just a pet.' Emma spoke the last word almost with contempt. 'He sired a lot of champions of course,' she added by way of compensation.

'It's Sandy's birthday on 29th October,' she went on. 'Jamie and I thought it would make a wonderful surprise present. You can get it done by then, I suppose?'

'Of course.' Sophie answered brightly, determined to ignore her haughty tone. 'How big do you want this portrait?'

I prayed Sophie wouldn't undersell herself and wandered away. Pat was putting up pictures of her own, papering the wall behind her with printed sheets showing the latest waifs and strays at Honeysuckle Farm looking for a home. I snapped my fingers under Gavin's nose, breaking Emma's spell and whatever fantasy he was weaving in his head.

'Don't drool,' I whispered. He blushed and went back to the newspaper he was reading.

I glimpsed a headline over his shoulder: *Batman Dies*. I should have known he wouldn't be reading anything sensible.

I was disappointed with Gavin; perhaps that was why I found him so irritating. When he'd rented his unit, or I should say when his parents, Mr and Mrs Hall, had rented it for him, the understanding was that he would be selling their collection of second-hand books. I'd been delighted at first. We currently have only one bookshop in Ashburton, a specialist dealing almost exclusively in classic comics and graphic novels. It's a wonderful place, full of beautifully crafted illustrated volumes. I'd bought a lovely book in there for Sophie's birthday. Gavin haunts the place, not because he appreciates graphic art, but because he's obsessed by superheroes and spends most of his time reading the adventures of mythical kingdoms and warrior queens, and not doing what he's supposed to be doing: setting up his own bookstall. Ashburton has a library but it's small and can't provide for everyone's needs. I was convinced that second-hand books would have really helped to drag the locals into *Old Nick's*. But I was hoping for books with general appeal. Trouble was, Gavin wasn't interested in mainstream and frankly, I doubt if his own collection of cheap and tawdry comics, mostly obtained from dubious sources on the internet, would be of much interest to anyone. I'm sure his parents had only forced him into renting space in the shop to prise him away from his computer, drag him from the darkened tomb of his bedroom into the daylight.

To an extent I couldn't blame him for his lack of enthusiasm. The Halls' book collection consisted of the kind of stock that charity shops end up throwing away: old and unfashionable cookery books, yellowing paperbacks, mostly turgid hospital romances, a few dry academic tomes from the days when Mr Hall was a student, out-of-date atlases and little else. Basically, they had cleared out the contents of their loft. I'd offered to take Gavin to the market in Newton Abbot, where he could see how some really thriving bookstalls had set up their businesses, but he wasn't interested. I looked at his shelves, only half-filled, most of the stock still in boxes, and sighed.

'Is there a toilet I can use here?' Emma's voice cut in suddenly. She and Sophie had finished striking their deal and judging by the grin on Sophie's face she was happy with her end of it. I was going upstairs myself and pointed her in the direction of the bathroom on the landing. I went on up to the kitchen. I'd replaced Nick's old cooker with a microwave and toaster, which was all we needed. Gavin had tried to persuade me into investing in an expensive coffee machine, but I told him if he wanted posh coffee he could buy it himself. As I extracted the milk from Nick's ancient fridge, I heard the bathroom door slam and looked out of the kitchen, down the stairs, calling out a goodbye to the descending Emma. She didn't answer. She was sniffing heavily, her hand up to her nose. Summer cold or hay fever, I wondered naively, or was she upset? I went to the bathroom myself.

I'd locked the door and was just about to flip up the lid of the loo when something glistening on its surface caught my eye. I bent down and peered at a line of very fine white crystals. It was the straightness of that line that riveted my attention. I switched on the bathroom light and hunkered down, peering. I wanted to be absolutely certain about what I suspected I was looking at. I could see a pattern of tiny cut marks on the lid's plastic surface. I flipped open the pedal bin under the basin. Sure enough, there was a razor blade and a little scroll of paper in there; it looked like one of Sophie's business cards, rolled up. And one end of it, I was now perfectly sure, had been stuffed up Emma's horrible little nose. No wonder she was sniffing.

The hot wave of anger that came up from the soles of my feet was so intense I found myself gripping the edge of the basin for support. How dare she? How dare that posh little cow bring her stash into my shop and snort her evil drug on my premises? And be so contemptuous of others that she didn't even bother to conceal the evidence; she didn't care who found out. I felt faint with anger and sat down on the edge of the bath. My mother had died of a drug overdose when she was twenty-three. It was one of the few things I knew about her. I was already older than she would ever be. I suppose that's why I was so angry, because of my mother, because of the waste. I wondered if Jamie knew about Emma's habit. Not my business, I warned myself resolutely, don't get involved. She would now be driving her little sports car through the streets of Ashburton under the influence of a dangerous drug. I ought to call the police and report her. But in the end I calmed down, swept the tiny remnants of her guilty secret away with

56

a cloth, binned it, and decided not to say anything to anyone; certainly not to those downstairs. Sophie would be celebrating getting her commission. I didn't want to ruin her moment.

But when I got down there, no one was celebrating. Something else entirely was going on.

'I tell you, it must have been her!' Sophie was saying loudly. 'It was right there on my desk, and now it's gone!' Gavin was on his hands and knees, searching for something under her desk.

'What's up?'

'Sophie's lost her inhaler,' Pat told me.

'I have not lost it,' she insisted. 'It was there, on the desk. No one else has been in here.' She rolled her eyes. 'It's not like we've had any customers.'

'Well, I did see Miss Hoity-Toity put her hand in her pocket,' Pat admitted, 'just before she went out.'

'But who would do that?' Gavin objected, standing up and dusting his hands. 'Who would steal an inhaler from an asthmatic?'

I could think of someone. I had no doubt that gin-guzzling, cocaine-snorting, horse-riding, sports-car-driving, thrill-seeking Emma could get high on just about anything.

Barely two hours after Emma had departed, during which time one customer had come in, wandered around and left without buying anything, Jamie himself arrived. Unlike his sister he was charm itself, asking after our welfare and EB's, introducing himself to Pat and Gavin, admiring Pat's wares and asking her questions about the animal sanctuary. We mentioned Emma's earlier visit, but I didn't say anything about the drugs. No one said anything about the inhaler. Sophie's mum had been phoned and had already popped in with a spare one from home.

'The portrait was her idea,' Jamie admitted. 'But that's not why I'm here. I'll come straight to the point,' he added briskly, perching his rear on the edge of Sophie's desk and folding his arms. 'I'm hoping you might be able to dig me out of a hole.'

'We'll try,' I assured him. We could refuse nothing to the handsome saviour of EB.

'We've got this fete up at the house a week from today,' he went on. 'I heard Sandy mention it to you. Well, it's more of an autumn country fair, really. We do it every year, to raise money for the lifeboats or some charity. Always brings in the crowds. This year it's for the air ambulance. Usual thing, you know, gymkhana, dog show, beer tent, all that. Well, we always have a tent for art and crafts. Dartmoor Guild of Arts come every year, put on a great display. Unfortunately, this year there's been some mix up over dates and they're not coming. They're already booked for somewhere else—'

'—leaving you with an empty art and craft tent,' I said.

'Exactly, bit awkward. So Sandy and I wondered if you ladies might be able to come along and bring your wares – and you, too, of course,' he added, turning around to include Pat and Gavin.

'Well, I don't do crafts, as such,' I warned him. 'I sell antiques and collectibles.'

'That would be fine. In fact, Sandy's got a few mates in the antiques trade. We can invite them along too. And if you know of anyone else who . . .'

He saw Sophie and me exchanging glances. 'We'd waive the normal stallholder charges, of course,' he went on. 'You'd be doing us a favour. Perhaps, if you do well on the day, you might consider making a small donation to the charity?'

'Well, in that case—'

'Good, so you'll come?' he asked, turning round to include all of us.

'I'll come,' Gavin said instantly.

'That's fixed, then. Can't tell you how grateful I am. Any news on your van, Juno?' he asked. 'Has the insurance chap turned up?'

I explained I was still waiting for the insurance assessor to come, my local garage playing host to the burnt-out wreck, but that I was getting new wheels in the meantime.

He raised his brows. 'Oh yes?'

'Peugeot Partner,' I told him.

'Excellent.' He left, well pleased with the success of his mission, as suddenly as he'd come.

There followed a brief argument with Gavin, who was intent on bringing his collection of comics to sell at the fete, about the unsuitability of his stock for such an occasion, but he remained obstinate; he was determined to come along.

'I don't see why my comics shouldn't sell as well as Pat's knitted sheep or Juno's old tat,' he argued.

'This is a country fair, not a fantasy convention, Gavin,' I pointed out. 'Perhaps some mainstream books would be more suitable, you know, appeal to a wider range of interests? You'll probably sell more that way.'

'Gavin has got a point,' Sophie said reluctantly. 'There will be families there, and lots of kids read comics.'

'These aren't for kids!' Pat snatched up the fantasy novel that Gavin had been reading.

'*The Sword of Virangha*,' she read out loud. 'Look at this female on the front. She's got nothing on except a metal bikini.'

'She's a warrior queen,' Gavin said hastily, a telltale blush beginning to tinge his cheeks, 'she's wearing armour.'

'I don't fancy her chances going into battle in that,' Pat went on remorselessly, 'it only covers up her rude bits.'

Gavin snatched the book out of her hands. 'Mr Westershall extended the invitation to include me, so I'm coming. And anyway,' he added childishly, 'you can't stop me.'

'I think we're missing the point,' I said before hostilities could escalate. 'If we all go next Saturday, who's going to look after the shop?'

There was a moment's gloomy silence. It was obvious that no one was going to volunteer to stay behind. It was equally obvious that it wasn't a good idea to close the shop on a Saturday. Whilst the fine autumn weather continued, Ashburton would be full of visitors.

The silence was broken by the mad jangling of the bell above the shop door. Ricky and Morris struggled in through the doorway, each carrying what looked like the severed halves of a naked female corpse but turned out to be a dress-shop mannequin. 'This is Mavis,' they chorused, grinning. 'Where do you want her?'

I pointed them in the direction of my unit in the stockroom. Then I turned to grin at the others. 'We *will* go to the ball, Cinderella,' I promised, and then followed, to talk nicely to my Fairy Godmothers.

* * *

Sunday morning I finally became the owner of White Van and took it for a spin up the A38 to Newton Abbot. A large market town, it has in abundance things that Ashburton doesn't have, like supermarkets, charity shops and takeaways. It is the kind of town that guidebooks describe as 'bustling'. Holidaymakers in their thousands pass through its railway station every year: change at Newton Abbot for Totnes and Plymouth – or for Dawlish, Teignmouth and the delights of the English Riviera. Famously, it boasts a racecourse, which on occasional weekends when the horses aren't running hosts a giant car boot sale.

As my ignorance about antiques is profound, the only chance I stand of making any profit is to buy cheap from people who know even less about them than I do. Boot sales can be quite good in this regard. I picked up half a 1960s coffee set, a Torquay pottery milk jug, a few pieces of nasty but collectable Goss ware, a sandalwood writing slope with a broken hinge, some strings of coloured glass beads that Pat could break down into earrings, and a cast-iron boot scraper: the sort of original feature that rich people doing up old houses will pay silly money for. I also invested in a box of paperback books in reasonably pristine condition, in the hope I could talk some sense into Gavin about putting them on his shelves.

As I was about to leave, I found a cardboard box full of electric light switches. The man who sold them to me was surprised I wanted them. After all, he said, they were just rubbish he'd found in his garage. It was true, many were plastic and broken and would be thrown away, but as I gleefully handed over my five pounds and gaily lied that my partner was an electrician and collected old switches, it occurred to him, judging by his slight frown, that he should have inspected the

I bent to stroke it. Oriental breeds of cat are very vocal, they like to chat. 'Hello,' I said, 'who are you?'

The woman shut the tailgate of her car and wandered over, the lead in her grasp. She was tall and slim, dressed in cords and a padded body warmer, her hair – in the dim light I couldn't tell if it was blonde or grey – worn in a French pleat. I judged her to be in her late sixties. 'He's Toby,' she informed me in a pleasant, cultured voice, 'just giving him a walk.'

I asked if he was Siamese, a breed I knew was easily trained to walk on a lead.

'Yes. He's a lilac point,' she confirmed, bending to scoop him up. 'Time to be on our way.'

I was close enough to her car to see that the back was piled high with bedding. I wondered if she and her cat were sleeping in it. 'Going far?' I asked.

'Yes. Goodnight,' she answered, pleasantly, but as a definite end to the conversation.

'Well, goodnight,' I said, and returned to my van.

She also went to her car, put the cat in the back on the pile of bedding, and sat in the driving seat. But the car hadn't moved when I turned out of the car park, its driver sitting motionless, and I had the feeling she was waiting for me to go, to be out of sight before she moved on.

Running away, I thought to myself, she and her cat are running away, and for the rest of the night, until sleep claimed me, I couldn't get them out of my mind.

I was alone in the shop with Gavin. It was the afternoon before the Moorworthy fete and I was in the storeroom sorting out what stock I was going to take with me. Was it worth taking a fluted carnival glass bowl with amber lustre, I wondered, and risking it getting broken en route? I decided it was and was carefully wrapping it in bubble wrap when I heard the bell jingle on the shop door as someone came in.

I didn't rush because I knew Gavin was sitting at his post, although as he was deep into one of his fantasy comics it was debatable whether the sound would have penetrated his consciousness. Then I heard his voice. 'I want you to leave me alone,' he was saying loudly. 'I've told you to stop coming in here.'

The reply, whatever it was, was spoken too quietly for me to hear. Curious, I crept into the corridor and peered into the shop. The man muttering inaudibly to Gavin was exactly as Sophie and Pat had described: ferrety-looking, a skinny man in jeans and an old denim jacket, thinning brown hair brushed across his head failing to conceal the red scabbiness of his scalp. His neck and hands were peppered with scabs too, as if he was suffering from some unfortunate skin condition. He was older than Gavin and, despite his general seediness, had an air of menace about him, like a small-time crook. I couldn't hear what he was saying, but I realised he wasn't purposely whispering. His voice was just very soft; a collection of breathy, sibilant sounds came from his lips, the sounds a snake might make if it could speak.

'I've told you, no,' Gavin's voice was edgy with panic.

'Anything wrong?' I asked, strolling into the shop. I stopped and smiled innocently at his companion. 'Did this gentleman come in to buy something?'

He slid a glance at me, hissed something inaudible and slipped out, not bothering to close the door behind him. I walked over and shut it, turning to study Gavin, who looked paler than usual and slightly unwell. 'Who was he?'

'No one,' he mumbled, averting his gaze, 'just a creep.'

'Does this creep have a name?'

'Croaker, that's what he calls himself.'

I folded my arms. 'Do you want to tell me what that was about?'

He shook his head. 'Nothing – it's nothing.' He blushed deeply. 'He's just a pervert.' Flustered, he began to tidy his table in an effort to cover his discomfort, hastily sliding comics into a box.

'If he's bothering you, we could call the police. You don't have to put up with—'

'No! No, I'll sort him out,' he cried hastily. 'Honestly, Juno. I'll make sure he doesn't come in here again.'

'Gav, if you're in any kind of trouble—'

'I'm not!' He gave me a steady stare, lifting his chin in defiance. 'It's fine, really.'

'OK.' I held up my hands in a gesture of surrender. 'But you can tell him from me that if he comes in here again upsetting anyone, I will call the police.'

'I've told you, I'll deal with him.'

I let it go at that, but I was dubious about Gavin's powers to deal with the creepy Mr Croaker and resigned myself to the fact that I might not have seen the last of him.

CHAPTER SIX

The wisdom of letting Ricky and Morris look after *Old Nick's* whilst we were at the fete was something I pondered more than once on our drive to Moorworthy House. It wasn't that they couldn't be trusted with handling customers, or cash; it was their fondness for putting their own stamp on things that had me worried. They could rearrange my stuff as much as they liked, had already done so in the intervening week as they produced a clothes rail with more and more vintage garments to fill it. But if they started tinkering with Sophie's or Pat's stock it would not go down well. I needn't have been concerned. Sophie had almost none left after her visit to the arts centre, and during the week she'd been busy dashing off quick watercolour sketches of Dartmoor and comical cartoons of farm animals to sell at the fete. There wasn't time to get them framed, just mounted and cellophane-wrapped.

She rode with me in White Van. Pat had nobly volunteered to take Gavin and his boxes of comics in her old station wagon. We arrived before them – quite a long time before them, as it turned out; Gavin wasn't ready to be picked up at the promised hour and had to be rousted out of bed whilst Pat sat drumming her fingers on the steering wheel.

The fete was taking place on the vast lawn at the back of the house, with a central arena for the gymkhana, dog shows and livestock competitions. A beer tent and pavilions housing flower and vegetable shows and cake competitions vied for attention alongside tents selling locally produced cheese, cider, honey and even Dartmoor gin and chocolate. In a marked-off area stood a Punch and Judy show for children and a bouncy castle, while a colourful bunch of helium balloons bobbed like a big bouquet over the face-painting stall.

The Craft and Antiques tent was situated nearest to the house, which was a bonus as far as I was concerned as the ballroom had been set up for lunches and teas. The long windows were thrown open, the terrace scattered with garden tables and chairs. Admittedly the Portaloos were way over the other side of the fair, but you can't have it all.

As Jamie had asked, I'd contacted some other traders to see if they could help fill the empty stalls. Tom and Vicky Smithson from Exeter had readily agreed, and when Sophie and I arrived in the tent, they were already busily dressing their table. Their stock was infinitely superior to mine, mostly delicate pieces of china and small items of highly polished silver. I gazed enviously at an arrangement of dainty vinaigrettes and snuffboxes. Tom and Vicky had been in the antiques trade a long time, they knew their stuff. I only wished the same could have been said of me. I had begun to educate myself when I started working with Nick; I just hadn't got very far.

Once Sophie and I had unloaded our boxes, I parked the van in an adjoining field and trudged back to the marquee. The sky was clear blue overhead, the air already warm, a perfect day for a garden fete. Further down the lawn a painted sign warned visitors to *Beware of the Ha-Ha*. The trees in the woodland had turned a deeper gold, a reminder that summer was over. In a few short weeks we would be turning back the clocks; there were not many of these long, golden afternoons left.

I lingered by a stall selling locally pressed apple juice, sipped the proffered samples and chatted to the young couple running it. Devon used to be famous for its orchards and they owned one just outside of Lustleigh. They talked passionately about the revival of old varieties of apple; varieties with lovely names like Sweet Coppin and Fair Maid of Devon, or Pig's Nose and Hangy Down. They were also selling pork and apple sausages, jars of apple chutney, and slices of apple pie served with thick clotted cream. I resisted. It was too early in the day to start being naughty and I had to get back. I contented myself with a sample of sausage speared on a cocktail stick and moved on.

The marquee had begun to fill up in my absence. I'd barely begun to lay out my own wares when Uncle Sandy came in, accompanied by one of his antique dealer chums and I heard a soft groan from Vicky Smithson, whose table was on my right. 'Oh no, not Barty!' she muttered to herself. I craned my neck to see Sandy's companion, a florid individual in a natty sports jacket. Sandy was introducing him to other traders and there was a lot of loud guffawing going on. I turned to Vicky. 'Friend of yours?'

'Not exactly friend, no,' she answered softly. 'Oh God, he's coming this way! Has he got this table next to mine?' She groaned again and clasped my arm. 'Whatever you do, don't let him get you in a confined space.'

Vicky, a slim and attractive sixty-something, favoured the approaching Barty with an engaging smile and submitted herself graciously to his embrace. She then introduced him to me. 'Eddie Bartholomew,' he said, pumping my hand with enthusiasm, 'but everyone calls me Barty.'

'Juno,' I responded, as coolly as I could.

'Juno, eh?' He rolled a lascivious eye over my body. 'How apt!'

Fortunately, Sandy, after enquiring if we were happy with the tables we'd been given, bore Barty off to meet his other comrades and I was able to get on with setting out my stock.

I took my jacket off. It was already warm inside the canvas tent, and stuffy; a sickly smell of fudge was wafting in from the tent where it was being made. The public address system whined and coughed as it spluttered into life, a hearty voice announcing the day's events. Later, we were promised, there would be a display by the Dartmoor Majorettes and a performance by Bovey Brass Band. Inside my skull a faint headache began to beat a warning tattoo. It was going to be a long, hot day.

If Gavin's fantasy magazines and graphic novels didn't strike me as suitable for a country fair, I have to say that Barty's stock struck me as even less appropriate: arms and militaria.

I know some people are fascinated by medals and wartime memorabilia, but there were far too many nasty-looking knives and weapons on his table for me to feel comfortable with all the children around. One of these children was Gavin who, having plonked his magazines down on his table in two untidy piles, more or less abandoned his stall for the day, assuming that Pat would look after it. He spent ages poring over Barty's weapons and came back brandishing a short, curved sword with a wicked-looking blade and even more lethal point.

'You haven't bought that?' I asked, horrified.

'Of course I have!' He unsheathed it with a slither of metal and brandished it aloft. 'The Sword of Virangha!' he cried proudly.

'Don't wave that thing about in here,' Pat told him crossly, 'you'll have someone's eye out!' The tent had become far too crowded for him to be messing about with a lethal weapon.

'Put it away somewhere safe, Gavin!' I hissed at him. 'Why don't you go and lock it in the station wagon?'

'Good idea!' he agreed readily. He swaggered off, the scabbard stuck through the belt of his jeans, and that was the last I saw of him.

Pat sold two of his comics for him in his absence. Better still, she had a good day herself, selling several pairs of handmade earrings as well as knitted toys and animal doorstops. She has a real talent for creating animals with comic expressions and she'd sold a frowning pug and three particularly bonkers-looking sheep before I made my first sale of the day. Meanwhile, Sophie was doing well with her watercolour sketches and greetings cards. Her hedgerow paintings attracted great admiration, although they're a bit expensive for an impulse purchase. She didn't sell one, but four people walked away with her business card.

I just wished I was doing half as well. I did sell a brass shell case – to Barty, of all people – a few glass brooches and the boot scraper. Unfortunately, I couldn't resist a mother-of-pearl hatpin from one of Sandy's chums, which wiped out most of my meagre profit.

It became oppressively hot in the tent during the afternoon, and we took it in turns to make our escape and walk around the fete in the fresh air. Not being interested in small girls jumping fat ponies over bales of straw, and teenagers in short skirts twirling batons even less, I turned my back on the arena and headed for the house. Here I found Vicky, who had somehow escaped before me, enjoying tea on the terrace. I joined her in a pot of Earl Grey and a plate of dainty sandwiches.

'Any trouble with the abominable Barty?' I asked.

'Not really. Thank God, I've got Tom between us to act as a buffer!'

Whilst we sat watching the crowds of people milling about in the sunshine, thankful for a while to be separate from them, Jamie came up with a young woman on his arm who he introduced as his fiancée.

Jessica was a pleasant young woman with soft brown hair and infinitely better manners than her future sister-in-law. She seemed a little shy and clung to Jamie's arm with obvious adoration. I couldn't believe he could be marrying such a sweet girl for money. I tried to imagine this English rose when she was older: the mistress of Moorworthy House, the gracious hostess in twinset and pearls. But there was something about her that didn't quite fit. Her pretty floral dress was appropriate for a garden party, but I couldn't see her mixing with the country landowners set, couldn't quite see her in jodhpurs and waxed jacket, like Emma.

'Emma not here?' I enquired, after we'd engaged in a little polite conversation.

Jamie shrugged. 'Oh, she'll be around somewhere.'

Stuffing something nasty up her nose, no doubt. Jamie was concerned that we were having a good day, that we thought coming to the fete had been worthwhile. We assured him that it had, and he went off to attend to something, leaving Jessica to sit and drink a cup of tea with us.

I was right about her as it turned out. She wasn't a country girl at all. She lived in London where she worked as a PA. I asked how she and Jamie had met. They'd been introduced at some company event, apparently. Sandy had once worked with her father who owned a pharmaceutical firm. 'I don't expect you've heard of it,' she said shyly. 'Dravizax.'

She was right, I hadn't. It sounded like the name of a villain from one of Gavin's graphic novels.

Jamie came back to claim Jessica as they were due to judge the Scruffiest Dog in Show together, and Vicky strolled back to the marquee. Before I went back in, I popped to the loo, a trip that took me to the other end of the garden. It was when I was returning from there that I spotted Emma, holding on to the bridle of a fidgeting bay horse whilst she stood in earnest conversation with a man I recognised as Moss. I didn't particularly want to say hello to her, and they seemed to be talking intently, so I just passed them by unnoticed and returned to the stifling canvas cave of the tent for the rest of the afternoon.

* * *

The final judging had taken place, the brass band had trumpeted its last, the crowds had dispersed and we were packing up to go home. Barty and his chums had already left, Vicky had almost packed her stock and Tom had gone off to fetch their car.

'Where's Gavin?' Sophie asked suddenly.

I realised I hadn't seen him for hours. His table was unoccupied, as it had been for most of the day. He'd shown no interest in it and I really don't know why he'd been so insistent about coming. Pat shook her head. 'He'd better come back and start packing up soon or I shall go home without him.'

'I haven't seen him since he went to put that stupid sword in the car.'

'He couldn't have done that. He'd have needed my car keys and he didn't ask for 'em. Not,' she added, 'that I'd have trusted that ninny with my keys. He'd probably drop them in the field and lose 'em.'

'He must come back soon.' Sophie was carefully stacking bubble-wrapped paintings in a box. 'Even he must realise it's all over. We could try his phone.'

I should have thought of that straight away but, unused as I am to the luxury of a signal, it's not always the first thing that occurs. After a few moments, Gavin's phone began to ring, loudly, inside the tent. Pat bent down behind his table, where his jacket had slipped off the back of his chair, and produced the ringing phone from his pocket.

'Moron,' I pronounced, as I terminated the call.

'Are you girls OK?' Tom had returned to the tent, ready to load up.

'We seem to have lost Gavin. He went off for a look around but that was hours ago.'

'Do you want me to have a scout about?'

'Oh, please don't trouble, he can't have got far.' As I said it, I realised that this wasn't true. Gavin could have gone anywhere. He might have decided to explore the house, although apart from the tea room it was strictly off limits to the public, or he could have gone for a walk and got lost. He could be anywhere.

'Let me check out the beer tent, make sure he's not passed out drunk,' Tom offered with a grin, 'and I'll check out the gents' loos, while I'm about it.'

'That's kind, Tom, thank you.'

As Vicky had packed up and could do nothing until Tom returned, she volunteered to box up Gavin's comics for him. Pat and I went off to retrieve our respective vehicles, leaving Sophie on guard in case he turned up whilst we were gone. We didn't want him wandering off again.

As we crossed the field where cars were parked, I saw a now familiar figure walking towards us. Not Gavin, but Moss. I had never spoken to the man, and other than just briefly with Emma, hadn't seen him since we'd left him standing in the road after my van caught fire. I thought I ought to thank him for waiting for the break-down lorry to arrive and overseeing its removal to the garage. 'Mr Moss!' I called out.

He saw me, halted in his stride and stared at me from pale blue eyes. He looked horrified.

'Mr Moss,' I began, 'I just wanted to thank you—'

He turned his back and headed off in the opposite

direction. As I called his name again, he quickened his pace. It was obvious from the rigid set of his shoulders and his lengthening stride that he didn't want to talk me. 'Well, I won't thank you, then, you miserable, rude old bugger!' I muttered. Takes all sorts.

There was still no sign of Gavin. Tom had had no luck in tracking him down. He and Vicky were loading up. Pat had stowed her stuff and was leaning against her station wagon looking fed up.

'It's pointless you hanging around,' I told her. 'I've got room in the van for Gavin's boxes; he can come home with Sophie and me.'

'I'll hang on a bit longer,' she insisted, but after a few more minutes of standing uselessly fiddling with her keys, she allowed herself to be persuaded and we decanted his boxes into White Van. 'You'd better take his rucksack,' she said, handing it to me. 'I don't know why he brought it. It's been sitting in the car all day.'

Pat's car trundled away across the grass, and Sophie and I began loading White Van. By now, the tent was almost deserted, the tables bare, the odd plastic carrier bag and sandwich wrapper left behind, littering the grass. 'That boy is a bloody nuisance,' I muttered, slamming the van doors shut.

'I don't like leaving you girls like this.' Tom came up, looking at his watch. It was close on seven o'clock. It would be light for a while yet, but the sun was sinking lower, the sky over the moor blushing pink. 'Something is obviously amiss.'

'Not necessarily. If Gavin got fed up, I wouldn't put it past him to have hitch-hiked home.' But I was getting worried, and cross that the wretched boy was inconveniencing so many people.

'Let's see if we can find the organisers,' Tom suggested. 'They must be around somewhere.'

We split up, Sophie and I to go up to the house in search of Jamie, Tom to check the other tents and talk to some volunteers gathering litter into bin bags, to ask if anyone had seen Gavin. Vicky was to stay with the cars and phone us if he arrived.

We found Mrs Johnson and a team of ladies in the ballroom. Every scone had been scoffed and they were clearing up after tea. We described Gavin and our predicament. She hadn't seen him and assured us, her face as starched as her apron, that no member of the public would have got past her and her team into the rest of the house. She suggested that we speak to Mr Jamie, who she believed was in the drawing room. Our quickest way, she added pointedly, was to go back outside and along the terrace.

We passed the balustrade, an evening scent drifting from the flower-filled urns. But before we reached the drawing room's open windows, we heard Jamie's voice, loud and furious. 'In broad daylight?' he was yelling at someone. 'With all these people about? Are you out of your mind?' I wondered if he'd caught Emma snorting cocaine from some horse's nosebag. Whatever, this was not a good moment to approach. We veered off, across the lawn.

'I don't suppose he went into the wood.' The trees were ahead of us, a dark tracery of branches with the sun melting gold behind them.

Sophie frowned. 'It's fenced off, isn't it?'

'Didn't Jamie say there was a path, that part of it is open to walkers?' There was certainly a gate in the fence that separated the trees from the lawn. As we approached, we could see a sign hung on it: *Please keep to the path*. I swung it open.

Sophie hung back. 'Do you think we should?'

'Yes, I do. He might have gone in there and sprained an ankle or something.'

The gate shut with a little click behind us. It was quiet under the trees, and growing dim. I yelled Gavin's name. There was no reply, just a frantic rustle amongst the leaf litter from some tiny creature I'd frightened. The path was directly ahead, wide enough for us to walk side by side: bare earth scattered with bark chippings, a pale strip against the surrounding undergrowth. It was well maintained, with no ruts or stones to trip on. The setting sun sent shafts of gold into the surrounding shadows and gilded gnats danced a ballet in the dying light. We walked, stopping twice to call out Gavin's name.

The path veered around a high fence that blocked the way ahead. Signs on the wire warned trespassers they would be prosecuted. We followed the path for a hundred yards or so, before it ended abruptly, the wire fence cutting it off. We couldn't go any further. Sophie sighed. 'He's not here.'

I peered through the fence into the dusky woods beyond. The ground sloped away sharply, tree trunks jutting at odd angles from steep, rocky banks.

'You don't think he climbed over the fence, do you?' she asked.

I looked up. It was topped with vicious razor wire. 'I don't think he could have.'

'We might as well go back.' The gathering gloom was getting to Sophie. She sounded nervous. Something dark fluttered between the trees above us, but whether it was bird or bat I couldn't tell, its darting, flickering movement was so swift.

We began to retrace our steps. The shadows were thickening, reducing the green vegetation to a tangled mass of darkness. Something white caught my eye, about fifty yards from the path; it snagged my attention and held it. An oak had fallen long ago, a tree of great age and girth, its gnarled roots left exposed, its branching crown holding the stricken trunk at an angle, not allowing it to sink to the ground in rest. Tiny ferns grew along its mossy branches and something white, some object, was hooked over the slanting trunk. 'Stay there, Soph.'

As I made off through the undergrowth, she began to follow. 'Where are you going?'

'Stay there,' I repeated. There was no point in both of us crashing about amongst the vegetation. I picked my way between saplings and ferns that swished against my thighs as I brushed past. Even in the twilight I could see where someone had been before me. I followed a trail of snapped off branches and broken twigs. A terrible feeling of misgiving was growing with every step. A few yards further and I knew what I was looking at: the sole of a trainer, white, like the ones Gavin wore.

'Gavin?'

There was no answer, no moans or groans from the other

side of the tree. No movement from the shoe, or the jean-clad leg I could see as I drew close: all perfectly still. I leant over the stricken tree trunk. Gavin was lying face down. My first thought was that he'd broken his neck; he'd tried to leap over the trunk, caught his foot and fallen. 'Sophie!' I yelled. 'Ring for an ambulance. Then you'd better run back to the house, bring Jamie.'

'Have you found him?'

I clambered over the stricken trunk, clutching at twisting stems of ivy clinging to the bark and heaved myself over. I could hear the rustling of Sophie's steps as she hurried up behind me. 'Stay back, Soph!' I knelt down by Gavin's side and touched his neck gently, feeling for a pulse.

Sophie was on tiptoe, peering over the tree trunk, her voice tremulous. 'Is he dead?'

'I think so, yes.' I could smell blood; the leafy ground beneath his body was sticky with it. I gently turned him over and heard Sophie gasp. Gavin was dead, his eyes staring, a fallen oak leaf clinging to his pale cheek, and the Sword of Virangha sticking out of his chest, the handle between his clutching hands.

CHAPTER SEVEN

Call it a run of bad luck, but Gavin's was the third dead body I'd discovered in less than a year. Perhaps that's why Detective Inspector Ford favoured me with such a long and thoughtful stare before he spoke. 'We always seem to meet under distressing circumstances, Miss Browne.'

'We do,' I agreed foolishly. We were sitting in the study at Moorworthy House, facing each other across the polished surface of a wide mahogany desk. It was dark outside, and the room was lit by lamps, heavy brocade curtains pulled across the windows, the only sound the measured ticking of a clock. In the next room, the inspector's sidekick, Det. Constable DeVille, was talking to Sophie.

'So, Juno, tell me in your own words what happened. Begin with how you know the deceased.'

I explained that Gavin rented space in *Old Nick's*, that we'd all come to the fete, how keen Gavin had seemed to come with us, and how he'd bought the sword and then disappeared.

'I thought he'd gone to put the thing away in the car.'

'And you say he bought this weapon here, at the fete?' The inspector raised a sandy eyebrow. 'Who from?'

'His name is Eddie Bartholomew. I've never met him before. He's a friend of Uncle . . . of Mr Sandy Westershall.'

The inspector was scribbling down names. 'Do you know if Mr Bartholomew is still here?'

'Everyone had gone except for Tom and Vicky . . . Mr and Mrs Smithson. They stayed to try and help us find Gavin. They're not still waiting, are they?'

'We've taken brief statements and let them go home. Someone will be interviewing them more fully tomorrow.' The inspector smiled. 'Juno, tell me a bit more about Gavin. Have you any idea how he . . . how this terrible thing happened?'

'In the shop he was quiet, reading most of the time. He was really into all this fantasy stuff . . . superheroes and . . . I don't want to make him sound stupid,' I said awkwardly. 'Actually, he was very intelligent, but . . . impressionable – immature, I suppose. I can imagine him running about in the woods, brandishing that dreadful weapon, stabbing himself.' I found I was fiddling with the lid of a silver inkwell and stopped. 'Sorry, but he was accident-prone.'

'That's all right.' The inspector smiled. 'I wanted your honest assessment. So, as far as you're aware, he didn't quarrel with anyone during the day?'

'Well, as I say, I didn't really see much—' I stopped and stared. 'You don't think someone else stabbed him?'

The inspector spread his hands in an almost defensive gesture. 'I would be very surprised if this turns out to be anything other than a bizarre and horrible accident,' he responded gently, 'but I have to keep an open mind. At this stage I can't rule out foul play.'

I suddenly felt sick. I must have looked a bit green because the inspector paused to ask me if I was feeling all right. I assured him I was, and he carried on.

'It's a pity that so many people had already left the fete before this poor young man's body was discovered. Mr Westershall will be supplying us with a list of stallholders, and we shall be speaking to them all. Other than that, all we can do is broadcast an appeal to anyone attending the fete to come forward. There were hundreds of people here today. Someone may remember Gavin, may remember seeing him go into the woods.'

I thought of him lying there alone, bleeding, frightened, unable to call for help. 'Do you think if we'd found him earlier—'

The inspector was shaking his head. 'We'll have to wait for the pathologist's report but I'm certain that death would have been instantaneous.'

Instantaneous? Did that mean that there wasn't even a moment, however fleeting, that Gavin knew he was dying? Tears stung my eyes and I blinked them away. 'His poor parents, they don't know yet, do they? Who will tell them?'

'Don't worry about that, Juno,' the inspector reassured me. 'You can safely leave that to us.' He stood up, clearly my signal to go. 'And if you think of anything else—'

'Actually, there is something – something that happened yesterday.' I went on to tell him about Gavin being visited by the man who called himself Croaker, and what Gavin had said about him.

'Croaker?' he repeated, his sandy brows raised in surprise. 'Creeping Ted Croaker?'

I wasn't familiar with the sobriquet, but I described him as well as I could. The inspector was nodding. 'You know him?' I asked.

'He's a particularly unpleasant species of low life. Not violent, though. We put him away a couple of years ago for trying to sell Ecstasy tablets at the school gates.' He paused for a moment. 'Tell me, was Gavin on drugs?'

'No!' I was shocked at the idea. He often seemed like he was away with the fairies but that was a different matter. I'd certainly never seen him high on anything. As far as I knew he didn't even drink.

'Well, thank you. That's useful information,' he told me as he walked me to the door.

'We shall talk to Mr Croaker.'

Jamie was pacing in the hallway outside and as I left the study he came towards me and enfolded me in a hug. 'God, Juno, this is so bloody awful! You poor girl, it must have been a terrible shock finding him like that.'

'Mr Westershall.' The inspector's voice called to him from the study door.

'Yes, one moment, Inspector,' he called back. 'Juno, Sophie's in the drawing room with Jess, waiting for you. Please go in, let Jess give you a drink.'

Sophie had obviously been sobbing; she was white as a wraith, her dark eyes huge in her little face. She clung to me and sobbed some more. I could have enjoyed a good sob myself, but somehow, like a big sister, I felt I had to keep it together. Jessica, wide-eyed and obviously horrified at the afternoon's events, was doing a great job with the tea and sympathy. There was no sign of Emma.

'Unless you'd like something stronger?' she offered.

'Better not, I've got to drive home.'

I accepted tea with gratitude but neither Sophie nor I wanted to linger. Moorworthy House had lost its curious charm. We drove in silence. For hours our attention had been focussed on police and ambulances and answering a thousand questions. Now the shock was sinking in we were too numb to speak.

'It's horrible,' was all Sophie would say. 'Poor Gavin.'

White Van juddered over a cattle grid as the woods on either side gave way to open moor. The night was black around us, tiny pinpricks of gold from some isolated dwellings the only lights that showed. Our headlights probed the road ahead, picked up the white backside of a ewe sitting on black tarmac. I slowed to a stop. She got slowly to her feet and ambled across in front of us to join a knot of others, scruffy pale shapes huddled in the shelter of granite boulders on the verge.

I kept thinking of Gavin's face, of that moment when I'd turned him over. He'd looked so childlike, that oak leaf clinging to his pale cheek, his blue eyes staring at the sky. I'd never really noticed that his eyes were blue before.

'Sophie,' I began thoughtfully, as we turned onto the Ashburton road, 'do you remember seeing Gavin without his glasses? Ever remember him not wearing them?'

She thought about it. 'He was very short-sighted,' she responded slowly. 'He told me once that he'd tried contact lenses but didn't like them. No, I've never seen him without his specs.'

'No,' I agreed, thinking about it some more, 'neither have I.'

* * *

The last thing we wanted to do when we got back was to unload all our stuff. It was already late and we both longed to get home. But we didn't want to leave our worldly goods in White Van overnight either, so I parked outside the shop. The first things that confronted us when we opened the van doors were Gavin's rucksack and jacket and his boxes of stock. We placed all his things on his table. We didn't know what else to do with them. As I put the jacket down, I felt the hard lump of Gavin's phone in the pocket. 'The police might want this,' I said, drawing it out. 'I'll ring Inspector Ford in the morning and let him know I've got it.'

'Sunday tomorrow,' I yawned when we had unloaded everything. 'I'll come in and sort this stuff out.'

Sophie said she would come in too. 'Will you ring Pat?' she asked anxiously. 'She doesn't know what's happened yet.'

'Yes, but in the morning.' I rubbed my hand over my face. I was so tired suddenly. 'Why stop her getting a good night's sleep?'

When I got home, the house was in darkness. Adam and Kate were already in bed. They opened *Sunflowers* for breakfast, and except in the winter months that meant on Sundays too. I tiptoed up the stairs and let myself into an empty flat, silent and dark. It must be good, at times like these, to belong to someone, to have someone to come home to.

I could see a red eye blinking in the darkness before I switched on the lamp in the living room. I pressed the button on the answering machine, but I already knew who the message would be from. Ricky and Morris were bursting to tell me about their day in the shop, curious to know how I'd got on at the fete and worried that it was so late and I hadn't rung.

I knew I could ring them anytime, but they'd want to know every tiny detail of what had happened, and I wasn't sure I could face a barrage of questions right now. Perhaps it was better not to have anyone to talk to, after all. It occurred to me that in South Korea, where my cousin Brian served as a diplomat, it would be breakfast time and he would certainly be up and about. But he had enough on his plate; I didn't want him worrying about me.

I dropped down on the sofa and slumped there, too tired to get up and go to bed. I felt empty, as if someone had drained all the blood out of me. A soft chirruping noise and a thump from the bedroom told me that Bill had been on my bed and was obviously fed up of waiting for me to join him. His black shape slid sinuously around the open door and in one long leap he landed on my lap.

'You'll get me in trouble,' I told him softly, 'being up here all the time.' He wasn't my cat. He belonged to Adam and Kate but preferred to spend his time with me. Cats are like that, they choose their own people. He gazed at me from his one green eye and pushed his head against my hand, rubbing me with his cheek, marking me as his own. It seemed I belonged to someone after all.

CHAPTER EIGHT

Feeling ragged after a rotten night's sleep, I rang Inspector Ford and told him I had Gavin's phone.

'We've been looking for that.' His voice betrayed the weariness of a man who'd been up all night too. 'Gavin's father seemed to think he should have had his mobile on him.'

'It was in his jacket. Sorry. We'd packed up all his things before we knew what had happened to him. How are Gavin's parents?'

The inspector sighed. 'As you might expect. His father did the formal identification late last night.'

'It must be dreadful for them.'

'Yes,' he agreed sadly. 'I'll send someone over for the phone.'

'Can I ask you something?'

'Of course you can. I can't promise I'll be able to answer it.'

'When I found him, Gavin wasn't wearing his glasses. They must have come off when he fell. Have you found them?'

'No. They can't have fallen far. But looking for a pair of specs on a woodland floor is a bit like looking for—'

'—a needle in a haystack.'

'Precisely.' He thanked me for calling him about Gavin's phone and rang off.

Next, I phoned Pat, who listened to me in growing horror. She became very agitated, her voice turning to a low-pitched moan, convinced the whole thing was her fault because she hadn't given Gavin the car keys so that he could put the sword away.

'Please don't think that,' I begged her. 'I don't believe he had any intention of putting that sword in the car. He went off into the woods by himself so he could swagger about and pretend he was Robin Hood or someone.' Pat didn't sound convinced, but she calmed down. She'd brought her remaining stock home with her after the fete and planned to come into the shop to put it all back. I said I'd see her there.

I didn't need to ring Ricky and Morris because no sooner had I put the phone down than it rang, and Ricky's commanding voice was blasting down the line, demanding to know how the previous day had gone. I began to tell him, forced to stop so that he could put the phone on loudspeaker and Morris could hear it all. They listened pretty much as Pat had done but without the self-recrimination, constantly stopping me to ask questions, and declared their intention of coming down to the shop that morning to see me. I put the phone down. It seemed the whole world was coming to *Old Nick's* that morning.

Pat got there before me. Her pale eyes were watery and her nose was red. She's not the huggy-kissy sort, but she let me fold her in a big hug. She's thin and strong, all bone and sinew, no softness in her body at all. I could feel her heart beating in her flat chest. 'If only I'd . . .' she began, voice trembling with emotion.

'Stop it. It wasn't your fault. Gavin should never have bought that sword. Bloody Barty,' I went on in disgust, 'should never have bloody sold it to him. Weapons like that shouldn't be on sale, especially to impressionable young twerps like Gavin.'

Unconvinced, Pat blew her nose. 'What are we going to do with all his stuff?'

'Give it to his family I suppose, at some point.' I patted her arm. 'C'mon. Let's get it stowed out of the way for the moment.' We put the boxes and rucksack out of sight on the floor behind Gavin's table. I placed his jacket over the back of his chair, which made it look as if he had just popped out for something and would be coming back.

We began to sort out our own stuff, working in subdued silence. It was difficult to think of anything to say. Trying to cheer each other up seemed wrong when Gavin was lying dead in a hospital mortuary. But in spite of myself, a laugh escaped me before I could stop it. I clapped a guilty hand over my mouth. 'What's she doing there?'

I couldn't believe that I had been so wrapped in woe that I hadn't noticed her, and hadn't seen her the night before either, when Sophie and I dropped off our things. Mavis, the shop mannequin, had moved from my unit in the storeroom into the doorway at the back of the shop, half-blocking the corridor. In her arms she carried the sign that pointed the way to *Antiques and Collectibles*. The words *Vintage Clothes* had been added to the sign in felt pen. Mavis now wore a 1960s yellow mini-dress which zipped up the front, a long, straight black wig and a hippy hat. A macramé bag dangled from one shoulder and she sported huge pink sunglasses.

'That looks good,' Pat said, after we'd stared at Mavis for a moment.

'Yes, it does,' I agreed, wondering what else Ricky and Morris had been up to while we were away.

Sophie came in, pale and heavy-eyed and we exchanged hugs and sorrowful greetings. Her huge dark eyes shone with tears, but she smiled at the sight of Mavis. 'Can you believe we didn't notice her last night?' I asked. 'C'mon, let's have a look,' and we all trooped into the storeroom.

My unit had been transformed. A Spanish shawl, black, deeply fringed and dramatically embroidered with roses, had been pinned at an angle across one white wall, and as well as the hanging clothes rail, which was now stuffed with clothes, a hatstand and a folding wicker screen had made their appearance.

'This is great!' Sophie exclaimed. 'People can try things on now.' She grabbed a white, baker's boy cap from the hatstand, jauntily placing it on her dark head, and admired her reflection in a full-length mirror that Ricky and Morris had brought in. On the folding screen hung a plastic mac in swirling, psychedelic colours, a pair of white knee-length boots placed neatly beneath it. A dressmaker's dummy wore a feather boa and a starched net petticoat.

'My mum used to have one of them,' Pat cried, fingering its stiff frills. 'I've got an old photo of her going out to a dance with a beehive hairdo and a big taffeta skirt.'

Sophie had grabbed the white boots and was sitting on a little chair, rolling up the legs of her jeans. I was still looking around me. My shaded lamps had been draped with gauzy scarves and a drop-leaf table pulled to the centre of the room and opened out. Several pairs of long kid gloves lay on its dark glossy surface, together with a top hat, a pair of opera glasses, and an open biscuit tin full of buttons. A garden trug was filled with ribbons, braids and lengths of fringe, the sort that Morris used in making theatrical costumes, and a vase was stuffed with curling ostrich feathers.

'What do you think?' Ricky's voice demanded suddenly from the doorway. He and Morris were standing there, laden with carrier bags.

'It's a bit over the top quite frankly,' I told him.

'The style is Early Tarts' Boudoir.' He dropped the bags and advanced on me, arms outstretched. 'Are you all right, darlin'?' He enveloped me in a cashmere hug and a miasma of menthol cigarettes, mints and citrus aftershave. 'What a horrible, terrible thing to happen.' He released me and descended on Sophie. Morris, I noticed, had laid a consoling hand on Pat's arm and was whispering to her solicitously.

For a while the talk was all of Gavin and whether he could have stabbed himself accidentally. 'If anyone could do it, he could,' Ricky said frankly. 'D'you remember, Maurice, when he was a kid, we had him in the pantomime?'

Morris nodded mournfully. Every few years, he and Ricky wrote and directed the Ashburton panto. '*Dick Whittington*, it was,' he confirmed. 'He was one of the rats. He went wrong in the middle of a dance routine and sent all the others tumbling over like dominoes.'

'God, he was hopeless!' Ricky shuddered. 'Always two steps behind everyone else.'

'Poor boy.' Morris began blinking a lot and took off his round, gold spectacles, polishing them on his jersey.

Sophie threatened to start crying again so we changed

the subject, forcing ourselves to behave as if everything was normal. Morris volunteered to go upstairs and make us all a cup of tea. He extracted a brick wrapped in foil from one of the carrier bags. 'Banana bread,' he explained, 'just baked.'

I love that man. 'So, what's in all these bags, then?'

'More stuff for sale.' Ricky pulled out a black dress, its layers heavily beaded.

'This isn't from the sixties.' I took it from him and held it up. 'This is earlier – forties, I would think – and it's an original.'

'That's the point,' he said. 'It is an antique. We can't send it out on hire, the fabric is too fragile – rips if you so much as look at it. And everyone was smaller back then,' he added. 'This won't fit anyone now – well, not the strapping great tarts you see these days – might just as well sell it.'

'If you're sure . . .' I said, doubtfully, holding it up for a closer look.

'Same with those white boots,' Ricky went on. 'No one can fit into them these days.'

'What size are they?'

'It's not the shoe size, it's the calves. Skinny legs those dolly birds had . . . Oh, hello! I stand corrected,' he said as Sophie stood triumphantly in the boots and began parading about in them. 'Sparrow's Ankles has got 'em zipped up. Mind you, look at them calves,' he went on, nodding at her legs, 'no fatter than a pair of sauce bottles . . .'

We were all laughing as Morris appeared with a loaded tray of tea and buttered banana bread. And it was in that moment that a voice cut through our merriment like an arctic wind and froze it on our lips.

'Enjoying ourselves, are we?'

Detective Constable DeVille, Inspector Ford's sidekick, known to all who loathe her as Cruella, had come in through the shop and was standing in the storeroom doorway. She's a striking-looking young woman with ebony hair in a sleek bob, an almost unnaturally pale face, and huge, violet-blue eyes. But her bid for beauty is ruined by a small, downturned mouth that gives her a permanent look of disapproval. Today, it seemed, she had a sidekick of her own. He was a broad-shouldered individual with brown hair shaved to stubble and the solid, stocky build that should make criminals think twice about grappling with him; he looked like a rugby player. She introduced him as Detective Constable Dean Collins. He gave a silent nod of greeting.

'You've left the door of your shop unlocked,' Constable DeVille went on, in the voice of a headmistress addressing naughty schoolchildren, 'and there are three handbags in plain sight.' She might as well have added it would serve us right if they got nicked.

No one said anything. We all felt chastened, not by leaving our bags unguarded but by our laughter, by being caught out in behaviour that seemed inappropriate in the tragic circumstances. She should have arrived half an hour before when we were weeping like drains.

'We've come for Gavin Hall's phone.'

'It's in the shop, I'll get it.'

The two detectives trailed after me, and as I took the phone from Gavin's jacket pocket, DeVille was ready with a plastic evidence bag open in her hand and I dropped it in. Collins had picked up one of Gavin's magazines and was leafing through it. Cruella scowled over his shoulder. 'Is this the sort of stuff he sold?' she asked, picking up another.

'Is there any more news,' I asked, 'about what happened to Gavin?'

'We're keeping an open mind at present.' Her voice told me to mind my own business.

I persevered. 'Have you found his spectacles yet?'

DC Collins glanced up from his comic. 'Forensics found them this morning, on the path. He must have dropped them.'

Ricky appeared from the storeroom at that moment carrying a short, white fake-fur jacket freckled with black spots. 'You know, Constable DeVille, you'd look sensational in this!'

Cruella's black brows arched upward and her little mouth quivered. For a moment she struggled, not sure if she was being mocked. I caught a twinkle in her colleague's eye. He folded his lips to hide a smile. If only she had laughed, treated the whole thing as a joke; instead she flung the comic back on the table and glared. 'Come on, Collins. We've got what we came for,' and she marched out. Collins, who looked as if he would have liked to peruse his comic for a bit longer, put it back and followed her. He nodded a goodbye to me and, as he passed the shop window, I could see he was grinning.

I turned the key in the lock after him so that we could enjoy our tea in peace.

'You're evil,' I told Ricky as we trooped back into the storeroom.

'S'not my fault she can't take a joke.' He looked at the fur jacket and sighed. 'The sad thing is, she *would* look sensational in this.'

'Can I try it?' Sophie mumbled through a mouthful of banana bread. She was still wearing the cap and boots.

'Too big for you,' he told her frankly. 'You stick with the cap and boots.'

'I can't afford them,' she sighed soulfully, turning tragic dark eyes upon him. She caught a warning frown from me. 'I'll have to save up,' she added quickly, unzipping the boots and wriggling her feet out.

'Yes, you will,' Ricky told her flatly. 'But you can keep the cap,' he added, winking at her.

'You look fab.'

'Oh, thank you!' She spun around to take another look at herself in the mirror.

'Did you see we'd sold a painting for you yesterday, Sophie?' Morris asked coyly.

'No!' she squeaked. 'Which one?'

'You'd better go and look in the book,' Ricky recommended, and she rushed out into the shop. Pat, during all this, had seated herself at the table, and was carefully selecting lengths of ribbon from the trug, laying each strip out methodically.

'Aren't these trimmings precious?' I asked Morris, watching her. 'Don't you need all these for costumes?'

'I've got miles and miles of the stuff,' he assured me, 'and these are just odd bits.'

'I want a word with you, anyway, Pat,' Ricky began ominously, making her stop and look up. 'Your country panoramas—'

'What's wrong with 'em?' she demanded, immediately suspicious.

'You're not charging enough for them.'

I cheered. I'd been telling Pat this for ages. Her country panoramas are created from felt and wool, delightful scenes of fields and cottages, with knitted trees and woolly sheep, little dressed figures of shepherds and farmers, each scene contained in a deep box frame behind glass. 'They must take you hours and hours,' Morris said.

'If I make 'em too expensive, I won't sell them,' Pat told him.

'And you won't sell 'em if you make them too cheap,' Ricky argued, mimicking her local accent. 'People equate cheap with tat. They won't value your work if you don't.'

Pat was shaking her head. 'Look, I sold one yesterday,' Ricky went on, 'and I whacked another fifteen quid on the price. The customer walked off with it, perfectly happy.'

Pat, who suspected Ricky of winding her up whenever he opened his mouth, scurried off into the shop to check the veracity of this in the ledger.

'Sell anything for me?' I asked, ever hopeful.

'Nah, sorry!'

'Take no notice of him, Juno.' Morris bustled up to me. 'We sold a pair of brass candlesticks and a very pretty ribbon plate.'

Sophie rushed back in, pink with pleasure: one of her most expensive paintings had been sold, an autumn hedgerow scene. 'Who bought it?' she demanded.

Ricky shrugged. 'Oh, some pair of old tarts.'

'They said they had the perfect place for it,' Morris added.

There was something about Ricky's shrug, Morris's coy smile. A little cat's tail of suspicion twitched in my mind. I leant in close to him and murmured, 'Would that perfect place be in your breakfast room or over the mantelpiece in your lounge?'

Morris placed a finger against his lips. 'Don't spoil it for her,' he whispered, as Sophie went rushing back into the shop to choose a replacement to hang on the wall. 'It's in the music room,' he confessed, when she'd gone out.

'I'm not going to find that ribbon plate hanging in there as well, am I?'

'Don't be silly,' he admonished me, patting my hand, 'that's in the downstairs loo.'

Later, much later, when I was back in the flat on my own, feet up on the sofa, radio playing softly, my diary open on my lap, I found myself thinking about spectacles. I was supposed to be going through the diary, reworking the shop rota for next week. With no Gavin, I had spaces to fill. Fortunately, Sophie would be starting work on the bull portrait for Sandy Westershall's birthday and so would have to be in the shop most of the time. At least, I hoped she'd be starting work on it. She'd announced during the afternoon that she didn't want to do it any more, after what had happened to Gavin, and it took a stern talking-to from me and Ricky to persuade her that she couldn't afford to pass up the opportunity. I understood how she felt. I didn't want to go back to Moorworthy House again either, or even think about the place, but she would have to toughen up, put her feelings to one side. Business was business.

Pat had already done more than her fair share in *Old Nick's* last week and I knew she was needed at Honeysuckle Farm. But I had a full week's work ahead of me and didn't know how I was going to manage extra hours in the shop. My attempts to wrestle with the diary weren't helped by the sudden appearance of Bill, who leapt on the sofa and settled down on top of the pages, obliterating them from view. I gave him a brief summary of how helpful this was, and he responded by purring like a buzz saw, tucking his paws under and closing his one eye.

I gave up on the diary and lay back, eyes closed, listening to the rasping rhythm of Bill's purr. My mind kept drifting back to spectacles. Morris wore his all the time, but peered over the top of them mostly, only really using them for sewing or reading. Sophie was supposed to wear hers, but was too vain, so coped without them unless she really needed them. Nick used to wear his, but only when he was working on the fine details of some restoration work. But Gavin wore his all the time. When he was in the shop, when he was cycling, I had never seen his face without them, never seen him put them down on a table, or fold them and tuck them away in a pocket. He was very short-sighted. Without them his world must have been a blur. So if they had fallen off when he was larking around in the woods, waving that silly sword about, and his whole world turned fuzzy, surely he would have stopped to find them, there and then? He depended on them totally. He couldn't have carried on through the wood for another fifty yards to the place where I had found his body. He would have been forced to stop; unless of course, he was running away from something, or from someone – running for his life.

CHAPTER NINE

I didn't get to *Old Nick's* until closing time. Monday was a busy day, with five dogs to walk now that EB had fully recovered, Maisie to clean and shop for, a towering pile of shirts to iron for Simon the accountant, and a full afternoon's tidy-up of Mrs Berkeley-Smythe's garden. It was a large garden and she liked it kept tidy even though she was away on the high seas most of the time and rarely home to appreciate it. This meant that I fell in through the shop door just as Sophie was putting on her coat to go home. She'd had a quiet day: no customers, but she'd made a start on preliminary sketches for her portrait of the Old Thunderer. There'd been a phone call from Vicky Smithson, to ask how we all were, but otherwise she'd had no human contact and was looking forward to going to the pub that evening with friends. She invited me to join them, but I declined and offered to lock up the shop. I wanted to do some rearranging of my stock after the hostile takeover of my unit by the vintage clothes mafia.

I spent an hour in the stockroom, mooching about without achieving much, moving things around and then putting them back again, before I decided I might as well give up, go home and spend another thrilling evening watching auction lots on eBay. I had my eye on some pretty 1920s evening bags; unfortunately, so did a lot of other people. Staying up until the early hours, trying to slip in the final bid before the auction closed, only to be pipped at the post at the very last second, was a frustrating experience. But as well as the bags there was a job lot of hatpins for sale, complete with two pretty porcelain hatpin holders that I was determined to get my hands on, so I reckoned it was worth another night at the screen-face.

It was only as I went to switch the lights off in the shop that I realised someone was lurking in the lane outside the door. A hunched figure, a hand shading his eyes, was staring in through the glass. For a moment I thought it was Creeping Ted Croaker but realised the figure was too tall. The closed sign was on the door, but as he saw me, whoever it was, he began to rattle the handle.

'I'm sorry, we're closed,' I said, loudly enough for him to hear me from the other side of the door, but he started banging on the glass. Surely he realised it was too late for the shop to be open? But there was a grim purposefulness to his banging, and I knew I would have to open the door. Then I recognised him, although he seemed to have aged a hundred years since I last saw him, his features gaunt, his eyes sunken and wretched: the face of a man who had lost his only child.

'Mr Hall,' I breathed, when I had got the door open. 'Please, come in.'

'I'm sorry,' he began brokenly,' I didn't really expect anyone to be here . . . then I saw the lights . . . I just wondered if I could talk to you . . .'

I stood staring at him, unprepared for this moment.

'It was you, wasn't it, who found my poor son?'

'Yes,' I said, recovering my wits. 'I'm so very sorry... Look, please . . . would you like to come upstairs? We could sit down . . . I could make some tea . . .'

He didn't answer, just stared around him, his gaze finally resting on Gavin's jacket hanging on the back of his chair. 'How is your wife?' I asked him in the silence.

He dragged his eyes away from the jacket and stared at me, his gaze almost unfocussed. He spoke slowly, as if his thoughts were happening in slow motion, as if he were sleepwalking. 'She . . . her sister has come to stay. She's with her now.'

I wasn't sure what to say next. Mr Hall had picked up one of the comics from Gavin's table and was staring at it, turning the pages over slowly as he spoke.

'He was supposed to go to university, you know. He got top grades in his A levels. But Gavin didn't always get on with his peers. His mother and I thought perhaps, it might be wise, give him a little experience of the world before he went . . . but now, I wonder, if Gavin might not have—' His voice broke and he stood with the magazine shaking in his hands.

'Please, Mr Hall,' I begged, touching his arm tentatively, 'I think it might be best if you sat down. Here,' I brought a chair up behind him and he sank down into it, the magazine dropping to the floor. I picked it up as Gavin's father sat with his head in his hands and wept, his shoulders shaking piteously.

'Would you like a drink of water?' I asked, after I had let him sob a while.

He looked up, wiping his streaming eyes with the heels of his hands. 'No, thank you.' He took a deep breath, steadying himself. 'I'd just like you to tell me what happened.'

I told him, as gently as I could, about our day at the fair, about the last time I had seen Gavin, heading, as I thought, for the car, and how Sophie and I had found his body in the woods.

'And the man who sold him this dreadful weapon . . .' He leant forward, gripped my wrist with a sudden force that made me wince, and stared intently into my face. '. . . does he know what happened to my son as a consequence?'

'I'm sure he does,' I answered. Cautiously, I put my hand over his gripping one and he released me, muttering an apology. 'But I think if you wanted to know more about that,' I went on, 'the correct person to speak to would be Inspector Ford.'

He stood suddenly, as if by some inner prompting, and then looked around him, lost, as if he didn't know why he'd got up, as if he wasn't sure where he was.

'Mr Hall, if there is anything I can do . . .' I left the rest hanging, as we all do, when we know that there is nothing we can do, nothing that will make the loved one live again.

He touched the cover of one of the graphic novels on Gavin's table. 'He was so into all this stuff,' he said bitterly. 'I'll come and get rid of it all . . . sometime.'

'There's no rush.' I picked up Gavin's jacket and held it out to him. 'You'll want to take this.'

For a moment I thought he would hug it to him, bury his face in it, breathe in his dead child's smell. Perhaps if I had not been standing there, he would have done. 'And there's his rucksack,' I said, producing it from under the table.

He shook his head. 'That's not his.'

'Are you sure? He took it to the fete with him. It was in the car.'

'That's not Gavin's,' he said emphatically. 'His backpack is blue, not black, and it's up in his room. I saw it this . . .' His voice cracked again. 'Thank you, Juno, for talking to me . . .' and he rushed out of the shop, leaving the door open, the bell jangling. He was away, down Shadow Lane before I could call out to him, poor man.

I looked down at the rucksack in my hands and put it back on the table, unclipping the plastic cover. On the inside of the flap a name and address had been carefully painted in block capitals: OLIVER KNOLLYS, 4 DAISON COTTAGES, ASHBURTON. I frowned, fingering the white-painted letters. Who was Oliver Knollys and why did Gavin have his rucksack?

Judging by the weight, there was something inside. I decided to have a look, undoing the drawstring and peering in. Whatever was in there was cushioned, enclosed in a cloud of bubble wrap. I took off the top covering. I could see white metal, hinged and folded legs, tiny rotor blades: a toy helicopter, perhaps? I lifted it out to get a better look.

It wasn't a helicopter. It might be a toy, but if it was, it was a very expensive one. I returned it carefully to its bubble-wrap nest. I knew Daison Cottages, passed them every week on my way to the Brownlows. I didn't know what Gavin was doing with the contents of Mr Knollys' rucksack but I intended to find out, and the only way to do that was to return it to its owner.

CHAPTER TEN

Daison Cottages are not really cottages at all. They are council houses, built after the war for agricultural workers. Like all council houses constructed back then, they are solid, well built, and have large garden plots. These stand in an isolated group of four on the road towards Owlacombe Cross, separated from the roadway by a low stone wall and surrounded on all sides by fields. At some time during the Thatcher era they must have been sold by the council and acquired by their owners. Since then, some have been resold and various degrees of gentrification have taken place. Of the four identical houses, originally painted cream, one is now pistachio green, and one pink, giving the whole row the appearance of a block of Neapolitan ice cream. The third cottage, still vanilla flavour, has sprouted an unconvincing Grecian portico and has a front door painted blue, with flowering baskets hung on either side. It matches the blue-painted wheelbarrow sitting on the front lawn, filled with pink petunias. Pretty, but undeniably naff. It's the last house, number four, which seems to have undergone no change at all, the cream-painted walls grubby and slightly sad, the front door a dull brown and the wire fence separating the garden from the adjacent field set in concrete posts that look original. This is Chez Knollys.

The garden gate was rusty and squeaked when I opened it, a cracked concrete path leading to the front door. The strips of lawn on either side could have done with a trim and the scruffy rosebushes were overgrown. There was no sound when I pressed the doorbell, so I rapped the brass pixie knocker for backup. As neither of these attempts produced any answer from within, I wandered around the side to the rear of the house.

The back garden was long, a washing line strung down its entire length, a solitary floral nightdress billowing gently in the breeze. There was a large vegetable plot on one side with some old cold frames, a water butt and a wizened apple tree. I picked up a fallen apple, hard as a conker and bright green – a cooking apple, probably. Apart from a few dishevelled dahlias, the rest of the garden was grass, except at the far end, where a small patch of wildflower meadow had been sown. I wandered down to take a look. Earlier in the summer, poppies and cornflowers would have glowed amongst tall, rustling grasses ticking and buzzing with insects. Now it was mostly gone, just a tangle of brown stems and rattling seed pods. Beyond the garden fence was a paddock, three ponies watching me from the far end, swishing their tails.

The neighbour with the blue wheelbarrow out front had constructed an imposing length of fence separating the two back gardens, the panels topped with sections of trellis, the whole lot stained a fashionable shade of green. It made the divide between the two neighbours abundantly clear: *We are not like that shabby lot next door*, it seemed to be saying. As I walked back up the path towards the house, it spoke to me.

'Can I help you?'

I had to draw close to the trellis and peer through a diamond-shaped hole to see who had spoken. I could see part of a woman's face through the lattice work, her brown hair wavy and short. 'Are you from social services?' she asked.

Well, I didn't say I was and I didn't say I wasn't. She just made her own assumptions and went plunging on. 'Only, I've phoned your department more than once.'

'Oh?'

'Well, I worry about the old lady.'

'Mrs Knollys?' I ventured.

'There's only that young lad to look after her, and he's still at school. He's away all day and that poor old soul is bedridden. In fact, I've never laid eyes on her.' She stopped, apparently expecting some response.

'Ah!' I said. 'So there is no Mr Knollys?'

She shook her head, 'Only young Oliver.'

So Oliver Knollys was a schoolboy. 'I'm afraid these days it's not unusual for a child to be the sole carer in their family,' I told her, shaking my head sadly.

'I'm sure he does his best, bless him,' the neighbour went on, 'but I've never seen a doctor, or a district nurse go in . . . or a carer . . . or anyone.'

'Have you lived here long?'

'About eighteen months now.'

'Well, I'm here to have a chat with Oliver,' I told her, with the voice of one who has arrived to take control of all problems.

'He won't be back from school yet.' She seemed slightly ruffled, as if she thought I should already know this.

'Do you know what time he gets home?'

'About half past four.'

'You've been most helpful, Mrs . . .'

'Hardiman,' she told me, 'April Hardiman.'

'You've been most helpful, Mrs Hardiman. I'll come back.'

'And what did you say your name was?' she asked.

I didn't. Damn. 'Juno,' I said, turning to smile at her. 'Juno Browne.'

As I reached the front gate and turned to close it, I could see Mrs Hardiman watching me from her living-room window. She must have run back through the house to get a proper look at me. Obviously the diamond-shaped view was not sufficient. I gave her a cheery wave. I don't know whether I make a convincing social worker. I generally look a bit scruffy so I'm sure I fit the bill.

I had an hour before Oliver was due home, time to drive down to *Old Nick's* and check on the takings, possibly pick up a few groceries whilst I was in town. For the first time I switched on White Van's radio, something I'd been reluctant to do because of what happened when Sophie did it in my last vehicle. This time there was no conflagration, just the local news. There had been a double murder at Dartmoor Prison, so the newscaster told me, and a riot during which prisoners had set fire to their cells. But police were not looking for anyone else in connection with the tragic death of nineteen-year-old Gavin Hall, she went on, who died in a stabbing at the weekend, and whose death was being treated as unexplained but not suspicious. She started blathering about the weather, but I switched her off.

I drove back to the shop, and after the briefest of hellos to Sophie and Pat, ran upstairs, sat on the bare floorboards in the living room and picked up Nick's phone.

Unfortunately, it wasn't picked up on the other end by the person I wanted to speak to, but by Det. Constable DeVille. Inspector Ford was at the prison, she informed me, investigating a double murder, what did I want? I didn't want to speak to her. I asked if the inspector could phone me back. There was a weary sigh at the end of the line. She would leave a message – she was obviously doing me an immense favour – but I shouldn't anticipate a response any time soon. The inspector was busy. She hung up.

But I was barely halfway down the stairs before the phone rang and I doubled back on myself to pick up the receiver. 'Juno Browne?' It was a man's voice, but not the inspector's. 'This is Detective Constable Collins. You phoned the station just now.'

It took me a moment to realise who was speaking: Detective Constable Collins, he of the burly, no-nonsense physique and twinkly eyes, the sidekick's sidekick. He must have been earwigging on my conversation with Cruella. 'The inspector won't be free for hours,' he went on. He definitely wasn't a Devon man. His flattened vowels suggested a northerner to me – well, north of Bristol, anyway. 'I wondered if there was anything I could help you with, Ms Browne?' Meaning: he was curious to know why I'd phoned. Whatever, it was nicer talking to him than Cruella. I asked him if what I'd heard on the radio was correct, that they thought Gavin's death was an accident.

'Well, there are no prints on the weapon except for Gavin's and those of Mr Bartholomew who sold it to him,' he explained patiently. 'There's no sign of pursuit, no evidence that anyone had been fighting with Gavin, or chasing him. There's a clear mark on the trunk of the tree where his foot had slipped. And . . .' He hesitated.

'Go on.'

'The pathologist confirms that the weapon's angle of thrust—'

'Dear God,' I moaned.

'Sorry, but you did ask. Shall I go on?'

'Yes, please.'

'The weapon's angle of thrust is consistent with the wound being self-inflicted. When he hit the ground, the blade was forced into his body.' Constable Collins allowed me a few moments to ruminate over this before he spoke again. 'You found him, Juno. Don't you think it was an accident?'

'It's his specs that bother me. They were found so far from his body.' I told him I couldn't believe that anyone as blind as Gavin could have carried on running after he'd dropped his spectacles, not unless all the fiends in hell were on his tail.

Constable Collins did a bit of silent ruminating himself. Then he said, 'I'll make sure your concerns are passed on to the detective inspector.'

It was the best I was going to get and a damn sight more than I'd have got from Cruella DeVille. At least he'd listened. I thanked him and put the phone down. Then I headed off down the stairs. If I didn't get a move on, I was going to miss the bus from school.

* * *

Most kids in Ashburton attend South Dartmoor College. I passed clusters of them in their uniforms dawdling home in the way that only adolescents can dawdle, as I drove up to Owlacombe Cross. I climbed the hill, following a road twisting between overgrown hedgerows until I was forced to brake sharply, the way ahead blocked by a twisted knot of kicking feet and flailing fists. I couldn't see the target at the centre of this affray, but whoever it was, he was outnumbered. I blasted my horn and the group scattered. Four lads, about fourteen years old, shot off in different directions, two of them scrambling through the nearest hedge. I opened the van door and yelled after them.

'Olly Nolly!' they chanted as they escaped, laughing. 'Olly Nolly!'

A small skinny figure was curled up in the road, lying on his side in a foetal position, knees drawn up protectively, elbows tucked in. I couldn't see his face because he had sensibly buried it in the schoolbag that he was clutching to his chest. I could only see short, spiky fair hair and one pink ear.

I leant over him. 'It's all right, they've gone now.'

He moved cautiously, uncurling like a little hedgehog, and one blue eye stared at me apprehensively. I had expected the owner of the rucksack to be older, a sixth-former perhaps, but I had no doubt that this skinny little lad was the one I was looking for. I held out my hand to help him up. 'Oliver Knollys, I presume.'

CHAPTER ELEVEN

Oliver Knollys had a split lip, torn trousers, a bloodied knee and probably a black eye brewing, but it still took a lot of persuasion to get him into my van and let me drive him the short distance home. It was only when I showed him his rucksack caged in the back he agreed to slide into the passenger seat next to me.

'So, what was all that about?' I asked.

'Nothing,' he hunched a shoulder, feigning unconcern. 'They're just smegheads.'

'Do they bother you a lot?'

He dabbed at his bleeding lip. 'Sometimes.'

'Have you told anyone you're being bullied?'

He didn't answer, didn't look at me.

'A teacher?' I prompted.

He gave a little snort of laughter. 'That'd make it worse.'

'Your grandmother, then?'

He looked taken aback. 'How do you know about my grandmother?'

111

I told him how I'd tried to return the rucksack to him earlier and had talked to his neighbour.

'Nosy cow, she is!' He turned to look at me suddenly, blue eyes wide with alarm. 'You aren't going to tell no one, are you? I don't want people coming round the house. I don't want anyone upsetting my nan.'

'I won't tell anyone if you don't want me to.'

Oliver stared unconvinced.

'I promise.'

He frowned. 'Who are you, anyway?' By now we were pulling up outside his house.

'Juno. I was a friend of Gavin's . . .'

He lowered his head. 'I know what happened to him,' he told me, fiddling uncomfortably with the strap of his schoolbag. 'They told us in assembly at school.'

'He used to be a pupil at South Dartmoor, didn't he?'

'Then they gave us a lecture about carrying knives.' He swung the van door open. 'Can I have my bag now?'

'Not just yet. We're going to patch you up first.'

He froze like a startled rabbit. 'You're not coming in?'

'We won't disturb your nan,' I assured him. 'She needn't even know I'm in the house.'

I pointed to his reflection in the rear-view mirror. 'You don't want her to see you like that, do you?'

'Well, all right,' he muttered, and led me reluctantly up the front path and around the side of the house, his schoolbag thumping on his shoulder. I held on to his rucksack. He dug a key from his pocket and let us through the back door into a large, square kitchen. A scrubbed pine table took up the middle of the room, an original oil-fired range set against

112

the wall with clean washing hanging around it on an old wooden clothes horse.

'D'you want to sit down, Oliver? We need to get that dirt and gravel out of your knee.'

'Call me Olly,' he said, rolling up the leg of his trousers. 'Only teachers call me Oliver.'

I swung open the door of a fridge almost as old as Nick's. 'Any ice?' I pulled a tray of ice cubes from the tiny freezing compartment, bashed some out into the sink, grabbed a handkerchief from the clothes horse, wrapped some cubes in it and handed it to Olly. 'Hold that against your lip.' It had stopped bleeding but was puffing up ominously. I asked if there was a first-aid kit in the house.

'There's some stuff up in the bathroom cabinet,' he mumbled. 'I'll get it.'

'Sit!' I commanded. 'I can find it.'

'Nan will be having her nap,' he said anxiously.

'I'll be quiet as a mouse, I promise.'

'I'll make her tea in a minute,' he said, then added pointedly, 'when you've gone.'

I was getting curious about Olly's nan. He seemed terrified of disturbing her. Or was it Nan herself he was terrified of? Was he being overprotective or was she some kind of gorgon?

I crept up the stairs. The door of his bedroom stood open, the bed tidily made. It looked like the room of a much younger boy; the Thunderbird wallpaper was probably an embarrassment to him now, much of it covered up by film posters. I listened outside Nan's door, which was shut: no sound from inside, no muffled television or radio, no enquiring voice. She must have been sleeping. The bathroom was pink-tiled, with a frilly curtain at the little window and a crocheted loo roll cover sitting on the windowsill, a medicine cabinet with a speckled mirror over the sink. I came downstairs armed with scissors, cotton wool, plasters and a bottle of TCP.

In my absence Olly had grabbed the rucksack and was checking out the contents. On the table lay a cloud of bubble wrap, and a few inches above it, four little motor blades whirring softly, the drone hovered like a giant dragonfly.

'It's working all right, then?' I don't like drones. I think they're a bloody nuisance. But I'd never seen one working at close quarters before and it was fascinating. Olly's fingers were busy on the controls as he sent it higher, circling the kitchen, before bringing it back to the table for a controlled landing.

'That must have cost a lot,' I said.

He shook his head. 'I made it.'

'You made it?' I cleared a little space amongst the bubble wrap to put down the things I carried.

'It's not difficult,' he informed me nonchalantly, 'I got the parts off the Internet.'

'In a kit?' I knelt before him and began dabbing gingerly at his bloodied knee. 'Sorry, this might hurt a bit.'

'Yeh, but some of the parts were a bit crap, I had to modify 'em.'

'Do you want to do this kind of thing when you leave school? Electronics?'

'Nah! I'm going to be a chef.' He watched me picking grit out of the wound. My teeth were on edge, but he was remarkably stoical about the process. 'You got a boyfriend?'

114

I don't currently have a man in my life. Men tend to want to murder me. 'Actually, there's a vacancy in that department at the moment. Did you want to apply?'

He shook his head and grinned, his face flushing faintly pink. 'I'm too young for girls.'

'How old are you?'

'Fourteen. But I look younger, don't I? People are always telling me.'

He was certainly still a child, no sign of the volcanic eruption which must shortly take place in his hormones. His skin was clear, cheek soft as a girl's, his voice a childish pipe; a skinny pixie of a boy, with spiky hair and sticky-out ears. There was something old-fashioned, almost quaint about him. Perhaps it came from living alone with his nan, being her sole carer. I looked around me. The kitchen was clean, the washing aired. When I'd opened the fridge I'd noticed the remains of a shepherd's pie in an enamel dish. He put me to shame. I felt quite moved at the idea of this little lad coping on his own. 'Do you get any help with your nan? You're entitled to support, you know, from the council.'

'We don't need any help,' he answered defiantly. 'Besides, Nan doesn't like anyone coming here. Look, thanks and all that, but you'll have to go now. I need to give Nan her tea.'

'I wanted to ask you a few things about Gavin. Look, now you don't look quite so scary, why don't you go and check on your nan, see she's OK? She might like a cup of tea.'

He agreed reluctantly and limped upstairs. I heard him knock on the door, calling softly.

It opened and then closed as I binned the bloodied cotton wool. He came down a few moments later.

'She's all right, for a few minutes. She sleeps most of the time,' he went on, 'or watches telly. I leave her sandwiches for lunch before I go to school, and a flask of tea. We have our proper meal in the evening.'

'What's wrong with her?' I asked.

'She's old.'

Old age isn't a disease, but I decided not to pursue it. I reckoned if her grandson was only fourteen, she couldn't be very old, anyway. 'I won't keep you long,' I promised. 'You knew Gavin from school?'

'Not really. I mean, I knew him to look at, he was a prefect. But he was years above me, he left last year.'

'But you were friends?'

'He was all right.' His eyes became shiny suddenly and he looked away. 'It was horrible what happened to him. Was he really just messing about with a knife?'

'That's what the police think. Actually, it was a sword. He was carrying it when he jumped up on a fallen tree and slipped.'

He was silent a moment, taking this in. 'I was out in the field one day, flying the drone. Gav was going by on his bike and stopped to have a look. Course, he wanted to have a go with it.' He grinned suddenly. 'He was hopeless with the controls. Anyway, he wanted me to go up Moorworthy with him, fly it around up there.'

'You mean where the big house is?'

'That's right.'

'When was this?'

He rubbed his nose reflectively. 'Weeks ago, the school holidays had just started. I told him we couldn't fly it over

116

private property, it's against the law. But he said he just wanted to look in the woods.'

'Did he say why?'

Olly's gaze slid away, eyes hidden by pale pink lids and fair lashes. 'No.'

He was holding out on me, but I knew I mustn't press him too hard, I didn't want him to clam up altogether. 'How did you get there? Gavin didn't drive.'

'We cycled up to Buckfast, picked up the path to Holne Chase. We walked the last bit, Gav wanted us to hide our bikes in the woods. When we got to the gates, we flew the drone up over that long wall, and over them woods, but there were too many trees for us to see much. We couldn't see the entrance to the mine—'

'That's what he wanted to see, the entrance to the mine?'

He nodded.

'Where were you when you were doing this?'

'On that bit of common, across the road,' he said.

'Sorry, Olly, I don't know anything about drones. I can see there's a camera on it.' It was mounted in the centre, a shiny black eye at the junction of the four legs. 'But how do you see what the camera is seeing?'

'It sends pictures to my smartphone. We watched on that.'

'Right. But you couldn't see what Gavin wanted to see?'

'The trees grow too thick. He wanted me to bring it down low, fly it amongst 'em, but it's too risky. So I brought it round, over a field and then we saw the bloke with the gun so—'

'Whoa!' I stopped him. 'What bloke with a gun?'

'When we flew the drone over this field – still on Moorworthy land, like – he was standing there with a shotgun, pointed right at us. He must have been watching it flying above the trees. He was going to shoot it out of the sky. D'you want to see?'

'You've still got the film on your phone?'

'I downloaded it onto the laptop. Come on.' Suddenly fired with enthusiasm, he hopped across the kitchen and into the living room. I followed him and sat at the table as he woke up the laptop and began keying in passwords and other mysterious stuff. The living room had the chilly feel of a room that is not used much, the wallpaper and curtains dating back to the sixties. Apart from a few china ornaments on the windowsill, the only objects of interest were an upright piano and a music stand. After a few moments Olly angled the screen of the laptop so I could see.

At first I was looking through blades of grass, an insect-eye view, and then as the drone rose higher, it gradually revealed the scruffy turf of the moor, boulder-strewn, with Gavin in his specs, grinning, waving up at it. He looked as if he was really enjoying himself. I felt a tug in my chest at the sight of him; I had never seen him looking so happy. The drone crossed the grey ribbon of road and the wall, going higher again, almost brushing the treetops. Then I was looking down over the impenetrable green mass of trees in full leaf. 'The entrance to the mine is under there somewhere,' Olly told me, 'but we couldn't see . . . so I brought the drone back over and . . . there he is!'

I found myself looking down into the face of a man in a sagging tweed jacket and flat cap, his shotgun raised, aiming straight at the drone. 'That's Moss!'

'D'you know him?'

'I suppose you could say I've met him.'

'I pressed *home*.' It seemed as if the film speeded up, going backwards over the trees, back over the wall, over the road, until the drone landed amongst the grass. 'It's a control that brings it straight back to the launch point,' Olly explained proudly. 'I reckon that bloke would have shot us right out of the sky.'

'Some people will go to any lengths to protect their privacy,' I pointed out.

'I told Gav, you're not supposed to fly it within fifty metres of private property. But you're not supposed to shoot at people either, even if they are trespassing.'

'I don't know if the law applies to drones.'

'I didn't mean the drone.'

I stared. 'You don't mean he shot at *you*?'

Olly's face was deadly serious. 'We was just packing up, had got the drone back in the bag, and we heard a shout, and there was that bloke coming towards us with the shotgun, yelling and waving. So we legged it. He fired over our heads.'

My very brief acquaintance with Moss had given me the impression he was a bit odd, certainly uncommunicative, but he must be an absolute nutter to fire a shotgun in the direction of two young boys, even if he was aiming high to frighten them off. 'What did you do?'

'We kept running. Then we hid in the woods. We had to wait ages till we were sure it was safe to come out, that he'd gone.' He gave a grim little smile. 'Then we had to cycle back home. We were knackered.'

'Did you tell anyone what had happened?'

'You mean, like the police?' He shook his head. 'I didn't

want anyone round here, asking questions. My nan—'

'Yes, I understand, but, after all this, you were happy to loan the drone to Gavin on the day of the fete?'

'Didn't loan it to him, did I?' he responded bitterly. 'He was dead keen to go back to this place, wanted me to go with him. But I've got Youth Band on a Saturday morning. I told him, I'm not missing band practice just to go to some crappy garden fete.'

I pointed to the music stand. 'So, you're the musician?'

He shrugged. 'Not really. I wanted to play the clarinet, but when I tried to join the band, they said they had enough clarinets. They couldn't get anyone to play the bassoon. No one wanted to play it, so I said I'd have a go. And I like it, it's sort of sad-sounding.'

'Yes, it is.' I'd have liked to have heard him play. 'But getting back to Gavin—'

'He pinched it, didn't he?' Olly said in disgust. 'I come home from school on Friday night, he'd got in here, must've found where I keep the spare key. He's left me a note. He said he was sorry, but promised he'd take care of it and bring it back on Sunday. I thought, he'll wreck it if he tries to fly it in them woods, he'll crash it into a tree.'

'Didn't you try and get it back?'

'I don't know where he lives, do I? I mean, I know his parents live in one of them posh places up on Druid somewhere, but I've never been to his house, don't know his address. When he didn't bring it back on Sunday I tried his phone. I was going to try again, when I got back from school, but then they told us he was dead, so . . .' He tailed off.

'He didn't fly the drone on Saturday,' I told him. 'It was locked in the car all day. Perhaps he thought better of trying it once he'd been in the woods himself . . . Olly,' I began tentatively, 'you really don't know why he was so keen to go back to Moorworthy House? He didn't tell you?'

He looked down and picked silently at a scab on his finger. 'This is really important, Olly.'

He wouldn't look at me. 'I don't want to get in any trouble.'

'You won't, honestly. Only I'm not sure that Gavin's death was really an accident—'

'I've told you I don't know.' He looked straight at me then, his little pointed chin lifted obstinately. 'I want you to go now.'

'Olly—'

'I want you to go,' he repeated firmly, closing the lid of the laptop. 'I've got to give my nan her tea.'

I know what I should have done. I should have called Inspector Ford straight away and reported the incident of Moss firing the shotgun. I should have betrayed Olly's confidence and told him everything he had told me. The police have to investigate any incident involving a firearm. But somehow, I didn't; somehow I didn't think Olly's nan would like her house filled with policemen. Besides, I needed to gain Olly's trust. He knew why Gavin was so keen to go back into the woods, to find the entrance to the Moorworthy mine. So, even when I had the perfect opportunity, when the inspector phoned me that evening, I held back.

I'd got out a map of Dartmoor when I got home and spread it on the kitchen table, much to the delight of Bill, who immediately sat in the middle of it. I'd locked him out of the flat that morning, but as always, he found his way back in. I think he has a network of secret tunnels behind the wainscot like one of Beatrix Potter's mice. Anyway, his entry into the flat is made easy for him at the moment because my bathroom window has been stuck open about six inches for months, letting in considerably more fresh air than I want, particularly when I'm naked and wet. I keep complaining to Adam, who promises he will get round to fixing it, but as the sash cords are broken and he's probably not capable of dealing with them himself, I doubt if this will be any time soon.

Despite Bill parking his furry body amongst the contour lines, I managed to locate the road to Moorworthy, tracing it with my finger until I found the house. The woods were marked as a green-coloured wedge. The thin end of the wedge must have been where Sophie and I had entered, through the little gate in the grounds. The footpath was just visible, if I squinted until my eyes hurt, as a tiny broken line. It was fenced off now, but originally it would have gone right through the woods, disappeared under Bill's tummy for a bit, and emerged close to a farm building close by. The words 'Moorworthy Mineshaft, disused' were written within the green shape of the woods. The farm building was marked as 'Applecote Farm, abandoned'. The footpath led away from the farm, across open fields to 'Applecote Pit, mineshaft, disused'. I reckoned the distance between the two disused mineshafts could not have been more than a mile.

The phone rang. It was Inspector Ford, to warn me that the coroner would be contacting me to ask me some questions about Gavin.

'Will I have to give evidence at the inquest?'

'Not necessarily,' he said. 'But she will want to ask you questions about how you found Gavin's body.' It was good of him to call me himself. Other police officers might have left such a call to one of his underlings. 'Collins tells me you were concerned about Gavin's glasses.'

He listened politely as I explained my theory about Gavin being chased. 'There's no evidence of any pursuit,' he told me. 'Of course, from a forensic point of view, it doesn't help that so many visitors to the fete decided to explore the little woodland during the course of the afternoon. We've been contacted by some, but no one saw Gavin or noticed anything untoward.'

This was understandable. I wouldn't have found him myself if I hadn't been looking for him.

'Oh . . . excuse me a moment.' The inspector must have turned his face away from the receiver. I heard his voice, slightly muffled, calling to someone. 'Dale! Where is Collins?'

'On paternity leave, sir,' a cheery voice replied.

'Has that started already?'

'Last night, sir – a little girl – mother and baby doing well.'

'Excellent. Are we sending any—'

'Flowers for the new mother, sir, present for the baby – all in hand.'

'Thank you, Constable . . . Sorry about that.' He returned his attention to me.

No need to apologise, I was fascinated. So Detective

Constable Collins was a new daddy. How sweet. I just hoped the baby looked like her mother.

'Forensics were able to trace the route that Gavin had taken,' the inspector went on, 'when he departed from the main path. It was evident from ferns and other plants that had been cut with something sharp, some sort of blade, rather than just broken off. This rather supports your theory that he had gone into the woods to play with the sword.'

'He'd been swiping at the undergrowth with it?'

'It seems so.'

'Just messing about?'

'Well, he didn't need to clear a path,' the inspector pointed out dryly. 'He was walking in lightly covered woodland, not hacking through tropical rainforest.'

So Gavin had just been fooling around. I could imagine him swaggering and swiping the heads off innocent plants. I began to feel vaguely idiotic.

'And let's just suppose this was murder,' the inspector went on, 'what was the motive? Why would anyone want to kill Gavin Hall?'

I'd asked myself the same question over and over. 'Did his phone reveal anything?'

'We've found nothing suspicious so far,' he answered, 'just some rather strange conversations about Batman.'

Inwardly I groaned. 'Gavin was obsessed with superheroes . . . What about that strange man who came into my shop . . . creeping someone or other?'

'Creeping Ted Croaker? Yes, we still intend to interview him, find out what his connection to Gavin was, but he seems to have gone to ground. We can't find him for the moment.'

'Well, if he comes to the shop again—'

'Please get in touch. Well, good luck with the coroner, Juno.'

This was my moment, before the inspector rang off, to tell him about the incident with Moss and the shotgun. But I didn't, I let him go. I left the phone, moved Bill and folded up the map. I still didn't know why Gavin had been so keen to go to the Moorworthy fete, or why he had wanted to search for the entrance to the mine with Olly's drone weeks before I was even aware that it existed. But I was convinced Olly knew, and the little sod was damn well going to tell me.

CHAPTER TWELVE

I arrived at Maisie's next morning, too late to prevent a flood. The smell of hot, wet washing hit me as soon as I opened her cottage door.

'It's the machine!' she wailed at me, standing in the kitchen, a shallow puddle of hot soapy water spreading towards her furry slippers. Jacko lapped at it experimentally then thought better of it.

'You've forced the door again, haven't you?' The washing machine was wide open, water dribbling from its rubber seal, sodden washing in a steaming heap on the floor. I moved Maisie firmly out of the path of the encroaching flood. 'Why don't you sit down? I'll deal with this.'

'It wouldn't let me have me washing,' she moaned dramatically, tottering towards her chair. 'I thought it had finished but the door wouldn't open.'

I sloshed through the puddle and switched the machine off. The red light stopped flashing.

'You changed the programme again,' I told her, pointing

to the dial. 'Now, you know we don't use that one. I've painted the only button you need to use with your red nail varnish, remember? You don't need to touch anything else.'

Her face flushed with indignant innocence. 'I never touched anything!' At ninety-four, Maisie can lie with the mendacity of someone ninety years younger.

'It must have been Jacko, then.' I scooped her wet washing into a bucket and reached for a mop.

'I told our Janet I didn't want that washing machine,' Maisie said petulantly.

'Our Janet' was her daughter, who lives up north. She had bought her mother the new machine after the old one collapsed from exhaustion. 'I wanted one just like the old one.'

'I know,' I sympathised as I finished mopping, 'but they don't make that sort any more, Maisie. You've broken the lock again. We'll have to get that fella to come and fix it. Give him a call.' I picked up the bucket of laundry. 'I'll wring this lot out and hang it on the line. And don't come onto this wet floor,' I warned her, 'in case you slip.'

I lugged the bucket into the garden. Wet washing weighs a lot. As I wrung out each garment and pegged it on the line, I thought suddenly of Olly's garden, of the single floral nightdress blowing in the breeze.

'You ever know a family called Knollys, Maisie?' I asked when I came back inside. 'They lived up Owlacombe way?'

'I went to school with a Fred Knollys.' She was sitting safely on the sofa by now, her feet up on a stool, making a big production number of behaving herself. 'He's dead, years ago. Now, he married . . . what was her name?'

'I've met a little boy called Knollys,' I told her, sitting

down. 'Oliver.' I smiled. 'Olly Knolly, they call him.'

Maisie suddenly laughed, bringing her hands together in a single clap of delight. 'That's it!' she cried, remembering. 'Dolly Knolly we used to call her! Dorothy was her real name.' She frowned. 'She still alive? She must be my age.'

'Olly only has his grandmother, but I think she must be younger than you.'

Maisie was shaking her head with the certainty of one who can remember years ago, even if she can't remember yesterday. 'No. There was no grandson. There was a granddaughter, and she was no better than she should be.' She rolled her eyes in disapproval. 'Now, she had a babby . . . now let me think. Course, he killed himself.'

'Who did? Fred?'

'No. Not Fred!' she snorted, as if she was talking to an idiot. 'The son! I'll think of his name in a minute. Suicide. Ever such a fuss, there was. Vicar only let him be buried in the corner of the churchyard. Mind you, this was years ago, be different now.'

'Are we talking about Oliver's father?'

Maisie looked blank. 'Who's Oliver?'

I began to wish I hadn't started this conversation. 'The grandson.'

'No! I told you, there wasn't any grandson, just the girl.'

I gave up after a couple more minutes, still unable to sort out the Knollys' family tree.

Fortunately, there were other people I could ask, and I'd be seeing them that afternoon.

* * *

Jamie Westershall was waiting in *Old Nick's* when I popped in at lunchtime, standing behind Sophie, admiring the progress of her portrait of the Old Thunderer, whose magnificent head was emerging from the white background of the thick watercolour paper like a ghost through the mist: his staring dark eye, the moist pinkness of his nose. His horns and curls were as yet unpainted, just faint strokes of Sophie's pencil, the background of field and woods a hazy wash of green.

There was something almost proprietorial about the way he was leaning over Sophie's shoulder, as she sat smiling up at him. But Sophie brings out the protective instinct in men.

I don't seem to have the same effect, possibly because I'm tall enough to look most of 'em in the eye and spit in it if necessary. They both looked up as I came in, spell broken.

'Ah, the gorgeous Juno!' Jamie came swiftly forward to give me a hug. 'Just wanted to see how you girls were after that terrible business the other day.' He sighed. 'Of course, I blame myself,' he added sadly.

'Why on earth should you?' It was looking more and more as if the only person to blame for what had happened was Gavin himself.

'I wanted to get the whole wood fenced off years ago, when we first discovered there were rare bats in the old mineshaft, but there was a lot of fuss from local ramblers about the right of way through the woods being kept open. In the end we came to a compromise, just fenced off part of it, but now I wish I'd stuck to my guns.'

'It's not your fault, Jamie,' Sophie assured him solemnly. She gave him a long-lashed blink, her dark eyes turned on him, full beam.

'No, it's not,' I added. 'Gavin shouldn't have been messing about with a lethal weapon. The police seem convinced it was an accident.'

'Of course it was an accident!' Jamie's eyes widened in surprise. 'What else could it have been? But listen, that's only part of the reason I came. I'm hoping that you haven't been put off Moorworthy House altogether. As you know, this portrait is a present for Sandy's birthday. Quite a big birthday, the old devil is seventy this year and we're throwing a party. I was hoping that you, Sophie, as the artist, would come along. And you too, Juno, of course.'

Sophie glanced at me, taken aback and uncertain. 'That's wonderful, thank you,' I put in hastily, before her little mouth had a chance to open. I knew she was reluctant to go back there again, but I didn't want her to blow my chances of taking another look around.

'We'll both be delighted. This could be very good for business, Soph,' I added. 'You might pick up another commission.'

'Just what I thought,' Jamie agreed. 'So you'll come? It's the 29th of October.'

'We'll be there,' I promised.

'Excellent.' He strode to the shop door.

'By the way,' I called out to him, 'I saw Mr Moss at the fete. I tried to thank him for getting my van taken to the garage, but he didn't give me the chance.'

'Moss?' he laughed. 'He's a bit of an oddball. He's worked on the estate for years. Believe me, he wouldn't bother about being thanked, especially by a young lady. He'd be covered in embarrassment, I expect. He barely ever speaks. Anyway,' he looked at his watch, 'must dash. Oh,' he paused as he opened the door, 'nearly forgot to say, this party is fancy dress.'

'Any particular theme?'

'Oh, hell, now, what is it? Emma thought it up.' Jamie frowned, drumming his fingers on the edge of the door. 'I know!' He snapped them, remembering. 'Legends of the Silver Screen. That won't cause any problems, will it?'

'None at all,' I told him, as Sophie grinned at me. 'That's absolutely perfect.'

Autumn had really arrived. In the distant woods bronze had mellowed to gold, acorns were dropping, rusty flakes of leaves falling on pavements; there was smell of woodsmoke, and any gust of wind was likely to bring down a painful shower of conkers, still in their spiky green jackets. But mostly what alerted me to the changing season was the increasingly chilly air blasting through my bathroom window. I called in at *Sunflowers*, when I came away from *Old Nick's*, to speak to Adam, my landlord. I could see his bearded figure through the window as I crossed the road. He spotted me and tried to hide behind the counter.

As the cafe was empty, I felt I could be direct. 'I've got just two words to say to you, Adam,' I told him as he lurked beardily behind the cake cabinet. 'Bathroom window.'

He held up his hands in apology. 'I know, Juno, I'm sorry. I'll get round to it.'

I reminded him that I'd heard this before. 'There's a bloke who advertises repairing sash windows in the Ashburton magazine. Shall I just call him in and send you the bill?'

'No, I'll do it,' he insisted. 'I promise.'

'This week?'

He sighed, rubbing his face with weariness. 'This week,' he promised reluctantly.

'Thank you.' I turned to go but he stopped me.

'Do me a favour,' he said, lowering his voice, 'only Kate's not here.' He pointed to an empty table, where a copy of *The Times* lay open at the crossword page, a woman's padded jacket slung over the back of the chair. 'That customer went into the ladies' loo a good half-hour ago. You wouldn't pop in there, check she's not been taken ill or something?'

'Perhaps she's wriggled out the back window,' I told him, grinning. 'Done a bunk, left you her jacket in lieu of payment.'

'Well, brilliant! She only had a coffee.'

I marched up to the ladies', opening the door a little cautiously. Standing in the tiny space occupied by the basin was someone I recognised immediately. I'd only seen her once, at night in a dimly lit car park, but she'd been difficult to forget. In the light of day her face was even more striking, with large, shrewd grey eyes, high cheekbones and a thin, slightly prominent nose. Her hair turned out to be more blonde than grey, and she seemed to be in the process of putting it up, arms raised, a hairpin pressed between her lips. On the edge of the basin was a washbag with a toothbrush sticking out of it, a pink towel, and a smaller zipped bag that I guessed contained make-up. There was a smell of expensive perfume.

'Excuse me.' I pretended I wanted the toilet and wriggled past her. She smiled pleasantly as I closed the door, but if she recognised me, she didn't reveal it. As I slid the bolt, I could hear her hastily zipping up her washbag, gathering up her things. I decided I might as well use the loo after all, and by the time I came out, the mystery lady had gone. Back in the cafe, I found the padded jacket had been taken from the chair and Adam was picking up three pound coins that she had flung on the counter in payment for her coffee as she left.

'She was all right, then?' he asked me. 'She certainly left in a hurry.'

'She was just having a wash and brush-up.' I frowned. I was willing to bet she'd left in a hurry because she had recognised me; she obviously didn't wish to be engaged in conversation. Who cleans their teeth and does their hair and their make-up in the cramped space of a cafe toilet except someone who has no access to better facilities? Like someone sleeping in a car? The good leather handbag and the expensive perfume suggested someone with money. Was this elegant, respectable-looking woman really living rough? And why was she hanging around Ashburton? Curiouser and curiouser. I was intrigued.

'I suppose you want a coffee now?' Adam offered ungraciously.

'Only if it's free,' I answered sunnily, 'and there's a raisin flapjack with it.'

He muttered something inaudible as he turned to the coffee machine.

CHAPTER THIRTEEN

'So, we'll be all right for costumes, then, me and Sophie, for this party?'

'I expect we can find you a couple of old rags,' Ricky muttered, his fag pursed between his lips as he sat at the breakfast-room table.

'After the last hour I've spent up that rickety ladder, scouring your loft for a box of spats you were so convinced was up there, and turned out to be down in your spare bedroom, you'd better come up with something fabulous.'

'Don't you worry, Juno,' Morris passed me a cup of tea, 'you leave it to us. You'll be the belles of the ball.'

'Damn right,' I told him, helping myself to a biscuit.

'No news on poor Gavin?' he asked.

I shook my head, mouth too busy with biscuit to respond.

'The police must be satisfied it was an accident,' Ricky said.

'Well, there's still the formality of the inquest, but yes, I suppose they are.'

There were a few moments of thoughtful silence as we all

sipped our tea and munched. Ricky's fag lay untouched in the ashtray.

'You don't know someone called Creeping Ted Croaker, I suppose?' I asked.

They had never heard of him but there are circles not even Ricky and Morris mix in. Then, of course, I had to explain who he was.

'You don't think he was involved in Gavin's death somehow?'

'Difficult to see how,' I admitted, 'unless he knew Gavin was going to the fete and followed him into the woods. But Inspector Ford says Croaker is just a small-time drugs pusher, not a violent character.'

Morris shook his head solemnly. 'You can never tell, not when drugs are involved.'

'It's funny you going up to Moorworthy House again,' Ricky said, 'for this party. Maurice and I have been asked to do another concert there in a few weeks.'

'You mentioned you'd done one there before.'

'We've been there a couple of times,' Morris put in, 'fundraising events.'

Ricky laughed mirthlessly. 'They could do with a few funds themselves. That place is falling apart. It's got dry rot, needs a new roof. I remember the old man telling me.'

'Jamie's uncle?' I asked.

He nodded. 'Very strapped for cash, they are.'

'They don't behave like it.'

'That's your landed gentry for you,' he said, picking up his cigarette, 'fur coat and no knickers. They gave us a grand tour of the house once, didn't they, Maurice? It's all very lovely on the ground floor, but the further up you go, the shabbier it gets.'

Morris was nodding. 'They've got a real damp problem, the ceiling in one bedroom was grey with mould.'

'Don't talk to me about mouldy ceilings, you should see the state of my kitchen.' Another thing I had to tackle Adam about. Stoically I resisted taking a second biscuit from the packet Morris was waving about under my nose. 'I wanted to ask you something. I've met a young friend of Gavin's, Olly Knollys. Did you ever know anyone called Knollys?'

Morris took off his specs and began cleaning them on a corner of the tablecloth, frowning thoughtfully. 'The name rings a bell.'

'Course it does!' Ricky poked him with his fag fingers as if to wake him up. I suddenly felt like Alice at the tea party: Ricky was the Mad Hatter and Morris was the Dormouse. 'Abigail! Our Princess Jasmine!'

'Princess Jasmine?'

'We were putting on *Aladdin*,' Ricky explained. 'Abigail Knollys was playing the princess. Only seventeen, she was—'

'Pretty girl,' Morris interrupted, shaking his head sadly, 'pretty girl.'

'There was a lot of fuss when we cast her. Some people felt she was a bad example. She'd got herself knocked up the year before, had a baby boy. She was still at school, in the sixth form, wouldn't say who the father was.'

'When was this?'

Ricky shrugged. 'Ten years ago?' He glanced at Morris for confirmation. 'Twelve? Anyway, poor maid never got to play the part because she and her mum went out

Christmas shopping in Exeter and got wiped out in some pile-up on the A38.'

'Shortly afterwards, her father killed himself,' Morris added sadly. 'Couldn't cope with the loss of his wife and daughter, I suppose.'

'Right,' I said. 'So, in a short time, this baby boy, who I assume must be Olly, had lost his mother and both grandparents. His father is absent, unknown. So, who was left to look after him?'

'His great-grandma,' he answered. 'Dorothy.'

'Dolly Knolly?'

Morris chuckled. 'That's what they used to call her.'

Ricky frowned. 'Is she still alive? She must be over ninety.'

So, Olly's nan was really his great-grandmother, ninety-something years old, bedridden and left alone all day whilst he was at school. His neighbour was right to be concerned.

I glanced at my watch. Olly wouldn't be home yet. But if Gavin could find out where he kept his spare key, I was damn sure I could.

It was underneath a small stone tortoise in the back garden. Not the most original of hiding places. Fortunately, Gavin had replaced the key there after he'd borrowed the drone. I'd parked the van way down the road, where I was sure no one would see it, and managed to creep up the path without being observed by Olly's neighbour. There was washing blowing on the line, a different nightdress this time, pink, and a pair of large floral knickers, plus two school shirts and grey socks. Olly had been busy with the laundry. I fitted the key into the lock and it turned with a satisfying click.

I let myself into the kitchen and looked around. An upturned cereal bowl and a spoon lay on the draining board, otherwise the room looked exactly as I had last seen it. The house was quiet as a grave, no sound, not even the ticking of a clock. It felt strange. I softly opened the door into the hall and then into the living room. The curtains were pulled back, but grubby nets filtered the light from outside, turning it grey. There was sheet music on the music stand, and an instrument case, lined in red plush, lay open on the floor, the bassoon, disassembled into its various parts, placed inside in tidy compartments. The drone must have been put away somewhere, and the laptop. On the mantelpiece I noticed some family photographs and went in for a closer look. A pretty blonde teenager smiled back at me, a baby in her arms, a man and woman, her parents I assumed, on either side. There was also a photo of a woman wrapped in a floral pinafore, a basket of washing on her hip: a woman with strong, tanned arms and thick, iron-grey hair that looked as if she'd chopped it short with shears, the front held back by a single hairgrip. She faced the camera boldly, an indomitable face but not without humour. Could this be Dolly Knolly, I wondered, Olly's nan? Well, it was time I met the lady. Feeling a little as if I might be in the Bates Motel, I quietly climbed the stairs. I hesitated for a moment outside the closed bedroom door, before I called out Mrs Knollys' name, and knocked.

Fifteen minutes later, Olly came home. He stopped in the doorway at the sight of me sitting at the kitchen table and his face blanched white.

'What are you doing here?' His voice rose in panic. 'You can't just . . .' His eyes flicked beyond me to the stairs. 'My nan—'

'You haven't got a nan, Olly,' I told him flatly. 'Putting her washing on the line is a clever touch, but no one has slept in that bedroom for a long time.' Her bed was stripped, blankets folded, the room cold, unlived in. But I'd known before I'd knocked on the bedroom door, as I'd climbed the stairs, felt that sense of nothing alive in the house, nothing breathing under that roof at that moment but me.

He stood transfixed, staring, blue eyes wide with terror, mouth hanging open in shock.

'There's no one in this house but you, Olly,' I carried on remorselessly. 'Your nan is dead. And I want to know what you've done with her body.'

CHAPTER FOURTEEN

I didn't expect him to faint. I thought he might start yelling, attack me, or panic and run away, but I did not expect the kid to pass out in a dead faint, flat on the kitchen floor.

It was only momentary. He started to come round almost immediately and I was able to help him up onto a kitchen chair. I felt dreadful. My stupid remark about where his nan's body was buried had only been a joke. I'd assumed she was safely tucked up in a care home somewhere. 'Take some deep breaths,' I told him as I fetched him a glass of water and placed it in front of him. He glared at me across the table, his face white, his body shaking.

'I'm not going into a children's home,' he vowed, his eyes brimming. 'I won't. I'll run away!'

'It's all right,' I told him softly. 'There's no need to be afraid.'

'What are you doing here, anyway? I never asked you to come.'

'Olly, you shouldn't be living here alone. You're not old enough.' I was wondering how on earth he'd managed to slip through the net. When his great-grandmother had been taken into care surely someone in social services would have picked up on the fact that there was no one at home to take care of him.

'You got no right,' he went on, 'breaking into my house—'

'Listen, Olly. My mum died when I was a baby, just like yours. I don't remember her at all. For a while, I was in care—'

'Was it bad?'

'I don't remember much about it,' I admitted. 'I'm sure nothing terrible happened to me. But I'm also sure that once I'd left it behind, I wouldn't have wanted to go back again. All I'm trying to say is, I understand how you feel. You can trust me.'

He gazed at me silently, eyes wide, like a frightened animal. At any moment I felt he might bolt, make a run for it. 'So, what happened to you?' he asked.

'My mother died of a drugs overdose. I must have been two or three at the time. I was taken into care. Like I said, I don't remember much about it. Then my cousin found me and sent me to boarding school.'

'Boarding school?' he repeated, horrified.

'He was a diplomat in the Far East – still is. He couldn't care for me. But in the holidays I'd come down to Devon and stay with another cousin, Cordelia . . . But Olly, we're not talking about me. Now, why don't you tell me what happened?'

He swallowed nervously. It took him a few moments to get his thoughts together. 'When Grandpa died . . . killed himself . . . there was just Nan and me living here. We were all right. We looked after each other. We didn't need anyone. Then Nan got ill . . .' He stopped, looked down at the table.

141

'Is she in a home?' I spoke in a quiet voice, gently. I didn't want to scare him.

He wouldn't look up at me. I was staring at the top of his head, his pink scalp visible through his spiky blonde hair.

'Is she dead?'

He nodded, his eyes still fixed on the tabletop.

'When did she die?'

'Last year.' His voice had sunk almost to a whisper.

'And you've been living here on your own since then?'

He sniffed.

'Did she die in hospital?'

He shook his head. 'Here.'

'When the doctor came,' I began, still trying to work out when things had gone wrong, 'didn't he realise that you were here on your own?'

Olly muttered something.

'What did you say?'

He looked up at me, dashing away glistening drops of tears with the back of one hand. 'She's buried in the garden.' He began sobbing helplessly. I foraged a tissue from my jeans pocket and gave it to him, waited for the sobs to subside, but he went on weeping unashamedly, an outpouring of suppressed anguish that continued for several minutes. I kept handing him sheets of kitchen paper from the roll by the sink, but every time the poor kid tried to stop crying and draw breath he started over again. 'She didn't want to be buried in the churchyard,' he gulped eventually, 'not after what happened to Grandpa . . . she wanted to be buried in her own garden . . . she wanted to be near to the paddock and the ponies . . . she used to give 'em carrots . . .'

'Olly,' I breathed, finally catching on. 'Are you telling me *you* buried her, that no one knows she's dead?'

He nodded, swallowing back another sob. 'Please don't tell! They'll put me in care. I don't want to go in a home!'

I sat back in my chair, gaping at him. 'But how on earth did you manage it . . . you could only have been . . . what, twelve or thirteen. Did anyone help you?'

'She was away, that nosy woman next door, on holiday, so I could dig the hole without being seen. All day it took me. I did it proper, you know, deep.'

'Is she *in* anything?' I asked, aghast.

'I wrapped her in her eiderdown, took her down the path in the wheelbarrow. I gave her a pillow and put her gold necklace round her neck and a bunch of flowers in her hands and her prayer book. And I put in things she'd like . . . you know, like you see in graves on those history programmes on telly. They put in swords and pots and stuff. I put in photos of Grandma and Grandpa, and an old teddy that used to be Mum's. Then I covered her up with a coverlet, and earth and I sowed wild flowers over the top of her. I thought she'd like that . . . wild flowers. They're good for the bees. She was so worried about the bees . . .' He stopped, staring at me, waiting for me to speak. But I was speechless. 'I've done a crime, haven't I?' he asked, his voice rising pathetically. 'Burying her in the garden?'

'Well . . .' I breathed at last. 'I don't think there's any reason why someone can't be buried in their garden if they wish, but . . . you see, every death has to be registered, officially. The doctor has to sign a death certificate, to say what a person died of. And if you're saying that no one else knows . . .' I puffed out my cheeks in a sigh. 'So, how did she die?'

'I went up with her tea one morning and she wouldn't wake up. Course, she'd been in bed for weeks. Just too tired to get up, she said. She wouldn't have the doctor, dared me to ring him.'

'And you're absolutely certain she was dead?'

'Course she was!' he cried indignantly. 'She was lying stone cold in her bed for two days whilst I waited for that old cow next door to get off on her holiday!'

'And ever since,' I said slowly, just to be sure, 'you've lived here alone and kept up the pretence that she's still alive. And no one knows?'

'I don't want them to take me into care. Her next door, she'd bring in the social services if she knew.'

'But you can't keep this up for ever!'

'Just until I'm eighteen,' he told me innocently. 'They can't put me in care then.'

'I don't know how you've managed it,' I admitted, shaking my head. I couldn't believe he'd kept this secret for over a year without something going wrong. He'd been incredibly lucky.

'I stay out of trouble. I never bunk off school, I do all my homework,' he told me solemnly. 'I don't give no one a reason to come round here, asking questions. I feed myself proper, like Nan taught me—'

'But how do you manage for money? What about the bills?'

'Oh, I started forging Nan's signature years ago,' he said nonchalantly, a touch of pride in his voice. 'She wanted me to do it,' he added hastily, 'her eyes were bad. She couldn't see to write. Course, she'd never go to the optician. I used to write all the cheques and sign forms for school and everything. Then we put all the bills, electric and council tax and that, online. Dead easy. I set it all up for her, on the laptop.'

'What about cash?' I asked.

'Grandpa left me his money. I get it from the post office, I've got my own account.'

'What about your nan's pension?'

He blushed, red, to the tips of his ears. 'Well, I couldn't stop it, could I? Not without telling them she was dead . . . I don't spend it on rubbish. I'm ever so careful. Just on food . . .'

'And the bassoon?'

'That's not mine,' he responded defensively, 'it belongs to the band.'

'And the laptop and the drone?'

'I am allowed Christmas presents!' he answered indignantly.

'You're committing fraud, Olly.'

He bit his lip. 'I'll be in trouble, won't I?'

'Perhaps, a bit,' I responded evasively. 'And you've got no other family?'

He shook his head. 'Nan left this house to me in her will. There was no one else to leave it to.'

'Have you got a copy of that will kept safe somewhere?'

'Yes, this house is mine.'

'Well, not quite.'

His pale eyes narrowed. 'What do you mean?'

'Your nan can't leave you anything if she's not legally dead. When a person dies their will has to be sorted out by lawyers, go through a process called probate. But she can't be legally dead without a death certificate. D'you see?'

'What am I going to do?'

145

'I don't know,' I admitted hopelessly.

'They won't want to dig Nan up, will they?' he asked anxiously. 'If anyone finds out?'

'Well, of course they will! There will have to be an autopsy, to make sure she died of natural causes.'

'You gonna tell?'

'No. No I'm not,' I promised after a moment. 'I give you my word.'

He let out a breath. 'Thanks.'

'But,' I added, leaning across the table towards him, 'there is a price for my silence.'

His eyes grew round in horror. 'That's blackmail, that is.'

'It most certainly is,' I assured him. 'You can tell me everything you know about Gavin, for a start. Why did he want to look in that mine on the Moorworthy estate? And don't try telling me that you don't know because I don't believe you.'

Olly bit his lip, hesitating. 'He said that a friend of his had been killed there . . . about a year back. Fell off a cliff or something.'

'In the woods?'

'He got over the fence one night, he was trespassing.'

'Did he tell you this friend's name?'

'Gavin just called him Ben,' he replied, shrugging. 'I don't know how he knew him, but it wasn't from our school.'

'And he didn't say why Ben had gone there?'

'No, he didn't. But he didn't believe he'd fallen off a cliff. He thought someone had pushed him.'

I considered this for a moment. Olly suddenly got up and opened a kitchen drawer, took something out and threw it on the table in front of me. 'And these aren't mine.'

I picked up a pair of wire cutters.

'I found them in a pocket of the rucksack,' he said. 'They must be Gav's.'

I squeezed the handles of the wire cutters experimentally. If Gavin intended to cut through the wire fence in the woods, he would have needed something more powerful, heavier. I doubted if these were man enough for the job. I considered them for a moment, then pulled Olly's spare key from my back pocket.

'I'm holding on to this.'

'Why?' he demanded indignantly.

'Because you need me. Your next-door neighbour is very concerned about you and your nan. She was ready to phone social services when I talked to her. Don't panic!' I added, seeing the alarm flare up in his eyes. 'She took me for a social worker. We'll let her go on thinking that's what I am. If she sees me coming in and out whilst you're away at school, she'll believe that I'm looking after your nan and there's nothing to worry about.' I sighed. 'Somehow, I'll find the time to pop in here a couple of times this week, and I'll make sure she sees me going in and out. That should set her mind at rest.'

Olly gave me a long, considering stare. 'Why are you helping me?'

'Because you're going to help me, Olly. What's the flying time of that drone of yours?'

'Half an hour if the batteries are fully charged.'

'Then get 'em powered up, ready for the weekend. You and I are going back to Moorworthy. We're going to take a second look.'

147

CHAPTER FIFTEEN

Some people think Dartmoor is unspoilt wilderness, untouched by man. But tin has been mined here since the Bronze Age, and copper and silver; and granite quarried. Over the centuries great oak forests have been cleared. The land has been ripped open, patched and pitted and scored with scars. Mining has created wrinkles in the landscape, long deep gullies, which, once the ore has been exhausted, are abandoned to gorse and scrub, to thorns, ferns and nettles, so that it becomes difficult to see them from above: from a drone, for example, especially when, as with the Moorworthy mine, there are also surrounding trees.

It's not that I'm interested in mines. Dark holes in the ground, natural or man-made, do not fill me with enthusiasm. I went caving with a boyfriend once, in Pridhamsleigh Cavern nearby. It was easy going, though horribly muddy, as far as the main cave, but I wasn't mad enough to go deeper in. And no attempts of his to persuade me how wonderful it would be to squeeze my body through narrow fissures in the rock or dive under pools of icy black water could convince me otherwise. And I *know* that the screeching and wailing heard down there is caused by the wind and not the ghosts of lost cavers, but I was still scared shitless.

No, my only interest in the mines of Moorworthy lay in finding out what Gavin was up to.

I'd have liked to have phoned his parents and ask if they knew anything about the death of his friend Ben, but I didn't want to intrude on their grief; and if they'd asked why I wanted to know I wouldn't have been able to tell them.

On Thursday I managed to find time to drop in at Olly's house, parking on the verge outside his neighbour's and waving to her cheerily when she saw me. I didn't see the owner of the property; he was at school. I let myself in through the back door, and as I went through the garden my eyes strayed instinctively to the far end, where Dolly Knolly was sleeping peacefully, surrounded by her ceremonial grave goods, beneath her coverlet of flowers.

I wandered down to where she lay and stood looking over the hedge into the field behind. It was a peaceful spot, surrounded by fields that swept upward to a copse of birch trees on the hill. I could hear rooks calling, the occasional bleat of sheep from distant pastures. I could understand her wanting to be buried here, where she had lived so long, rather than in the town churchyard. The ponies came down the field, pushing their heads over the hedge, gazing at me expectantly beneath long forelocks. I fed them fallen apples from Dolly's garden, the soft hair around their muzzles brushing my open palm.

I stayed in the house half an hour and had a good snoop around. Olly must have suspected I would do this because he'd locked his bedroom, and his nan's. There was a third bedroom with a double bed and a dressing table in it, but the drawers had been emptied.

As I was in the house anyway, I took down the grubby nets in the living room and put them in the washing machine, with a note to Olly to hang them straight back up, damp, when he got home.

He was a remarkable boy. Most fourteen-year-olds, given money and complete freedom from adult control, would be living in squalor by now, surrounded by coke cans and pizza boxes, bunking off school, money all spent on computer games, getting into trouble and high on drugs. But not Olly. I looked around his neat and tidy home, his school shirts carefully hung on hangers on the old clothes horse, and I could have wept for him, for his neat and lonely little life.

His terror of social services seemed to have come from the indomitable Dolly, who'd threatened to put him in a home if he misbehaved, and been fed by television reports of the terrible abuse suffered by children in some of these places. His whole life was now dominated by the fear of being found out, the danger of putting a foot wrong. He had no friends at school. He dared not invite anyone home, in case they discovered his secret. He dared not visit them, in case parents asked questions. The only time he seemed to interact with others was when he attended his youth band rehearsals once a month. He spent his evenings, weekends and school holidays completely on his own. And he was entirely without self-pity.

He just got on with it. But it wasn't good for him. He was learning to lie and to be a loner. What Olly needed in his life right now was a responsible adult, and I had no idea where I was going to get one of those.

The coroner phoned me next morning, a softly spoken lady, Mrs Drew. She asked me if I could see her in her office, which meant a trip down to Plymouth. Fortunately, she had a window of opportunity that afternoon, which suited me because I wanted to get it over with. This was partly because I wasn't looking forward to the interview, but also because the city of Plymouth is just too big, noisy and too full of concrete and traffic for my taste. The sooner I was in and out the better.

Mrs Drew was very sweet and sympathetic, treading carefully with someone who had been through, as she put it, a traumatic experience. She asked me to tell how I discovered Gavin's body in my own words and listened without interrupting; then she asked me to go over several points again. She was armed with photographs and little diagrams of the scene showing the exact position of Gavin's body, provided by the police. She asked if I felt these were an accurate reflection of how I remembered things. I said that I did. I said nothing about drones or wire cutters. She told me that she would call me to give evidence at the inquest, but that this may not happen for several months. All I would be required to do was tell the court exactly what I had told her.

'All the evidence so far points to this tragic death being an accident,' she told me. 'Of course, the presence of the weapon is disturbing, but again, the evidence points to the wound being self-inflicted. However, I may direct the jury to record an open verdict.'

'I see.'

'No death certificate may be signed until after the inquest has taken place,' she told me apologetically. 'However, I am satisfied that no further evidence can be gathered from Gavin's body, so I will be issuing an order of release so that his parents can bury their son.'

'I'm sure that will be a comfort to them,' I told her, and she smiled.

And that will be it, I thought unhappily, as I made my way down the stairs from her office. Accidental death, open verdict, what does it matter? It will be finished with, tied up neatly, no further investigation deemed necessary. It will be done. Case closed.

CHAPTER SIXTEEN

I collected Olly after his band practice on Saturday morning, dropping his bassoon back at Daison Cottages and picking up the drone. It was a fine day, with a clear blue sky that would offer it uninterrupted views. It was almost lunchtime by then, so we stopped off in Holne and I treated him to egg and chips in the community cafe which, like the only shop in the tiny village, is run by local volunteers.

When we came to the gates of Moorworthy House, I drove on past. I wanted to tuck White Van out of sight of the road. But before I could find a likely spot, we were forced to slow down to a crawl behind a rumbling beast of a lorry piled high with black, plastic-wrapped bales of silage. Its swaying tailgate bore the legend 'Moss and Pike', its green paintwork thickly coated in dust. Some wag had written 'clean me' underneath the name with a finger. We trundled along behind it for about a mile.

'It stinks!' Olly complained, his hands over his nose.

'It's silage,' I told him. 'It's fermenting. If you were fermenting, you'd stink.'

He shook his head. 'Silage doesn't stink like that!'

I had to admit the fumes wafting our way from the back of the truck were particularly noxious. In addition to the fermenting silage, periodic belches of grey smoke from the exhaust pipe added to the unpleasant ambience. I dropped back, away from the fumes, veering off the road when a muddy track into the woods opened suddenly on our right, bringing White Van to a squelchy halt in the golden shade of some beech trees. 'This'll do.'

We clambered out and walked through the woods onto open ground. The moor stretched away into the distance, the purple flowers of heather gone with the end of summer, the green bracken ferns turning to rust. Ollie knelt on the grass and set up the drone, fixing his phone into the control unit so that we would be able to see what the camera was seeing. He switched the drone on and red lights flashed on its four rotors. A central light turned green. 'Ready!' he called out. It rose into the air, a giant insect, buzzing faintly.

I had the map out and pointed in the direction I wanted Olly to fly it. 'Over the road,' I told him, 'down towards the farm.'

He sent it soaring into the blue until it hung above us no bigger than a sparrow, its tiny red lights winking. I crouched behind him, watching the screen over his shoulder as the drone flew over the road and across the fields opposite, the hedgerow appearing beneath it as a crooked line of dark green.

'Look!' Olly cried. 'There's that stinky old lorry we were following just now!'

We were looking directly down on the lumbering beast, on its piles of black plastic bales.

It had turned off down the track to Applecote Farm. 'What's it gone down there for?'

He brought the drone down for a closer look. 'I thought you said it wasn't a farm no more.'

'It's not operating as a farm. No reason why it shouldn't be used for storing silage, though.'

He giggled. 'Let's buzz it!' And before I could stop him the drone shot forward, dropped in front of the truck and hovered before the windscreen. The driver and his passenger, both thickset individuals, the driver wearing a green knitted hat, gaped, astonished.

This was not what we'd come to see. 'That's not a good idea, Olly.'

He sent the drone rocketing off at an angle, soaring higher, his fingers working the twin controls with practised ease. It whizzed away over the chimneys and slate roof of the old farmhouse. A motorbike was parked in the farmyard, a small knot of people gathered near the doors of a cowshed. Without any prompting from me, Olly sent the drone swooping down for a closer look.

Three men were talking, one wearing a trilby and a sheepskin jacket, one in a flat cap, and the third, the owner of the motorbike, clad in leathers and black helmet. The truck jerked to a stop beside them, the driver leaning out of his cab, yelling, jabbing his arm skyward. They looked up, saw the drone, and began pointing. The driver shook his fist. Clearly, they were not pleased at being observed.

'Time we weren't here,' I warned Olly.

He sent the drone around in a curve. As we passed over the farmyard again, we saw the biker racing for his bike,

155

sitting astride it. Olly pressed *home* on his controls and the drone came swooping back across the road like a returning falcon and landed neatly in the grass.

He picked it up and we jogged smartly back to the safety of the trees and climbed, a little breathlessly, into White Van. I decided we'd better abandon our search for Moorworthy Mine and beat a hasty retreat. Olly struggled to fit the drone into the rucksack as I backed down the muddy track, and hid it beneath his seat. I turned the van and sped off down the road.

'What if they catch us?' he asked, eyes wide.

I shrugged. 'We're just driving along. There's no reason for them to think the drone is anything to do with us.'

It turned out I was being just a smidgen overconfident. Suddenly the motorbike roared into sight in the rear-view mirror, a gleaming black predator racing up behind us, only slowing when it was close on our back bumper. Then it swung out into the road, riding alongside so that the biker was able to turn his helmeted head and get a good look at us. We couldn't see his face at all, masked behind his mirrored visor.

'It's a Harley Davidson!' Olly breathed, awestruck at the sleek, powerful machine riding beside us.

I speeded up. The bike overtook, swerving in front of us, slowing and settling there, forcing us to slow again, hogging the centre of the road, making it impossible to overtake. The road ahead was narrow, hugged on either side by high green hedgerows. All we could do was carry on, stuck behind the bike for another half-mile.

I heard the thundering of the truck before I saw it, looming up behind, filling up the rear-view mirror, massive and menacing. For a moment I glimpsed the driver, his beefy red face, green woolly hat pulled down over his head like a tea cosy; then all I could see was the chrome bulwark of his bumper, the teeth of his radiator grille blocking the entire back window as it closed up behind us, growling. We were trapped, the bike maintaining a slow and steady speed just in front of us, the green walls of the hedgerow rising on either side. The truck nudged us, gently, bumping us forward.

'What are they doing?' Olly cried in alarm.

'They're just trying to intimidate us, that's all. Frighten us.' Or very possibly kill us, I added silently. This was a lonely road, a good place to stage an accident. The truck bumped us again, harder this time, jolting us forward, making us rock in our seats like crash dummies. Olly stared at me, white-faced in fright. 'Hold tight!' I yelled. There was an unhealthy crunching sound from the rear of White Van as they bumped us again.

'Bastards! I've only had this van five minutes!' I tried to pull out around the bike, but the biker weaved across the road, preventing us from getting past, cutting off our escape.

The truck dropped back in preparation for a more powerful, more violent shunt. 'To hell with this!' I gritted my teeth and put my foot down hard. We hit the rear wheel of the Harley Davidson and sent it slewing onto its side, sparks flying as the mudguard scraped along the tarmac, the driver skidding on his back before flailing to a halt in the hedgerow. The truck behind was forced to swerve to avoid hitting him, its giant tyres bouncing over the back wheel of the bike as it lay on the ground. As we sped away it jammed to a halt, blocking the road slantwise, the driver's cab crashing into the bushes.

Olly gave a yelp of delight and punched the air in triumph. I swung the van off the road at the next turning, a lane so narrow that the hedges brushed the van on either side. It would be impossible for the truck to follow. Judging by the bumps and ruts, and the grass growing up the middle, it was a track not much used and I had no idea where it was going to come out.

'You don't think we've killed him, do you?' Olly asked, as a blackberry briar thwacked against the windscreen. 'The biker, I mean?'

'I wouldn't think so. He wasn't doing any speed for one thing.' For another, when he came to rest, the bushes must have cushioned the impact. If he'd slammed against a drystone wall it might have been a different story. 'But you know what?' I asked him as poor White Van bumped and rattled down the rutted lane. 'Right now, I really don't give a shit.'

Back in the safety of Olly's kitchen we reviewed the film from the drone, watching the group of men talking in the farmyard. We couldn't make out the face of the individual in the trilby hat but the tall, loose-limbed figure in the sagging tweeds and flat cap was definitely Moss. Besides, his was one of the names painted on the truck, which was unlikely to be coincidence. So what were Moss and friends up to? They disliked being spied upon by the drone so much they were prepared to play lethal games to warn us off. They could have killed us. They had to be up to something. And whatever they were up to, Applecote Farm was on Jamie Westershall's land. Was he a part of it? Was he the masked rider on the bike?

I didn't like to think that might be true; but whoever that was, he'd got a good look at me and Olly.

'Tell me something,' I asked, as he placed a steaming mug of hot chocolate by my elbow and slid back into his seat at the kitchen table. 'The first time you went out with the drone, with Gavin, did Moss – you know, the old guy with the shotgun – get close enough to get a good look at you? When he was chasing you, did he get close enough to Gavin to see his face?'

Olly thought about it, silent for a moment. 'Perhaps,' he said eventually. 'Gav kept turning around to see if he was still behind us. Why?'

'I'm just wondering if Moss would have recognised Gavin if he'd seen him again at the Moorworthy fete.' And if he had, would he have followed him into the woods and killed him?

'Are we going back there again?' he asked excitedly. Now that time and distance had recovered him from his fright, he was talking about the whole incident as if it was a great adventure.

'*We* are not going anywhere.' It was too dangerous. Even I wasn't irresponsible enough to involve a fourteen-year-old boy with thugs who were prepared to run us off the road. As it was, the bumper of White Van was buckled and the back doors dented. I didn't want Olly getting buckled and dented too. 'Look, I may have to call the police and you've got to stay out of trouble, remember?'

'Oh, yeah, right.' He looked disappointed but didn't argue.

'Look, we'll take the drone out again,' I added, trying to cheer him up, 'somewhere safer next time.'

'Tomorrow?' he asked hopefully.

'Sorry, I can't tomorrow. I'm working.'

'But tomorrow's Sunday,' he objected.

'Yeah, well, no rest for the wicked. So, what do you do with yourself on Sundays?'

He shrugged. 'Homework,' he answered miserably. 'But I've only got history and I don't have to hand that in till Tuesday.' He stared down at his finger and began picking at a cuticle. 'I might weed the veg patch. I'm growing kale. It's good for you. Nan always grew cabbage. She didn't hold with kale.'

'You must miss her.'

'We used to have a laugh. I go down the end of the garden and talk to her sometimes. You know, just tell her what I'm doing, tell her what's going on.' He flicked a sheepish glance at me. 'Stupid, aren't I?'

'Not at all. I think you should talk to her any time you feel like it. But don't you get lonely, living on your own?'

'Not really. I don't like other people much . . . Oh, you're all right,' he added graciously.

'Thanks.' I tried not to feel overwhelmed by the compliment. 'Tell you what, I'll pick you up in the morning, take you to Honeysuckle Farm, to the animal sanctuary. They can always use a volunteer up there. You like animals, don't you?'

'Yeah!' His sharp little face brightened. 'Are you hungry? I picked some blackberries out of the hedge yesterday, made a crumble. There's loads of it left. Do you want some?'

Silly question. He got a dish out of the fridge and put it in an oven in the Rayburn. 'It'll take a few minutes to warm up. I haven't got a microwave.'

'Let me guess. Your nan didn't hold with microwaves?'

He nodded, grinning.

'Was it your nan who taught you to cook?'

'We always used to cook meals together, right from when I was small. Then, for the last year, it was just me doing the cooking. But she didn't like anything fancy. I couldn't get her to eat anything foreign, not even pasta.'

'A bit frustrating when you want to be a chef.'

'Well, I think I do.' He rubbed the side of his nose thoughtfully. 'I can't make my mind up. I might play the bassoon. It's hard, isn't it, working out what you want to do with your life?'

Certainly is. So far, I haven't managed it.

'Or I might just do science. I can do anything I want,' he added, giving a smug little grin. 'I'm a genius, me. I got the same birthday as Albert Einstein.'

And just for a moment I understood what made other boys want to kick him.

Albert Einstein, in case you're wondering, was born on 14th March. This makes him a Pisces, like Olly. Like Sophie, like Morris, like Cordelia. I am always surrounded by them, these romantic, imaginative, sensitive, dreamy, muddled, vulnerable, hopeless, bloody irritating people: me, an organised, practical, down-to-earth, sane and sensible Capricorn.

As a Capricorn, of course, I am not remotely interested in astrology. The only reason I know anything about it is because I absorbed it by some kind of weird osmosis as I was growing up. My cousin Cordelia, whose life was tragically cut short, was a real wise woman. She practised astrology in a little shop in Totnes, giving consultations on horoscopes.

And in the wee small hours, when any sensible Capricorn should have been asleep, I lay awake thinking about Gavin. I bet he was a Pisces. I was still trying to work out what had happened to him that day. Suppose he'd gone to Pat's car, intending to put the sword away, to get out the rucksack containing the drone and wire cutters so that he could get through the fence, then discovered the car was locked. What did he do? He didn't come back to ask Pat for the keys so perhaps he decided to go for a walk in the woods, reconnoitre, find another way in? Or just mess about with the sword? And at some time during all this, did he and Moss encounter one another? Did Moss challenge him, chase him, cause him to fall on his sword, or did Gavin panic and run?

Bill leapt onto my pillow suddenly and began to tread about in my hair, purring seductively. I don't know how he got in because Adam had finally got around to fixing my bathroom window and it was shut. I put up with Bill's rasping lullaby for a bit before yanking my hair out from underneath him so that I could turn over. I drifted off to sleep with no questions answered and dreamt of Dolly Knolly at peace in her bed of earth, beneath the borage and the honeywort, the field poppies and corn cockle, the meadowsweet and the butterflies.

CHAPTER SEVENTEEN

On Sunday I promised to help with the fat fairies. Ricky and Morris had spotted me in the week doing errands when they were sunning themselves at a table outside The Old Library Cafe and had begun yelling embarrassing things like 'yoo-hoo!' and 'cooee!' to attract my attention. Attempting to ignore them was useless so I'd sat down and let them buy me a coffee and recruit me to help them on Sunday with a sudden demand for costumes.

First of all, I dropped Olly off at Honeysuckle Farm. It's not as pretty as it sounds. Years ago, some idiot thought it would be a good idea to demolish the seventeenth-century farmhouse and replace it with a concrete bungalow. A barn and other old farm buildings remain, but it's hardly picturesque. Visitors arriving at the gate have been known to turn away in disappointment. Because, although the animals are fed and well-cared for, their pens and enclosures scrupulously clean, what visitors to an animal sanctuary expect is a cafe and a gift shop, easy parking and civilised loos. All that requires investment: money. And money is what Pat, her sister Sue and brother-in-law Ken, who devote their lives to caring for injured wildlife, unwanted pets and abandoned farm animals, do not have, and are never likely to have. So, although they were surprised, they didn't question the arrival of an enthusiastic little helper who wasn't looking for payment. My last sight of Olly, after I'd made the introductions and was driving away, was of him crossing the yard in a pair of oversized wellingtons, running to keep up with Ken. I'd promised to pick him up later, when I'd finished with the fairies.

But first I made a slight detour. I backtracked, turning the van up over the hill to Buckland, past the lovely thatched cottages and church, on to Holne Chase and the Moorworthy estate. The early morning cloud had fled, leaving an open sky, the moon a chalk sketch against the clear blue.

I'd packed my rucksack and put it in the van along with walking boots, maps, compass and binoculars. I wasn't planning on any serious hiking, but I never went walking on the moor without the essentials. I drove past the impressive gates of Moorworthy House and pulled in half a mile further on, by the track that led to Applecote Farm.

The gate was closed, a five-bar steel gate, rails twined with barbed wire, a heavy chain wound about its locking bar, finishing with a weighty padlock; and a sign, 'Private. Keep Out', just in case you didn't get the message. The track was wide enough to take a tractor or a lorry, a simple earthen road that would have been muddy most of the year but had dried to dust after the long hot summer. It led straight down to the farm. I could see the stone chimneys of the farmhouse, its roof and upstairs windows. Strangely, for a farm that was abandoned, there was a whisper of grey smoke coming from the chimney.

I could have climbed over the gate, with extreme caution, but anyone on the track could be seen from those upstairs windows and I didn't want to risk being spotted. I contented myself with placing my hands carefully on the gate and rocking it with my weight, just to feel it move, just to hear the metal clang, a tiny act of rebellion. Then I got back into the van and drove on.

I pulled in again a few miles further on, on a small gravelled space by the verge. I put on thick socks and laced on my leather walking boots, enjoying their chunkiness, their weight, as I crunched gravel underfoot. A wooden signpost pointed across the moor to stone circles and distant tors, but I was heading back the way I'd come, towards Moorworthy.

I left the road, heading across the short grass, picking my way between granite boulders scattered like dinosaur bones, following pony tracks between gorse bushes and twisted hawthorns, and jumped a tiny stream. I was heading for a steep rise, a tumble of rocks on its summit. The air was fresh and I was breathing harder than I should have been by the time I'd climbed to the top.

But it was a great viewpoint, rising above the stunted rowan trees that grew all around it, their clusters of berries red as lipstick, and vicious blackthorns heavy with sloes, and showing me a far-reaching sweep of open moorland and rocky tors, of distant blue hills. I sat my bum down on a rock and looked through my field glasses. They were powerful, but small and neat, easy to slip in a pocket, an expensive gift from cousin Brian. I began sweeping from left to right until I found what I was looking for.

You couldn't spot it from the road, but from here it stood out as a dark irregular line crossing the landscape: a steep bank, topped with hedgerow, the border between the pastures of Applecote Farm and the open heath. It would have been built a hundred years ago or more, to prevent valuable dairy or beef cattle from wandering onto the moor.

The hedge bank enclosed the farmland as solidly as a wall. But walls have weaknesses, points of entry. It might offer me a back way in, a chance to get into the Moorworthy estate unobserved, to take a proper look at Applecote Farm, and Moorworthy Mine, and what might be going on there.

But it would have to wait for another day now. I'd promised this day to Ricky and Morris and I was already late. I turned and began to jog back the way I had come, towards the roadside where I had parked the van.

As my parking spot came into view, I could see a jeep had drawn in behind it. Someone was walking around my van, taking a lot of interest in it. Someone was surveying the damage, trying the doors. I'd already packed my damn binoculars back in the rucksack, thinking that I'd finished with them and I could only just about make out a figure in a flat cap before he climbed in the jeep and drove away. But I was sure it was Moss.

I waited a few minutes before I set off down the road. I didn't want to catch up with him. I slowed down as I came to the turn off for Applecote Farm. The gate was open, and I just glimpsed the back of a silage lorry as it trundled down the track.

'The DOs are doing *Iolanthe*,' Ricky explained as I arrived.

Dartmoor Operatic Society, known hereabouts as The DOs, are generally held in great affection because of the enthusiasm with which they tackle the works of Gilbert and Sullivan. Their voices still sound lovely, but most of them are far too old to be gondoliers, pirates or little maids from school. Ricky says they really ought to be known as the DON'Ts, but that's typical of him.

'They don't usually hire costumes from you, do they?' I asked. For years they'd got their togs from a G and S specialist in London.

'No, but they're not happy with what they've been sent.'

'Well, the men's costumes are all right,' Morris interrupted, coming into the workroom carrying a plastic skip full of rolled-up ribbons. 'It's the ladies that are the problem.'

'Specifically, the fairies,' Ricky went on, eyes twinkling with mischief as he held up an example of the costumes sent.

'Oh!' I exclaimed. 'They sent costumes for *real* fairies!' Obviously, the costume company in London didn't appreciate that there was not a fairy in The DOs under the age of fifty. The dainty little outfit held up by Ricky, flimsy and transparent in places, would have suited a slender young sylph but was not suitable for the bingo wings, sausage-meat arms and cellulite-dimpled thighs of the ladies of The DOs chorus.

'They are not happy,' Ricky said. 'They've asked us to help 'em out.'

'How many fairies are there?'

'Twenty.'

'We can't possibly make them all new costumes in the time,' Morris sat down, taking the lid off the skip. 'So we asked ourselves, what have we already got a lot of? We had a look at the ball dresses from *Cinderella* but . . .' He shook his head, pulling down the corners of his mouth. This idea was obviously a no-no.

'Then we thought of those Victorian nightdresses we've got dozens of,' Ricky went on, 'we thought we'd put wings on them. Well, they looked more like angels from some bleedin' school nativity than fairies—'

'So, then we thought—'

'So *then* we thought,' Ricky carried on, 'about long petticoats. We've got hundreds of them. We could team each one with a pretty white blouse, and make sashes to go round the waist . . .'

'Coloured sashes—' Morris put in.

'Coloured sashes. With wings. And trim the petticoats and blouses with flowers and ribbons.'

'We might even have time to make them little bonnets,' Morris added. 'They'll look very pretty and demure.'

'Course, half of them will keep their specs on, which will ruin the effect,' Ricky finished, 'but at least they won't look like something in a geriatric porn video.'

'So, where do I come in?'

Morris shoved the skip of ribbons in my direction. 'You're making flowers from ribbon, please, Juno. We'll need a couple of hundred.' He peered at me over his half-moon specs. 'You remember how to make them?'

I did. So all day, between cups of tea and pieces of cake, I sewed pink ribbon, blue ribbon, lilac ribbon, lemon ribbon, red ribbon – if a colour came in ribbon, I made flowers from it, whilst Ricky cut twenty pairs of wings from very stiffly starched net and Morris rattled away on the sewing machine, creating sashes.

They didn't talk much – well, comparatively. I didn't want to be drawn into discussion about Olly and fortunately they'd forgotten our talk about his family and didn't ask.

I didn't mention what had happened the day before with Messrs Moss and Pike. I had a story ready about how the van came to grief, but I'd parked it up the drive a bit and, so far, they hadn't noticed it. Mostly I kept quiet, working away at my ribbon flowers until my fingers were sore.

They did ask how things were going at the shop, specifically if I was selling any of their vintage clothes. I had to admit I didn't know. I'd hardly been near *Old Nick's* all week. Sophie had been holding the fort. But now she'd finished the portrait of the Old Thunderer, she wanted a day off. It would be my turn tomorrow.

At the end of the day, Morris offered me supper, but I declined. I had to go and fetch Olly.

He was full of it, sliding into the van beside me, bursting to tell me about ferrets and hedgehogs, ducks, baby owls, donkeys and all the other critters he'd dealt with.

'D'you know, they've got a llama?' he asked me excitedly. 'They just found it one morning, tied to the gate. They don't know where it came from. Anyway, it's a lady llama, so they could put it in the paddock with Bam-a-lam and he doesn't mind it. Bam-a-lam's a ram,' he explained. 'Ken says he's an old bugger, butts anything that moves.'

'Oh, I know Bam-a-lam.' He was a black-faced ram sporting particularly impressive headgear. He'd been useful to me more than once. Any dog who took it into its head to start chasing sheep needed only half an hour in a pen with Bam-a-lam to seriously go off the idea.

Olly pulled a rumpled paper bag from his pocket and began chewing a rather limp sandwich.

'Didn't you have those for lunch?'

'We all had roast dinner,' he told me happily. 'Chicken and peas and carrots and roast potatoes and cabbage. Pat cooked it. And apple pie and ice cream.'

I tried not to think of the Moroccan tagine, whose spicy aromas I had been savouring all day as it cooked slowly in Morris's oven, and which I had turned down so that I could pick Olly up; not to mention the glass of red wine. 'Would you like to go there again?' I asked.

'Ken says I can go anytime. So I'm going to go at half-term, every day.' He chuckled. 'That'll be better than going to bloody Lanzarote.'

I could only assume that was where one of his classmates had boasted of going. I let him out at Daison Cottages and he waved to me cheerily as he bounded up the garden path. I was glad he'd enjoyed himself. As I turned White Van towards home, I tried to remember what food I had in the fridge for my supper; or if I had any at all.

My luck was in. When I got back home there were several offerings on the table on the landing outside my door – two promising plastic boxes and three interesting-looking objects wrapped in foil. There was also a ladder leading up into the loft. I could hear voices coming from the roof space and footsteps thumping about, so I stood at the foot of the ladder and hallooed upward.

Kate's little face appeared framed in the hatch, her black plait swinging down towards me like Rapunzel. I thanked her for her offerings.

'Veggie curry and homity pie,' she informed me, 'and a couple of cheese scones.'

'Fantastic. What are you doing up there?'

'Adam's worried about your kitchen ceiling, about where the damp's coming in. He thinks we might have dry rot. So he called in Roy the roofer. Hang on.' She climbed down the ladder. 'Go up and have a look whilst I make him a coffee.'

Well, if I must. I climbed the ladder obediently and stuck my head and shoulders through the hatch. There was no sign of Adam, just a thin man in overalls who must be Roy the roofer.

He beamed when he saw me, showing large front teeth, like a beaver. 'Hello! You must be the lady in the upstairs flat.'

'Yes, I am.' I climbed into the loft.

'Well, as I explained to Kate, there is nothing much to worry about. No dry rot, I could tell that immediately, just a few slipped slates where the rain is getting in.'

'Well, good, I suppose.' I frowned. 'But I don't know anything about these things. Why would damp give you dry rot?'

'Ah, well, there has to be a certain amount of moisture present,' he informed me, 'because dry rot is, in fact, a fungus.'

'I see.' For the first couple of minutes I was genuinely interested. But Roy's high-pitched nasal monotone could render the most fascinating subject boring. After a minute or two my eyes glazed over, quickly followed by my brain.

'I could tell at once there was no dry rot in here because there was no dust,' he intoned. 'Well, I don't mean your usual dust. To the uninitiated it looks like a brown powder, but it is, in fact, the fungal spores . . .'

I wondered where the hell Kate was with his coffee. I suspected her of deliberately taking her time. I endured at least twenty minutes as Roy aired his knowledge. 'The

171

fungus draws all the moisture out of the wood, you see, in fact, eats it from the inside . . .'

I was convinced by the time that Kate finally appeared with his coffee that there wasn't a thing about dry rot I didn't know.

'I have seen rafters disintegrate with a single hammer blow . . .' he was saying as her head finally appeared through the loft hatch. It was too late. I had lost the will to live by then.

I glared at her and she gave me a guilty look as she handed Roy his coffee.

'They call him Boring Roy,' she admitted when he had finally taken his leave.

'Well, you might have warned me before you encouraged me to go up there with him.'

'Sorry, but I knew if he had no one to talk to, he'd follow me down to the kitchen.'

'How on earth did you manage to get him to call on a Sunday evening?'

'Oh, he offered. I think he's lonely.'

'I'm not surprised.'

'Sorry.'

'I forgive you,' I told her magnanimously as I gathered up the offerings from her kitchen, 'but only because of these.'

CHAPTER EIGHTEEN

I was late opening *Old Nick's* next morning, didn't get there until ten o'clock.

At least there was no queue of customers waiting outside: fat chance of that, frankly. I didn't like being forced to waste the entire day waiting to serve non-existent customers when I had more urgent things I could be doing. But it was my turn. Not for the first time I cursed Nick for leaving me the shop.

Then I stepped inside, let the door close behind me, experienced a moment of total quiet, absolute calm, and realised that a day in the empty shop was just what I needed: a day without rushing around, a day when all I could do was sit and literally take stock. I looked around me and let out a breath I didn't realise I'd been holding in.

For a start, the shop looked fantastic. The portrait of Old Thunderer stood on an easel in Sophie's window. She'd done a magnificent job. You could almost touch his matted hair, feel his hot breath, almost smell him. Pat's window looked great too. Soft, knitted shawls in rich autumn colours lay in undulating folds on the wide windowsill, whilst suspended above them on fishing line hung stuffed felt pumpkins and cute, funny little witches on broomsticks, which she'd obviously crafted herself. It was a good job she was more awake to the sales opportunities of approaching Hallowe'en than I was. Even Mavis the mannequin was sporting a witch's hat. It was just a pity all this talent and enterprise would go largely unnoticed in the quiet of Shadow Lane.

I locked the door behind me whilst I nipped up to the kitchen and made myself a coffee. Then I brought it down, turned the sign on the shop door to *Open* and sat at the counter for an overdue look at the ledger to see if I'd taken any money that week.

My day had not started well. I'd overslept, gone rushing out of the house without breakfast and walked the dogs through the woods. Schnitzel the sausage dog had run off amongst the undergrowth and I'd lost him for half an hour. When the smug little *Schweinehund* deigned to return he'd obviously been rolling in badger shit and I had to clean him off before I could take him home. This made me late returning the dogs, which pissed off one owner, who was waiting to leave for a dental appointment and gave me a right earful.

I had dumped the last of my doggy charges and was driving back towards town, trying to make up time, when I was forced to screech to a halt. Amongst the shaggy heads of old man's beard that twines itself amongst the yellowing leaves, the clusters of blackberries and tight clumps of green ivy flowers buzzing with wasps, and all the other things one expects to see in an autumn hedgerow, there was something big and blue that definitely shouldn't have been there: Judith-Marianne in her dressing gown, attempting another escape from Oakdene Nursing Home, was stuck in the bushes.

As I climbed out of the van, she began trying to attract my attention, waving ineffectually with one hand, the only part of her that wasn't completely hitched up on surrounding thorns. 'Help! Oh, help!' she was mewing softly. I surveyed her for a moment, wondering whether it would be easier to pull her forward into the lane or push her back the way she'd come, into Oakdene's gardens. I decided on the former. I reached cautiously through the cat's cradle of branches, trying not to snag myself on the surrounding armoury of thorns.

'Silly me!' she kept repeating. 'Silly me!'

'Well, you've got that bit right.' A long bramble, vicious with thorns and laden with juicy berries was tangled in her woolly blue sleeve. I unhooked it cautiously, leaving a purple smear. She began singing softly to herself, rocking backwards and forwards, her blue eyes staring into a place and time that had nothing to do with here and now. It would have been much easier if she'd kept still. As soon as I'd unhitched her from one lot of thorns, she was getting caught up on others.

I was beginning to think my attempt to rescue her was hopeless and I'd have to call the cavalry, when it arrived in the short, curvaceous form of Barbara the care assistant and her colleague with the ponytail, whose name turned out to be Camille. They'd bustled along the lane in the hope of catching Judith-Marianne before anyone had realised she was missing. Between the three of us we managed to ease her

175

free of enclosing brambles and pull her gently through the hedge onto the road.

'Sleeping Beauty,' she told us solemnly as we were standing on the road, picking off bits of twig and flakes of leaves that crowned her silver hair and clung to her dressing gown.

'Yes,' I agreed, as we checked her over for scratches, 'you were just like Sleeping Beauty, imprisoned by thorns.' She frowned at me, picking at some thread of her unravelling memory, trying to place who I was.

'This is Juno,' Barbara told her. 'Remember? She found you the last time.'

'Are we going back to the hotel?' Judith-Marianne asked suddenly.

Camille took her arm. 'That's right, back to hotel.' She spoke with a Polish accent.

'Do we have to dress for dinner?'

'Yes. We must get you dressed. But we have breakfast before dinner,' Camille told her. 'There's lovely breakfast waiting for you.'

Barbara turned to smile at me as they began walking their docile prisoner back to Oakdene. 'You've changed your van.'

'Yes, I have,' I sighed at its bent doors and buckled bumper. 'I'm not having much luck with vans, lately.'

I sat behind the shop counter, going through the sales ledger, copying out my sales and adding up my takings, which did not take long, and then counting up sales of vintage clothes for Ricky and Morris, which took a bit longer. I found that the money in the cash box was all mine, Pat and Sophie having already sensibly removed anything owing to them, so I counted out Ricky and Morris's money and pocketed the rest.

It was only as I picked up my shoulder bag and wondered why it weighed so much, that I remembered the package I'd grabbed off the hall table that morning before I'd rushed out of the front door. It seemed like I'd been waiting ages for it to arrive. Feeling like a kid at Christmas, I tore open the padded envelope and unwrapped my job lot of hatpins and their two porcelain holders. I'd been successful in my bid for them on eBay, although I'd lost out on the 1920s handbags. I inspected each pin carefully. Some were small and dainty, some were long with wicked points and weighty, knobby ends. None of them was very expensive, but sold individually they'd fetch far more than I'd paid for them, and they'd look pretty displayed in their holders, once I'd given each of them a jolly good scrub with a child's toothbrush, followed by a buffing up with some silver polish: that was my evening sorted.

I remembered I was supposed to have phoned my mechanic. Dave is a proper, old-fashioned mechanic, who'll have a go at anything. He'd managed to smuggle my van through its MOT on the last two occasions. I don't mean White Van, the bent and battered one, I mean the previous one, the burnt-out hulk. I explained White Van had been in an accident.

'You're not having a lot of luck, are you?' he commented.

No, I'm not, Dave, funny you should mention that. Apart from the fact that Green Bastard Hat in the truck had smashed one of my rear lights and buckled my bumper, the newly dented back doors didn't line up as they had before. They were sticking slightly when I tried to open them and as there was no way I was going through another experience like the one I'd had with EB, I wanted them fixed.

'I'll have to pay you,' I told him. 'This isn't an insurance job.'

That reminded Dave that the assessor had finally turned up at the garage and declared my burnt-out hulk a write-off. I'd had to wait nearly three weeks for that assessment. Still, now at least the cheque would be in the post.

A thought occurred to me. 'Dave, when my van was brought in, the day it caught fire, you don't remember the name on the break-down truck?'

'Yeh, it was Moss and Pike.'

'Are they a local firm?'

Dave thought a moment. In the background I could hear the ring of metal beating on metal, a radio playing, someone whistling along to the music as he worked. 'Well, they've got a depot in Moretonhampstead,' he shouted a little above the noise, 'but they've got depots all over, I think. Anyway, I can't do your van today,' he went on, 'I've got a rush job on a beaten-up Harley Davidson.' He chuckled grimly. 'Not as beaten up as its rider, though.'

'Really? A friend of mine rides one of those,' I lied blithely, 'you can't tell me the name of the bike's owner?'

'Westershall.'

A cold, hollow feeling settled inside my stomach.

'Look, Juno, we're busy, I gotta go. Bring your van in in a day or two and I'll see what I can do.'

'Thanks, Dave,' I said as I disconnected. 'Cheers.'

Westershall. My feeble brain was grappling with the horrible idea that Jamie really was the bike rider who'd tried to run me off the road when it received another confusing blow. Standing outside in Shadow Lane, studying the portrait of the bull in the window, was Jamie himself. I tried to gather my scattered wits as he walked into the shop.

'Hi, Juno,' he began, and stopped, frowning. 'Are you all right?'

'Er . . . yes, fine.'

'You look a bit flustered.'

'No, I'm fine, thanks.' I rummaged for a smile. 'How are you?'

'I'm good.' He certainly didn't look like someone who'd recently been thrown into a hedgerow or had any kind of close encounter with a hard surface. He was staring at my head.

'Do you know you've got stuff in your hair?'

'Stuff?' I hadn't bothered to check the mirror since I'd come in the shop. I put up a hand to my hair and pulled out a little twig with two leaves attached. Well, I had been dragging an old lady through a hedge backwards. I checked with my fingers for any other detritus. 'Anyway, what can I do for you?'

He jerked a thumb in the direction of the window. 'The portrait is fantastic. Old Sandy is going to be over the moon. As a matter of fact, I was hoping to see Sophie. Is she about?'

'Day off. Can I help?'

'I was hoping she might be able to get it framed for us. Emma was going to arrange it but she's a bit *hors de combat* at the moment.'

'Not well?'

'She got a bit smashed up,' he explained, with a rather fixed smile, 'got thrown from her steed.'

Enlightenment dawned. 'Nothing serious, I hope?'

179

'Scrapes and bruises mostly. She jarred her neck rather badly, but nothing broken.'

'She'll be all right for the party, will she?' I did my best to sound solicitous. I was feeling a whole lot better, myself. That cold, hollow feeling in my stomach had melted away, realising that Jamie had not been the rider of the motorbike, and that the steed that had thrown Emma was not a horse, but a hog.

'Oh, God yes!' he answered cheerfully. 'Take more than a fall to make her miss Sandy's birthday bash. But she can't drive for a day or two. So I was hoping that Sophie could get the portrait framed. I'm afraid I haven't got much of an eye for that sort of thing.'

'Of course, she'll be delighted to do it. I'll give her a call.'

'Would you mind, Juno? Only, I've got to dash.'

'Leave it to me.'

He thanked me and made to leave, but as he reached the shop door, he suddenly turned as if he'd thought of something. 'That is your new van parked down the road, isn't it? The white Peugeot—'

'—with the missing rear light and buckled bumper? That's mine.'

He nodded, as if confirming something to himself, his lower lip caught between his white teeth in a strange smile. 'What happened?'

That cold feeling settled in my stomach again. There was an intensity in his gaze that told me his question wasn't a casual one; this was what he'd wanted to know all along. 'Some fool rear-ended me,' I said after a moment.

'Did you get his number?' His blue eyes held mine.

'No,' I answered steadily. 'It was parked at the time.'

He raised his eyebrows. 'So, no witnesses?' he asked lightly.

'No,' I assured him. 'No witnesses.'

His smile as he left was enigmatic. I couldn't read it at all.

I phoned Sophie as soon as he had gone and gave her the news about the framing. She asked if Jamie had left any money and when I told her he hadn't, she moaned down the phone. 'It's going to be so expensive. Something that size will want double-mounting, and they'll need a wide moulding on the frame to do it justice, something heavy and gilt.'

'Well, they'll pay you for it.'

'Eventually, but I'll have to shell out for it upfront. My usual framing guy is away on holiday and I'll have to go to Newton Abbot to get the job done.'

Excellent, I thought, and offered to drive her there. Newton Abbot has as many charity shops as Ashburton has antique shops. Whilst Sophie was taking ages choosing mounting board and mouldings, I could give them all a quick tour. Not only could I hunt for stock for my unit, I might find some jeans. I refuse to pay silly money for denims I'm going to scrub floors and walk dogs in. And needing ones with extra-long legs only adds to the expense, so pre-loved ones are fine. I told her I would take her the following afternoon and resigned myself to rearranging my timetable all over again.

Three ladies came into the shop then, all together, probably the biggest crowd of customers the shop has ever experienced, and for the next half-hour they happily exclaimed over this and that before they went out with two of Pat's little witches, a watercolour sketch of Haytor, three of Sophie's greetings cards and a pair of handmade earrings.

I must confess to a slight stab of envy as I wrapped the earrings in tissue paper. I had taught Pat how to make them and now she sold quite a lot. I could have done with some small and steady sales myself. I thrust such ignominious feelings aside. Her profits went to the animal sanctuary; she gained nothing from her hard work, except the pleasure of doing it. I told myself off in no uncertain terms.

Whilst the three ladies had been looking round, I had noticed a fourth person gazing in Pat's window. It was the mystery lady. This time she didn't look quite as well groomed as when I'd last seen her. Perhaps she hadn't been able to make use of a cafe toilet. Her hair was not arranged in a French pleat but hanging down over one shoulder in a plait, wispy ends making it untidy. Perhaps because there was a wind blowing that was the raw side of fresh, she huddled in her padded jacket, her hands thrust into her pockets. She looked a bit more bag lady than mystery lady, to be honest. I really wanted to go out and talk to her, but I was trapped by my chattering customers, and when I glanced at the window a second time, she had gone.

I realised I was bloody starving, what with no breakfast and lunchtime approaching. Ricky and Morris always brought cake – where were they when I needed them? I popped upstairs to the kitchen, in the hope that there might be some crumbs of comfort somewhere. I found half a packet of Hobnob biscuits in the cupboard and some cheese triangles in the fridge. Perfect. I took the lot downstairs and hid them under the counter so that I could ditch them quickly if a customer came in.

I tore the fiddly silver paper off the cheese triangle and made myself a Hobnob sandwich.

The customers had distracted me from thoughts about my conversation with Jamie. I still wasn't sure what to make of it. Did he know that it was my van that had caused Emma to come off her bike or was he merely suspicious? I wondered what she'd told him about the accident. When he asked about witnesses, was he just trying to protect his sister or was that a warning to me to keep quiet? And whatever she, Moss and the other man had been doing at Applecote Farm, was Jamie any part of it? I'd prefer to think he wasn't, but I was far from sure.

I sat at the counter, munching, gazing distractedly at Gavin's bookshelves and thinking how empty and dismal they looked. I would have to do something about them.

I brushed myself off for crumbs, fetched the box of books I'd bought at the boot sale and placed them on an empty shelf. They looked good but only filled about a quarter of it. I would go through Gavin's boxes of stock, I decided, pick out anything remotely saleable, and fill the shelves up. I picked up the first box, opened it and began taking the books out. There was a newspaper, a copy of the *Dartmoor Gazette*, folded on the top. *Batman Dies* – I remembered the headline. Gavin had been reading the article that day when Jamie had invited us all to the fete. I tossed it to one side.

Then, for some reason, I picked it up again and opened out the folded page. *Batman Dies in Bat Cave* was the full headline. It turned out to be more sensational than accurate. I read the article twice.

An open verdict was recorded today at the inquest into the death of Ben Luscombe of Buckfast, whose body was found on the Moorworthy estate last November. Mr Luscombe, who was twenty-one, was found at the foot of rocks near a disused mineshaft known locally as Moorworthy Pit. A keen member of the Devon Bat Society, it is believed that Mr Luscombe entered the estate without permission to monitor a colony of rare greater horseshoe bats in woods nearby. It is believed he lost his way in the darkness and fell to his death. The post-mortem revealed that he had recently taken cocaine.

Estate owner, James Westershall, made the following statement. 'The woods are fenced off to protect roosts of rare bats and Mr Luscombe was trespassing on a site of special scientific interest. We are only too happy to assist members of the local bat society with the National Bat Monitoring Programme, but visits are strictly by appointment. The old mine workings are dangerous and, sadly, Mr Luscombe paid the price for entering the woods unaccompanied. We are very sorry for his death and our thoughts are with his family at this time.'

Mr Alec Pedrick, local secretary of the Devon Bat Society paid tribute to Mr Luscombe. 'Ben was a passionate conservationist and did important work for the British Bat Survey and National Bat Monitoring Programme. He will be sadly missed.'

The newspaper was dated the previous June, which meant the inquest referred to an incident that was now almost a year old. As I looked up from the article, I just caught sight of the mystery lady hurrying past the window, carrying a large laundry bag, and I realised she had probably spent the last hour in the launderette two doors down. I had missed my opportunity to speak to her. But that didn't matter now. There was someone I wanted to speak to more urgently. I grabbed a copy of the local phone book from under the counter and began looking for the number of Mr Alec Pedrick.

CHAPTER NINETEEN

Alec Pedrick was a bearded man in his fifties, who welcomed me warmly into his cottage. I'd found his address on the Widecombe road, just up the hill towards Buckland.

'It's kind of you to see me at such short notice, Mr Pedrick.' I'd driven straight there as soon as I'd closed up the shop. It was good to get inside, into the warm. It was dark under the trees and growing misty.

'Call me Alec.' He offered me tea and I followed him into his kitchen, passing two young children sitting on the floor in the living room, engrossed in the television. 'I'm only looking after the grandkids till their mother picks them up after work,' he told me, 'so it's no trouble, no trouble at all.' He smiled, waiting for the kettle to boil. 'So, you were a friend of Gavin's? Terrible tragedy, that was,' he added, shaking his head. 'Terrible.'

I sat in the chair that he indicated, next to the orange glow of a wood-burning stove. The kitchen was cosy, book-filled, as if it also served as a study. 'I didn't realise Gavin was interested in bats.'

'Well, to be honest, I'm not sure that he was,' he admitted, taking the seat opposite me. 'He never joined the society as a member, but he did come along with Ben two or three times. Nice lad, but a bit of a dreamer, I thought.' He laughed. 'I mean, he seemed more excited about being out in the woods at night than interested in the bats. We go out to monitor bat numbers, but he was always chatting on about Dracula and werewolves and stuff like that.'

'That sounds like Gavin.'

Alec stretched out his legs towards the glow of the wood-burning stove and crossed his ankles, making himself comfortable. 'Do you know that there are eighteen different species of bat in this country and sixteen of those are found in Devon? And,' he went on, warming to his theme, 'Devon has the largest population of rare greater horseshoe bats in western Europe.'

'And some of those are on the Moorworthy estate?'

He nodded. 'There's a large roost in Moorworthy Pit.'

'Is that what Ben was interested in, monitoring the numbers of greater horseshoes there?'

'Well, not quite,' he admitted. 'We've known about the greater horseshoe bats for years. Course, we still monitor their numbers. But a couple of years back there had been sightings of barbastelles. Now they are very rare,' he told me, holding up a finger, 'threatened as a species. And they don't roost in caves or mines, they roost in hollow trees.' He stood up, searched his shelves for a book and began leafing through it until he found a picture. 'There!' he showed me. 'That's a barbastelle. See?'

I've always thought bats were ugly little buggers and

187

the barbastelle was no exception. It had a squashed-in, leathery face like a tiny gorilla's. 'And these have been seen in Moorworthy woods?'

Alec nodded enthusiastically, taking back the book. 'They like mature trees, broad-leaved woodland. Ben was very keen to carry out a transect of the area . . .'

'Transect?' I repeated.

'It's just a walk, really,' he explained. 'You walk for an hour, traversing a specified area, carrying a recording device. You can analyse the recordings later and identify the bat species present. Well, the society had always had free access until then, no problem. But shortly after the discovery of the barbastelles, Mr Westershall had the woods fenced off.'

'Do you know why?'

Alec shrugged. 'He said it was dangerous, said some old shaft had opened up that no one knew about and he had a duty to protect the public. Well, there was no argument, really, was there? I mean, you can't quarrel with public safety. Anyway, it's all on his property, so what could we do? But Ben was furious, he—' His mouth clamped shut suddenly as if he was afraid to say more, afraid his emotions would betray him. He stared into the flames of the wood-burner.

'He went back there, didn't he?' I prompted. 'The night he died?'

Alec nodded. 'What they didn't say in that newspaper report was that he'd been chased out of those woods before that night. He'd got through the fence under cover of darkness.' He chuckled in spite of himself. 'He took wire cutters with him. He was determined to carry out this transect.

188

He said he saw lights coming from the old mineshaft, from Moorworthy Pit – before he was spotted and had to leg it.'

'Is that possible – the lights, I mean? The shaft is disused, isn't it?'

'Hasn't been worked in a hundred years,' he confirmed. 'But someone was there.'

We were both silent for a moment, thoughtful, the only sound the crackle of logs in the wood-burner and the distant tinkling of music from the television in the next room. Then Alec spoke again. 'My grandfather was a tin miner, you know, and his father before him. And *he* worked at Moorworthy. The old shaft in the woods, where the greater horseshoes roost now, was shutting down, even in his time, so then he worked at Applecote Pit.'

'On the farmland next door?'

'That's right.' He shot me a keen glance. 'Do you know how it's done, tin mining? A lot of it is open work, you know, open-cast. Been going on for centuries on the moor, like that. But sometimes they sink a shaft, deep, maybe fifty feet, like Moorworthy. Applecote was open-cast for a century or more,' he went on, 'then they sunk shafts from the bottom of it – that's what they used to do if they kept finding ore, and maybe dug an adit—'

I stopped him. 'Adit?'

'Sorry.' He smiled. 'An adit is just a tunnel – it gives a level access to the shaft for the workers. Sometimes they'd be forced to dig one to drain water off, if they were working down deep enough.'

'Where exactly was Ben's body found?'

'At the foot of some rocks.' Alec laughed softly, but it

was a bitter, mirthless sound. 'He was determined to go back to that shaft in Moorworthy, find out what was going on. He was convinced the bats were being threatened. He'd have been nowhere near those rocks where they found his body. They were over half a mile away, surrounded by open ground, there are no bats there.'

'The inquest said he'd lost his way in the dark.'

'It was a full moon that night and Ben wasn't stupid. He'd have known where he was going.'

'The inquest said—'

'That he was high on cocaine?' Alec's lips pursed angrily. 'That boy never took drugs in his life. If there was cocaine in his system, it was because someone forced it on him.'

'You think he was murdered?'

'I do.' His voice shook. 'Someone killed that lad and threw his body off those rocks.'

'I'm sure that's what Gavin thought,' I said. 'He leapt at the invitation to go to the Moorworthy fete. I think he saw it as an opportunity to discover what happened to Ben, take a good look around in the woods, but . . . someone stopped him.'

Alec was nodding grimly.

'Did you ever talk to the police after Ben was killed? Tell them his suspicions, about the lights that he had seen coming from the old shaft?'

'I did. They said it was just all hallucinations, part of his drug-taking.' He snorted in disgust. 'It makes me sick to think about it.'

I hesitated before I asked the next question. 'So, who do you think killed him?'

'Westershall of course, it was his land he was on.'

'You mean Jamie?'

He nodded grimly.

I had gone over the circumstances of Gavin's death again and again, but I had never considered Jamie as a killer. Despite the warmth from the fire, I felt cold.

'But, let's just suppose that Jamie – or, anyway, one of the Westershalls – was responsible for Ben's death, why not drop his body down a mineshaft where no one would ever find him? Or leave him at the foot of Haytor? They could have dumped him anywhere on the moor. Why leave his body on their own doorstep?' I frowned. 'Who found him, anyway?'

'Jamie Westershall.'

'Now I'm confused.'

Alec leant forward intently. 'Listen, a lot of people knew what Ben was up to. He was a blogger, and in contact with Bat Conservation groups all around the country. He had family and friends, a girlfriend. He would soon have been reported missing and the police would have been given a pretty good idea of where to start looking. Now, whatever the Westershalls are up to, the last thing they would want is police searching all over their estate. Much better if Jamie Westershall contacts *them*, tells them there's been a tragic accident, he's found a body, and takes them straight to it.'

'It's still taking a risk.'

'Oh, I don't think Mr Westershall is averse to a risk.' Alec leant back in his chair. 'And another thing, he's been denying people access to his land, saying it's dangerous – you read what he said at the inquest. Well, there was quite a lot of protest at the time, but finding Ben's body proved his point

191

for him. No one was going to raise any objections after that. He can do what he likes—'

There was the sound of someone coming in, a footstep at the front door, a woman's voice calling out, and children scrambling, yelling, to greet her. Alec's daughter had come home. It was time I left. 'Well, thanks for seeing me, Alec. I'm sorry if talking about Ben's death upset you.'

As I rose to go, he stood and gripped my hand. 'You be careful,' he whispered urgently. 'Whatever's going on in that place, they've killed twice to keep it a secret. You be careful.'

I placed my hand over his. 'I will,' I promised him. And I left, not knowing what to think.

CHAPTER TWENTY

In Newton Abbot I bought two pairs of jeans, a silver caddy spoon I found in a box of old cutlery, an oak tea trolley with barley-twist legs, various pretty plates and a Moorcroft saucer; but when I went back to the framers where I had deposited Sophie an hour and a half before, she was still making up her mind about frame mouldings, so I dumped my haul in the van and went hunting again. This time my trawl of the charity shops brought me a willow pattern meat dish with a hairline crack in it and some decent paperback books, which would fill up another few inches on Gavin's empty shelves. Not as big a haul as I had been hoping for but at least it was something. And the caddy spoon and the Moorcroft were good finds.

At least Sophie had finished when I went back to the shop a second time. The framer promised to have the job done the day before Sandy's party.

Of course, she wanted to know what had happened to White Van. I filled her in on some, but not all, of the details.

I didn't tell her anything about Olly's domestic situation, but I told her the rest.

'You should have called the police!'

I knew she'd say that. 'What's the point? I can't prove anything. Even if I could prove that Moss and Pike's lorry went into the back of me, I can't prove they did it deliberately.'

'You could have been killed.'

'Jamie knows about it,' I went on. 'He knew my van had been involved in Emma's accident when he came into the shop yesterday.'

'Are you sure?' Like me, she didn't want to believe that the brave and handsome saviour of EB, the charming rescuer of damsels in distress, could be up to anything dodgy. 'Why didn't you ask him?'

'I don't know.' I had replayed that conversation over and over in my mind. Why hadn't I asked him what the hell his sister was up to, what was going on at Applecote Farm? Why hadn't he asked me why I was flying a drone over his property? Instead, we'd just stared at each other, like poker players trying to avoid a show of hands.

Sophie slanted me a dark look. 'This party's going to be interesting. Are you sure you still want to go?'

'Of course I want to go. I want to find out what's bloody going on!'

Perhaps, I realised, when I was thinking about it later, Jamie didn't say anything because, like me, like a poker player, he was considering his next move.

The following morning I saw the mystery lady again. I was up early, walking the dogs. The woods had turned to marmalade

194

gold, sunlight pouring through translucent leaves like stained glass in a church window. The dogs raced through crunchy piles, paws scattering the leaves and sending them flying. I found her car parked by Cuddyford Cross, empty, tucked in by a farm gate. I peered in the back, at a folded sleeping bag, pillows, a shopping bag full of sachets of cat food. But no sign of the lady herself, or her cat.

I followed the lane down to Great Bridge and peered over the old stone wall. The River Ashburn, from which Ashburton takes its name, rises on Rippon Tor and flows down the valley, right through the centre of the town before it joins the Dart at Buckfastleigh. From the bridge I could look down onto the rushing water, fallen leaves like tiny boats swept along on the flood.

Then I took the dogs up steps to the Terrace Walk. It's a strange name for what is basically an earthen path traversing a sloping field. But the view from there is one of the most beautiful around Ashburton, across the wooded valley to the foothills of the moor. In summer the distant woods are just masses of green. But in autumn they become a tapestry of russet and brown. I could pick out the rusty gold of horse chestnuts, the lime glow of poplars and the bright firecracker red of maple against the deep, dark green of holly and spruce.

The view from this muddy path is so beautiful that over the years benches have been put there to allow people to sit and drink it in. Many of these have fallen into disrepair, their wooden seats entangled with bindweed and brambles, or rotted away. But there are one or two benches that are still useable, and seated alone on one of these, gazing across the valley, her cat sitting upright on her lap, was my mystery lady. Mist had filled the depths of the valley, and it lay in a milky layer so that the trees seemed to float above it. She was rapt in a view that was magical, quiet, until my tumbling, rushing dogs broke the spell by barking.

Schnitzel and EB made a beeline for her bench. They wanted to be friendly, to say hello.

I managed to grab Sally the Labrador by the collar before she could follow. As the dogs approached, her cat rose up on its legs, back arched, and became a spitting puffball of angry fur. Mystery Lady grabbed it and stood up, holding it clear of EB and Schnitzel, who were bouncing excitedly around her feet, trying to jump up.

'I'm so sorry!' I cried out to her, shouting at the two yapping hooligans to come back to me. She didn't turn around but began walking away up the path. 'Do you need help?' I called at her departing back, as I started fastening leads on collars. She walked on, ignoring me. 'You're sleeping in your car.'

That stopped her. She turned to look at me, stared hard. 'Am I?' she asked, arching her slim brows.

'Are you in some kind of trouble?' I asked. 'Can I do anything to help?'

'You can learn to mind your own business,' she responded in a controlled voice, turned and marched swiftly away down the field.

I didn't attempt to follow. 'We know when we're not wanted, don't we?' I said to my canine companions.

The last part of the Terrace Walk goes through a small wooded area until the path emerges at the top of Roborough Lane, which in turn leads back into town. As I walked the muddy path under the trees, I could tell I was approaching so-called civilisation by the number of nasty little doggie doo-doo bags littering the ground. It's as if people who have picked up their pet's poo can't bear to carry it as far as the nearest receptacle. But that's not the only kind of refuse lying there. Drink cans, broken bottles, chip papers and various other kinds of nasties littered the ground. I kept the dogs on short leads, didn't want one of them cutting a pad on something sharp.

After I'd taken the dogs back, I popped into Chloe Berkeley-Smythe's place, cleared a pile of junk mail from behind her front door and watered her house plants. The cross on her kitchen calendar showed she wouldn't be returning from her cruise for a few more weeks, so the pre-arrival clean of her house could wait. Chloe paid me a retainer to keep an eye on her place whilst she was away. As she spent most of her life cruising, this suited me very well.

She only stayed at her home in Ashburton for a few weeks, usually just enough time to unpack her cases, launder her clothes, and repack before she was off on her next adventure. She was the most indolent and pleasure-loving person I had ever met and great fun to be with.

Maisie, on the other hand, hardly ever left home, but she got her pleasure in other ways. As I let myself into her cottage, she was happily engaged in her favourite blood sport. 'But how can you tell there's something wrong with my computer,' she was asking someone on the phone, 'when I haven't got a computer?' There was a pause, a protest from the other end of the line. 'Well, you never asked me!' She slammed the receiver down with an evil chuckle.

'How long did you keep that one going, Maisie?' I asked, fending off an imminent attack from Jacko with my boot.

'Ooh, a few minutes,' she responded happily. 'Few minutes they couldn't be pestering someone else. That'll teach 'em to ring me up, telling lies.'

She was slacking. I'd known Maisie torment call-centre employees for twenty minutes or more before they finally realised what the dear little old lady on the end of the line was up to.

She was resplendent in her black, beaver lamb coat with the fur collar, circa 1953, and a slightly dusty black velvet beret. These were her going-out clothes. I had rung her earlier and told her to be ready. I reckoned she could do with a change of scene and was taking her out for a little drive.

'Where would you like to go?' I asked, although I knew the answer already.

The parish church of St Pancras in Widecombe is often referred to as the Cathedral of the Moor, not just because of its perpendicular windows and tall tower, but because of the way it sits in the landscape, amongst a patchwork of fields that seem to be there just to show it off, to act as a green backcloth to its loveliness; and despite the Devil's attempts to smite it with a bolt of lightning, it has stood firm for five hundred years.

Widecombe Fair had been held earlier in the month, but the fame of Uncle Tom Cobley and his grey mare meant that the tiny village of Widecombe-in-the-Moor was full of visitors whatever the time of year. And it was one of Maisie's favourite places. After a little totter around the churchyard and the village green, Maisie's hand clinging tightly to my arm, and a wander around the National Trust shop, set in the old sexton's cottage, where she could draw in her breath in disgust at the price of the tea towels, we settled down for tea in the little cafe overlooking the green.

'We were talking about you the other day,' she informed me cheerfully as we sipped our tea, 'at my church coffee morning. There was a new woman there, turned out she's a neighbour of old Dolly Knollys'. Remember, we were talking about her? Up Daison Cottages?'

I was all ears, my attention dragged from our picturesque surroundings. I couldn't remember the woman's name, just her face peering through the diamond-shaped hole in her trellis. 'What did she have to say?'

'Oh, just that poor old Dolly was all alone except for that great-grandson of hers, and he was at school all day, and how worried she was,' Maisie rattled on. 'And then she said she'd met this great big tall girl with a mass of curly ginger hair, who'd come to call on her—'

Excuse me. *Ginger?*

'And Nelly Mole said that could only be Juno Browne cos there wasn't anyone else fitted that description round Ashburton . . . and we all said, yes, that's right. And then old Tom Hopkins said that you wasn't a great ginger girl, you was a flame-haired goddess, and Nelly Mole said to him, "You should be ashamed of yourself, Tom Hopkins, talking about goddesses, and you a Christian and a bell-ringer too." Well, poor old Tom, he blushed beetroot—'

'Maisie, can we just forget Tom for a moment, what did she actually say?'

'Who?' she asked blankly.

'Dolly Knollys' neighbour.'

'Oh, 'er! Nothing.'

'Nothing?'

'Well, only that you was calling in from time to time, but that she didn't think it was enough.'

Olly's neighbour had already stopped me on one of my visits, hailing me over the garden fence, asking how things were. I think the poor woman was only trying to be neighbourly; she offered to pop in on Dolly herself, keep the old dear company, and I had quite a job persuading her that this was not a good idea. She sleeps a lot, I'd said, and she gets very confused and distressed when she meets strangers. Best left alone. But I could tell she wasn't convinced. As I took Maisie back to the car, I made a mental note to try to call in at Daison Cottages more often.

We drove back through Holne Chase and Buckland, and stopped on the brow of the hill where we could get a clear view of Buckland's church tower and its clock, another of Maisie's favourites. The clock face has no numerals; in place of them, letters spell out the words 'My Dear Mother'. I have no idea why. You have to start at nine o'clock and read clockwise for 'My Dear', and then go back to nine and read anticlockwise for 'Mother'. I've no idea about that either.

'It's A past E,' Maisie chuckled, and we had to sit and wait until R past E so that we could hear the clock chime 'All Things Bright and Beautiful' on the quarter hour. We drove on down the hill, slowing down to gaze lustfully at the huddle of picture-perfect thatched cottages set in a little glade.

Maisie pointed out bare trees, the dark clumps of abandoned rooks' nests set high up amongst the mesh of branches.

'Rabbits' nests – that's what I used to tell our Janet when she was a little girl,' she said. 'I told her they were rabbits' nests.'

And I laughed, although she'd told me a hundred times before.

Next morning, I did her shopping in Ashburton and walked along the lane behind St Andrew's church, Jacko trotting jauntily on the lead, so that I could visit the garage and fix a date with Dave for the repair of White Van.

In the garage yard I nearly changed my mind at the sight of a massive flatbed truck, piled with black silage bales, 'Moss and Pike' written clearly on its tailgate, 'clean me' etched beneath it in the dust. I crept up the side of the vehicle and peeped cautiously around. Sure enough, Green Bastard Hat was standing talking to Dave. It was the first time I'd seen him outside of his cab and been treated to the sight of the considerable paunch bulging over the belt of the jeans he was struggling to keep hitched up.

I slipped back along the side of the truck and began to write on the dusty tailgate with one finger. I got so absorbed in what I was doing that I didn't spot him coming until it was almost too late. 'Here!' he shouted. 'What are you up to?'

I didn't know if he would recognise me as the driver of White Van. He hadn't got a good view of me, as Emma had, but he took a step towards me. Jacko gave a warning growl, his lip writhing back to show his teeth.

To give Green Bastard Hat credit, he wasn't a man to underestimate the crunching power of a terrier's jaws, even when the terrier in question is barely above ankle height. He hesitated, and in that moment Dave himself came around the truck, wiping his hands on an oily rag.

'Everything OK?' he asked, glancing from me to GBH.

'Hi, Dave!' I said brightly. 'Can I talk to you about my van?'

'Yes, let's book you in. Step inside the office.' He waved his hand in the direction of his workshop and I walked past Green Bastard Hat, Jacko still growling and muttering curses in his direction. GBH gave an impatient snort, got up into his cab and drove off with an angry grinding of gears and hissing of brakes. Through the grimy window of the office I watched him depart. He hadn't read what I had written on the back of his truck, wouldn't see it now until he reached the end of his journey. Then he could read two names: 'Gavin Hall' and 'Ben Luscombe', and a very large question mark, inscribed in the dust.

'You've got a customer,' Pat whispered excitedly as soon as I got in the shop door. She jerked her head in the direction of the storeroom. 'Back there,' she added, rolling her eyes.

'Well, who is it?' I asked, puzzled by the dramatics. 'Someone we know?'

She stifled a giggle with her hand. 'Go and see!' She tried pushing me in the direction of the storeroom.

'All right, I'm going!' I squeezed past Mavis in her witch's hat and down the corridor, peering around the door frame a bit cautiously. There, admiring her reflection in the full-length mirror stood Detective Constable Cruella

DeVille, wearing the white fake-fur jacket with the black spots. I stopped in the doorway, watching her as she turned the collar up, then flipped it back down, turning her head from side to side. She saw my reflection and a faint flush coloured her pale cheeks.

'It really does look good on you,' I told her honestly.

'Yes, it does,' she agreed, with a slight note of defiance, 'even though you and your friends were laughing at my expense the other day.'

'You mustn't mind Ricky,' I told her.

'Oh, I'm used to it,' she sighed, taking the jacket off and looking at the price tag.

'What is your name?' I ventured. 'Your first name?'

'Christine,' she told me flatly. 'And that doesn't help, having to sign myself C. DeVille.'

'I'd enjoy it. And I think you should too.'

She almost smiled, a tug of her tiny mouth. Was this a crack in the ice, the first hint of a thaw? I wondered.

'That's what Dean says.'

'Is Dean your boyfriend?'

'My colleague,' her little mouth twisted again. 'Detective Constable Collins.'

'Ah!' I wanted to ask how the paternity leave was going but thought perhaps I'd better not. I came up with a more serious question. 'Tell me, are the police aware that Gavin Hall and Ben Luscombe knew each other?'

'Ben Luscombe?' she repeated.

'He died at Moorworthy Pit a year ago, supposedly the victim of a fall.'

Her dark brows drew together. 'Supposedly?'

'Yes. He and Gavin were friends.'

'So?'

'Well, doesn't it strike anyone as odd that two young men should die in horrible accidents, both on the Moorworthy estate, about half a mile from each other?'

'Accidents happen and these were over a year apart.'

'But I think Gavin tried to get into the woods because of what happened to Ben. They were both convinced that something was going on in the mines there. And they both ended up dead.'

DeVille stared at me impassively, her violet gaze icing over. No hint of a thaw now.

'So what did they think was going on?'

'Well, that's just it,' I admitted lamely, 'I don't know.'

The violet-eyed Medusa continued to stare. 'Then what exactly are you saying, Miss Browne?'

God, she was learning from her boss! I could hear him in her level voice, see him in the intensity of her stare. Yet, if Inspector Ford had been asking the questions, I wouldn't have felt quite so foolish. 'It just seems to me that their deaths have been too readily dismissed as accidents when there could be a connection between them.'

Cruella hunched a shoulder. 'Because they knew each other doesn't mean their deaths have to be connected. Ben Luscombe was wandering about in a dangerous place at night, and he was high on drugs . . .'

'His friends don't believe that.'

'And Gavin Hall,' she went on inexorably, 'was messing about with a dangerous weapon.'

'But . . .'

She silenced me with a shake of her head, pitying me. 'It's natural to want to find a reason when a death occurs, to make sense of a tragedy that seems senseless—'

I cut her off. 'Did that come out of some police training manual for dealing with the bereaved?'

I knew I was being rude, but her condescending tone irritated me.

Her little mouth twisted and she eyed me with hostility. 'Inspector Ford is a very busy man,' she told me, 'but I will pass on your concerns.'

'Thank you,' I responded, and gave her back a little smile, like hers, a tiny tug of the mouth.

She glanced at her watch as if to indicate she had wasted time enough on me already and I held out my hands for the jacket. 'If you're buying that, I'll find something to wrap it in.'

'No need, I can put it straight in the car.'

I charged her the full ticket price. I didn't feel like being generous.

Ricky and Morris had asked me to go and help fit the fat fairies. The whole fluttering flock was descending on them in the afternoon, and they could do with an extra pair of hands to make sure that each fairy got the right blouse and petticoat. Some of them looked very pretty in their frills and coloured sashes. Morris had looped lace and ribbon around each hemline, tying them up with little knots of silk flowers made by yours truly. They all had wings made from glittery net and tiny hats or headdresses to perch on their hair. It's true, there were a few sagging bosoms and unsightly bulges that weren't exactly fairy-like, and as Ricky had prophesied, some of them would be wearing their bifocals, but on the whole I thought they were a success, and I am sure when they all come tripping onto the stage in *Iolanthe*, the audience will be delighted.

But as I was down on my knees, pinning up a hem, I became aware of being stared at, and an increasingly hostile atmosphere. I looked up to see a lilac fairy fixing me with a baleful glare. It was Olly's next-door neighbour.

'Are you working here?' she asked, obviously upset. 'I thought you were a social worker.'

'I'm just helping out.' I felt at a disadvantage on my knees and scrambled to my feet, brushing cotton threads from my jeans. I tried a smile, but it got no response. 'I think there's been a misunderstanding. I work freelance. Some of my work involves care of the elderly, like Mrs Knollys. You met Maisie Biddle at the church coffee morning the other day,' I went on as she continued to glower at me, 'she's a client of mine.'

'Oh, yes, I did,' she admitted, her hackles lowering a little. 'But when we first met you gave me the distinct impression you were from social services.'

'I think you just assumed. I'd been asked to call in by one of the mothers at Olly's school,' I lied gaily. 'Now, have you got all the bits you need for your costume? Gloves, yes?' I caught her arm and steered her in the direction of Morris, who was trying to fit fairy bunions into dainty shoes and called, 'Next!' in a very determined voice.

He gave me an old-fashioned look over his little gold-rimmed specs. 'And what was all that about?' he asked me later, when we had sent the fairies home clutching their respective costumes.

'Nothing,' I assured him.

'She's up to something,' he said to Ricky.

'Yes,' he agreed, eyeing me narrowly, 'and what's worse, she's not telling us what it is.'

'I am not up to anything,' I assured them, trying to sound indignant. They weren't fooled.

'You're not getting into any trouble, are you, Juno?' Morris asked anxiously.

'Me?' I asked innocently. 'Noooo.'

Well, not yet anyway.

CHAPTER TWENTY-ONE

St Andrew's Church was packed for Gavin's funeral, local people turning out to support Gavin's parents who were well known in the town, and there were representatives from Gavin's old school. Sophie, Pat and I sat in a pew towards the back, and across the aisle, Jamie Westershall cut a lonely figure in black suit and tie. He nodded a greeting at me as he came in. I suppose he felt obliged to pay his respects. Emma obviously didn't feel such an obligation, or maybe she was still recovering after her accident. I saw him glance over his shoulder as new arrivals came in from the back of the church. As he turned to face the front again, I caught a glimpse of his expression for just a moment. He looked disconcerted, I thought, and began to flick through the pages of the order of service with unease.

I turned back to see who had entered and found myself staring at Detective Inspector Ford.

I must have been staring for a few seconds, because as he inclined his head in a greeting, he gave me a slightly quizzical look. Embarrassed, I turned back to face the front. Was it routine for the police to attend a funeral when there had been a suspicious death? It was on the television. TV coppers are always turning up at the victim's funeral, convinced that the murderer will turn up to gloat. Except that, according to Cruella, they didn't believe Gavin's death was a case of murder.

The service was pitiful and mercifully short. Not the celebration of a life fulfilled but a lamentation for a life cut short. Poor Mrs Hall sobbed uncontrollably, and by the time we had struggled our way through 'The Day Thou Gavest, Lord, Is Ended', Pat was sniffing, surreptitiously wiping her eyes, and Sophie was in floods. I let the two of them go out ahead of me as the mourners filed out of the church. I wanted to talk to Inspector Ford.

'I'm surprised to see you here, Inspector,' I told him frankly.

'Just paying my respects, Miss Browne.' His manner was friendly but guarded, as always.

'So, the case of Gavin Hall is now closed, I take it?'

'Not officially, not until the coroner's ruling, but,' his shoulders lifted and fell in the slightest of shrugs, 'unofficially, yes. We are satisfied that we have pursued all lines of enquiry.'

'Detective Constable DeVille told me the same thing.'

I sensed he wasn't really listening to me. His concentration seemed fixed on someone else. Following the direction of his gaze I saw Jamie Westershall making his way out through the mourners. 'Excuse me, Miss Browne,' the inspector said politely, and walked swiftly after him.

CHAPTER TWENTY-TWO

It took a long time to get ready for the Legends of the Silver Screen party. Ricky, who insisted on doing my hair, made me sit for hours with a head full of huge curlers, which frankly I thought was the last thing I needed. Meanwhile, Morris got Sophie ready. She emerged from his ministrations wearing a full-skirted black dress with white polka dots, a stiff petticoat underneath, and a bright-pink belt. She wore pink pumps and ankle socks, and tiny net gloves. A small pink hat perched on her dark head between two round black, cardboard ears. She was the prettiest, sexiest, most sophisticated Minnie Mouse you ever saw.

I was poured into plum-coloured velvet that fitted like a second skin from the very low neckline to the knee, where it suddenly flared out in a cascade of sparkling net, forming a train, which dragged on the floor behind me. Long black satin gloves completed the outfit, and my hair, released from the curlers, was brushed into glossy, rolling waves and swept over one shoulder. Then Ricky flung a pale mink stole around my shoulders.

'You look amazing!' Sophie breathed in awe. 'Who are you supposed to be? Jessica Rabbit?'

'Jessica Rabbit?' Ricky repeated, scandalised. 'Jessica fucking Rabbit!' he cried again, unable to believe his ears. 'She's Rita Hayworth!'

'I'm Rita Hayworth,' I repeated, just to be sure she knew.

'Now, listen, you!' Ricky pointed a warning finger in my face. 'You're not Miss Marple or Sherlock bleedin' Holmes, so don't get carried away up there this evening. No crawling about in the woods, understand? Not in that dress! Nor,' he added, waving his finger in Sophie's direction, 'you neither!'

'I'm not going near the woods,' Sophie protested with a shudder. 'I never want to go in them again, not after what happened to poor Gavin.'

'That's right,' Ricky nodded gravely. 'Just don't let Rita Hayworth lead you astray.'

'She was well known for that, was Rita,' Morris added.

The dress was tight about my knees and it was difficult not to step on the train. 'I'm not going crawling about anywhere. I can barely walk.'

'Take smaller steps!' Ricky cried. 'You can't stride about like a bloody Amazon! Oh my God! Shoes!' he exclaimed. 'What are you wearing?'

I raised the hem of the dress to reveal the flat leather pasties I find so comfortable. Ricky shuddered. Morris disappeared, giggling, and returned bearing high-heeled sandals in gold. 'The only thing in her size,' he told Ricky in a mournful whisper.

I tried them on and tottered about until I got the hang of them and my inelegant steps were pronounced passable by the two doyennes of Hollywood fashion.

'And don't get covered in dog hair!' Ricky ordered as a final caution.

I assured him that we weren't travelling in White Van but were borrowing Sophie's mum's car for the evening. And Sophie would be driving. She didn't really drink. Half a glass of Prosecco would be more than enough for her, whereas it certainly wouldn't be enough for me. Then, after hugs and kisses and more promises to behave ourselves, we were allowed to go.

'Have you got your inhaler?' I asked Sophie, before we set off.

She held up the dinky pink handbag that Morris had given her. 'In here.'

'Legends of the Silver Screen?' Ricky rapped on the car window, grinning. 'Just count the Marilyns!'

There were three, actually: three Marilyn Monroes in varying degrees of age and sadness. Emma was not one of them. She looked stunning, her hair drawn back in an elegant chignon, her dress a long sheath of ice-blue crystals. She looked very cool, very Grace Kelly, except that the surgical collar she was forced to wear rather spoilt the effect. Any momentary guilt I might have felt for her suffering evaporated when I thought of her riding her motorbike alongside White Van, looking in. She knew I was the driver, knew I had a child beside me on the front seat, but she'd still tried to trap us in a deadly game of cat and mouse. Remorse withered at the memory of Olly's terrified face.

'You've been in the wars, I hear.' I put on my best

solicitous smile as I received her frosty greeting in the hall. She was on meet-and-greet duty with Uncle Sandy and other than dart me with an icy, cat-like glare, she couldn't really make a response. Besides, there were too many Legends of the Silver Screen trying to pile into the hall behind us for us to be able to linger. We were forced to grab a glass of something bubbly from a proffered tray and move on into the ballroom where a lot of Legends were standing about, glasses in hand, and we could take a really good look as we drifted around introducing ourselves.

There was a brunette, a friend of Emma's, with piled-up hair, lots of eye make-up and a long cigarette holder, who made a really good Audrey Hepburn, whilst Jess wore a white hospital smock and had somehow turned her hair into a stiff, upright column and sprayed one wriggly streak of it silver. She was, she told me giggling, the Bride of Frankenstein. I liked that about her, that she'd gone for something fun, rather than for glamour.

She wasn't the only one who'd come as a film character rather than the legend who might have portrayed it. An older lady had gamely painted her face green and come as the Wicked Witch of the West and there was a Snow White as well as a Cleopatra.

Most of the men just cheated. There were at least a dozen in dinner jackets, including Uncle Sandy, all claiming to be James Bond, and one in a white tuxedo who said he was Humphrey Bogart. Jamie wore a leather jacket and fedora and carried a whip, as Indiana Jones; there was an elderly Beau Geste, a rather rotund John Wayne, a Charlie Chaplin and a whippet of a fellow in white tie and tails who assured me, with a blast of truly appalling halitosis, that he was Fred Astaire. 'Are you Ginger Rogers?' he asked, grinning at me. 'We could dance cheek-to-cheek later.' Now there was something to look forward to.

'I thought she was Rita Hayworth,' Uncle Sandy approached, glass in hand. I dutifully gave him a birthday peck on the cheek. 'Well, whoever you are, you're absolutely magnificent,' he went on, looking me over. 'My word! But where's your little friend?'

I pointed out Sophie, who was chatting with a young man who could have been James Dean. 'Oh, look at that!' he exclaimed. 'Minnie Mouse! Isn't she cute? Mind you, with her looks, she could have come as Liza Minnelli.'

Well, she could if she had borrowed longer legs.

'And then,' Sandy went on incorrigibly, 'she could have worn the bowler hat and suspenders! Ah well!' he added, his voice laden with regret. Then he turned back to me, his eyes brightening. 'Now, you run a little antique shop.'

'Well, I wouldn't exactly describe it as—'

'We've got a few bits and pieces around the house you might find interesting. There's a fine collection of oriental ceramics upstairs, in one of the bedrooms. I'll show you later on, if you like,' he promised, patting me on my arm, and sailed forth to greet another of his guests, saving me the awkwardness of a reply. Whilst I would certainly have loved a tour around the house, visiting any of the bedrooms in Sandy's company was not on my agenda.

After a lot of preprandial mingling, Jamie tried to call the party to order by raising his voice. This had no effect at all and so he silenced the babbling horde by cracking his whip.

This had the desired result and caused Fred Astaire, who had been narrowly missed, to hop about a bit.

'Sorry! I've always wanted to do that,' Jamie admitted, grinning. I assume he meant cracking the whip, not flogging Fred Astaire. 'Anyway, we're here tonight to celebrate Sandy's birthday and . . . where is the old devil?' he asked, eyes searching the crowd. Sandy declared his presence, lurking rather closely behind Audrey Hepburn. 'Ah! There you are! Emma and I have got you a rather special present.'

A waiter, obviously ready for the signal, bore an easel into the room, the portrait covered by a cloth and Sandy, after a bit of prompting, performed the great reveal. The picture of the Old Thunderer was greeted by a genuine gasp of delight from Sandy and a burst of applause from the assembled throng. Sophie was dragged forward to receive her plaudits as artist and for several minutes she and the portrait became the centre of attention.

Then the dinner gong sounded. I had assumed that, as there were so many of us, any food would be in the form of a buffet, but I was wrong. The enormous dining room contained a table the length of a bowling alley, covered in white damask, and sparkling with cut glass and silverware. Sophie was dismayed to discover we weren't sitting together. She, the feted artist, was much nearer Sandy at the top of the table than I was. I waved to her as I sat down, bundling armfuls of sparkling net under the table. I wasn't seated anywhere near Emma, thankfully; she and her cronies were giggling together at the far end.

Sitting directly opposite me was Barty Bartholomew, looking truly awful in straining blue spandex as Superman, already crimson in the face and rather less than sober. He boggled at me across the tablecloth. 'Are you Jessica Rabbit?' he asked, grinning.

He got a dig in the ribs from the Wicked Witch of the West on his right. 'Don't be ridiculous, Barty! She's Rita Hayworth.'

'And every bit as gorgeous!' Barty leered on, unabashed.

Next to me on the right was an empty chair, and I was just thinking I was condemned to spend the evening trying to drag conversation out of a po-faced and reticent Beau Geste on my left, when a bronzed hand grabbed the back of the chair and Jack Sparrow thrust himself into the seat. He must have been a late arrival because I hadn't noticed him in the ballroom. And I would have. I could tell he was Jack Sparrow, and not just any old pirate, because as well as the boots, baggy shirt, bandana and hat, he'd gone for the Johnny Depp eyeliner. I don't know if I should be worried about myself, but I find something rather attractive about a man in eyeliner. Well, this one anyway. He grinned at me as he sat down and proffered his hand. 'Jack Sparrow,' he said.

'Rita Hayworth.' We shook. I tried to see the printed place name, wondering what his real name was, but there were too many flowers and wine glasses in the way.

'Is that your real hair?' I asked, eyeing his dreadlocks.

'No, this comes off with the hat.'

'A gentleman should remove his hat at the dinner table,' Barty told him, a little sulky at his arrival.

'Couldn't possibly.' Jack nodded towards Beau Geste and John Wayne. 'And they're keeping theirs on.'

Making conversation as the chilled avocado soup was

served, I learnt that the pirate on my right was a friend of Jamie's, had studied with him at agricultural college, lost contact, and bumped into him quite by accident a few weeks before.

'Are you a farmer too?' I asked.

'No, I'm just here temporarily. I'm based in London. I work for the Department of the Environment.'

I was barely halfway through my delicious pale green soup, and had started to tell Mr Sparrow about how I'd met Jamie, when I became aware of a disturbance under the table. There was a lot of rustling amongst my net as if a mouse had got in there. Something slyly touched my ankle and began to slide up and down my calf. Bloody Barty was playing footsie. I glared at him, but he just continued to ogle me, grinning, and rub his foot up and down my leg. He was relying on the fact that a woman in company won't generally embarrass herself or others by making a fuss. He was about to learn he had mistaken his woman when I was saved the bother of retaliation. He suddenly let out a snort like a wounded buffalo and grabbed his shin.

'Sorry!' Jack Sparrow held up his hands helplessly. 'It's these swashbuckling boots, I do apologise.'

Barty muttered ungraciously, something about his being more careful, and sulked through the rest of the soup.

I smiled at Jack Sparrow. He smiled back but there was a slight wariness, a look of caution, almost, that lurked in his grey eyes, as if he was weighing me up carefully. 'You were saying . . .' he reminded me.

'Was I?'

'About the dog in the van . . .'

'Oh yes.' I don't remember too much about the rest of the meal. There were lots of courses and they were all delicious, and I have no idea how many times my wine glass was refilled, but by the time we got to the brandy posset with marrons glacé, Jack and I were definitely flirting. Perhaps he had decided to throw caution to the wind. Suddenly Beau Geste opened up. He leant across the table to Barty and asked a question that grabbed my attention.

'Barty, you didn't get any more trouble from the police, did you, over that unfortunate business of that young idiot with the sword?'

Barty had also had his wine glass filled several times and appeared to have difficulty remembering. 'Oh! Silly little ass who stabbed himself?' he cried at last. 'No, no.'

'His name was Gavin.' My voice cut into the conversation more loudly than I had intended. 'His name was Gavin Hall and he was nineteen.'

Beau Geste had the grace to look uncomfortable. 'Oh, knew him, did you?'

'I went to his funeral yesterday.'

The room had suddenly gone quiet. I decided to lob another pebble into the pool of silence and see if it caused any ripples. 'And he was a friend of Ben Luscombe, another young man who died on this estate.'

Jamie rose hastily. 'We've certainly had our fair share of tragic accidents. We're very sad, of course. But we're here to celebrate a happy occasion. So, if I could ask everyone to raise their glasses . . .'

There was an instant response, an exhalation of pent-up breath, the relief of people happily moving on from an awkward moment. They raised their glasses. We all toasted Sandy on his birthday and he made an amusing speech about how wonderful it was to have so many friends sharing his day with him, and how lovely all the ladies looked, and he finished by declaring that as it was his birthday he was jolly well going to drink brandy and smoke a cigar, inviting all the gentlemen at the table to join him, and promising the ladies they would find coffee and petits fours awaiting them in the drawing room.

We ladies dutifully withdrew, my exit made slightly less graceful by having to tug a bunch of sparkly net from under the leg of Beau Geste's chair as I got up to leave.

Sophie caught up with me on the way to the drawing room and we began to compare notes. 'I wish I'd been sitting near you,' she complained bitterly. 'I don't like the way Sandy keeps looking at me.'

'He's imagining you in a bowler hat and suspenders.'

'What?'

'Don't worry about it. I think he and Barty are about level-pegging in the dirty old man stakes. Barty was trying to play footsie under the table.'

'You seemed to be doing all right whenever I looked at you, heads together with that good-looking pirate.'

'He's nice, isn't he?' I was hoping we might get our heads together again later.

In the drawing room we found ourselves beckoned over by the Wicked Witch of the West, who patted the empty cushions of the sofa next to her. 'Come and sit with me, girls,' she called out, pouring coffee that had been left on a tray on the table in front of her.

'And you, my dear,' she added to Sophie, 'talk to me.

I'm thinking of asking you to paint my bulldogs.'

I made my excuses, left the two of them chatting and headed for the guest cloakroom. Going to the loo was a more complicated process than usual: it involved stripping off long gloves and being very careful with an ocean of sparkly net. I put myself back together again and was heading back to the drawing room when I heard gales of girlish laughter coming from behind the library door, which was slightly ajar.

'I thought she was Jessica Rabbit!' a voice was shrieking loudly.

I lurked, ears straining.

'Who on earth invited her?'

'She's a friend of the artist woman.' Emma's voice was sour.

'So, I suppose I can understand inviting *her*,' chimed in someone else. 'But what does the other one do?'

'I like her!' I recognised the voice of the Bride of Frankenstein. Thank you, Jessica.

'She owns a shop, apparently.'

'So, I'd heard she was some kind of cleaner.'

'Well, I wish I had her figure.'

'It was Jamie who invited her,' Emma added. 'Sandy had told him to make sure there was some fuckable totty at his party.'

'Oh, charming!' cried the first voice.

'He meant someone not like us,' Emma assured her smugly. 'Anyway, come on girls, heads down, let's have a race!'

Intrigued, I pushed the library door a fraction wider. I was treated to the spectacle of two Marilyn Monroes, Audrey Hepburn, Snow White and, alas, the Bride of Frankenstein, each armed with a tube of paper, bending over the desk, racing to see who could snort white powder up her nasty little nose the fastest.

I slammed the door shut, which caused them all to shriek, first with terror and then with hysterical laughter. I stalked away, or rather minced, as swiftly as my tight skirt and trailing net would allow.

As I approached the drawing room I slowed down. The hall was deserted. I cast a quick look around me and headed for the door of the study, where I'd been interviewed on the day of Gavin's death by Inspector Ford. I didn't know what I expected to find, but a chance for a poke around seemed too good to miss.

The study was quiet and lamp-lit, heavy curtains drawn across the window. I stood still and looked around me. There were pictures on the wall, which I had not noticed when I was in the room before: engravings of mine workings on the Moorworthy estate, the earliest dated 1860. They showed the mineshaft in the woods, and the shaft at Applecote Farm and several underground passages connecting the two.

There was also a set of photographs, mostly featuring Sandy, who was obviously receiving an award of some kind, shaking hands with another man, the pair surrounded by self-satisfied men in dinner jackets and bow ties. The caption beneath mentioned Dravizax, the firm Jessica had said belonged to her father.

'Can I help you, miss?'

I nearly jumped out of my skin. Like Creeping Ted Croaker, Mrs Johnson seemed to possess the demonic power to materialise, silently, from nowhere. I hadn't heard her come in and she was standing right next to me.

'No, I'm . . . um . . . I was just interested in . . .' I blundered uselessly. 'This is a lovely room.'

'There's coffee in the drawing room.' She held the study door open, forcing me to leave.

'Yes, I know. Thank you,' I swept past her and carried on across the hall. I could feel her gaze drilling into me, right between the shoulder blades. She must have been satisfied I was going where she'd told me to because when I reached the living room door and turned around, hand on the handle, she had already disappeared.

The eyes of the ancestors stared from their portraits. But there was no one else about.

I gathered up my sparkly train and quickly nipped up the grand staircase. I came to the first landing, my hand resting on the oak bannister next to an impressively carved pineapple. For a moment the suit of armour and I stared at one another. I resisted the impulse to lift the visor of his helmet and check there was no one inside. I looked left and right. Which way to go? I turned right along a wide corridor, passing a series of doors separated by brass console tables and ornately framed mirrors. I stopped by a door that was open and poked my head inside.

I wondered if this was the bedroom that Sandy had mentioned earlier. It was certainly oriental in style, hung with Chinese wallpaper decorated with birds and flowers. A Japanese lacquer cabinet stood against one wall, whilst on the mantelpiece were placed two Canton vases and an Imari bowl. Whoever had put the collection together obviously didn't distinguish between Chinese and Japanese. There were several Nanking blue and white plates on the walls, but the pride of the collection was a chrysanthemum flower teapot, only a few inches high, and probably worth more than the rest put together. Very carefully, I picked it up for a closer look. Then I heard a man's cough in the corridor outside and hastily replaced it.

I needed a hiding place. I didn't want to be caught in here, especially not by Sandy. I tiptoed across the room to a closed door, which I hoped led to a lockable en suite, and opened it. It was a cupboard, but someone was coming into the room, so I had no choice but to duck inside. I waited in complete darkness, my breath held, trying to listen for muffled footsteps on the Chinese carpet.

The door opened and a light flipped on above my head. 'Well, this is cosy!' Jack Sparrow remarked pleasantly, his hand on the light switch. 'May I?' He stepped inside.

It was quite a tight fit, requiring an adjustment of feet, elbows, hips and hat before he could wedge himself in. The net did a lot of rustling.

'How did you know I was in here?' I was whispering for some stupid reason.

'I saw you come upstairs.'

'No, I mean, in *here*?'

He grinned. 'All that net sticking out from under the door is a bit of a giveaway. Anyway,' he shifted slightly to avoid the prong of a coat hook sticking into his shoulder, 'I'm impressed. There's nothing like causing a sensation at dinner.'

'Talking about Gavin as if his death was just an inconvenience—'

Mr Sparrow leant in even closer. 'Listen.' His face was just an inch from mine. There was no levity in his voice now, no laughter in his grey eyes. 'I want to hear what you know about Gavin and Ben.'

'They thought something—'

He laid a finger to his lips. 'Not now. We'll be missed if we're not careful. We're not exactly an inconspicuous couple—'

'Who are you?' I asked.

'Jack Sparrow.'

'No, what's your real name?'

He grinned. 'Nathan, Nathan Parr.'

I confessed that I wasn't really Rita Hayworth and we shook hands awkwardly in the confined space.

'And what are you doing here? You said you worked for the Environment Agency.'

'I do. Officially I'm down here as part of a survey into pollution along the River Dart.'

'And unofficially . . . ?'

He hesitated. 'Let's just say that I didn't bump into James Westershall by accident.'

'Is this about drugs?'

His dark brows drew together in a frown. 'Why should it be about drugs?'

'Because in this house they treat cocaine as if it's an after-dinner mint. Emma's a user and Ben Luscombe was found—'

The door swung open suddenly, making us both jump. 'Playing sardines?' Jamie asked, his brows raised quizzically.

'We're just getting acquainted,' Nathan told him coolly, sliding his arms around my waist. I gave a silly little laugh.

'I was just rounding up people for the fireworks,' Jamie responded. 'I thought I heard voices in here. So, if you two can bear to tear yourselves away . . .'

He stood back and we trailed past him, doing our best to look sheepish.

'You go on down,' Nathan murmured to me, 'I'll catch you up in a moment.'

The gentlemen had not lingered too long over their brandy and cigars and the sitting room had filled up in my absence. Sophie waved to me through the throng. 'Don't worry,' she whispered, patting her little pink handbag. 'I've saved you some petits fours.' Judging from the way the bag was bulging she must have slid an entire plateful in there.

The room was so warm now that someone had flung open the long windows onto the terrace and a few people had drifted out to look at the stars. I decided I could use some air and drifted out myself. After a few moments, Nathan Parr leant on the balustrade next to me.

'Can we meet?' he asked softly. 'Are you free on Tuesday evening?' He named an isolated pub on the moor. 'We can talk more freely there, less chance of being overheard.' He glanced at his watch. 'Look, I'd really love to stay and dance with you till dawn, but I have to go.' He raised my gloved hand to his lips and kissed it. 'Till Tuesday.'

'I'm not sure I'll know you without the hat and dreadlocks.'

'I'll wear a red carnation.'

'You might not know me either. I don't usually look like this.'

'You don't?' he asked in mock sadness.

'My hair is usually . . . um . . . wilder.'

'Wow!' he grinned. 'I'll look forward to that,' and walked away.

I felt mildly triumphant. At last there was someone interested in hearing about Gavin and Ben Luscombe, prepared to take their deaths seriously. He was also a very attractive pirate and I was not at all unhappy at the thought of a little swashbuckling in his company. If things went well, we might even go as far as a jolly roger.

Jamie came out at that moment and announced that fireworks would be starting in five minutes, and that the place to view them from was the terrace, but if people wanted to wander down onto the lawn, he warned them, please beware of the ha-ha.

'We don't want any broken necks. Also, it's getting a bit chilly, so some of you might want to grab a coat or something before the fireworks start.'

I went inside and reached for the mink stole I'd left draped over the end of the sofa. I snatched it up just before Emma grabbed it. 'Mine, I think,' I told her, smiling sweetly. She glowered, her pupils mere pinpoints, then shrugged, a painful manoeuvre she obviously regretted, and stalked away.

'Well, I'm getting a coat,' Sandy announced loudly. 'I feel the cold these days. I blame it on these damned pills the doctor keeps giving me.'

'You're just getting old, you fool,' the Wicked Witch of the West informed him flatly.

'You're right, Margaret, m'dear, you're right,' he admitted, shaking his head.

A few minutes later I stood on the terrace with Sophie whilst rockets shot upward in golden, fizzing streaks and

227

exploded in sparkling starbursts. I saw the figure of Sandy close by, suddenly silhouetted in a dazzling burst of brightness, wrapped up against the cold in a sheepskin coat and trilby hat, looking as he had when I had seen him standing outside the shed at Applecote Farm, just before Moss and Pike's lorry had tried to run me off the road. I tried not to stare. Sophie was shivering. I wrapped one end of the mink stole around her shoulders and watched the dying glitter of the fireworks as they fell to earth over the dark masses of the woods, and the place where Gavin and Ben had died.

CHAPTER TWENTY-THREE

Never trust a pirate. The bastard stood me up. On Tuesday evening I drove all the way out to this damn pub in the dark and sat for two hours in a deserted and almost silent bar, nursing half a sour-tasting cider, waiting for him to show up, and receiving unwelcome glances from two fat blokes playing pool. At first, I thought I'd got the time wrong, then the place. And it was only then it got through to my dim brain that I didn't even have the man's phone number. I'd obviously got carried away on the bubbly at the party and the whole assignation was just a fantasy.

Sophie and I had not stayed long after the fireworks. James Dean wanted her to dance, so I sat down between the Wicked Witch of the West and the eldest Marilyn, and watched them join the jigging horde on the ballroom floor.

'Not dancing?' WWW asked me.

'Difficult to move at all in this dress,' I admitted.

'It is lovely. Did you get it from those two old reprobates up on Druid Lane? What do they call themselves, Sauce and something . . .'

'Sauce and Slander,' I told her. 'You know them?'

'They've done a couple of fundraisers for my charity. In fact, I've got a ticket for a concert they're doing soon.'

'They did say they were doing a concert here,' I remembered. We chatted on for a bit. She turned out to be neither Mrs Superman, nor Mrs Beau Geste, as I thought she might be, but a widowed aunt of Jamie's. 'Is Sophie going to paint your bulldogs?' I asked when we had exhausted the family connections.

'Florence has just produced a litter,' she answered with the beaming smile of a proud grandmother. 'I thought it might be fun, you know, a portrait of mother and babies. Sophie's coming to my house to make sketches and take photos. Come with her and have a cup of tea.'

'Well, thank you, Mrs . . . I will.'

'Call me Margaret.' She patted my arm. 'You're a good 'un. I like the way you spoke up about the death of your friend, put Barty and Geoffrey in their place—'

Fred Astaire came bounding up at this moment and tried to claim me for a dance he said I'd promised him and vowed he wouldn't take no for an answer.

'Oh, do fuck off, Robert!' Margaret commanded him, causing the eldest Marilyn to give a startled hiccup. 'We're trying to have a conversation.'

Poor Fred shrank visibly, mumbled an apology and left, muttering something about coming back later.

'Well really, Margaret!' Marilyn protested. 'Language!'

Margaret favoured her with a long stare. 'Why are you got up like an old tart, Betty?' she demanded amiably. 'Who are you supposed to be?'

'Marilyn Monroe,' she responded, a red flush of embarrassment creeping up her neck.

Margaret gave a witch-like cackle and turned her attention back to me. 'No, you're a good 'un, I can tell. That one over there,' she nodded in the direction of Emma, who was dancing with Charlie Chaplin, 'she's a bad 'un, even though she is my god-daughter and I shouldn't say it.' She sighed. 'I don't know the half of what she gets up to and it's probably just as well.'

She was right about that. I doubt if she knew about the after-dinner cocaine. I was still angry about it, disappointed in the Bride of Frankenstein.

'Is Charlie Chaplin Emma's boyfriend?'

'Boyfriend?' Margaret's shoulders shook as she chuckled. 'She can't keep 'em, my dear. She's got the fiend's own temper. Men don't like it. I told you, she's a bad 'un.'

'And what about Jamie?' He was dancing with his whip twined around Audrey Hepburn's waist. 'Is he a good 'un, or a bad 'un?'

'That's a good question,' she answered me sadly. 'I've never been able to tell.'

Sophie flopped down into a nearby chair at this point. She was a bit wheezy and I judged it was time to be going home. Anyway, it seemed that Charlie Chaplin had now been abandoned and James Dean had been dragged away from her by an obviously possessive Emma. 'Eddie!' she'd hissed furiously, beckoning him to her. 'Eddie!' He'd scuttled obediently across the dance floor. I told Sophie to forget him. He was obviously a lap dog.

We made our excuses and left, carefully avoiding being

spotted by Fred Astaire. When we got to the car, I asked Sophie if she felt well enough to drive.

'Well, I'm more sober than you,' she responded, dropping the pink handbag into my lap. So I let her steer our way down the darkened moorland road and tucked happily into the petits fours.

Next morning, Sunday, I took Rita Hayworth back to Ricky and Morris. She was carefully sheathed in plastic to avoid contact with any dog hair in the van, but actually, cat hair was more likely to be a problem. I had dutifully put the dress on a hanger before I went to bed, and hung it on the bedroom door, but the train was so long it reached the floor and lay in a big frothy cloud on the carpet. When I got up next morning, I found Bill, who'd been strangely absent from my bed all night, blissfully nesting in the middle of it. I didn't mention this to Morris and Ricky when I gave it back. In any case, they were more interested in who'd been at the party and what they'd worn than anything else. I gave them the details over coffee and croissants, adding good wishes sent from Margaret the WWW.

Then I drove to Olly's, making sure my arrival was clocked by his fairy neighbour, and offered him a trip up to the moor to fly the drone around. He said it was too windy for the drone, so I asked him what he'd like to do instead.

'Could we go to a supermarket?' he asked, eyes alight. 'A big one?'

Ashburton doesn't have a real supermarket. If he and his nan had wanted to shop in one they would have had to catch a bus; I suppose in Olly's mind a visit to a supermarket still represented a day out. So I took him to Newton Abbot, where there were several such cathedrals of consumerism, and told him to take his pick. He shopped like a thing demented, racing up and down the aisles with his trolley, buying new school trousers and stationery as well as stocking up on tins, cleaning materials and foodstuffs. 'It's all so cheap!' he squeaked ecstatically as he loaded up his trolley. It was true; the small independent shops of Ashburton could not compete in terms of price. Even I bought a few groceries and a T-shirt.

After a milkshake and sticky bun for Olly and a coffee and croissant for me we escaped the supermarket and I got my reward for taking him shopping: the racecourse was holding a boot sale. I wandered around, happily accruing an armful of paperback books, a box of china ornaments, a brass coal scuttle, a three-legged oak milking stool and a set of pretty pine shelves, which, even if they didn't sell, would look good on the wall in the shop and be useful for displaying other stuff. Olly helped me carry my spoils, along with a science annual he'd bought and a book about unexplained phenomena.

'I nearly bought a jigsaw,' he told me, as we were loading our booty into White Van.

'The man was trying to sell it to me, but I told him, I got lots of jigsaws. Nan used to like them. She'd got really old ones that were her mother's – you know, wooden ones with funny old pictures on – and he said if ever I wanted to sell them—'

'If ever you want to sell them,' I told him firmly, 'you sell them to me.'

'Why did you buy that box of stupid china animals? They can't be worth much.'

'No, most of them aren't,' I agreed, 'but if you turn them upside down, some have a magic word on the bottom.'

'What's that?'

'Wade. These little animal figures are collectors' items.'

'Are they worth a lot, then?'

'Just a few pounds each, but that's more than I paid for them.'

Olly digested this in thoughtful silence for a few moments and then stuck his head in unexplained phenomena for the rest of the journey home.

When we arrived back at Daison Cottages, his neighbour was weeding her front garden. As we drew up, I saw her sneak a look at her watch. We had abandoned Nan for hours.

'Just stocking up,' I called to her as I struggled up the front path laden with supermarket carriers and a giant pack of toilet rolls. And then I added to her in a low, conspiratorial voice. 'Some of the essentials were running low.'

'Such a good job you're here,' she answered, but her expression was sour. I got the feeling that the milk of human kindness had curdled.

I'd planned to suggest a walk up on the moor when we got back, but after cruelly abandoning Nan for such a long time, I thought we'd better stay indoors, so Olly and I sat and played Scrabble. I won. For a genius his spelling isn't very good.

Monday was Hallowe'en. Just an ordinary busy Monday: dogs, Maisie, Brownlows, shirts, shop. Pat did quite well with pumpkins and witches. I sold nothing at all. Late in the afternoon, Pat came in lugging a box from the orchard at Honeysuckle Farm. Showers of apples had been brought down by the wind, she told me, and there were basketfuls to be picked up before they rotted in the wet grass. Olly had started his half-term holiday and was helping out.

'So, who are this lot for?' I asked, as she dumped a second box on the shop floor.

'You and Sophie,' she answered breathlessly. 'Them's Lambournes, they're eaters,' she pointed at the apples in one box. 'The others are cookers. Can't you use 'em?'

'I know someone who can,' I assured her. And so I spent that evening seated at the big scrubbed table in Katie's kitchen, happily chatting as we cored and sliced until nearly midnight whilst the saucepans on the stove became steamy cauldrons of spice-scented stewed apple. She told me to drop into *Sunflowers* next day for a free lunch.

I took the Tribe for their usual walk in the morning and decided to take them home along the Terrace, where I had last seen the mystery lady enjoying a quiet moment with her cat. She wasn't there this time, but I still put the dogs back on their leads before we went through the little woodland that would take us down to Roborough Lane. I was trying to keep them away from any broken glass that might be littering the muddy path, so my eyes were fixed on the ground, rather than looking ahead.

Nookie the husky growled suddenly, stopping still, the silver fur around her neck bristling in a stiff ruff. She was staring off into to the trees, and as I peered between the ivy-covered trunks, I could see two figures standing. Lurking, you might say. Two men, one in a dark duffle coat, the other in a leather jacket. They were looking around furtively, casting anxious glances over their shoulders; but they didn't see me. Something passed between them. I couldn't see too clearly, but I'm sure money changed hands, and then something else.

The other dogs had picked up Nookie's alertness. EB began to bark, and then Schnitzel, Boog and Sally all joined in. I had to haul back hard on their leads to stop them rushing forward.

Startled by the raucous cacophony of noise, the men parted company, hastening away in opposite directions. Leather Jacket cast a glance over his shoulder, and I saw his face clearly. His hair had lost the quiff he'd worn when he'd danced with Sophie at the party, but it was James Dean, alias Eddie. The other man also risked a look behind him; none other than Creeping Ted Croaker. So, what was this unlikely pair up to that they had to move away sharpish at the sign of anyone's approach? The dogs were sniffing the ground inquisitively and I just snatched something that Eddie had dropped before Schnitzel's snout got to it. It was a clear, self-seal packet glistening with white crystals, like sugar. Except of course, it wasn't sugar and it wouldn't have done Schnitzel any good at all.

We dog walkers come prepared with pockets full of plastic bags. I fished one out, dropped the little bag of goodies into it and tied it up tightly. At the top of Roborough Lane I deposited the bag, along with a few others I had collected, into the evil-smelling red bin that stood there for the purpose. I shoved it down firmly, squishing it amongst the other parcels of dog poo. Let Eddie fish it out if he dared.

I tried phoning Inspector Ford to tell him I had seen Croaker, but as usual, he was unavailable. Even Cruella wasn't around to speak to. I left a message, without much hope that anyone would get back to me soon. So I was surprised later in the day when the inspector phoned back. They had found Creeping Ted and taken him to the police station for a little chat.

'Unfortunately, we had to let him go again,' the inspector told me. 'To begin with, he denied ever knowing Gavin Hall, but when we told him three different witnesses could swear to him speaking to Gavin in your shop, he admitted that he did. He said he'd come in because he was interested in the classic comics that Gavin was selling. That's rubbish, of course, but sadly, there's no law against it.'

'So we still don't know what he was up to?'

'He was almost certainly trying to sell Gavin drugs – or trying to recruit him.'

'Recruit him?'

'To sell drugs for him,' the inspector explained. 'Mr Croaker is desperately trying to claw his way up the supply chain.'

'I don't think Gavin would have got involved in selling drugs,' I said frankly. 'What about Eddie, do you think he's one of Croaker's recruits?'

'We've arrested Eddie Coates for possession on more than one occasion. But we have no evidence that he's supplying it to others.'

'Someone supplies it to Emma Westershall.' I told him about the little cocaine-snorting party I'd witnessed on the

237

night of Sandy's birthday. 'And Eddie was there that night.'

The inspector sighed in a way that told me this was not evidence. 'Well, we'll have words with Eddie, next time we catch hold of him,' he said wearily, and bid me goodbye.

I dropped into *Sunflowers* for my promised lunch and ate parsnip and apple soup so thick it was almost solid, followed by spiced apple cake with clotted cream. It was all delicious and I hoped there would be plenty of leftovers.

I spent the rest of Tuesday looking forward to meeting Nathan Parr in the evening and finished work early so that I could glam up. Alas, Rita Hayworth's glossy waves were long gone and the wild curls were back. I did the best I could with spritz and set out in nicely fitting jeans, ankle boots and a caramel silk shirt, to meet my pirate at the pub in the middle of the moor.

It was when one of the pool players came over and offered to buy me a drink that I decided it was time to leave. It was getting late by then and I still faced the drive home. I left a note with the girl behind the bar. Just in case a man came in and asked for me, I told her. It read: *Came. Waited. Went. Rita Hayworth.* And beneath my name I wrote my phone number.

During the evening the weather had finally broken. A gale had blown in from the west and rain was flinging itself in fitful gusts against the steamy windows of the pub. Outside, beyond the lighted haven of the car park, the night was black. Cursing, I turned up the collar of my jacket and ran across the uneven concrete to White Van, dodging puddles as I went. The wind was strafing through the trees, stripping the branches. Leaves clung wetly to the roof of the van and to my windscreen. I climbed in and got the windscreen wipers going, swishing them aside. The rain rattled on the roof, danced in the light of my headlamps and bounced up from the tarmac. I shivered. It would be a while before the van warmed up and as I turned out onto the moorland road, I cursed Nathan Parr alias Jack Sparrow several times over.

The headlights questioned the darkness ahead, picking out the road, the whiteness of granite boulders scattered on the grassy verge and the occasional shine of animal eyes, but beyond, the moor lay in darkness, sky black as molasses, no moon, stars blotted out. I drove slowly, as always on the moor at night, for fear of hitting wandering sheep or cattle. Now and again the golden lights of a lonely house glimmered in the distance, a welcome reminder that light, warmth and comfort existed out there somewhere.

The roaring wind stirred the gorse and heather into a shifting sea, buffeting the van as it crawled across the exposed moorland. I wasn't in any danger of getting lost; I was clinging to the only road I could, which would take me around the edge of Holne Moor, past the gates of the Moorworthy estate, and down the hill into Ashburton. My delicious apple-filled lunch seemed a long time ago now and I wondered if the Indian takeaway would still be open when I got back into town.

I was not far short of the gates of Moorworthy House when I hit something, or rather, something hit me. I felt it thump, bounce off my nearside wheel. I'd seen nothing in the headlights. Whatever it was must have come at me from the side, and it must have been small: a rabbit or a farm cat, perhaps a pheasant or a badger. I pulled up on the verge and got out, peering into the rainy dark. I couldn't bear the thought of leaving an animal injured. I fetched the torch from the glovebox and shone it back the way I'd come, peering through the slanting rain. There was nothing lying in the road, no sad little furry corpse. I crossed over, hunching my shoulders against the chill, against the fat wet drops rolling down inside my collar. I swept the torch beam up and down the verge, probing the bushes for any sign of an injured creature. Around me the moor was a wild thing, roaring wind thrashing the heaving gorse bushes, flailing and swishing the bracken, blowing my hair across my wet face so that I had to clutch at handfuls, drag it out of my vision.

I was caught suddenly in the headlights of an approaching vehicle. I ran to the verge out of its way and it pulled up behind me, quenching its tyres in wet gravel. For a moment I thought it might be Nathan, but the figure that climbed out of the driving seat was not him. It came towards me, silhouetted by the headlights behind. I could see only a stooping figure in a flat cap, but as he drew close and I pointed the torch in his direction, the glaring white light revealed the lugubrious features of Moss.

'What are you doing here?' he demanded loudly, eyes narrowed against my torch beam.

I had to raise my voice above the roar of the wind. 'I thought I'd hit something.'

He grabbed my arm. 'Put that torch out and dowse them headlights!'

I pulled away, wrenching my arm from his grip. 'Just a minute!'

'For the love of God, maid!' he cried, shaking me. 'They're coming! If you value your life, do as I say.' He pushed past me, opening the van door, switching off the engine and ripping out the keys. Then he slammed the door shut and thrust the keys into my hand.

'Down!' he told me. 'Get down in the ditch there, where they won't see you.' I stood goggling at him like an idiot. 'Quick!' he shouted, wresting the torch from my grasp. 'They mustn't see you.' He began to hustle me towards the ditch. 'There's too many dead already.'

The anguish in his voice, the desperation on his face, told me this was not a moment to argue. I did as I was told, hunkered in the ditch behind gorse bushes, out of sight of the road, seconds before the glaring lights of a large truck appeared around the bend. It thundered towards us, water spraying sideways beneath its heavy tyres and rumbled to a stop a few feet from Moss's Land Rover. I heard the cab door open and someone jump down onto the roadway on the passenger side.

'Something the matter, Moss?' It was Jamie's voice, but cold and authoritative, stripped of bonhomie. As I peered between the bushes, I saw the shadows of his legs scissoring across the road as he walked in front of the headlights. The driver in the cab was just a hunched shape slumped behind the steering wheel, but I was willing to bet he was wearing a green hat.

'I saw the van parked, sir,' Moss responded. 'Just thought I'd take a look around. But there's no one about.'

'Hang on, that's Juno Browne's van, isn't it? I recognise the number plate . . . and look at the back bumper! What the hell is that bloody woman doing up here?'

'If it is hers, she's long gone, sir.' Moss laid a hand on bonnet. 'Engine's stone cold,' he lied. 'And I think she's had a bit of a knock to this nearside wheel. Forced to abandon it, I reckon. She must've got a ride home.'

'Let's hope you're right. She's turning into a nuisance. We might have to do something about her. Look, just have another check around, will you, Moss? Make sure? There's too much at stake to leave any loose ends. We'll carry on.'

I saw his shadow cross the road in the glare of the truck's lights, heard the slam of the cab door. The truck growled into life again. As it roared past, tyres hissing on the wet road, I could see the back piled high with the rounded shapes of silage bales, light glimmering on black plastic.

'Stay down!' Moss yelled in my direction. After what seemed like an age cramped in the narrow wet ditch, scratched by the thorns of tossing gorse, he told me it was safe to stand up. 'They've turned off for the farm.'

'What the hell is going on?'

'Stop asking questions.' He handed me back the torch. 'Get home and stay away from here.'

'You said there'd been too many dead already.' I squinted into the rain, trying to read his face beneath his dripping cap. 'What did you mean?'

'You don't want to know.'

'Moss, what happened to Gavin?'

'I tried to warn him, all right?' His voice was broken, hoarse, shouting above the wind. 'I tried to scare 'em off, him and the other lad!' He headed back towards his car.

'The other lad?' I yelled after him. 'Do you mean Ben?'

'I'm not saying no more.' He pushed past me. 'My

242

family's been loyal to the Westershalls for years, but it never used to be like this. You don't want to let them catch you up here, maid.' He wrenched the car door open. 'Go home!' He climbed inside and drove off.

I watched his tail lights disappear. I was clutching the keys he had thrust into my hand so tightly they had dug an impression in my palm. I hurried to the van and got in. I was soaked, shaking with the cold, water running off the ends of my hair. My hands were icy and for a few moments they trembled too much for me to get the key in the ignition. I fished an old towel I used for wiping muddy paws from the back of the van and dried my face and hands with it. I breathed in deep; the doggy smell was comforting. I got going at last, headlights on, heater full blast, windscreen wipers swishing into action.

And as I passed the end of the lane that led to Applecote Farm, drove by the gates of Moorworthy House and trundled on down the hill towards the safety of Ashburton, I wondered why the hell anyone would be hauling trucks full of silage around empty farms at night. I wondered about Nathan Parr who just happened to have been placed next to me at dinner and who'd lured me to spend the evening alone in an isolated pub. And I wondered about Jamie. Was he a good 'un or a bad 'un? I think I had the answer to that now.

CHAPTER TWENTY-FOUR

Driving down the wooded hill towards Ashburton I had other things to worry about. The trees at the roadside shifted like restless giants. They came down in gales like this. I had to steer around branches wrenched off by the moaning wind, fearful that any moment a great trunk might fall across the road in front of me or come crashing through the roof of the van.

When I got home, I ran myself a hot bath. I was still shaking, from fear as well as cold, and I spent a long time soaking in the glistening bubbles, staring through clouds of steam, thinking of Jamie and what he'd said to Moss about having to do something about me. I didn't like the sound of that. And what about Nathan? Was he who he claimed to be, or had Jamie planted him next to me at dinner to find out what, if anything, I had said to the police about Gavin's death, or to discover what I'd been up to with the drone? But if Jamie had set Nathan on me to spy, why hadn't he turned up at the pub? Was Nathan a good 'un or a bad 'un?

I slept badly. Even in my dreams I could hear the wind that had ripped and roared up on the moor. Down in the town it buffeted the houses like a drunken fist, smiting at chimneys and rooftops, rattling doors and windows, trying to get in.

I did not want to get out of bed next morning, leave its snuggly warmth, but there were five waggy creatures waiting expectantly for me to take them for a walk so I was forced to drag myself from under the duvet, despite Bill's best efforts to pin me down. Half of me wanted to drive them up onto Holne Moor, let them race around on the common land where I had stopped last night, just beyond Applecote Farm, and have a nose around. The other, more sensible half reminded me I had a full morning and not too much time. So we just followed the course of the river through the town and into the woods. Barely more than a stream for most of the year, after the storm it was swollen and muddy, choked in places by rafts of twigs and leaves.

The gale had blown itself out, but in the wood the trees still stirred. A few odd leaves clung like golden pennies to bare and dripping branches, but most lay on the ground in soggy heaps, their crunchy crispness lost. The dogs didn't care, snuffling amongst the sodden leaves. The wind stirred them up, ruffled their fur, excited them like kids in a playground, and the rain released fresh smells, wet smells, the earthy pungent tang of the forest floor and the creatures dwelling in it. For the dogs the world was new again.

Back in town, Tribe delivered, I checked in at *Old Nick's*, and had a brief chat with Pat.

'That Olly's a nice lad,' she told me approvingly, 'very

eager. And you say he lives all alone with his nan?'

'Yes,' I said, hoping to turn the conversation in another direction.

'My mum knew old Dolly Knollys. I'd have thought she would have been dead long ago.'

'Mmm.' I nodded evasively. 'I'm glad Olly's being useful. I can't hang about, Pat. I've got errands to run for a few people. I'll be back here lunchtime to take over.'

I hurried out of the door before she could chat further. I threaded my way between the wheelie bins in the side alley, stepping over the puddles, emerged into Sun Street and bumped slap into Jamie Westershall.

'Hello!' he cried, grinning. 'Just the girl I was coming to see. Time for a coffee?'

For a moment I stared, unable to reconcile the smiling blue eyes, the easy charm, with the man standing in the road last night.

'Well . . .' I stumbled, 'I'm really short of time, I—'

'Oh, come on!' He grabbed my arm. 'Just a quick one, look, there's a place right here.' His grip on my arm was firm, almost tight. He steered me through the door of the coffee shop and we sat down. For a moment we stared across the table, considering each other. 'I've been worried about you, Juno.'

'Oh?' We paused, as the waitress came and took our order. 'Why?'

'I found your van abandoned on the moor last night. No sign of you. I wondered if you were all right.'

'Just a puncture,' I lied, with what I hoped was an airy shrug. 'Luckily, someone I knew came by and gave me a lift back into town.'

His brows lifted slightly. 'When I drove back a little later your van had gone.'

'We got the puncture fixed.'

'You came back to do it? Couldn't you and this friend have done it there and then?' His voice was light, but his blue eyes, narrow with suspicion, never left mine.

'We had to come back into town to fetch a toolbox.'

'Bit risky, I'd have thought, driving about the moor at night without proper tools. It makes me wonder what you were doing up there at all, Juno, on a terrible night like that.'

'Well, I'll tell you,' I volunteered, deciding to take the risk. 'I went to meet your old pal from agricultural college, Nathan Parr, alias Jack Sparrow.'

'Yes, I remember the two of you getting acquainted in a cupboard.'

'Well, Mr Nathan Parr invited me out for a drink in a pub up on the moor and then stood me up.' I waited to see his reaction, watched for any flicker in his blue eyes, but his gaze was unwavering. 'I don't suppose you would know anything about that?'

He laughed. 'Of course not, why would I?'

'I just wondered if it might have been someone's idea of a joke.'

'Certainly not mine. Nathan had to leave the party early for some reason and I haven't seen him since.' He took a sip of black coffee and sat back, studying me reflectively. 'So, he stood you up, eh? Poor old Juno!' His shoulders shook with silent laughter. 'And everything seemed so promising back in that cupboard.'

His smugness, his amusement, convinced me that he

knew more about this than he was saying. He'd set me up with his friend, I was sure of it. But then for some reason, he'd called him off.

'It just seems a bit strange, you know, Juno,' he went on, all trace of humour vanishing, 'finding your van parked on my land like that, especially after the little stunt you pulled at Sandy's party. I'm wondering if you've got something on your mind.'

'I didn't bring up Gavin's name,' I pointed out.

'No, but you brought up Ben Luscombe's. What was the point of that, Juno? He was trespassing. He took cocaine—'

'Like your sister.'

For a moment it was as if I'd struck a match; anger flared in his eyes. Then the flame died down. He smiled, but I could see the muscles in his jaw were tight. 'Emma likes to experiment. She's not an addict.'

'And Jess?'

He bit his lip, furious. 'Jess doesn't take drugs.'

'No? Well, she was snorting something up her nose at Sandy's party.'

He leant forward across the table and spoke softly. 'You'd better be careful what you say.'

'Had I?'

'There's a young boy who keeps flying a drone over our land. I don't suppose you know him?'

I felt a shiver of disquiet but managed a smile. 'Why would I?'

'Just that he was spotted with you in your van.'

'And you would know this, how?'

'We both know how,' he answered steadily. 'Tell your

young friend that it's illegal to fly a drone over private property and I'm prepared to take steps to protect my privacy.'

'Is that what you did with Gavin? "Took steps"?'

'The police are satisfied his death was an accident.'

'I'm not.'

'Don't meddle, Juno,' he warned me softly. 'Don't meddle in things that are none of your concern.' He flung a note down on the table to cover the bill, stood, ready to leave.

'You don't think another accident on the Moorworthy estate might arouse suspicion?'

He gripped my wrist suddenly, his face bent close to mine. 'Don't cross me, Juno,' he warned and strode out, letting the door slam behind him.

I watched him go, watched the swagger of his broad shoulders as he set off down the street. I don't like being told what to do, I don't like being threatened. I was glad I'd made him angry.

Late that afternoon, when I was in the shop, I got a distress call from Olly, just back from Honeysuckle Farm. He was crying, almost hysterical. I had to tell him to calm down before I could make sense of what he was saying.

'It's her, next door!' he sobbed.

'Mrs Hardiman?'

'She's coming in. She was round here earlier . . . come to the back door . . . she says, she says . . .'

'Take a breath, Olly,' I recommended. 'Now, what did she say?'

'She says she knows you ain't a social worker. She says something funny's going on . . . And she says, if I don't let her come in and talk to Nan, she'll ring the police—'

'What did you say?'

'I told her Nan was asleep, so she said she's coming back at five o'clock and she ain't leaving till she's seen her. What am I going to do?' he cried piteously.

I looked at my watch. It was already nearly four. 'Bake a cake,' I told him.

'What?'

'Bake a cake. Lay the table, nicely, as if we're having guests to tea. Get out your Nan's best cups. I'll be there as soon as I can.'

'But what are we—'

'I'll think of something,' I promised him. 'Don't panic.'

I put the phone down knowing I had an hour to find Olly a great-grandmother. As I ran to the van I was going through my options. Maisie was no good, Olly's neighbour already knew her. Chloe Berkeley-Smythe would have been up for it, would have considered the whole idea of impersonating someone else a hoot, if she'd been persuaded it was a joke; but she was on the high seas, and anyway, no one in their right mind would believe she lived in a council house. I briefly considered Morris in drag, but this was too hideous an idea to contemplate. Anyway, I would have been forced to let him and Ricky into Olly's secret and I had promised him I wouldn't tell.

I was halfway up the road towards Owlacombe Cross when I saw her. She wasn't wearing her blue dressing gown, but beige trousers and a flowery top, and for a moment I didn't recognise her. I pulled up next to her and wound the window down. She peered in at me, giving me a bright but questioning smile.

'Hello, Judith-Marianne!' I leapt out and opened the passenger door.

'Are we going out to tea?' she asked as she slid into the seat.

'It's funny you should ask that,' I said, securing her seat belt. 'But we *are* going out to tea. Yes, we are.'

We got Judith-Marianne installed in Nan's chair just a few moments before we heard the determined footsteps of Olly's neighbour marching up to the kitchen door. I welcomed her inside whilst Olly put the kettle on. Two halves of a fragrant Victoria sponge lay on a wire cooling rack, and he had spread one half with jam.

'Now, we must clear up this misunderstanding,' I began, putting on my best smile. 'Do come in . . . er . . .'

'April,' she reminded me, looking around the kitchen as if she expected a gang of terrorists to come leaping out from somewhere. 'April Hardiman.'

Single repetitive notes on the piano drifted through from the living room.

'Let me introduce you to Mrs Knollys.' I guided April into the living room. 'She got up out of bed especially so that she can meet you.'

Judith-Marianne had moved from the chair and seated herself at the piano, where she was prodding each of the keys individually with a forefinger. 'This isn't in tune, you know,' she told us as we came in.

'No, I'm sorry, Nan.' Olly had followed us in, carrying the jam sponge on a plate, its golden top dusted with icing sugar. 'It's been out of tune for quite a while now.'

'This is April,' I said, as she continued to test each note repetitively. 'She lives next door.'

Judith-Marianne did not look up, ignoring April's proffered hand. 'April, May, June,' she said, as she played each key. She scowled in frustration. 'Out of tune!'

'You play piano, then, Mrs Knollys.' April's face was fixed in a determined smile. 'I'm musical, too. I belong to the Dartmoor Operatic Society.'

There was no response. Judith-Marianne just stared.

'That's right,' I pitched in recklessly. 'April is playing a fairy in their production of *Iolanthe*.'

April then proceeded to warble a snatch of some tune about fairies tripping lightly hither and thither. The effect on Judith-Marianne was extraordinary. It was as if the fog in which she wandered like a lost child miraculously lifted. Suddenly she was with us, present in the moment. She joined in with April's warbling. She knew every note and every word. She had become the person that she used to be. As they chirruped and trilled ecstatically together, Olly rolled his eyes at me in alarm. 'They're getting on too well,' he hissed at me in a whisper. 'She,' he jerked his head in April's direction, 'will want to come back.'

He needn't have worried. Judith-Marianne then tried to accompany them both on the piano, but it was so badly out of tune that after a few faltering notes, she stopped, screaming in vexation and began banging the lid up and down. She burst into tears and April backed away, horrified.

'It's all right, Ju . . . Dolly.' I took her by the shoulders and steered her, still sobbing, from the piano stool to the armchair. 'We're going to have a cup of tea. Look, Olly's made a cake.'

'It's your favourite, Nan,' Olly told her bravely. 'Victoria sponge.'

'Do sit down, April.' I indicated a chair. 'And afterwards,' I promised, 'Olly can play us a tune on his bassoon.'

He began shaking his head.

'Now, don't be shy, Olly.' I directed him a warning glance. 'You know how much your nan loves to hear you play.'

'I'll fetch the teapot,' he muttered furiously and stomped off into the kitchen. By the time he came back, order had been restored. Judith-Marianne was silently contemplating the sponge cake, lost in the fog once again and ignoring April's attempts at making polite conversation. I poured the tea while Olly cut the sponge, handing slices around and for the next few minutes we all nibbled politely.

'Your garden is looking very pretty, Mrs Hardiman,' I commented, by way of filling the void, 'especially for this time of year.'

'Not for much longer,' she sighed. 'The dahlias are almost over now.'

'Bishop of Llandaff,' Judith-Marianne crumbled a morsel of sponge between restless fingers.

'What's that, Nan?' Olly asked apprehensively.

'Bishop of Llandaff,' she repeated, dabbing crumbs from her plate with a wet forefinger.

'It's a variety of dahlia,' I cried, catching on. 'The Bishop of Llandaff is a variety of dahlia. That's right isn't it, Dolly?'

'Would you like to come and see the dahlias in my garden, Mrs Knollys,' April offered politely, 'before the frost gets them?'

Judith-Marianne paused, crumbs on fingers, and scowled

at her. 'No! Shut up!' Her moods, it seemed, changed as suddenly as the weather. April's smile had taken on a rigid quality, like the grin on a ventriloquist's dummy.

'I think it might be time for that tune now, Olly,' I said hastily.

'Oh, right!' He opened the case and assembled the instrument from its various compartments. April and I watched him, fascinated. Judith-Marianne took no notice at all and helped herself to more cake.

The bassoon is a very long instrument and the player wears a shoulder strap to help support the weight. Even with this help, Olly had to sit down to play, the end of the bassoon balanced on his shoe. He licked his lips nervously, tried a few experimental notes, fussed with the reed in the mouthpiece, and then played a simple tune.

It was lovely. I didn't recognise it, but Judith-Marianne did. She began to la-la softly in time.

After a few moments, April rashly tried to join in too.

'No! No!' Judith-Marianne threw her plate to the floor, scattering crumbs and icing sugar. 'Not you! Not you!'

'Dolly!' I cried. 'That's not very nice!'

She burst into tears.

'That's quite all right.' April hastily bent to pick up the plate from the carpet. Olly stopped playing, disengaged himself from the bassoon and slightly nervously went to comfort his nan, patting her on the shoulder. April handed the plate back to me. 'Perhaps I should go now,' she whispered. 'It was very nice to meet you, Mrs Knollys.'

'I'll show you out.' I led her down the hall towards the front door. 'I do apologise for Dolly,' I said softly. 'You can see how difficult she is.'

'Oh, I understand,' April assured me, nodding wisely.

'The way she reacts to visitors sometimes . . . well, it just makes life more difficult for Olly.'

She was nodding furiously now, like a toy dog in a car's rear window. 'I think that boy's a marvel!'

'Oh, he is!'

She was hopping from foot to foot, desperate to get away, so I kept her talking another ten minutes. I wanted to be sure she wouldn't come back in a hurry. Every minute or so, Olly appeared in the living room doorway. He seemed to be trying to signal something to me, but I ignored him. 'I apologise again for Dolly.'

'Don't you think,' April suggested tentatively, 'that Oakdene is where she really belongs?'

'Oh, you are so right, April!' I agreed. 'And don't worry, I'm sure she'll be there before much longer.'

We said our goodbyes and I finally closed the door on her. I leant against it, letting out a groan of relief.

'Has she gone?' Olly appeared in the living room doorway.

'She has.' I looked at my watch. 'It's time I got Judith-Marianne back to Oakdene. Is she all right? She's gone very quiet.'

'Of course she has,' Olly answered. It was only then I noticed how pale he was looking, his blue eyes huge with shock. 'She's dead.'

CHAPTER TWENTY-FIVE

'What happened?' I was desperately feeling Judith-Marianne's veined wrist for a pulse. Finding none, I touched her neck.

'I've done all that,' Olly told me, watching my efforts. 'She'd quietened down a bit, so I got the dustpan and brush. I was brushing up the icing sugar,' he pointed to the carpet where she'd thrown the cake, 'and I looked up, and she was sort of slumped over, like she is now. I thought she'd just nodded off. I got a bit worried after a few minutes, and you were still talking . . . so I tried to wake her up.' He watched me as I tried to find her heartbeat.

'She's gone, isn't she?'

'I'm afraid she is.' I sat back on my heels and studied her, eyes closed, her head drooping towards her chest. She looked entirely peaceful. 'Poor old soul.'

'Can't we use her?' he asked suddenly. 'Can't we pretend she's really my nan, get the doctor to come, sign a death certificate—'

'I'm afraid it doesn't work like that. A doctor can only

sign a death certificate for a patient he knows, someone he's been treating, otherwise there has to be an autopsy. We couldn't risk it. We don't know who her real doctor is. What if we phoned the surgery and her real doctor turned up and knows she isn't the person we're pretending she is?'

'Well, what are we going to do then?' he demanded, trembling voice rising high in excitement. 'I'm not putting her in with my nan!'

'No, no, I wasn't going to suggest that,' I assured him. 'I've got to get her back to where she belongs . . . Listen, go outside, sneak down the front path and see if April's closed her front curtains.' I hoped she might have done, it was already dark outside. But Olly came back to report the curtains were wide open. He could see April in the light of her television, her gaze fixed upon the screen.

'Well, we'll have to risk it.'

We sneaked down the front path, Judith-Marianne loaded gently into the wheelbarrow. 'It would have helped if you'd got this bloody wheel oiled,' I hissed as it squeaked unrelentingly at every turn. Olly kept looking over his shoulder, making sure April was still transfixed by her television programme. We made it as far as the gate, bumped the wheelbarrow into the road behind the van and round to the passenger door where, with a great deal of difficulty, we loaded our burden carefully into the front seat. I buckled her in.

'Do you want me to come?' Olly asked, obviously praying that I'd say no.

'You stay here. Wash up the tea things and get on with your homework. You know nothing about this, understand? Absolutely nothing!'

'What if you get caught?'

'I won't,' I promised, with a lot more certainty than I felt. 'Now, did you get that phone number?'

He passed me a scrap of paper. 'I looked up their website on the laptop.'

'Good boy.' I took the paper from him. 'And don't worry about April.' I watched her, illuminated by the flickering glow. 'She won't be back in a hurry.' I promised to phone him as soon as I could and buckled myself in the driver's seat. 'Right then, Judith-Marianne,' I said to the silent figure by my side. 'Here we go.'

I drove very slowly and carefully. It was stupid, looking back on it: it didn't matter to poor Judith-Marianne how I drove, but I was trying, in some idiotic way, to drive with reverence. She had done Olly and me a good turn, saved our bacon, and I was determined to treat her with respect. I kept glancing her way, her head nodding gently as we drove along, her eyes closed peacefully, still hoping that she might suddenly stir into wakefulness, into life, even though I knew her poor old heart had given up and she'd never wake again. I slowed the van to a halt on the brow of the hill and pulled out my mobile phone. I dialled the number Olly had found for me and waited for someone to pick up, my eyes still fixed on Judith-Marianne.

'Oakdene,' a crisp voice answered, and I asked if I could speak to Barbara or Camille.

It was dark by the time I drove through the gates. The windows of the care home were lit up and I could see the evening meal taking place in the dining room, residents gathered around the tables. I drove quietly by, around to the tradesman's entrance. As I rounded the corner, I saw Camille hovering nervously by the path, her big forehead pale in the gloom, her hands clutching the handles of a wheelchair. I stopped beside her and wound the window down.

'Pull up by kitchen door,' she instructed softly. 'Is safe. Boss is serving dinner with residents.'

'Where's Barbara?'

'She help boss. But she knows.'

I parked the van as directed and Camille wheeled the chair to the passenger door. Carefully, gently, we loaded Judith-Marianne into it.

'Where you find her?' Camille asked. 'In road again?'

'Yes.' Well, at least that part of it wasn't a lie. 'I was bringing her back and she suddenly passed out. When I realised she was dead I thought I'd better phone and speak to you. I don't want you girls to get in trouble because of her running off again.'

'Thank you,' Camille said devoutly. 'If she found dead in road it would be very bad. We might lose job.'

We wheeled Judith-Marianne into the garden, to a little wooden bench under a cherry tree. 'This her favourite place,' Camille told me as we lifted her onto the seat. 'She often sit here.'

'You won't leave her out here long?' It was dark and getting cold. I didn't like the thought of leaving her there. I wanted to wrap a blanket around her shoulders.

'Soon as you're gone, I run in, tell boss I find her room empty. We will all search. Soon we find her here.'

'You're sure you'll be all right?'

'Yes. Best you go. Quickly.'

I took a last look at the little figure sitting on the seat. I reached out and touched her soft, silver hair. 'Did you know that she could sing?' I asked Camille. 'And play the piano?'

'No,' she answered sadly. 'I never knew that.'

'Thank you, Judith-Marianne,' I whispered and kissed her on her forehead. I hurried back to the van and drove slowly down the path and out through the iron gates.

CHAPTER TWENTY-SIX

No news is good news. At least that was the way I was looking at it. All night I was expecting some feverish call from Barbara or Camille telling me that something had gone wrong, that the doctor had been suspicious about Judith-Marianne's death, that he wanted a post-mortem. But when Barbara finally phoned, late the next morning, it was to tell me that everything had gone according to plan, and the doctor was happy that she had died of natural causes. No post-mortem, no inquest. All was well. I'd relay the good news to Olly later on.

I drove up onto Holne Moor. It was a beautiful day, calm, clear and still, a complete contrast with the wild night when I had last driven up there. I stopped where I had stopped then, searching around for whatever it was that might have hit my wheel, but there was no evidence of any collision with wildlife, no furry corpse, no carrion-pecked offal lying in a heap by the roadside. It remained a mystery.

A bigger mystery was what the hell had happened to

Nathan Parr. I was still sore about him standing me up, hoping that it hadn't been part of some plot of Jamie's, that there was some genuine reason why he'd failed to show at the pub and that, sometime, he would get in touch.

I decided not to turn around but to carry on up the road for a few miles. I had an hour free, and the thought of going straight back to the shop was depressing. I would follow the road as it looped around Venford Reservoir and take a look at the water. On my way back, I might grab a quick sandwich in the little cafe in Holne.

A mile further on I slowed to a stop. To the left of the road a ribbon of blue and white police tape was stretched between the gorse bushes, marking off a section of ground that fell away steeply, the short grass scattered with boulders. A metal sign had been set up at the verge, an appeal for witnesses to a fatal road accident that had occurred at this spot on Tuesday evening. A car had come off the road and crashed. It seemed no other vehicles had been involved. Police were appealing for anyone who had been driving this road on Tuesday evening to get in touch.

I got out of the van and a man walking his dog hailed me with a wave. I bent to pat the black and white sheepdog snuffling around my boots. 'Do you know what happened here?'

He pointed to a distant house, just visible through a screen of bare trees. 'I live up there.'

It must feel isolated. No wonder he liked to chat to strangers. 'Someone must have reported it early. I was out walking the dog yesterday morning and the police were already here. They were just taking the car away.'

'And the driver was killed?'

He nodded. 'You can see the tyre tracks. He must have been driving at one hell of a speed to come off the road there. Mind, it was a filthy night. Police think he must have been drunk. He hit those smaller rocks,' he said, pointing, 'the car must have flipped over and slammed into that great lump of granite. He wouldn't have had a chance. The front of that car was mangled—'

A sickening sense of dread was settling inside me. 'Could they identify him?' I asked.

'Not from the body. That had already been taken away when I got here. They were just loading the car onto a lorry. It was a nice little Jag, too. Complete write-off, of course.'

'Of course,' I repeated dumbly.

'Personalised number plate,' he went on. 'It's funny the things that stick in your mind. I suppose it's because I'm a golfer—'

I frowned at him. 'What?'

'The number plate – N12 PAR,' he responded brightly. I must have just stared at him because he felt it necessary to explain. 'Golf, you see? Par?'

'Yes, I understand,' I said. 'I get it.'

I got it. I understood why Nathan hadn't turned up for our meeting at the pub, and that he wouldn't be getting in touch. I understood Jamie's barely concealed laughter when I had told him Nathan had stood me up. He was laughing because he knew that Nathan was already dead; and because he had murdered him.

My first thought was to contact Inspector Ford, tell him everything, beginning with Moss and Pike trying to ram my van with their lorry. For that was what had happened to Nathan, I was sure. They must have lain in wait for him, in that monstrous truck, run him off the road, caused him to crash. And when I'd seen them on Tuesday evening, when I was crouching in the ditch behind the gorse bushes, they were returning from the scene of his murder. But how could I tell the inspector about what had happened without involving Olly? He was the only one who could verify what I said. They might want to speak to him, to his parent or guardian.

Instead, I phoned the police number advertised on the sign at the site of the accident. I explained that I had been driving on the road that night, that I had seen a vehicle coming from that direction, a Moss and Pike lorry being driven very fast and, in my opinion, recklessly. I had been forced to swerve to get out of its way and nearly ended in a ditch. No, I didn't get its registration number. Was it definitely a Moss and Pike lorry? Yes, it was. The officer thanked me very much. They would certainly investigate.

I was late getting back to the shop, and by the time I arrived, Pat was getting fretful.

I apologised and she shot me a sideways glance over her clicking knitting needles. 'Everything all right?' she asked.

'Fine.' I felt spaced out, numbed by Nathan's death. I didn't want company. 'You go on home, Pat.'

'You look awful.' She rolled up her knitting and stabbed her needles into her ball of wool. 'You sure you can cope?'

'I think I just need an early night.'

She didn't look convinced but had to get back to the

animals and so left. I was glad she'd gone. I didn't feel like talking, didn't want to answer questions. I spent all afternoon messing about with my stock. By the time I turned the sign on the shop door to 'Closed' and locked up behind me, the weather had turned dank and dismal. It just about matched my mood. A low mist skulked over the rooftops and the slick cobbles shone with wetness, with drops of moisture too fine to see except where they danced in the haloes of lighted street lamps. I turned up my collar. I needed some cash. I'd have to walk to Ashburton's only cash machine.

Most of the shops were locked and in darkness, their sensible owners having already called it a day. Just one or two antiques dealers, ever hopeful, were bringing in the stock they displayed outside their shops on the pavement. We exchanged goodnights as I went by.

I crossed the road into St Lawrence Lane. The whole town seemed deserted. Perhaps everyone else knew something I didn't. By habit I cast a glance over my shoulder as I fed my card into the cash machine. I caught a flicker of movement at the corner of my vision, a pale shape that was there one moment and not the next. When I swung around for a proper look, the street was empty. But all the time I typed in my pin and waited for my cash I felt a tickle of unease at the back of my neck, a sense of being watched. I stuffed the card and notes straight into my pocket, not bothering to fiddle with the zip of my purse and bag and carried on down St Lawrence Lane.

Someone fell into step behind me. I walked on, past the tower of St Lawrence's Chapel, and then dropped down on one knee, pretending to tie a lace on my trainers. A burly figure yards behind suddenly stopped and peered into the window of a shop. The shop was in blackness, he wouldn't have been able to see much. But I could see him, lamplight shining down on his overhanging belly, his fat face, his green woolly hat. My heart throbbed in panic.

I pretended not to have seen him, stood up and carried on. I quickened my pace and so did he, his heavy footsteps pounding the pavement. As I reached The Silent Whistle I peered in through the lighted windows. This early in the evening no one was inside, no chance of losing him in a packed bar. Instead I crossed the road and walked on past a terrace of houses. At the end of the terrace I had a choice. If I could lose GBH now, just for a few seconds, when he reached the corner, he wouldn't know which direction I had taken. I ran.

I heard a muffled curse behind me. Footsteps broke into a shambling jog. Green Bastard Hat was heavy, but he wasn't fit. He was no runner. I knew I could outrun him. I could veer right, but then I'd have no choice but to fling myself into the traffic of the dual carriageway that bypassed the edge of town. My best chance of losing him lay straight in front of me. I sprinted across the road and headed for Love Lane.

But sometimes, what seems to be the best choice turns out to be the worst. Love Lane is long and straight with just one dog-leg turn towards the end, and so narrow it's possible to touch the stone walls rising on either side without stretching. Like a running track, Love Lane was a place where I could build up speed, leave GBH puffing along behind. Except that a single wet leaf on the ground betrayed me. I skidded, my feet slid from under me and I landed flat on my back, winded, my breath shocked out.

The fat bastard could move faster than I thought. I was still scrabbling to my feet when he grabbed me, his fingers closing over my arm. I turned and punched him hard in his flabby gut. He doubled over, belching like a deflating balloon. But he didn't release his grip. He cursed, grabbed a fistful of my hair and slammed my face into the stone wall.

I felt the force ricochet down my spine. Rough stone scraped against my jaw and cheek.

I tasted blood. He pinned me against the wall, his grip on my hair tightening. He was out of breath, his chest heaving as he pressed his foul body against mine. 'You got to learn to mind your own business,' he rasped into my ear. I slammed backward and downward with my foot, scraping his shin. He swore. He was pulling my hair out by the roots. 'You've been poking your nose where it don't belong. We've had the police round the depot this afternoon, wanting to look at all our trucks. Someone had reported seeing us on the moor the other night. I know that was you, bitch. I got to teach you a lesson.'

I let my body sag, heavy and limp, as if I'd fainted. As he shifted his feet to keep hold of my dead weight, I twisted around, my hand held rigid, fingers poking out straight, and jabbed him in the belly. He yelped and staggered back. I was free, but not for long. He grabbed me clumsily and dragged me onto the floor, rolling his entire grizzly-bear bulk on top of me, crushing my ribcage. His face hung over mine, his bristling double chin like a blancmange rolled in ash, his breath stinking of beer and fags. 'Seeing as you're rather tasty . . .'

One hand slithered between our bodies, groping for his belt. I squirmed, spat in his face and he sat back, knees like boulders pinning my arms to the ground. He raised one mighty fist to swipe me across the face.

The blow never landed. Something parted the air between us. Something that made no noise beyond a soft thunk as it embedded itself in the wall and sent a chip of mortar flying. Instinctively, we knew what it was.

GBH growled. 'What the fuck . . . ?'

'Let her go,' a calm voice commanded.

We stared at the figure illuminated by the solitary street lamp: an elderly woman with a handbag under one arm, a cat tucked under the other and a pistol clutched firmly in her right hand. It was slightly surreal.

'What the fuck . . . ?' he repeated.

'Please don't oblige me to fire this gun again, my cat doesn't like it.' The mystery lady waved the pistol slightly, indicating to GBH that he should back off. The cat wriggled, making an unholy yowling noise as if he was revving up for a fight and she clamped him to her side more firmly.

'Where the bloody hell did you come from, Grandma?' GBH demanded. 'You're not going to shoot me—'

'I won a medal for pistol shooting in my youth,' she informed him coolly. 'It was only a bronze, but you don't want to take any chances, do you?'

He made a move, a slight raising of his hand, and a bullet drilled through his outstretched palm. 'Fuck!' he screamed, clutching his hand and rolling away in agony.

'Your vocabulary is quite limited, isn't it?' My mystery lady kept her sights fixed on him as he staggered to his feet, sobbing and swearing. 'I'd get going if I were you,' she advised. 'I'm a little out of practice, we can't be sure where I might shoot you next.'

'I'll fucking kill you!' he spat, reeling against the wall. 'Both of you!'

'Oh, do get along!' She sounded bored.

GBH shambled off, vowing vengeance. We could still hear him gibbering with pain long after he had disappeared from sight.

'Are you all right, my dear?' my saviour enquired as I staggered to my feet.

'I think so.' The skin on my cheek had been scorched by a blowtorch and my spine ironed flat by tank tracks but otherwise I was fine.

She put the cat down, his lead looped around her wrist and let him wander, sniffing, as she knelt to dig the bullet from the wall with a penknife she produced from her handbag. 'You didn't see where that other shell case landed? I do think it's important to tidy up after oneself, don't you?'

I began to peer vaguely at the ground around me, my feeble brain still trying to process what had just occurred.

'Ah! There it is!' She stooped and picked it up, dropping both cases into her bag and closing it with a soft click.

'Thank you!' I breathed belatedly. 'But how did you . . . um, come to . . . ?'

'I was taking Toby for his evening walk, when I saw you run hell for leather across the street and dive down here, chased by our primitive friend. I thought I'd better investigate.'

'Well, I'm very glad you did. Thanks again.'

'You're welcome . . . er . . . ?' She raised her brows enquiringly.

'Juno.'

'Juno.' She held out a slim hand for me to shake. 'Elizabeth,' she said, and smiled.

CHAPTER TWENTY-SEVEN

'I was married to George for thirty-six years,' Elizabeth began. We were sitting at the kitchen table in *Old Nick's*, each with a mug of coffee, the cat Toby curled up on the seat of the chair next to hers. I was holding a swab of cotton wool, soggy with TCP, gingerly dabbing at my cheek from time to time. 'It's funny,' she sighed, 'how you can live with someone all that time and never really know him. He was in finance, I was a teacher. We lived very comfortably. I knew he gambled of course, but he'd always persuaded me that his losses were small. "My little vice", he used to call it. It was only when we retired that I realised how bad things were, that all of our savings were gone. I had some money, some investments of my own. He begged me to help him, promised me on his life that it would be the last time.' She gave a brief, bitter smile. 'It wasn't, of course.'

She took a sip of coffee. The kitchen was warm and quiet, the only noise a slight hum from the electric heater I had brought up from the shop and she looked around her pensively. 'You have no idea how lovely this is, sitting in a room instead of in a car with the roof a few inches above my head.'

'We could have gone to my flat. But this was closer.'

'This is fine.' She fondled Toby's ears reflectively and he mewed in his sleep. I wanted her to carry on with her story, and after a few moments, she spoke again, her voice steady and calm.

'In the end, everything went – our weekend cottage, our cars, my jewellery. But it wasn't until George died that I discovered he had remortgaged the house, that the property we had lived in for over thirty years was no longer my home, that I would have to get out. And he still owed money to some very unpleasant people. It didn't matter that he was dead, that the stress of it all had killed him. As far as his creditors were concerned, I was liable. And the money I had in my own name was far from sacrosanct. Their methods were . . .' she paused, a frown puckering her delicate brows, 'intimidating.'

'Didn't you go to the police?'

'I thought about it. But the problem was that, technically, the law was on their side. I soon realised I'd be lucky to be left with the clothes I stood up in. I'd be reduced to living in temporary accommodation on some endless council housing list. At worst, I would be on the streets. Well, I thought, if I'm going to be homeless, let it be on my own terms. I cleared out what was left in my account, and sold everything, all I owned, anything I could turn into cash. It was when I was going through the loft that I found my father's pistol – the old Luger Parabellum.' She smiled. 'I thought it might come in useful one day.'

'It certainly did.'

'I bought the old car and disappeared.' She gave an elegant shrug. 'I simply vanished, left the house empty, dropped the keys into the bank, and left London with no forwarding address. Left all my old life behind. So far, no one has followed me.'

'You had no family? No friends?'

She was quiet for a moment, gone inward. 'No one to speak of,' she said at last.

'And you've been living in the car all this time?'

She smiled. 'Occasionally I treat us to a night in a guest house, but I have to watch the pennies. Of course,' she gave a wry smile, 'I did things all wrong. What I should have done was to have invested in a camper van. But they are rather expensive.'

'What made you come here?'

'George wouldn't countenance the idea of living in Devon, strictly a Home Counties man. But I've always been attracted by the area, so I've been driving around, trying to find the right place for us to settle. I keep being drawn back here for some reason. Ashburton has the right atmosphere.' She smiled again, mocking herself, 'the right *vibe*.'

'You're welcome to sleep on my sofa,' I told her, although I wasn't sure what Toby would make of Bill, and vice versa.

'No, no. The floor here will be fine. I have plenty of bedding in the car.'

'If you're sure? You've got a choice of two rooms. The floors are clean, just recently laid.'

'It will be absolute luxury. I shall be able to spread myself out. What I would love,' she added tentatively, 'is a bath.'

'Help yourself. And don't feel you have to get up early in the morning. I'll leave a note for Sophie and Pat downstairs so that they'll know I have a friend staying. You won't be disturbed.'

'Thank you.' There was a moment's pause. 'Now it's your turn.'

'My turn?'

'To tell your story. All that carrying on in the lane back there, I still don't know what it was about. Please don't tell me that was an angry boyfriend!'

'I'll tell you everything—' I stopped suddenly as a new thought occurred. I glanced at my watch. So much had happened since I left the shop at closing time I couldn't believe it was barely eight o'clock. I looked at Elizabeth. 'How would you feel about a change of plan?' I asked.

'Very well,' she agreed, somewhat doubtfully. 'What?'

'We're going out. There's someone I want you to meet.'

Olly listened with eyes wide, his mouth slightly open, as Elizabeth recounted to him the same story that she had told me.

'So you see, Olly,' I said when she had finished, 'Elizabeth needs a place to stay. And you need a grown-up living here with you – then,' I added quickly as he opened his mouth to object, 'you won't need to worry about your neighbour, your teachers, or anyone else finding out that your nan isn't living here. You can stop worrying about being taken into care.'

Olly scowled, jerked his head in Elizabeth's direction. 'What's she know about my nan? You promised you wouldn't tell.'

'I haven't. That story is yours to tell, or not. It's up to you.'

'I know only that your nan isn't here,' Elizabeth said calmly. 'We have to be able to trust each other. If the wrong people found out where I was living, that could be very bad for me. I'm trusting you to keep my secret, and I promise you can trust me to keep yours, whatever it is.'

Olly frowned, unconvinced. 'So, what would happen, then?' he asked, looking from her to me.

'What I suggest, if you're agreeable,' Elizabeth said slowly, 'is that Juno, Toby and I go away now, and then I return in about an hour in my own car. I'll park where we can be sure your neighbour will see me arrive. You can come out and make a great fuss of greeting me, as if you haven't seen me for a long time. In the morning, I will introduce myself to your neighbour, telling her that I'm your aunt, that I've been living abroad, but that now your nan is so ill, I've come back to look after you both . . .'

Olly thought about this for a few seconds. 'What room will you sleep in?'

'Whichever room you'd like me to sleep in. Then, after a little while, preferably on a day when your neighbour has been out, we'll tell her that we've moved your nan into Oakdene.'

Olly considered this plan with a furrowed brow, fidgeting unhappily. 'You're a teacher, ain't you?'

'I was a teacher,' she corrected him.

'What you teach?'

'I taught a variety of subjects, but music primarily.'

His face brightened. 'You play piano?'

'Yes. I hear you're learning the bassoon. Perhaps I could help you, if you want me to.'

275

At that moment, Toby, who'd been lying in idiotic bliss next to the Rayburn, stretched, flexed his paws and rolled over, displaying his cream-coloured tummy. Olly giggled.

'It looks like Toby's settled in already,' I said.

'You know, Olly, this need be only a temporary arrangement,' Elizabeth assured him. 'You can throw me out, any time you like.'

He slid a glance at me for confirmation. I nodded. 'All right,' he agreed grudgingly. 'We'll give it a go.'

Elizabeth solemnly shook hands with him on the agreement, and then she and I buzzed off, cat under her arm, so that she could return and put her plan into action.

CHAPTER TWENTY-EIGHT

On Friday morning, I went to Ashburton library. I asked the librarian if she had any maps of old tin mines in the area and she came up with an absolute beauty. It showed me the positions of all the known shafts on the Moorworthy estate, including the shaft at Applecote Farm. What it didn't show, unfortunately, were any underground tunnels that might link them. But I got her to photocopy it for me and took away a copy.

I met Elizabeth, as planned, for coffee. She wore a silk scarf at her neck, her face beautifully made-up, hair in an elegant French pleat. She laid leather gloves and handbag on the table as she sat down. Despite being dressed in jeans and sweater, she looked immaculate. I looked like a woman who'd been smashed into a wall. I had a fine black eye, purple with yellow and green around the edges, and my jaw and cheek were freckled with scabs where I'd made contact with granite. I'd had to make up a silly story to explain my appearance to Pat and Sophie. The librarian had looked at me askance and when I told Maisie I had fallen and landed on my face, she just said, 'Bollocks! You've been in a fight!' I was going to have to come up with a more convincing story: I was seeing Ricky and Morris later on.

'How does it feel?'

'Sore.' I asked her how the first night went.

'Oh, fine. Breakfast was a little tense, but Olly was happy to accept a lift up to the animal sanctuary. He hinted I could start running him to school when the half-term holiday is over.'

'Make him walk,' I recommended. 'Where did you sleep?'

'In a room I believe belonged to his grandparents. There's a double bed in there.' She laughed softly. 'The decoration is a bit grim.'

'I'm sorry.'

'I'll survive. And Toby is in seventh heaven. He hasn't stirred from the kitchen range all night.' She sipped her coffee. 'I'm getting the piano tuned, by the way. Oh, I know I'm buying affection,' she added, holding up a slim hand in defence, 'but music is common ground between Olly and me and I want to take advantage of it.'

'Sounds sensible.'

'And I introduced myself to our neighbour as promised. Mrs Hardiman.'

'And?'

'Perfectly charming.'

'You or her?'

Elizabeth gave a low laugh. 'She did take a little winning over, but I got there in the end. She's invited me in for coffee next week.'

'Are you going to be all right living there?' She seemed so elegant, so effortlessly chic. 'Dolly's old house doesn't seem like an appropriate setting for you, somehow.'

She reached across the table and laid a hand on mine. 'My dear, I shall be happy to live there as long as Olly is prepared to put up with me. I have three things I thought I would never have in my life again – a garden, beautiful country surroundings, and a piano. And,' she added wryly, 'the challenge of learning to cook on a range, although Olly has promised to help me with that one.'

'There's just one thing that worries me.' I leant closer to her and lowered my voice, 'The pistol.'

'I'll keep it well hidden. Olly will never know it exists.'

'Actually, that's not what I meant. Jamie Westershall knows about Olly. He made threats. I don't think he knows where Olly lives but it might be wise to keep that pistol handy.'

Elizabeth nodded. 'I will.'

'And I don't want him flying his drone anywhere near Moorworthy House.'

'That boy will come to no harm,' she promised solemnly, 'not while I'm around.'

She sat back and studied me silently. 'But you, you must be careful, my dear. This Westershall man sounds dangerous, don't provoke him. If you don't feel ready to go to the police, please leave well alone.'

It was good advice. I only wished I could have followed it.

I had never seen Ricky angry before. I've seen him throw a prima donna hissy fit hundreds of times, but I'd not seen the cold, quiet anger with which he studied me now, two

279

long fingers pressed against his temple, the cigarette poised between them sending a thin spiral of smoke above his head. He was wearing his specs and the lenses magnified his blue eyes, intensified his gaze. 'So, let's just have a brief resumé, shall we, Princess? The lorry driver in the green hat tried to run your van off the road and you didn't go to the police?'

I nodded.

He continued to glare like an angry hawk. 'Same bloke, same hat, attacks you in Love Lane and you still don't go to the police?'

'I can't prove anything.'

'It's the police's job to prove things, not yours.'

'You had a witness in the van – young Oliver.' At the edge of my vision, seated on my left at the table, Morris was also giving me a disapproving stare.

'I don't want to involve him.'

'You had a witness to the attack,' Ricky insisted, 'the old bird with the cat.'

'I don't want to involve her.'

'You didn't bleedin' want to involve us, did you?' he asked, disgusted.

Morris was silent but shot me a reproachful look over his specs.

I had gone to their place to help them sort out the first of a rash of requests for pantomime costumes, the panto season fast approaching. But so far, we hadn't done any work. My arrival had caused a stir. One look at my damaged face and they had accused me of not trusting them, infuriated by my feeble story of falling over, by my blatant lie. 'D'you think we're idiots?' Ricky had demanded. 'Who did this to you?'

280

In the end, I had told them everything. Well, not quite everything. I left out Olly's illegal burial of his great-grandmother; in fact, I didn't mention that she was dead. But I told them everything else. I had crumpled under the accumulated weight of their hurt feelings. They had been too kind, too generous, too absurdly protective of me over the years for me to keep them out now. And they might gossip about everyone and everything, but when it really mattered, I knew I could trust in their silence.

'Who is this old girl with a cat, anyway?'

Morris shook his head. 'You don't really know anything about her, do you?'

'Only what she's told me,' I admitted.

'She could be a psychopath, for all you know,' Ricky said.

Did I detect a touch of jealousy? Personally, I thought Elizabeth was one of the sanest people I'd ever met, but perhaps it was a good thing I hadn't mentioned her gun. I'd just said that Green Bastard Hat had run off when he'd heard her coming.

'Don't forget this yob in the green hat is still out there,' Ricky reminded me. 'He's still a danger to you. He needs locking up.'

'I think he'll be lying low for a while. In any case, he's working for the Westershalls. It's Jamie who's behind all this.' In my opinion, he was the one who needed locking up, him and his lunatic sister, the dangerous crackhead.

'But what's going on?' Morris asked. 'What's it all about, Juno?'

I wish I knew. 'All I know is that there's something going on at the Moorworthy estate that the Westershalls – and that

281

includes Sandy – don't want anyone finding out about. And maybe it's what got Ben Luscombe and Gavin killed.'

'What about this Moss character?' Ricky asked. 'You said he knew what was going on.'

'He does but he's not going to talk about it, certainly not to the police.'

'This lorry firm,' Morris continued frowning, 'Moss and Pike. Is the firm involved in what's going on, or just the driver?'

'You mean, is he using the firm's vehicle without their knowledge?' Ricky asked.

'I've only seen him hauling bales of silage about,' I admitted. 'There's nothing illegal in that. I've got to find out—'

'Stop right there!' Ricky pointed his fag at me like a smoking gun. 'You are not finding out anything. You're not to go near that place again, understand? It's too dangerous.'

'I don't think I'll be getting an invitation any time soon.'

'Well, we have,' Morris said suddenly. 'Got an invitation,' he added as Ricky and I stared at him. 'Sunday afternoon.'

'My God, our concert!' Ricky suddenly swivelled around in his chair to look at the calendar on the wall. 'Is that this Sunday coming?'

'It is, the day after tomorrow,' Morris responded primly. 'It's a good job one of us pays attention. Why do you think I made us rehearse everything last night?'

'All right, Maurice,' Ricky rolled his eyes, 'don't get a cob on!'

'Listen, Juno, maybe we could find out something,' Morris suggested, glancing sideways at Ricky, 'ask some questions.'

'What kind of questions?' I asked, alarm bells ringing.

Ricky was suddenly enthusiastic. 'There will be drinks and a bunfight after the show. It's going to be a big fundraiser. We'll have a chance to mingle, chat with the guests. If we keep our eyes and ears open, you never know what we might pick up.'

Morris tittered. 'I've always fancied myself as a Poirot.'

Ricky gave a shout of laughter. 'And I could be Miss Marple.'

My heart sank. 'Listen, boys, I really don't think that's a good idea.' I had a vision of disaster looming, of the two of them making pointed and unsubtle remarks that could only lead to trouble. I knew I shouldn't have told them anything.

CHAPTER TWENTY-NINE

On Saturday morning I rose early. I packed the map the librarian had copied, binoculars and all my usual hiking gear, plus a bottle of water, some nutrition bars, a waterproof poncho and spare socks. I was planning to be out most of the day, but home before it got dark. Elizabeth and Olly had invited me to tea. I'd phoned the night before to ask how the rest of Friday had worked out. Elizabeth had laughed. 'I went shopping and shocked Olly because I bought a bottle of gin. He now thinks he's living with an alcoholic. Apparently—'

'Dolly didn't hold with gin.'

'Or spirituous liquors of any kind,' she added.

'Well, you can put me down for one, as soon as I arrive. See you later.'

I drove up to Holne Chase, bumping the van over the gravel and onto the grass, parking so that, from the road, it was almost hidden by gorse. The day was dismal, still, a thin mist malingering above the ground. Trees, bent and twisted by prevailing winds, loomed out of it like skeletons, their boughs bare of leaves. The grass was green underfoot and damp, the rest of the world grey, the air chill on my cheek. Magpies chattered somewhere close, but I couldn't see them. I stuck to pony tracks weaving through the gorse until the rising tumble of rocks where I had sat a couple of weeks ago became dimly visible on my right. There was no need for me to climb it again, but to keep heading on, in as straight a line as I could. If I could have seen more than a few yards ahead of me, this would have been simple, but it's easy to become disorientated in the mist so I kept checking my bearings.

Just a mile or two distant, high on the moor where no trees grew, was a place where the ground never dried out, where peat-black soil held the water like a sponge and what looked smooth and green as a croquet lawn was semi-liquid bog. Unless the sun shone and showed you a glimmer of water lurking amongst the mosses on the surface, you could be boots full of liquid black mud and up to your knees after one mistaken step. Not the place to be walking on your own, to get lost, not in the fog.

Brown ponies, three who had escaped the autumn drift, cantered out of the mist, alarmed by my presence. Snorting, tails flying, they passed so close I could see droplets of mist like pearls on the hairs around their flaring nostrils. Forced to jump back I almost fell over and stood still, heart thumping, until the pounding of their hooves faded into silence.

I came at last to a standing stone, a lump of granite tall as I was, phantom grey, blotched and speckled with lichen. I'd seen it marked on the map. It meant I was still heading in the right direction. I sensed that the mist was lifting, that I could see further ahead of me now; the day was warming up. As I walked, the sky gradually lightened from grey to gold, low sun filtering through thinning mist.

When I came to the hedge bank I stopped, sat on a rock, drank water, munched a nutty bar and studied the obstacle before me. The foot of the bank was faced with stones, lumps of granite laid centuries ago, half-hidden by cushions of moss and bound together by roots of hawthorn and elder, which scrambled over the top of it and formed a sturdy hedge. Trees grew out of it: holly, blackthorn and mountain ash. The whole structure was roughly ten foot high. I walked beside it for perhaps half a mile before I came to a likely place for climbing up and scrambling through.

A jutting stone gave a step for my boot and ivy stems thick as rope offered handholds to haul myself up the bank. So far so good, but the gap in the hedge was narrow and defended on all sides by vicious spikes of blackthorn. I didn't fancy dragging myself through it, and dropped back down to the ground to look for a bigger breach in the defences.

I found it further on, a handy gap amongst straggling twigs of hazel. I could climb the bank easily enough, grabbing at roots and branches to haul myself up, but it was clear that my rucksack was going to be an encumbrance when it came to squeezing through the tangle. I'd better leave it behind.

At the foot of the bank I inspected the contents. I reckoned I didn't need the Ordnance Survey map any more; the smaller map from the library was more relevant now I'd reached the farm. It was a dry day and I wouldn't need the waterproofs. I was wearing plenty of layers and my jacket was protection enough. I put my field glasses around my neck, zipping them up inside my jacket. I pocketed my phone, keys, penknife and the folded library map. I placed the rucksack carefully at the foot of the bank where I could retrieve it later, then pulled myself up.

Wriggling through the hedge was an undignified procedure and I was glad there was no one there to see me squeezing my various body parts between twisted branches. As I emerged on the other side, struggling to keep my balance and simultaneously bend aside twigs that threatened to spring back and take my eye out, I noticed thin strips of something grey and white hanging from the twigs like tinsel. I reached out and pulled some off – thin strips of crinkled paper, like the contents of an office shredding machine. As I glanced along the hedge, I could see branches festooned with the stuff.

I dropped down and found more at the foot of the bank, white strips tossed amongst the tide of autumn leaves. I scanned the green expanse of an empty field. There was no sign of any fly-tipping, no telltale trail of refuse littering the grass, but I could only think that this paper had been blown here from some dump site nearby.

I set off, keeping to the concealment of the hedge, walking three sides of a rectangle rather than straight across the field to the gate. I had a few acres to cross before I reached Applecote farmhouse and I didn't want to be spotted and chased off the land by an irate someone with a shotgun before I even got close.

Half an hour later I lay on my front behind a scattering of rocks and looked through my binoculars. I had a clear view of the stone farmhouse, the yard and the sheds beyond, a clear view of the farmhouse door, of the wisp of smoke rising from the chimney. I could smell it, woodsmoke. Someone was burning logs.

The door suddenly opened and Green Bastard Hat filled the doorway, a fag between his lips, a mug in the hand that wasn't bandaged. He stood for a moment, squinting into the sun, before he took a last drag on his cigarette and lobbed the butt on the ground. Two dogs – rangy, lurcher types, one brown, one white – surged out on either side of him, tails wagging.

Damn. I should have thought about dogs. The air was still, no wind to carry my scent to them, but I knew they were aware of me. They stopped, staring in my direction, bristling with alertness. One began to bark. GBH growled at it to stop its row. I didn't dare move, even to duck down out of sight. I stayed so still that a blackbird, foraging amongst the leaf litter, turning leaves over with its beak, hopped close to my arm. The dog barked once, sending the blackbird into the air, chattering in alarm. Its tail wagged uncertainly, and then it was ordered inside and the door shut behind it. I breathed again.

I sprinted across the grass to the corner of the cobbled yard. There was a long cowshed down one side, and I slipped through the open doorway. Inside, the building seemed vast. My footsteps echoed on the concrete floor so that I halted in my stride and tried to tread quietly.

The shed was piled high with rows of silage bales, one black, plastic-coated roll on top of another, as sleek and fat as monstrous sausages. I trailed my hand along the surface of the nearest one. Silage bales are packed tight with chopped grass, the air extruded. They feel solid and smooth, firm to the touch. This one felt as if the material inside was loose. As I prodded with my fingers, I could detect something lumpy, crunchy inside and took out my penknife. The plastic was thick, heavy-duty, intended not to tear. I had to press hard on the point to make a small slit in the surface. Dust drizzled out, dry and grey and I rubbed it between my fingers. This wasn't silage. I opened up the slit some more. Tiny chunks of stone drizzled to the floor. I picked one up. It was concrete or some kind of aggregate, the sort of material you might find on a building site. I moved on to the next bale and made another slit. More gritty dust trickled out, tiny particles glistening, as if within the mixture there were fragments of glass. Further along the row of bales I tried again, thrusting the knife in. When I drew out the blade it was white with a chalky powder. It had a chemical smell. It might have been fertiliser or insecticide; but whatever it was, it wasn't silage.

There was a crunch of wheels in the yard outside, a vehicle drawing up. I took a peek around the bales. Doors slammed. Through the open doorway I watched Jamie climb out of the jeep, followed by Moss, and cross to the farmhouse. Any sensible Capricorn would have beaten a hasty retreat at this point. I ran to the farmhouse, flattened myself against the wall by the window and listened.

'I want that shed cleared.' It was Jamie's voice, loud and angry. 'We've got more lorry loads arriving next week. I don't want us falling behind schedule.'

'I need more help,' Green Bastard Hat whined. 'It's not easy working with one hand. It's all the fault of that red-haired bitch—'

'Yes, and you really fucked that up,' Jamie declared bitterly, 'scared off by some old granny with a gun—'

'She shot me—'

'I'll shoot you if you mess up again. You were supposed to get rid of her!'

I felt sick. I could only think of one red-haired bitch they might want to get rid of and I'm afraid it was me.

'I'll sort her out—'

'Make sure you do. And get those bales dumped.'

Time I made myself scarce. I dared not cross the yard again or walk the open track. I backed off, slipping around the blind side of the building and ran, heading for a thicket of sheltering bushes. I scrambled through a mass of hawthorn, fighting my way through thorns and twigs.

Then suddenly I was rocking back on my heels. I teetered on the edge of a deep, ragged tear in the rock, my boots sending small stones skittering down, bouncing into oblivion. A rocky gorge dropped away beneath my toes: Applecote Pit. I was on the very edge. My senses reeled as if I was balancing on a heaving swell at sea. I stepped back, still clutching at stems I prayed wouldn't break, as the shifting sea settled, the wave of nausea ebbed. I stopped looking down, raised my head to focus on a steady horizon, and across the mouth of the pit to the other edge.

A lorry was parked there, idle, its flatbed raised at an angle, as if its driver's last act before he had abandoned it there had been to tip its load, slide it over the edge into the depths below.

I braved another look down. The pit was deep but I couldn't see the bottom because of what was filling it up from below.

Silage bags, burst open like ruptured intestines, spilled their guts into a mass of rubble, broken brick and shattered timber. Pointed metal thrust through in spikes. Oil drums were tossed about like drink cans. And the whole mass was sinking into a slick black fluid that oozed around the edges, only visible here and there, like moorland bog lurking beneath moss and grass. A dry, throat-catching dust hung in the air, but worse than that was the smell, not just of concrete dust, of effluent run-offs and chemicals, but of something putrefying, rotting, something that had once been alive.

I backed away, threading my way out through the tangle of bushes and hit the ground beneath the weight of a charging bull, a ham-like hand smothering my scream.

'Quiet! Quiet!' a voice hissed urgently as I struggled. 'If you scream, they'll hear us and we're both dead. Understand?' I nodded slowly as I recognised the broad and homely features hanging over mine. 'D'you understand, Juno?' He relaxed his grip. 'OK?' he whispered, and took his hand away from my mouth.

'What are you doing here?' I breathed.

'I'm the policeman,' Detective Constable Dean Collins responded, grinning, 'that's my line.'

CHAPTER THIRTY

Spirituous liquor was just what I needed. I handed DC Collins back his hip flask.

'Better?'

I nodded my thanks, wiping my hand across my mouth, feeling a glow of warmth in my throat sliding down into my stomach. We'd retired to a hiding place, an old blowing house abandoned after the collapse of the tin mine, its turf roof long ago disintegrated, its stone walls ruined, the blackened granite furnace the only remains of a place where tin had once been smelted. It was a good place from which to watch the comings and goings at the farmhouse. Dean had been tracking the arrival and departure of the trucks through binoculars but the only visitors to the farm that day had been Jamie Westershall and Moss in the jeep. Together, we watched them depart.

'I thought you were on paternity leave.'

Dean frowned at me, puzzled how I knew. 'I am, in a manner of speaking.'

'So, what are you doing here?'

'You first.' He folded his brawny arms and stared at me. 'You'd better start at the beginning.'

So I did. When I got to the part about Moss and Pike's lorry trying to run my van off the road, he began shaking his head in disbelief. 'You should have called us, Juno.'

It was too late for that. I told him about Sandy's party and Nathan not turning up at the pub, and the conversation I had heard between Jamie and Moss as I hid by the roadside, how Jamie had threatened me next day and GBH had attacked me in the alley. I did not mention anything about boys burying their grandmothers or elderly ladies with guns.

'When I realised that Nathan was dead,' I said finally, 'I wanted to see for myself what's going on here.' I repeated the conversation I'd just heard, lurking outside the farmhouse.

Dean was silent, as if arranging his own thoughts. 'We're both here after the same thing,' he said at last. 'I'd been working with Nathan for some time, on and off. The Environment Agency got in touch with us last year.' He grinned ruefully. 'Waste crime wasn't considered a high priority here at the time, so Nathan got assigned to me. He was convinced something was going on here. When I heard he'd been killed, I knew he must be on to something. Thought it was time I took a look.'

'Please don't tell me that Nathan was murdered just because they're burying rubbish.'

'The illegal dumping of waste,' Dean answered gravely, 'next to people-trafficking and drugs, offers the biggest profits for organised crime.'

'Seriously?'

'We're not talking about fly-tipping,' he said earnestly, 'dumping the odd mattress and a bit of garden rubbish. This is big business. It costs companies hundreds of thousands every year to dispose of their waste legally. And the nastier the waste, the more hazardous the stuff is, the more it costs to dispose of. But if you can pay someone to take it away for you and dispose of it illegally, without all the proper rules and safeguards, it costs a lot less.'

'So, you're saying that all that stuff in the pit, that construction waste, could have come from anywhere in the country?'

'Courtesy of Moss and Pike.'

'Jamie's steward is called Moss.'

'Family firm.' Dean grunted. 'They've been caught more than once for illegal dumping, upcountry. They're just a gang of thugs, the kind of outfit that cruise around in vans, touting for business, looking for someone who's tearing down an old bungalow or ripping out a kitchen. Slip 'em a few quid and they'll cart your rubbish away for you, asbestos included. It won't cost you much and it's a lot less bother than taking it to the tip.'

'But people must know where their rubbish is likely to end up,' I protested. 'Or don't they care if it's spread across some farmer's field?'

He held up a thick forefinger. 'Ah, well that's the good bit! Even if you do care . . . even if you're a law-abiding citizen and you ask the blokes offering to dispose of your rubbish if they can prove they're registered waste carriers – anyone can buy a licence, perfectly legally, on the Internet. You don't even have to prove who you are. I bought one in my little daughter's name,' he added bitterly, 'and she's not a month old.'

'But you said they'd been caught.'

'The fines are small. Prison sentences are rare.' He raised the hip flask in an ironic toast. 'It's worth the risk.'

'And any rubbish can be baled up in plastic,' I said, thinking about it. 'People round here wouldn't take any notice. They'd just think it was hay or silage.'

Dean was nodding. 'That's the beauty of the countryside. You can move stuff around in broad daylight, no problem. And if you happen to know a greedy landowner with old mineshafts on his property who's only too happy to let you pay him to dump the stuff . . .' He shrugged. 'That's where the firm got lucky, when old Moss introduced his cousins to the Westershalls.'

'There's nothing like keeping things in the family.'

'Nathan was at agricultural college with Jamie Westershall. He said he was a bastard, the sort who's always banging on about heritage and tradition but who'd shit in his own nest for money.'

'But if the police know about all this, why the hell haven't you arrested them?'

Dean shot me a fierce look. 'Because there's more to this than a bit of demolition waste or herbicide . . . Look, the problem is, waste crime is usually committed on a small scale, so it gets dealt with by local police forces. To realise the extent of what's going on, nationally, you have to start joining the dots—'

'You need a national agency,' I said, 'like the Environment Agency. Enter Nathan Parr,' I added.

'And exit, unfortunately.'

We were both silent for a moment, lost in gloomy thoughts.

'And Inspector Ford knows all this?' I asked.

'Listen, the boss has got his hands full. He's Head of Serious Crimes for this whole area and with the crisis up at the prison he was happy enough for me to monitor the situation here, but that was all. But Nathan didn't want to prosecute a few thugs for dumping rubbish down a hole. He wanted to catch the people higher up, the people who are producing this waste, the polluters who pay criminals to dump it illegally. He had Westershall in his sights for a long time, ever since the murder of Ben Luscombe—'

'So you know Ben was murdered, then?'

'Let's just say we were suspicious,' Dean admitted, 'but we couldn't prove anything at the time. Nathan knew he'd be putting himself at risk if he approached Westershall openly, but he was convinced that the Moorworthy estate is receiving a big kickback from a major pharmaceutical company—'

'Sandy Westershall was in pharmaceuticals.' I told Dean about the photograph I'd seen on his study wall, of Sandy receiving a business award from some firm whose name I couldn't remember.

'Well, whatever the Westershalls are dumping for them, it's nasty stuff, not the sort of thing they'll risk throwing in an open pit like that building waste. They'll be hiding it somewhere else.'

'I know where it is.' I pulled the folded map from my pocket and opened it out. 'Moorworthy shaft.' I tapped my finger on the map. 'There. Ben Luscombe reported seeing lights coming from that shaft—'

Dean almost snatched the map from my hands. 'Where d'you get this?'

'Ashburton Library.'

'You're kidding!'

'No, I asked the librarian, she gave it to me.' He gazed at me, astonished. But then, he's a man, he probably doesn't ask for directions either.

'Moorworthy Pit is fenced off, because of the bats, supposedly.'

He frowned. 'Then how do we get into it?'

'We can get there through the adit.'

'Adit?' he repeated.

'This map doesn't show them, but there were tunnels dug so that the miners could get level access to the shafts. I saw some in old engravings up at the house. There's a tunnel connecting the shaft at Applecote with the one at Moorworthy, I'm sure there is.'

'And the entrance to this tunnel is somewhere down in this pit.' He jabbed at the map with his forefinger. 'Do you know where?'

'I didn't see it earlier, but I wasn't looking, I was concentrating on not being swallowed up by all that rubbish.'

'The entrance to this tunnel might be buried under it all,' he pointed out.

'There's only one way to find out.' I looked at my watch. 'It'll be dark in an hour or so.' I realised I probably wasn't going to be sitting down to tea with Olly and Elizabeth. 'We must try and find it now, while we still can.'

This time I knew about the pit and we threaded through the hawthorn with more caution. We stopped a few feet away from the edge, lay on our bellies and crawled. There was no one around, no work in progress. Despite Jamie's orders, GBH was not dumping bales today. There was still light draining from the sky, but down in the depths the pit was already deep in shadows. Dean shone his torch, sweeping the beam around its rocky walls. The mine had originally been open-cast; years ago men had dug their way down with shovels, creating ledges and stepping stones that allowed them to cut deeper and deeper into the granite. But there was no sign of a tunnel, no hole in the pit wall.

'Perhaps it's underneath us,' I whispered. 'Perhaps we need to be over there, on the other side, to see it.'

We crawled, keeping back from the rocky edge until we reached the place where the bushes had been cleared away to make open ground for lorries to roll up to the pit edge. It was a relief to stand up, to walk normally for a yard or two. Then we hunkered down again and swept the walls of the pit with the torch beam.

On the other side, the walls were not as clear. Nature had reclaimed crannies in the rock, wind-blown seeds taking root in tiny cracks, growing into straggly bushes. Ivy scrambled over ledges.

'There!' I pointed. 'Just to the right of that metal pole that's sticking up, d'you see?'

The circle of the light swung around the walls crazily as Dean tried to find what I was pointing at. 'Got it!' He lit up a dark rent in the granite, half-hidden by a tangle of dusty creeper straggling down from above.

'Look, we can clamber down to that ledge just above it—' I began.

I heard Dean sigh softly as he turned to look at me. 'Sorry, Juno, but you're not coming. It's too dangerous,' he went on hastily, 'and you're only a civilian. I'm responsible for your safety and I can't allow it. From here on in, I'm on my own.'

I must have gaped at him. 'Are you joking?'

'No. I want you to go back to the blow house, wait for me there—'

'I want to catch these evil bastards just as much as you do!'

'I know.' He laid a consoling hand on my shoulder. 'I know you do.'

I shook him off. The reasonableness of his tone was infuriating.

'Listen, if I'm not back at the blow house in two hours—' he began.

'Forget it, I'm coming with you! I owe it to Gavin,' I added as he tried to interrupt.

'Gavin's death was an accident,' he said quietly.

'I don't care. Maybe someone shoved that sword into him or maybe he did it himself, but the only reason he was in the woods that day was because of what had happened to his friend, to Ben. Accident or murder, his death is directly connected to what's going on here.'

'Juno—'

'You try and leave me behind,' I warned him, 'I'll go straight to Inspector Ford and tell him what you're up to.'

That shut him up. He frowned ominously.

'Because he doesn't know you're here, does he?' I persisted.

'Of course he does.'

I shook my head. 'If this were an official operation, there is no way you'd be here on your own. You'd be working in pairs and there'd be at least one other team on this.' His frown was like thunder, so I knew I was right. 'Detective Inspector Ford believes you're on paternity leave at this moment, isn't that so? And if I tell him what you're really up to, right now, together with what I know, this place will be crawling with coppers in five minutes. And that won't suit you, will it?' I added finally. 'Because you want to be the one to bring Nathan's killers down.'

He seemed lost for words. When he eventually came up with one to describe me it wasn't complimentary.

'Guilty as charged,' I smiled sweetly and waved an arm at the mouth of the tunnel opposite. 'Shall we?'

CHAPTER THIRTY-ONE

Dean couldn't climb with the torch in his hand and clambering down to the mouth of the tunnel was unnerving in the gathering dusk. One missed footing would mean a fall into the pit, floundering amongst filthy rubbish, amongst broken rock, ripped metal and shattered glass or sinking beneath that oily bilge never to surface again.

The ledge we reached was narrow, its rocky edges fallen away. We were forced to crawl on our hands and knees, inch our way forward, dislodging loose chippings and sending them bouncing down the walls into the pit below. Halfway along we stopped for a breather, sitting back on our heels. Dean switched on the torch and shone it along the path to the mouth of the tunnel. 'Just a few more yards, but be careful here.'

Something pale had caught my eye down in the shadows, something like a mask. I pointed. 'What's that?'

Dean shone the torch. I was startled into a gasp and he swore softly. Staring up from dead eyes was a screaming skull, bone-white and open-mouthed in horror: the face of Ted Croaker, sunk to his neck in an oily swamp, one rigid hand, a black and glistening claw, reaching up in desperation as he had tried to scrabble his way out.

'Do you think he fell or was thrown in?' I asked when I felt able to speak.

'I don't know, but he's been there a few days by the look of him, poor sod. Of course, when they've filled this shaft up, they'll just cap it off with concrete,' he went on. 'A few tons of earth on top of it, turf it over, and no one will know there's anything down here.'

I was still staring into the hollow eyes of Ted Croaker. 'Or anyone,' I added.

It was a relief to drag ourselves in through the mouth of the tunnel, to collapse, to sit there, getting our breath back. We sat for a few moments, our breathing the only sounds in the quiet dark. My stomach rumbled. I thought longingly of the nutty bars I'd left behind in my rucksack. I heard Dean chuckle in the darkness, then a rustle of paper and the unmistakeably attractive snap of a chocolate bar being broken in half. 'Here.'

I'd left my torch behind in my rucksack, so I switched on the light on my phone, its blue glow showing me what he was holding out, and took it thankfully.

'Enjoy it,' he advised with a grim laugh, 'it could be our last meal.'

We munched in silence.

'What's your little daughter's name?' I asked, after a minute.

'Alice.' There was love in the darkness, even in that one word. A moment later his features were lit by the colourful glow from his mobile. He scrolled down until he found what he was looking for and then passed it to me.

One bald, pink baby looks much like another to me, but I took it dutifully. I had to admit, Alice was cute. When the photo was taken, she must have been fresh out of the pod, her face red and crumpled, her tiny fist curled tight as a rosebud next to her little mouth, but she already had more hair than her father.

'You should be at home with her, Detective Constable Collins,' I reproved him, 'not sitting here in this dark hole.'

He murmured something unintelligible.

'Does your wife know where you are?'

'Gemma?' He gave a crack of laughter. 'Christ! No.'

'What did you tell her?'

'That they were short-handed at the station and needed me to go in. She knows that uninterrupted paternity leave is a pretty fantastic idea to begin with. She won't fret if I don't turn up till the morning.'

'Did Nathan have a girlfriend . . . ?'

'He'd just been through a divorce . . . Look, while we're asking personal questions, do you have a significant other?' he demanded crossly. 'Because he could do with a bloody good talking-to about the things you get up to.'

'I don't, as it happens.' I could hear an edge in my voice I wished wasn't there. The last time I'd felt attracted to a man, things hadn't worked out well.

'I heard about what happened with the Nickolai murder,' he began.

'Let's just say I'm not actively seeking a significant other at the moment,' I responded before he could get any further.

'Understood.' Dean flicked on the torch and shone it around the walls of the tunnel. Above our heads a cat's cradle of slanting timbers shored up the roof. They were ancient, festooned with cobwebs and some of them looked decidedly dodgy to me. 'It's high enough to stand up in here, thank God. I didn't fancy crawling on our hands and knees.' He rose to his feet and thumped a fist against one of the lower timbers, dislodging a century of dust. 'We'll have to watch our heads, though.' His coughing echoed around the walls.

I got up and fell into step behind him. What little light was coming from the tunnel mouth soon faded. Ahead the blackness was dense, thick, all light blotted out. But in the torchlight the walls around us glistened, tin-bearing ore buried in the rock showing here and there as silver specks and patches.

'I feel as if we're going slightly uphill,' Dean said after a while.

'These tunnels slope up a bit towards the entrance to allow water to run out,' I explained.

'It's quite dry in here.'

'There could be another tunnel beneath this one; the lowest adit was always for drainage.'

'You seem to know a lot about it.'

I only knew what Alec had told me and what I'd read in the library. 'I'm an expert,' I told him. 'I might write a book, *Tin Mining for Dummies*.'

'Well, Miss Expert, do you know how long this tunnel goes on for?'

'It can't be very long, not if it leads us into the Moorworthy shaft.'

'And we're sure about that, are we?'

Why is it that if someone asks if you're sure about something, you're suddenly not sure about it, even if you were perfectly certain about it before they asked? Dean noticed my hesitation and grunted. We carried on in silence.

It got steadily warmer, stuffier, as we went deeper into the rock. I started to find the heat oppressive, thought about shedding my jacket; but then I'd only have to carry it. Around us, the blackness was stifling, closing in around the torch's narrow beam. I'd decided to put my phone away, save it in case Dean's torch failed. The thought of being down here in blind black was too appalling to dwell on. I pitied the poor bloody miners who'd had to spend every day of their working lives down here.

'There's something up ahead,' Dean called out suddenly. He shone the torchlight on a plastic cylinder, white, dustbin size, lying on its side. The lid had rolled away and whatever had been inside it had seeped into the ground beneath our feet, dried into a dark stain.

The lingering smell was acrid, made me want to catch my breath. I pulled my scarf up over my nose. Dean rolled the thing over with one push of his boot to reveal a lot of labelling with some long, chemical-sounding names I did not understand, and a yellow triangle with a black exclamation mark which I did: *hazardous waste*. There was another label to indicate the contents were corrosive and flammable.

'This is what Nathan was on about,' Dean coughed, a hand to his mouth. 'Be careful where you step.' He aimed the torch back, directing the light towards the ground so I could pick my way. This stuff could probably melt boots.

Stack after stack of containers almost blocked the tunnel ahead, all displaying labels with cheery yellow triangles. Dean swore softly. He handed the torch to me, got out his phone and started taking pictures. *Chemical waste, medical waste*, I read as I edged my way past: *explosive; toxic; reactive.*

'Just small amounts of some of this stuff, if it gets into groundwater . . .'

He didn't need to finish, I got the point. *Acetyl Chloride*, I read, *Chromic Acid*. Chemistry had never been an interest of mine, so I was none the wiser. *Sodium Hypochlorite*, I'd heard of that one. It was not stuff you wanted to breathe in or splash on your skin.

'We need to prove where this stuff has come from.' Dean's camera flashed in the darkness. 'We need to find a company name.'

I wasn't enthusiastic about getting any closer to the containers. The lids all seemed to be safely shut but there must be a leakage somewhere. My eyes were watering, my lips stinging, I was starting to cough. Then, in letters designed for a cockroach to read, I found a printed name. *Dravizax.org*. 'Got it!'

Dean came to look over my shoulder. I pointed the light at the adjacent container and picked it out again. Now that I knew where to look, I could see it written on all of them. 'Dravizax, I remember it now.' Dean leant in close to take pictures. I could sense his mounting excitement. 'Their boss is pictured in a photo with Sandy Westershall,' I told him, my voice rasping. 'I saw it on the wall of his study . . .' My lungs were burning. I was finding it difficult to breathe.

Dean took the torch from me, grabbed my hand. 'Let's get out of here!'

We jogged on. I couldn't count the number of containers we passed, some stained brown at the edges, the plastic being eaten away by whatever was held inside. From somewhere amongst them I could hear an ominous trickling.

We didn't speak, tried not to breathe until we'd left the stacks of plastic drums behind. Ahead of us, tiny dark objects littered the ground like shrivelled leather purses: dead bats. The poor little buggers had flown too deep into the tunnel and been poisoned by the fumes.

Further on the air seemed to be cooling, clearing. At first, I thought we must be nearing the tunnel mouth, but Dean suddenly stopped and shone the torch beam upward over our heads. It was as if we were looking up from the bottom of a well, a stone-lined telescope with a circle of sky way above us. We could see a freckling of stars.

'Ventilation shaft,' I breathed. It would have been sunk when the mine was originally dug, to draw heat and fumes up from the rock face. It was criss-crossed by wooden rafters. Odd little pouches hung here and there, like old leaves clinging to a winter tree; sleeping bats. Disturbed by the torchlight and by our echoing whispers, they stirred and fluttered away.

'They must be the late sleepers-in,' Dean grinned. 'The rest will have gone a-hunting.'

We lingered for a while, breathing in cold, fresh air, gazing up at pinpricks of blessed light far above. Then we moved on, enlivened by the air, buoyed up by the evidence we had of the Westershalls' involvement with Dravizax. Now we just needed to get out.

The tunnel led us straight into Moorworthy shaft. It sloped down to the left, into the furthest reaches of the mine, down to the abandoned rock face. To the right it sloped upward, towards the entrance, to the way out. Our climb upward was made easier by artificially cut levels and pallets laid down to create a wooden walkway. Dean shone his torch over it. 'This looks recent. I bet they laid this down so that they could wheel in all those drums of shit.'

Our boots clumped noisily along it. Ahead of us the blackness was thinning. It might be night outside, but moonlight filtering through the entrance pierced the blanket of a deeper dark. A turned corner brought us our first view of the ragged rent in the rock that was the mouth of Moorworthy Pit.

Excitement and relief drained away. Dean swore fiercely as we stood and stared. A grill blocked the entrance, an iron screen of crossbars, set wide enough apart to allow bats to flutter in and out but not wide enough for anything larger, like us. Dean rattled the grill in vain and shone the torch beam over three separate padlocks. 'I don't suppose you happen to have a set of lock-picks about you?'

'Don't you?'

'Funnily enough, they're frowned upon in the police force.'

'Well, you're allowed to smash down doors. I've seen it on the telly.'

He gave a grim laugh. We were silent then, considering our alternatives. We could go back the way we came, past all the containers, climb back out of Applecote Pit. Or we could scale the ventilation shaft.

We looked at one another. 'Ventilation shaft,' we said as one.

Climbing the shaft was just a case of stretching between the uneven rafters that criss-crossed it in a ramshackle ladder. It should not have been difficult, at least not for a long-legged creature like me; anyone shorter would have been stuffed. But the rafters creaked ominously beneath our weight and were slimy with bat shit. It was difficult to find a place for hand or foot to rest without slipping. After a few minutes we were breathless with the effort, and sweating. We rested, clinging onto our respective perches, Dean a few rafters above me.

'Are we getting near the top?' I called up to him. It didn't seem to me we were making any progress at all.

'About halfway,' he called back. He reached up, his hand searching to find a grip on the rafter above him. His fingers locked on, he took the next step up with his boot. There was a sharp crack. I managed to dodge as the splintered halves of a falling beam barely missed my shoulder, tumbled down into the darkness, hitting the ground with a crash. Dean was hanging by his arms from the rafter above him like an ape, his legs swinging.

'You OK?' he yelled down to me.

'I'm fine.'

I heard him straining with effort as he pulled himself up by his arms until he could balance his body over the rafter above him, get a leg over it and sit up.

I wasn't hurt but the fallen rafter had created a gap in the ladder too long for me to bridge. I looked around at the walls of the shaft, wondering if I could edge my way over and climb up the rock instead. But it glistened, oily with bat shit and damp. It didn't look safe.

Dean had both legs locked around the rafter he sat on. He swung his body down, hanging underneath and stretched his arms towards me. 'I'll have to pull you up. It's the only way.'

'You're kidding.' Like a trapeze artist, he'd have to take the entire weight of my body and I'm substantial to say the least.

'Trust me. I trained in the circus.'

Very funny. But I didn't really have a choice. Muttering darkly about not dropping me, I reached up until his massive paw circled one wrist and then the other. Heaving and groaning, teeth clenched, he pulled me up until I was within clutching distance of the rafter above me, veins standing out on his forehead with the effort. As I grabbed the rafter and hauled myself up, he grasped my belt, helping to heave my body over until I could get my legs round it. I just prayed it would bear the weight of us both.

He sat up, grinning and wiped the sweat from his forehead with his sleeve. The mouth of the shaft was just a few feet above us. Dean climbed until he reached the top and stretched down an arm to haul me out. Solid ground had never felt so good. We lay on our backs in the damp grass, gasping like landed fish, heaving in the fresh air and staring up at a spangled veil of stars. I had lost all sense of time, had no idea how long we had been down in that tunnel, groping our way in the dark. It felt like days.

After the mine and the ventilation shaft, getting over the fence with its razor-wire top seemed easy. We just scaled the nearest tree, shimmied on our bellies along a branch and dropped down on the other side. All we had to do now was to creep quietly down the drive through the grounds to the gate and we'd be out. Safe. Free. Except that I knew we wouldn't. I'd already worked out what was coming next, knew it before Dean opened his mouth.

'Sandy Westershall and the boss of Dravizax,' he said, turning to grin at me. 'I want that photograph.'

CHAPTER THIRTY-TWO

We watched the lights of the house from behind a screen of rhododendron bushes, hoping to see them go out, hoping that the Westershalls might go early to bed. I didn't think it was likely myself, and all hopes were dashed when Emma's open-top car roared up the drive and quenched its tyres noisily in the gravel. Four people climbed out. I recognised Eddie, posh-boy drugs dealer, and Emma of course. I didn't know the other two. All four talked at the top of their voices as they weaved their way into the house and the door slammed shut behind them. A few moments later more lights flicked on downstairs and loud music began to blare from the windows.

Dean groaned. 'It looks like no one will be going to bed for a while.' We decided to work our way around the back of the house in the hope that it might be in darkness. The quickest way was to run across the garden, keeping well away from the windows and anyone who might chance to look out. The lawn was long and wide and running across it felt horribly exposed. 'Watch out for the ha-ha,' I warned Dean in a hoarse whisper as we scurried, almost bent double, across the wet grass.

'The what?'

'It's a hidden drop. Over to our right somewhere.'

We made it across the lawn and into the safety of the shrubbery, crawling in amongst sheltering shrubs. We stayed still for a few moments, watching and waiting. But we'd disturbed nothing except for a hunting owl, which hooted in a tree nearby, its call echoed by another, somewhere in the woods. We crept around the side of the building.

Lights were on at the back of the house and we could hear a radio playing. We sneaked to the kitchen window and peered over the sill. Mrs Johnson was busying herself at a granite worktop, in a vast kitchen that was strangely at odds with the rest of the house: functional and modern, all white walls and stainless steel like an operating theatre. Tray after tray of canapés was lined up on the surface and she was busy covering them with plastic film. At a central island, Moss perched on a stool, reading a newspaper, a mug at his elbow. It didn't look like either of them would be heading for Bedfordshire any time soon either. We hadn't seen any sign of Jamie or Sandy, but presumably they were in the house somewhere.

At Dean's signal we tiptoed away from the window. 'Let's find somewhere to wait until things quieten down.' We slipped down a path. A wooden door led us into a walled vegetable garden, and we crunched down a gravel pathway past serried ranks of cabbages. I could smell sage and fennel as we brushed past a bed of herbs. God, I was starving.

313

Further on we came to a standpipe with garden hose attached, turned the tap and bathed our hands and faces in the icy gush of water, rinsing lingering traces of contamination from our bare skin and cleansing our hands of bat shit.

We found shelter in a little wooden summer house with garden loungers stored inside; we grabbed the cushions and settled down comfortably on the floor. 'We might as well rest up for an hour or two,' Dean said, 'until they've all gone to bed.'

I awoke in the grey light of morning to the liquid song of a blackbird. For a moment I didn't know where I was. I sat up, staring around, rubbing my stiff neck. Dean was fast asleep on the cushions beside me and I shook him by the shoulder, hissing at him to wake up. He snored, stirred grumpily, blinked at me, uncomprehending for a moment, and then snapped into wakefulness. 'Christ!' he muttered, sitting up. 'That must be the longest I've slept since Alice was born!'

I thought we must have slept away our chance, but he was already staggering to his feet, stiffly stretching. 'C'mon.'

'They'll be getting up again soon,' I warned him as he peered out of the summer house and around the vegetable garden.

'Not if they went to bed late enough.'

The back of the house was still and silent, windows black in the grey gloom. I held my breath as Dean tried the handle of the back door. No luck. A few feet away a pane of frosted glass was set into the wall and the narrow transom window above it was ajar. Dean was considering it, eyes narrowed, calculating its size and I realised, with a sinking in my guts, whose backside would shortly be squirming through.

'I'll give you a leg-up,' he offered graciously.

I snagged my hair in the window-catch as I poked my head through the window, staring down at the windowsill below me, and the toilet beneath it, stretching down to brace my hands upon the sill as I wriggled my bum through the narrow gap. There was a water pipe running down the wall beside me and I transferred one hand onto it, so that I could swivel sideways, get one leg in, stand on the windowsill, then draw the other leg in after me. It was either that or crash headfirst down the loo. I stepped on the cistern, carefully on the rim of the loo seat, and finally, thankfully, stood upon the floor.

I opened the door and peered cautiously down the corridor. The house seemed to be sleeping, all quiet. From where I stood, I could see into the kitchen. I could also see a homely touch that had not been visible through the kitchen window the night before: a dog basket, a very large dog basket. Judging from the snores rumbling from within, it contained a grizzly bear. All I could see was a dark mound, which heaved with each snuffling breath. I crept down the corridor, my heart beating loud enough to wake it up.

As I hesitated in the kitchen doorway, the owner of the basket raised a black, doggy snout about an inch, studied me from a drooping eye and, after considering me for a moment, thumped its plumy tail lazily.

'Hello,' I whispered, in that soppy voice we reserve for dogs and small children. 'There's a good boy.' I crouched carefully, and reached out, praying I wasn't about to get my face ripped off. The dog, a Newfoundland, allowed me to stroke his head and licked my hand in greeting.

Just behind his basket stood an enormous fridge. I swung open the door, bathing myself in icy white light, and gazed upon shelves loaded with trays of canapés. I decided they wouldn't miss a few, peeled back a corner of plastic film, popped a prawn vol-au-vent straight into my gob and gave one to the dog. He sat up, suddenly awake and interested, licking his chops. I grabbed another two and we shared them in the same way. 'Now, you go back to sleep,' I mumbled, mouth full. I crossed the kitchen, shutting the door behind me so that my new friend couldn't follow me out, and drew back the bolts on the back door.

'What the hell have you been doing?' Dean demanded in a fierce whisper.

I swallowed hastily. 'Essential diplomatic negotiations,' I told him.

He frowned. 'Smells fishy to me! Now, which way is it?'

There seemed only one way to go, up a bare flight of servants' stairs with a metal handrail. We tried to tread softly but our boots clumped on the stone steps. We considered taking them off but decided that might hamper a quick getaway and carried on, on tiptoe.

At the top of the servants' stairs we found ourselves at the end of the wide passage that led down the hall to the grand staircase; mercifully, the floor was carpeted, a long Persian runner deadening our noise. The double doors of the ballroom stood open to our left. A grand piano occupied the far end of it, with rows of gilded chairs lined up to face it, ready for a recital.

We crept on until we reached the drawing room. The door was open, and I stifled a quick intake of breath. The four partygoers from last night were crashed out on the sofas, fast asleep. Eddie's cherubic features were squashed against the floral cushions, muffling his snores; Emma's legs, encased in black satin trousers, hung over the edge of another sofa, one silver high-heeled sandal trailing from her toes. The other couple were just a tangled heap on the carpet. Bottles lay scattered around the room and a stale smell of breathed-out booze hung heavy in the air.

We hurried on past, crossing the hall to the door of the study, turning the handle slowly, wincing at the soft click it gave on opening and slipped inside. The heavy brocade curtains were pulled back and the tall windows overlooking the lawn showed us that the sky was swiftly lightening, a faint glow warming the clouds above the horizon. I hoped no one in the house was awake and fancying an early breakfast.

Dean crossed swiftly to the display of framed photos on the wall. In one picture Sandy Westershall was shaking hands with the boss of Dravizax. In another, they were holding a big cheque between them, although it wasn't clear who was giving and who was receiving. Dean couldn't suppress a low chuckle as he framed each one in the lens of his camera and began snapping away. I was feeling jittery. Photographing the pictures was taking too long. It would have been quicker to nick them off the wall. I distracted myself by trying the

317

drawers of the mahogany desk that occupied the centre of the room. I pulled at each of the brass handles, but all the drawers were locked.

'Now can we get out of here?' I hissed, as at last he slid his phone back into his pocket.

He didn't answer. Sitting on the desk was a laptop. He lifted the lid and pressed a button. I groaned as the screen lit up and the blasted machine played a tinkling tune.

'I don't suppose there's a spare memory stick anywhere.' He tried to open the top drawer, then picked up a paperknife. As he bent to insert it in the lock, I heard a click. But it wasn't the desk drawer opening.

Sandy Westershall stood in the doorway, dressed in pyjamas and a silk dressing gown; behind him stood Mrs Johnson, pale and grim in a hastily buttoned housecoat, and Moss, who had completed his rustic ensemble with a shotgun levelled straight at us.

'Johnnie, fetch Master Jamie, will you?' Sandy ordered calmly, without turning his head to look at her. He kept his gaze fixed on us. His skin looked yellowish and blotchy in the early light; he reminded me of a lizard watching its prey. I expected his tongue to flicker from his lips at any moment. He walked into the room; Moss and his shotgun came in after him. Instinctively, Dean and I raised our hands.

'Step away from the desk,' Sandy ordered, and we backed towards the fireplace. He drew a tiny key from his dressing gown pocket, unlocked the top drawer of the desk and brought out a pistol.

'You can lower that shotgun now, Moss. I'd really sooner you didn't fire it in here.' He brandished the pistol in his hand. 'This is far more suited to the purpose. The good old Navy Colt.' He smiled unpleasantly. 'It's amazing the things dear old Barty can lay his hands on if you ask him.' He cocked it, and with an almost casual air, aimed it at my head. 'I'm very disappointed in you, my dear,' he sighed. 'Now, who's your friend?'

Neither of us spoke. Sandy pressed the gun against my temple and ordered Moss to go through our pockets. I could feel the round rim of the barrel digging into my skin. I was fighting to keep still, not to betray the fear I felt by trembling. 'Chuck everything on the desk there. Make sure you get their phones.' Dean must have made a slight move. 'You!' Sandy rapped at him. 'Keep your hands up!' With his free hand he picked up Dean's wallet and opened it. 'Detective Constable Dean Collins,' he read aloud, as Jamie walked in. 'Oh dear, that complicates things rather.'

Jamie took the wallet from him silently and read it for himself. He flicked a glance at Dean, and then at me, his blue eyes cold. 'Juno. I knew I was going to have to do something about you sooner or later.'

'Like you did something about Nathan Parr?' Dean demanded.

Jamie raised his brows. 'And what do you know about Nathan Parr?'

'I know that you killed him, you bastard.'

Jamie picked up Dean's phone from the desk and began scrolling through it. 'I trusted Nathan. I thought he was a friend,' he answered, his gaze fixed on the images on the phone.

'I expected loyalty. I didn't know he was a liar and a spy.' He found the photographs Dean had just taken, of the pictures on the wall, the drums of hazardous waste down in the tunnel. He held up the screen so that Sandy could see. 'I think we'll just erase these.' Our hard-earned evidence vanished with one push of his thumb. 'Parr got what he deserved.'

'And Ted Croaker?'

'He got greedy, thought he could blackmail us.'

'So you threw him in the pit,' I accused him.

'Like the garbage he was,' he responded smoothly.

'You can't expect to get away with this,' Dean warned him.

Jamie just smiled. 'Moss, drive down to the farm, fetch Pike up here, will you?'

'Moss!' I called to him as he turned to go. 'You know this is wrong. You said yourself, too many have died already—'

'I don't know what you're talking about,' he growled, flicking a nervous look in his employer's direction before he hurried from the room.

'How can you do this?' I asked Jamie. 'Three people dead. What gives you the right—'

'Don't you dare lecture me about rights,' he countered, suddenly fierce. 'What do people like you know about running an estate, about heritage and tradition, about keeping farms from going bust and this house from collapsing, about responsibilities towards your tenants, towards the countryside, the land—'

'Which you despoil by polluting it?'

That pulled him up short. He bit his lip, but he didn't want to show that I'd touched him on the raw. He sat back on the edge of the desk and studied the two of us reflectively. 'Now, Detective Constable Collins,' he said after a moment, 'I think it's time we had a conversation about how much you and your superiors know about our little operation here.'

Dean grunted. 'You expect me to tell you?'

'Yes, I do.' Jamie smiled. 'The only question is how much you're prepared to allow the lovely Juno here to suffer before you come to your senses.'

Dean shot me an anguished look.

'Tell him to get stuffed!' I recommended.

'It's easy to sound brave now,' Sandy said sadly. 'You'll feel a little differently, my dear—'

'Mr Jamie, the catering staff will be here soon.' Mrs Johnson spoke with perfect calm, reminding him of an inconvenient fact, unfazed apparently by whatever he and his uncle were proposing to do to us.

Jamie frowned, irritated. 'This early?'

'They've been told to come in early, sir, there's a lot to do before the concert this afternoon.'

Suddenly I realised. The piano in the ballroom, the rows of chairs, the trays of canapés: today was the day of Ricky and Morris's concert. As if on cue, a blue van came trundling down the drive and passed the window, heading around to the back of the house. 'Special Events Catering' was written on the side. The staff were beginning to arrive.

Jamie swore. 'We can't have all these people about. Johnnie, just keep them out of the way, in the kitchen. Offer them breakfast or something.'

She was about to go out when he stopped her. 'Miss Jessica is still tucked up in bed. I don't want her coming downstairs and seeing all this. Take breakfast up to her bedroom, will you?'

'Of course, sir,' she nodded and left.

'What's going on?' a weary voice demanded from the hall. A moment later, Emma stood in the doorway, wobbling unsteadily on her high heels. She was as pale as a corpse and clearly suffering the effects of last night's party. 'You'll wake up the others.'

Jamie swore softly. 'Shit! Emma, are they still here?'

'They slept over,' she responded, gazing around with eyes narrowed against the daylight, her pupils no more than pinpoints. She gestured at me. 'What's she doing here?' She scowled groggily at Dean and tottered into the room. 'Who's he?'

'Never mind, my darling.' Sandy turned towards her and I felt the release of pressure from the pistol as he turned away the gun. I let out a breath. 'They'll soon be gone,' he went on, as if pacifying a spoilt child. 'Now, why don't you go and wake up your friends and tell them it's time they went home?'

'But they might want breakfast,' she objected.

'Emma!' Jamie snapped. 'Just do as you're bloody told! Get rid of them.'

Moss returned at that moment, with Green Bastard Hat, who gave me a foul grin. He was obviously enjoying the prospect of a rematch.

'Perhaps all this had better wait until later, dear boy,' Sandy observed calmly, 'until after the concert. Lock 'em in the wine cellar till then.'

Jamie shook his head, 'Too many people around down here.'

'An attic, then.'

'What happened to Gavin Hall?'

322

Silence fell, as if they were stunned I had dared to speak. They all turned to look at me. 'What happened to him?' I demanded.

'It was his own fault,' Emma said petulantly.

I gazed at her in astonishment. '*You* killed him?'

She hunched a pettish shoulder. 'Eddie and I went into the woods just to . . . you know, take care of a little business . . . a little exchange.'

'Money for drugs,' I completed for her.

'Well, we didn't know the boy was there. He must have hidden when he saw us coming. He shouldn't have been snooping about.' She smiled. 'He was probably embarrassed about being seen with that stupid sword . . . anyway, he saw us. So what? There was no need for him to have run. We called out after him. I'd have paid the little creep to keep quiet, only . . . he leapt up on that tree trunk and . . .' She shrugged carelessly. 'That was that.'

I couldn't believe how little his death mattered to her. 'Didn't you try to help him?'

'It was obvious he was beyond help. And we didn't want to get too near him, frankly.' She giggled. 'He lost his specs as he was running away. I saw them go flying off. He was blundering about . . . you know, looking back on it, it was really very funny.'

Something exploded in my heart and in my head. I was on top of her, on the carpet, driving my fist into her face, punching her again and again. She tried to fend me off. Enfeebled by her hangover she could do no more than slap and scratch. I just went on punching.

Hands tried to drag me off, to wrench me away. Perhaps

323

Dean used the distraction to make a move. I'm not sure what happened but a shot rang out. I turned to see him falling, heavy and slow until his body hit the carpet and lay still. I struggled against restraining hands to reach him. I realised that someone was screaming. It must have been me.

CHAPTER THIRTY-THREE

I had a vague, half-conscious memory of being dragged upstairs; lots and lots of stairs.

My body felt battered and bruised as if I'd been thumped repeatedly. In a dull, sickening rhythm my aching head throbbed. The taste of blood was in my mouth, I felt around with my tongue. My teeth were all present but my lower lip was split. I was lying on a floor. I felt it hard beneath my body and my exploring fingers touched rough wood planking. I opened my eyes and shut them again, assaulted by bright, grey daylight. There was a strange smell coming from somewhere – earthy, like mushrooms. I pulled myself cautiously up onto my elbows and squinted around the room.

The walls on either side of me slanted steeply towards one end. A small round window was set high into the sloping ceiling, letting in the unforgiving light. I was in an attic, directly beneath the roof. Perhaps a servant had once slept in this room. It was empty except for a metal bed frame, an old chest of drawers and Dean. He was there on the floor beside me. I scuffled across the bare floor towards him. He was lying very still, eyes closed, a deep frown between his brows, both hands clutched to his right side, beneath his ribs. Blood had seeped between his fingers and dried sticky, and run down to stain the wooden floorboards. The sharp tang of his blood filled my nostrils. He was pale, skin clammy, his scalp shining with sweat beneath his stubbly hair. But he was alive, his broad chest heaving painfully at each shallow, ragged breath. I whispered his name.

He opened heavy-lidded eyes and he swallowed. 'Sorry, Juno,' he breathed.

'Let me see.' I moved his hands away gently from his wound and pulled up his sweatshirt. An evil red flower had bloomed across the white T-shirt underneath, dark in its centre. The wound was bleeding, but slowly. I ripped off my jacket and shirt, rolled the shirt into a pad and pressed it against the wound. Then I placed his hands back over it whilst I unknotted my scarf to bind round it and keep it in place. This wasn't easy. I had to slide the scarf beneath his back in order to tie it around him, a manoeuvre that caused him to draw in a sharp breath and swear. The wound began to seep. It was obvious he shouldn't move, couldn't walk.

I bundled up my jacket and slipped it under his head. 'You're going to be all right,' I lied.

I didn't know what was going on inside his body, what organs the bullet might have punctured, what bones fractured, what vital blood vessels severed. But at least the bleeding was slow. Maybe we had some time. 'I'm going to get us out of here,' I promised, touching his hand.

He smiled weakly. 'Green . . . hat . . .' he whispered, '. . . out there . . .'

I pointed questioningly towards the door.

He nodded and winced. 'With . . . gun . . .'

'Don't talk,' I told him. 'Rest.'

'Juno . . .' he began, with what was obviously a great effort, 'if you get out of here . . . tell my wife . . .'

'Don't you dare!' I hissed at him. 'Don't you start all that "tell my wife I love her" shit! *We* are getting out of here.' I squeezed his hand hard. 'Both of us. Understand?'

He gazed at me sadly. 'Whatever you say . . .'

'Good. Now shut up and let me think. Close your eyes. Concentrate on keeping pressure on this.' I indicated the makeshift dressing over his wound and watched him as he sighed and his lids sank to a close.

I stood up, tiptoed to the door and listened. I could just detect a tiny metallic rhythm, no louder than the ticking of a watch. I recognised that irritating, teensy-weensy, cicada-type sound you hear when someone sitting close to you is listening to music through headphones. Green Bastard Hat was at his post, but only just. Good. I didn't want him to hear me moving about.

I checked the round window. I'd noticed a row of them in the roof on the day I first came to Moorworthy House, squinting up at them from the terrace below. They were set into the tiles, behind a balustrade. They were for show and didn't open. There was certainly no mechanism for opening this one. And it was very high up; all I could see through it was sky, a dull grey blanket of cloud.

I turned to examine the room for anything useful. The

bed was no more than an iron frame without a mattress, not even any springs. The chest of drawers was old, probably Victorian, and heavy; two small drawers at the top, four bigger ones underneath, all with round wooden knobs for handles. I pulled out each drawer. Someone had lined them with wallpaper, pale green with cream flowers. But they were empty. Nothing I could use as a weapon or means of escape. No handy implement I could bash Green Bastard Hat over the head with. I stared in desperation around plain, painted walls.

In the corner, where the sloping ceiling almost met the floor, was a door about two feet high, the top edge sloping in line with the wall above it. I hunkered down for a look. Possibly it was the door of a cupboard, but as this was an attic, I thought it more likely that it gave access to the roof space. It could only be a small space, probably big enough to store a trunk or a suitcase or two. The door had no lock, just a plain brass knob. It turned, but whoever had last painted this room had glossed over door and frame together, effectively sealing the door shut. What I needed was something sharp enough to penetrate the coat of paint, and slim enough to slide between the frame and the door. I needed my penknife, which was lying useless on Sandy Westershall's desk.

I glanced over at Dean, watching the shallow rise and fall of his chest. He was still breathing, I didn't know if he was conscious, didn't want to wake him to a world of pain. Anything useful would have been emptied from his pockets downstairs. I wouldn't risk disturbing him. I sat with my back against the wall, thinking.

For the first time I noticed that the chest of drawers was set on wooden feet, only an inch or so high, meaning that there was a narrow space underneath. I lay down and peered under it. Something was lying in the dust, on the bare boards, something tiny but within reach of my fingers. I slid my hand underneath and managed to sweep out whatever it was. I picked it up and blew off the fluff. It was a key – not a door key or a key to the chest of drawers, but the kind of small, flat key that is used to open the locks on luggage, barely an inch long. I tested the end of it with my thumb. It wasn't sharp, but it was metal, and it was hard.

Holding it between my thumb and forefinger, I tried to force the end of the key between the little door and its frame. It wasn't sharp enough to pierce the skin of paint, but the edge was hard enough for me to scrape it away, a centimetre at a time. I began scratching at the paint repeatedly, tiny flakes falling off at first, revealing brown wood underneath. After a few minutes my hand ached from holding the key, from making the same tiny movement over and over. But suddenly the end of the key slid through into space. It was easier then, once I had made a start, scraping the paint off all around as I worked my way along the top of the door to the corner and then down the side. About halfway down I tried the brass knob again, thinking that perhaps I'd freed up enough of the door to make it move. But it wasn't until I had reached the final inch that I was able to yank it open.

The smell knocked me back, earthy like toadstools, the smell of a wet forest floor. It made me cough and raise a hand to shield my mouth and nose. I peered into the small, shallow space under the roof. I was looking up at rafters and the underside of original slates. A bright shaft of light, no bigger than a penny, pierced the dimness, shone through a hole where a slate had slipped to one side. I cast one glance back at Dean and then crawled through the door into the space beyond.

There was no room to stand up. I was on my knees. I poked a finger through the hole made by the slipping slate and managed to push it aside a little more. The circle of light became a triangle, big enough to put my hand through. I felt around, found the edge of the slate, felt the single iron nail that pinned it to the rafter, jiggled it about. It gave slightly but not enough for me to pull it out. I drew my hand back inside.

I was kneeling in what looked like orange-brown dust, the spores of dry rot. I recognised it from Boring Roy's description. The rafters above my head were shrunken and dry, deep crevices in the wood laced with tiny white filaments, delicate as strands of cobweb. Cotton-wool cushions sprouted here and there: the fungus that was gradually eating the timber away, crumbling it to dust.

I put both hands on a rafter and pushed hard. It creaked and rocked. I sat with my back braced against the wall, my hands against the floor. I bent my knees and kicked. The timber groaned. Fragments fell away – not splintering, not cracking loudly, but softly crumbling.

I gave another kick, both boots full on, and heard a tile slide down the roof outside. I paused, ears straining, in case above his music Green Bastard Hat had heard the noise I was making. I peeked back through the little door into the attic, but all was quiet and still – no angry footsteps, no sudden rattle of the key in the lock. Dean lay still as the effigy on a tomb. I didn't want to, but I closed the little door on him, pulling it shut.

Then I began kicking again, hard as I could. With each kick I felt anger getting stronger within me, pounding inside me with each blow. 'That's for Gavin,' I muttered. 'That's for Ben, that's for Nathan.' I felt as if my thigh bones would break but I could see the rafter sagging beneath my onslaught and I kept going. 'That's for Nathan, that's for Dean—' No, not for Dean, because Detective Constable Dean Collins was not going to die, not if I had anything to do with it. Baby Alice, she of the crumpled red face and tiny pink fists, was going to get her daddy back.

They had taken away my phone and my penknife; they should have taken my boots. I just had time to fling myself to the side as the rafter disintegrated, collapsing in splintered chunks around me, sending up a cloud of thick, powdery dust. A slate, falling inward, caught me a glancing blow on the shoulder. I coughed, retched, struggled onto my knees. Another slate dangled by its nail before my face and I yanked it out. There was a hole in the roof big enough for me to push my head and shoulders through and I stood up. Coughing, eyes watering, I breathed in fresh air. God bless you, Boring Roy.

I saw grey sky and the tops of bare trees. Rooks, like scraps of burnt paper, rose up, calling. In front of me the roof sloped down about four feet towards a narrow gutter strewn with broken slates. In front of that was a stone parapet, about a foot in height, ornamental stone balls along its length. I placed my hands on the slates to either side of me and pushed down, wriggling my hips through the hole, out onto the roof. I sat for a moment, getting my breath. Then I stretched my legs down the slope of the roof and lay back, letting my body slide down, very slowly, until my feet were in the gutter. I bent my knees and lowered myself carefully, turning my body sideways so that I could rest in the gutter on all fours.

I peered cautiously over the parapet. It was a very long way down. Parked cars lined up on the drive looked like toys. The audience for the afternoon concert had already arrived. I crawled along the gutter until I turned the corner of the roof and peered over again. Now I was at the back of the house, looking down at the flagstones of the terrace.

Below me the long windows of the ballroom were open. It was a grey, still day, curiously mild. Perhaps those sitting in the concert felt a need for fresh air, but the open windows allowed the sound of laughter and applause to float up to me. Ricky and Morris were well away. All I had to do was to get down there, where they were. Somehow.

The old wisteria had been climbing the wall for generations, its furthermost tendrils stretched to a third-storey window about ten feet below me. But those delicate stems would not support my weight. I needed to place my feet on stronger boughs, further down. I knew that if I lowered myself over the parapet, even at full stretch, I wasn't going to reach down far enough. I would be a couple of feet short. I needed a rope, and there was no such help to hand.

I sat down in the gutter and unlaced my boots, taking them off and stripping off my socks. They were covered in a thick layer of dust; so were my jeans, which I stripped off next. It was tricky getting out of them; I had to lie down in the gutter to wriggle them over my hips. I sat up and peered over the parapet again. I didn't want to do what I had to do next, but little Alice Collins was depending on me. I wondered whether I should put my boots back on. But for what I had to do next I needed to be able to feel with my toes, I needed the flexibility of a bare foot.

I took a deep breath and crawled up onto the parapet. My arms started to tremble and I felt sick, but I didn't have time for hesitation. Dean didn't have time. If I thought about it too long my nerve would fail. A foot away was a stone ball and I gave it an experimental shove. It didn't budge. I looped my jeans around it and tied them in a knot, like a scarf around the neck of a snowman. Then I wound the denim legs around my wrists. They would give me another two feet or so. I was sweating, though my mouth felt sucked dry.

I stretched one leg over the parapet, feeling for the wall with my foot, bracing my toes against the rough stone. This is the worst bit, I told myself. Remember when you did that charity abseil off Haytor? This is just the same. Except on the abseil, there were proper ropes and a safety harness, and instructors. My life did not depend on a pair of recently purchased, extra-long, pre-loved jeans. I do not pray to any conventional god. If I pray at all, it is to Cordelia. She is the saint who must intercede for me with heaven. I prayed to her now. *Don't let me fall.* And I swung my other leg down over the parapet.

For one horrible moment I dangled, legs flailing, arms at full stretch as I clung desperately to handfuls of blue denim, dreading the sound of tearing fabric, of ripping seams.

Good old Mr Levi. The jeans bore my weight as I clung, toes scrabbling until I found a foothold, a branch sturdy enough to take the weight of my searching foot, a slenderer stem within reach of my hand.

I let go of one denim leg and grabbed. My other foot found a place to rest. For a moment I just stayed there, breathing hard, my heart racing in my chest. Then I let go of my jeans with the other hand and grasped the stem in front of me. Applause floated up from the windows below. 'Thanks,' I muttered. I felt I deserved it.

Wisteria stems, when they are young and green, twine around each other. As they thicken and stiffen with age, the stems become twisted ropes, ideal for climbing. I clung tight with my right hand as I slid my left down as far as I could reach. I didn't want to look down, so my fingers fumbled blindly until they closed around a branch. Then I moved one foot and began to search for a lower foothold. I inched my way downward, hand and foot, hand and foot, placing each carefully, testing whether it would take my weight, before I dared to move on. Below me, I could hear Ricky playing the piano, Morris singing some fast-paced patter song, but I couldn't identify it, couldn't pick out the words.

I stopped to rest for a moment. My arms were shaking, my hands so slippery with sweat I was scared stems might slide through my fingers, leave me clutching at nothing but air. Autumn had stripped the wisteria of its leaves, leaving bare stems. Now and again a blackened, withered seed pod dangled in front of my face like an ancient runner bean. Wisteria seeds are poisonous, I remembered reading somewhere, and should not be ingested. I don't know why

334

this struck me as funny – hysteria, I suppose – but I let out my breath in a silent laugh.

I dared not look down, so I looked up. I was below the windows of the third storey, which meant I must be drawing level with the windows of the second. Making progress, slowly. The fall would still kill me, but I wasn't going to fall. As I clambered down the twisted stems of the wisteria thickened and felt stronger. I dared to move more swiftly. The windows of the second storey were above me now. I risked a peep down, down to the wide-flung French windows immediately below me, down to the stone-flagged terrace just waiting to break my back, to smash my skull. For a moment the world swirled dizzyingly and I clamped my eyes shut. I clung on.

Then I heard a voice, far above.

'Look up, bitch!'

Green Bastard Hat was leaning over the parapet, aiming a shotgun straight at me. I froze, staring up at the barrels. I was a sitting duck. He grinned, his finger on the trigger. Then two things happened at once. He leapt back, swearing, swiping at something in the air that seemed to be buzzing around his head like an angry hornet. And I experienced a sickening sense of movement as the stems that I was clutching began to tear themselves slowly from the wall. I clung on as a hundred years of growth peeled itself away from its moorings. Branches snapped, stems slid through my fingers as the old trunk groaned and the whole plant arched away from the wall, taking me with it, dangling me over the terrace like a fish on a hook. Then the old trunk snapped. I seemed to be surrounded by a moving mesh of branches that landed me in a heap on the terrace and as I let go, slid me bodily through the open windows of the ballroom. Miraculously, I landed on my feet.

I stood there in my T-shirt and knickers, bare-legged as any warrior queen, as two hundred people turned to stare at me. Ricky, hands poised over the keyboard, gaped open-mouthed. In the one still moment before all hell broke loose, Morris, standing before the piano, managed a little smile. 'Hello, Juno,' he said. 'Good of you to drop in.'

CHAPTER THIRTY-FOUR

You can explain away a lot of things. You can, perhaps, explain the unexpected delivery by wisteria of a wild-haired woman in her underwear, covered in blood. But you cannot explain the presence in a locked attic of a police officer suffering from a gunshot wound. More particularly, you cannot explain it to other police officers, who seemed to arrive, as if by magic, moments after I had made my entrance into the ballroom.

Later, when things had calmed down, I asked Inspector Ford how they had arrived so quickly. Apparently, the police had received an anonymous tip-off from someone illegally flying a drone over private property that a woman was clinging on halfway up the wall of Moorworthy House while a man on the roof was pointing a shotgun at her.

By this time, I was decently covered in a coat belonging to Margaret, Wicked Witch of the West, and Dean had been carried off to hospital in a helicopter, which arrived, spectacularly, on the lawn; the Westershalls had been arrested for murder, kidnap and conspiring to kill a police officer and Mrs Johnson and Moss taken away for questioning. The last I saw of Green Bastard Hat was as he was trying to escape across the lawn, pursued by a string of uniforms. Way out in front of the pack, gaining on him fast, was none other than Detective Constable Cruella DeVille. I had to hand it to her, she could leg it.

'Go, girl!' I cheered her silently. But she came to a skidding halt, arms windmilling, struggling to keep her balance on the edge of a precipice as GBH dropped out of sight a few feet before her. Apparently, he broke his pelvis. Ha-ha.

He did nick the next available ambulance, though. And as there was no way that Inspector Ford was allowing me to go home without visiting the local accident and emergency, I was driven to hospital in a police car. As we swept out through the gates of Moorworthy House I spotted a vehicle parked across the road, and standing anxiously on the verge, Elizabeth and Olly. They waved as I swept by. I waved back frantically and cried all the way to hospital.

Most of the blood I was wearing was not my own. It belonged to Dean. I kept asking about him but all anyone could tell me was that he had been flown down to Plymouth for emergency surgery. Inspector Ford promised me an update as soon as he heard anything. And he would take my statement next morning. Meanwhile I had a lot of bruises and scrapes to be attended to. Elbows, knees and knuckles had come off particularly badly. I went through an hour and a half of antiseptic, gauze and wincing before I was finally allowed to go home. The doctor wanted to keep me overnight for observation, but I declined. I asked the nice nurse if she would order me a taxi.

'You won't need one,' she told me as she swept back the plastic curtain of the cubicle I'd been treated in. Ricky and Morris were sitting in the corridor in their dinner jackets and bow ties. 'These two gentlemen have been waiting to drive you home.'

But the wrong man died that day. It should have been wicked Uncle Sandy who made an excuse to go into the study, who put the barrel of the pistol in his mouth and pulled the trigger, but it was Jamie.

'Too proud,' Sandy said sadly, as the police took him away. 'Like his father, always too proud.'

'I didn't know you were watching Moorworthy House,' I said naively to Inspector Ford when he visited me next day.

He responded with the ghost of a smile. 'Just because you have an uncanny, and some might say, unfortunate knack of discovering dead bodies, Miss Browne, does not oblige us to let you in on all of our secrets.'

I felt like a fool. 'No, no,' I mumbled, 'of course not.'

'But I would like to thank you, Juno,' he went on, 'on behalf of Constable Collins and his wife and daughter. What you did was very brave.'

I blushed and came over all unnecessary and mumbled something incoherent. 'And he's going to be all right?' I managed at last.

The inspector smiled. 'He is.'

'So, what happens now, to the Westershalls, I mean?'

'Sandy Westershall will be charged with the murders of Nathan Parr, Ben Luscombe, Ted Croaker and the attempted murder of Dean Collins. In addition, Emma Westershall is facing certain drugs charges. Pike is in hospital under guard and will be charged with your attempted murder. Meanwhile our colleagues in London are interviewing the board members of Dravizax.' I must have looked taken aback at all this because the inspector laughed.

'Mr Moss has been very co-operative – singing like a canary, in fact. His conscience was troubling him. I don't think Mrs Johnson has any trouble with her conscience, but she knows which side her bread is buttered – and your own statement corroborates theirs to an extent. What you and Collins discovered in Applecote Pit and the tunnel leading to the Moorworthy mine is just the tip of the iceberg. Moss and Pike have been dumping hazardous waste for Dravizax in holes all over the country. The Westershalls are not the only landowners receiving a kickback from them – and Dravizax is not the Westershalls' only customer, either.'

I felt sorry for Jess. Her fiancé was dead and her father would be going to prison. And she'd known nothing at all about what was going on.

'And Gavin?' I asked. 'Is anyone going to be charged with his murder?'

The inspector puffed out his cheeks in a sigh. 'If Emma Westershall is to be believed, his death really was an accident. Unfortunately, we have not so far been able to lay hands on Mr Eddie Coates to get his version of events, but we will. Let's just say our investigation into Gavin's death is not yet concluded.'

Poor Gavin. He should have been the hero of this story. He should have been the one to slay the evil giant Dravizax with the Sword of Virangha. I took Olly to meet his parents and we showed them the film taken by the drone, film that showed Gavin waving and looking so happy. Olly sent it to their computer, so that they would have it for ever.

I went down to Plymouth to visit Dean in Derriford Hospital. By then the Environmental Protection Agency had moved into the mines at Moorworthy to begin removing the hazardous waste and decontaminate the site. Alec Pedrick had been taken on as a consultant to advise them about the bats. Apparently, they were due to hibernate very soon and there were great concerns about disturbing their roost.

When I got to the hospital, Dean's wife, Gemma, was by his bedside, along with Alice. I held the baby for a few minutes. She was sleeping soundly, her little pink eyelids tight shut. She didn't wake, but when I moved her rosebud fist away from her mouth, I swear she smiled at me. Dean was going to be fine after a spell in hospital and plenty of TLC.

TLC: tender loving care. It sounds great, doesn't it? I often feel I could do with more of it myself. But after a few days of Ricky and Morris clucking round me like mother hens, during which time Ricky stole my diary and cancelled all my appointments for the week, I decided there's a limit to how much TLC I can take. But we did rescue my van, my rucksack, my phone and, eventually, my jeans. And the Wicked Witch of the West got her coat back.

'We knew something was wrong when you didn't turn up,' Elizabeth told me when I finally made it to tea. 'We knew you wouldn't let us down without contacting us.'

Olly nodded. 'We called you lots of times.'

'I was probably in a tunnel.'

'So we decided to phone your friend Pat at the animal sanctuary—'

'And she was worried an' all,' Olly interrupted, 'because you hadn't turned up in the afternoon for your shift at the shop. And she'd been trying to get hold of you—'

And she phoned Adam and Kate, I said to myself. I'd already heard all this from the various parties concerned, but I didn't want to spoil Olly's story. Kate had insisted on contacting the police, but until I had been missing for twenty-four hours the local station weren't prepared to consider me a missing person. So they phoned them again next morning, when I hadn't come home for breakfast.

'It was Olly's idea to search for you next morning with the drone,' Elizabeth went on. 'He was sure you'd gone to Moorworthy—'

'I had this feeling!' he declared dramatically.

'We thought if we flew it over the Moorworthy estate we might see your van.'

'I'd parked it on Holne Moor.'

Elizabeth smiled. 'I practically drove past it, but Olly spotted it. I thought you might have gone walking and got lost on the moor. But Olly wanted to fly the drone over Moorworthy House one last time – and there you were!'

'I buzzed him, that fat bloke on the roof, the one with the gun, I buzzed him with the drone.' Olly's face was alight, blue eyes brimming with excitement. 'Did you see it?'

'Of course I did,' I told him. 'If you hadn't done what you did, I'd have got my head shot off.'

'We've got it on film. We had to email a copy to the police so they could see it. It's ever so funny, all buzzing round his head. Do you want to see it?'

'Later,' Elizabeth said firmly. 'Let Juno eat her tea.'

She and Olly seemed to be getting on well. The house was more cheerful, somehow. Olly had always kept it tidy, but now it seemed brighter, more polished, as if it had lost its dusty corners, the rooms aired and more lived-in. There was a vase of fresh flowers on the kitchen table, and there were plans afoot to redecorate Elizabeth's bedroom.

I was sure Olly had shot up inches since I last saw him. Free from the fear of discovery, the burden of living on his own, he seemed to be blossoming. I asked Elizabeth how things were, later, whilst he was watching the new widescreen TV that she had bought.

'Bribery and corruption,' she admitted, 'but it works.'

I eyed her doubtfully. 'No teething problems?'

'Of course. But I persuaded Olly that we didn't always have to abide by Dolly's rules, we could make up new ones of our own, as long as we both agreed on them. And so far, it's working. Actually, I believe that he enjoys having someone to boss him a little, he feels more secure.' Toby, who'd been luxuriating in the heat of the Rayburn, decided to stretch his limbs and strolled over, leaping up onto Elizabeth's lap. She stroked his head pensively. 'We're happy here in Ashburton, Toby and me. I've joined the choir at St Andrew's and I plan to find a part-time job.'

'So you're going to stay?'

'There are important things to think about. Olly will have to decide on options for his GCSE exams soon. He wants to go on to A levels and university and the standard of his written English is dreadful. I've told him, it needs a lot of work. And I'd like to buy him a new bassoon. The instrument he has on loan from the youth band is pretty basic. He deserves a better one.'

'You think he has talent?'

'He has an excellent embouchure and, for one so puny, produces a pleasingly deep and mellow tone. The bassoon is not an easy instrument to play, which is why there aren't that many players around. A bassoonist is never out of work.' She laughed. 'Not that Olly is considering music as a career at the moment.'

'He still wants to be a chef?'

'No, at the moment he wants to be a vet. I think it's the effect of working at the animal sanctuary . . . By the way, I must tell you' – she lowered her voice so that Olly wouldn't hear – 'tomorrow, Prudence is coming to tea.'

'Who's Prudence?'

'Well, judging from the picture on Olly's phone, she's a rather scrumptious little thirteen-year-old. She plays the flute in the youth band.' She hesitated a moment, her expression becoming more serious. 'And we have moved Dolly to Oakdene, as far as our next-door neighbour is concerned.'

'So soon?'

'April was away for a few days. It seemed like the ideal opportunity.'

'And she has never questioned your being Olly's aunt?'

'Why would she?' She stroked Toby's head reflectively for a moment before she looked back at me. 'And I don't see any reason why Dolly can't continue to rest in peace beneath the flowers—'

'Ah!' I said, surprised. 'Olly told you about that bit?'

'He did. I was flattered, took it as a sign of trust. When the time comes . . . which is whenever Olly is ready . . . we simply tell April next door that Dolly has passed away peacefully at Oakdene. Of course, we'll have to kill her off officially in order to stop her pension—'

'What about the death certificate?'

She raised a delicate eyebrow. 'It can't be that difficult to get hold of a death certificate. I'm sure one can be purchased on the Internet if one looks hard enough.'

'You can get copies of existing certificates,' I agreed. 'But the problem is no original exists.'

'I'm sure with a little careful forgery . . .' She shrugged. 'I shall do some research into the subject.'

You know, I like Elizabeth.

After Olly had shown me the film of GBH on the roof five times, including speeded-up and going backwards, he played me a tune, Elizabeth accompanying him on the newly tuned piano. It was a piece they were practising for his music exam. It had taken Elizabeth some time to persuade him that he should enter for it, but she was confident he would pass. As I walked down the path, they were engrossed in going through it again, happily arguing over some minor detail. They didn't even realise I had gone.

'I don't know if I'm ever going to be any good at this antiques business,' I confessed to Ricky and Morris.

Morris looked at me anxiously across a plate of home-made

345

scones. 'Why do you say that, Juno? I thought you enjoyed it.'

'Well, yesterday, I went to the flea market and I picked up a really rare piece of Poole pottery that this lady was selling for a pound. It had been her mother's and she didn't like it. And I knew what it was really worth and how much profit I could make on it and frankly, I felt like a thief.'

'Oh, don't tell me—' Ricky began, rolling his eyeballs.

'So I gave her a fiver and . . .'

He groaned and pretended to bang his head on the kitchen table. 'Look, if the silly cow didn't know what it was worth, that's her fault. She could've looked it up on the Internet, same as you.'

'I know,' I conceded, 'and I know that the whole point of this business is to buy low and sell high and make a profit, but somewhere in the middle is what a thing is actually worth, its true value—'

'Which changes all the bloody time,' Ricky finished for me.

'It's true, Juno,' Morris agreed earnestly. 'Look at my teapots. Some of them are worth far more now than when I bought them, but some of them are worth a lot less. Antiques go in and out of fashion.'

'It's a game, sweetheart!' Ricky cried in exasperation. 'Dealing in antiques is just a bloody game. You take it all too seriously.'

'I suppose.' I wasn't convinced.

'A thing is only worth what someone is prepared to pay for it,' he insisted.

Morris patted my hand. 'Tell you what, there's an auction at Rendells later this week. Why don't we go together, see if they've got anything interesting?'

'Good idea,' Ricky nodded, lighting a cigarette. 'We can keep an eye on your bidding.'

'By the way,' Morris added. 'We need to ask you a favour. We've got a concert coming up in December at Ashburton Arts Centre. Someone had to drop out, leaving the organisers with a gap in their programme, so they asked us if we would put together a concert, you know, fill in. And we thought the proceeds could go to Honeysuckle Farm, what d'you think?'

'That would be wonderful! Pat will be delighted—'

'Blimey! That's something I'd buy a ticket for,' Ricky exhaled, 'to see Pat looking delighted.'

'Don't be rotten.' I frowned. 'What's the favour?'

'Well, as it will be near Christmas,' Morris rattled on excitedly, 'we thought we'd end the show with our potted pantomime—'

'Oh, great!' I loved their potted pantomime. The two of them played all the different roles and the whole thing lasted just ten minutes.

'So will you help us backstage with the quick changes?' Ricky asked.

'Of course.'

'We thought that we might do it again for our Boxing Day party—'

'You are coming, aren't you?' Ricky interrupted.

Of course I was coming. No one in their right mind would turn down an invitation for their Boxing Day party. The food and entertainment were legendary. 'Can I bring Elizabeth and Olly?'

He waved his fag airily. 'Bring who you want.'

That stopped me for a moment, because the person I

would have liked to have brought to their party was Nathan Parr. He had been on his way to meet me on the night that he was murdered. When police dragged his body from the wreck of his car, they'd found a red carnation pinned to his lapel. A thing is only worth what someone is prepared to pay for it and for the things Nathan valued he had paid with his life. I would like to have known him better, sorry that now that could never happen. I would never even see for myself what he looked like without that pirate hat.

My thoughts must have been written on my face because Ricky suddenly reached out a hand to cover mine. 'Don't be sad, sweetheart.'

I smiled at him, at both of them. 'I'm OK.'

'Talking of Christmas,' Ricky went on, in a very obvious attempt to distract me, 'have you thought about what you're doing in the shop? It's November already. You retailers have got to start thinking about these things. You've got to make a bid for the Christmas shoppers, you'll have to put some decorations up.'

'Pat and Sophie have got lots of ideas,' I admitted, sighing, 'but I haven't really thought about Christmas.' The only decision I had made was that I was going to take over Gavin's bookshelves. I was determined to have a bookshop in *Old Nick's*, and if no one else was interested in renting that unit, I would fill it myself.

'Well, we've had a wonderful idea, haven't we, Maurice?'

Alarm bells began ringing. Mentally, I braced myself.

'We can turn your back room into a winter wonderland – Santa's Grotto – bring in the parents with small kids – put on a bit of a show.'

'Well, I really don't think—' I began.

'Maurice will be Santa, won't you?' he rattled on. 'And I can be Professor Yule, in charge of the reindeer—'

'Reindeer?'

'Hasn't Pat got a reindeer?'

'No. She's got a llama . . .'

'Well, that'll do.'

It was only at that moment I realised they were winding me up. I didn't let on that I knew. 'What a wonderful idea,' I agreed. I selected a scone and helped myself to jam and a dollop of cream. I put the cream on first – this is Devon, we do things proper – then the jam. Then I took a big bite, sat back and let them prattle on.

ACKNOWLEDGEMENTS

My thanks go to Jenny Donaldson at Gnash! bookshop in Ashburton, for opening my eyes to the scope and beauty of the graphic novel. I'd also like to thank the Devon Bat Group for their very informative website, and for being there for the bats. I'd get nowhere without my agent, Teresa Chris, the team at Allison & Busby, and my husband, Martin, who locks me in the study and pours tea through the keyhole.

STEPHANIE AUSTIN graduated from Bristol University with a degree in English and Education and has enjoyed a varied career as an artist, astrologer, and trader in antiques and crafts. More respectable professions include teaching and working for Devon Schools Library Service. When not writing, she is involved in local amateur theatre as an actor and director. She lives on the English Riviera in Devon where she attempts to be a competent gardener and cook.

stephanieaustin.co.uk

The Girl's Guide to Being a Working Mum

How to be happy at work and happy at home

Caitlin Friedman and Kimberly Yorio

A & C Black • London

First published in the United States by Broadway, 2009

First published in Great Britain in 2009 by

A & C Black Publishers Ltd
36 Soho Square, London W1D 3QY
www.acblack.com

A CIP record for this book is available from the British Library.

ISBN: 9-781-4081-1566-4

This book is produced using paper that is made from wood grown in
managed, sustainable forests. It is natural, renewable and recyclable. The
logging and manufacturing processes conform to the environmental
regulations of the country of origin.

Design by Fiona Pike, Pike Design, Winchester
Typeset by RefineCatch Limited, Bungay, Suffolk
Printed in the United Kingdom by Cox & Wyman, RG1 8EX

Contents

Introduction

While we were in Seattle during our book tour for *The Girl's Guide to Kicking Your Career into Gear*, a woman approached us after a talk. She looked curious, but we read something slightly hostile in her expression as well.

'So you girls live in New York?' she asked.

We nodded, both wondering where she was headed.

'Wow. Don't you feel terrible leaving your kids?'

Though we felt like just shouting 'No!', the truth is much more complicated. We love our kids (Caitlin has toddler twins and Kim's son is in primary school) and miss them while we're gone. And many days we feel guilty, really guilty, about walking out the door. But this time, we had earned the right to go on the road. We certainly weren't feeling terrible about travelling to promote a book we spent two years writing. Our kids were being cared for by their *fathers* and, frankly, we had earned this time away.

In fact, if we had been completely honest, the woman would have probably been shocked. We *loved* touring for our book and the break it offered. For Caitlin, it was the first time in years that she could sleep uninterrupted and past 6:30 a.m. (when we didn't have to be up to do morning television interviews). And both of us were thrilled with the response the book generated, along with the opportunity to connect with the women we wrote the book to help. Sure, we flew on red-eyes, slept in uncomfortable hotel rooms, gave interviews at the crack of dawn, led lunch and evening workshops (often followed by late dinners with clients), and yet it still *felt* like a holiday.

Crazy? Sadly, not at all.

Being a working mother is tough. Juggling your parental, professional and spousal responsibilities while occasionally addressing your own needs is no small feat. When we admit we need help and look for support, the first suggestion we hear is work less – as if it's the most obvious and easily-done thing in the world and we must be brain-damaged not to have thought of it ourselves. Even if we could afford to give up the income and our careers, why would we want to? We love work and believe we are better mothers because of it. Society doesn't ask men to choose between work and family. Why should we?

And to think, we've come so far, we working mothers. We are no longer a minority, automatically receiving sideways glances of disapproval – or outright lectures – from friends, family and colleagues. We are an accepted, important and driving part of the work force. We can do as good a job as any childless colleague or married man with a stay-at-home wife. Our daily challenges are now the issues of national and political discussion – the availability of safe and affordable childcare, and health care for all children, as well as the endless juggling of family and work.

These are facts, but the reality somehow doesn't connect. The prevailing wisdom in this country remains that you need to make a choice between having a career and raising your kids. The perception remains that after having a child, the professional *you* will change as much as the personal *you* – even if you are the exact same employee you were before.

In 1998, journalist Betty Holcomb wrote a book called, *Not Guilty! The Good News for Working Mothers* published by Simon & Schuster. It's a substantial and superbly researched book that explores the scientific studies, the media and the public's impressions, as well as mothers' perceptions about what a 'good mother's' role in society should be. Her extraordinary research supports that we can work outside the home and still be good mothers. She writes about attitudes that make it harder for women not to feel squeezed all of the time, and of course as you can guess from the title, she writes about the guilt mothers have about going to work while also raising families. It's a great book and not only did we learn a lot, we were really taken aback. Almost everything she wrote more than 10 years ago still holds true today. What's going on? Why aren't society's attitudes toward working mothers changing? Why aren't there more resources for working mothers in 2009 to help us feel less time-pressured, less racked with guilt, and less overwhelmed by their responsibilities? And perhaps most importantly: Why do working mothers not only earn less than men but also working women who happen to be childless?

We wish we had the answers to these questions, but in the absence of a more quickly changing society, we can at least arm you with the tools and strategies to set yourself up for success at work and at home. Working mothers need support. And support is not that easy to come by. If you're not one of the very few who are blessed with an accessible, available, willing and competent family to help you, you are forced to juggle between paid childcare and spousal support. And that's after the baby is born. The challenges begin the day you get pregnant.

How do you schedule doctor's appointments so they don't impact on your working day? What if you're suffering from morning sickness? How do you manage to complete a day's work when you are too tired to even eat? How can you afford to be out of work on unpaid maternity leave?

Where's the help going to coming from? All too rarely from your employer or even your spouse (more on that in chapter seven). While we don't want to scare you off because we're just in the introduction and because this book is going to offer a number of solutions for you from women who are making it work – the sad fact is that working mums are often on their own. So much so that organisations are being set up to help them get the support and resources they desperately need.

We want you to be aware of what we're up against and armed with the tools and powers to be the best advocate for yourself and other mums. This book is designed to give you those critical keys to success. In addition to support (paid or unpaid) if a working mum can take a long-range view of things and not worry so much about each day, learn to ask for what she wants (and needs), delegate more, communicate well, sell her accomplishments, fight for what she deserves at home and at work, make time for herself and start saying *no* as much as she says *yes* then it is possible to have a satisfying career and a thriving family.

We aren't delusional. We know this is a tall order. But this book will offer inspiration and ideas that will make you more successful on every front. It is extremely difficult to keep your career a priority but it is also essential not to give up your goals and dreams because you are now a mother. We love our work and we love our children. We are not defined by either but by both and this book reflects our experiences and those from more than 100 other women who choose to be working mums.

In interviews with working mums, children of working women, therapists, human resource professionals, counsellors, and career coaches, we offer solutions that work for all involved: the partner, children, boss, employees and – most of all – YOU.

You've Got Nine Months to Get Ready. Hint: It Goes Quickly

Congratulations. You're pregnant or thinking about becoming pregnant. You are about to embark on the scariest and most unique nine months of your life. You've signed up for the pregnancy calendar and you eagerly watch the progress of your growing baby. You've cut down on or given up caffeine and alcohol, stopped eating runny cheeses and sushi and are busy stuffing your face with fresh vegetables and folic acid. You've bought every book on pregnancy and are busily scouring websites for all the news you need to know. In between all of this fun and excitement, you go to work. You, after all, are a career girl – a career girl who is also going to be a mum. You are thrilled by the prospect (and perhaps a little scared) and can't wait to shout it from the rooftops once that third month has passed. But don't start shouting yet. You've got a lot of planning to do first.

This chapter will give you the information and strategies you need to successfully navigate your pregnancy. After reading chapter one, you will be armed with all the tools you need to go on a work- and worry-free maternity leave. We inform you about your rights, the options for childcare and share resources and stories that you will support you in this very scary and exhilarating time in your life.

Good luck. The next nine months are going to be a whirlwind.

First Things First, Know Your Rights

This can get dense. And as with all legalese, you may just want to skip right over it. Don't. Don't even put it off until later. You absolutely must know your legal rights and options and here they are. All information was correct at the time of going to press, but we've included the relevant Web links so that you can keep up to speed with any changes.

In the UK, employers have a legal obligation to look after the health and safety of pregnant employees. They need to ensure that the pregnant person is not obliged to lift heavy loads, work in confined spaces or unsuitable workstations, work in stressful or violent environments, or be exposed to potentially harmful substances such as lead.

The Employment Rights Act of 1996 defines your legal rights in terms of ordinary maternity leave, additional maternity leave and statutory maternity pay. Part VIII is the relevant section, and you can read it online at www.opsi.gov.uk/acts/acts1996/ukpga_19960018_en_1, but here is a summary of the most important points.

Maternity leave (ordinary)

At the time of writing, as a pregnant UK employee you are entitled to a period of 26 weeks' ordinary maternity leave, regardless of length of service to your employer. To qualify, you must tell your employer – by the end of the 15th week before the week when the birth is expected – that you are pregnant, the week you are due, and the date you intend to start maternity leave. You can normally start your maternity leave whenever you choose, as long as it's no earlier than the beginning of the 11th week before the expected week of the birth.

Your employer must then inform you in writing, within 28 days of your notification, of your expected return date. However, you can change this date if you give your employer 28 days' notice.

During maternity leave an employee is entitled to all the benefits of the terms of her normal contract (except for remuneration). At the end of the maternity leave, she has the legal right to return to her original job. If the situation dictates that the original job is no longer available, the employer must offer a suitable alternative vacancy. If the employer cannot offer suitable alternative work, she may be entitled to redundancy pay.

Statutory maternity pay

Statutory Maternity Pay (SMP) should be paid if a woman has been employed by the same employer for a continuous period of 26 weeks or more (calculated from the 15th week before the expected week of the birth) and has average weekly earnings at least equal to the lower earnings limit for National Insurance contributions. SMP can be paid for up to 26 weeks, and is paid by the employer but partly (or, in the case of small companies, entirely) reimbursed by the state.

Additional maternity leave

An employee with 26 weeks' continuous service (calculated from the beginning of the 14th week before the expected week of the birth) is entitled to an additional 26 weeks' maternity leave. For the duration of this period her contract of employment continues but with limited terms and conditions. This means it is possible to be away from your job on maternity leave for around 52 weeks in total. If you are eligible for additional maternity leave, your employer will assume that you will be taking it. At the end of additional maternity leave, as with ordinary maternity leave, you are entitled to return to your original job or, if this is not reasonably practicable, to a suitable alternative job.

According to the Sex Discrimination Act of 1975, a 'period of legal protection' begins when a woman becomes pregnant and ends at the end of her period of ordinary maternity leave (or her additional maternity leave if she is entitled to it) or if, earlier than this, she returns to work after her pregnancy. If she is not entitled to any maternity leave connected with the pregnancy then this protected period ends two weeks after the end of the pregnancy. Within this protected period, a person is said to discriminate against a women if, on the grounds of her pregnancy, or the fact that she is exercising her right to take maternity leave, she is treated 'less favourably'. This would include, for example, not getting a job or being passed up for a promotion directly because of pregnancy. This discrimination also applies if the woman is suffering from an illness as a consequence of a pregnancy.

The Sex Discrimination Act also states that employers must offer a pregnant employee not only maternity-related remuneration, but also increase-related remuneration in respect of when she is not on maternity leave (eg standard pay increase for all employees), and bonus-related remuneration if she is on compulsory maternity leave. You can read the full text of the Sex Discrimination Act here at www.opsi.gov.uk/si/si2008/uksi_20080656_en_1.

The law can (and does!) change regularly, as do maternity pay and leave entitlements, so check regularly on the useful government website DirectGov (www.direct.gov.uk) for updates.

It can be a challenge to decipher how your employer will react to absences due to pregnancy, pregnancy-related health issues, and childbirth-related absences. If you are not aware of your rights and the laws and guidelines that are in place to protect you, you could face a maternity or parental leave that is cobbled together from sick leave, holiday entitlement or unpaid family leave. You do not need to do this! But meticulous planning is crucial in the early stages of your pregnancy. The goal is to set yourself up with all of the necessary information as soon as possible, so that you can make both a seamless exit and stress-free return to the workplace.

Save Your Time, You're Going to Need It

As your pregnancy progresses, you will begin to craft a birth plan. You'd be smart to create a maternity leave plan, too. Your goal is to maximise the paid time off and it quickly becomes a juggling act. Here are a few ways to stockpile your days:

- Schedule all doctors' appointments for off-work hours if you can. In the UK, you are entitled to take time off for doctor's appointments, so there's nothing wrong in being out of the office for this very legitimate reason, but as far as possible, show your boss and the team that you're still committed to getting your work done too. You want to demonstrate to the boss and team that your priority is still the job (even if it isn't).
- Go to work even when you're feeling ropey – provided that you can get the job done. It's better to show up and get something done then use up a sick day that you might need later.
- Do not go to work if you feel so lousy that you can't get your work done. Go to the doctor instead. While you may think you're being a trooper, you may be giving your boss a reason to deal with you harshly or treat you differently due to your pregnancy.
- Begin a savings plan: not for the baby's eventual university career, but for when you are on maternity pay at home taking care of the baby. Many mums-to-be don't realise that they can start a 'salary sacrifice' scheme that helps to provide to return-to-work childcare a few months down the line. For more information, visit www.childcarevouchers.co.uk.

Girl Talk

Elizabeth is an executive at a major national retailer in her sixth month of pregnancy. She is feeling absolutely great and starting to put her maternity leave plan together. Her company's paid maternity leave is based on years of service and she is one year shy of the ten year bonus of extra time off. As she's based in the United States, she's earned eight weeks of paid maternity and two weeks at half-pay. If she has a C-section she will get an extra two weeks paid. (This latter option is not available in the UK.)

She has four weeks of vacation and plans to use those as a back-up if she's not ready, but right now she's planning to come back when the ten weeks are up. She's recently been promoted so she plans to be available to the staff during her leave. She had a bad experience when one of her colleagues chose 'radio silence' as her maternity leave plan so plans to be as accessible as she needs to be.

Elizabeth has done everything to ensure that she will have a smooth maternity leave, including planning her delivery to coincide with the quietest time in retail, January. She is planning to be back in the office when things kick off in March. She's hired an additional person to support her number two while she's out and she's hoping for the best.

She does have a few worries though. Her husband would prefer that she didn't return to work, so she knows there will be a few struggles in the beginning, and secondly, and wisely, she realises that she has no idea how she's going to feel and what's going to happen after the baby is born, so her biggest plan is take a 'wait-and-see' attitude. She's planned as much as she can and she's hoping for the best.

The Paid-Leave Squeeze

The UK fares quite well in comparison to some countries in its provision of maternity leave and maternity pay, especially when compared to the United States which, along with Swaziland, Liberia and Papua New Guinea offers no paid leave to pregnant women at all. However, Sweden offers all parents 16 months' paid leave per child. In Estonia mothers can take up to 18 months' of paid leave, and Bulgaria is even more generous: mothers are entitled to 45 days' paid sick leave before the birth, two years' paid maternity leave afterwards, and the option of an unpaid third year of leave.

How Family-Friendly is Your Workplace?

Most of us expect that our employers and colleagues will be thrilled when we announce our good news. After all, having a baby is a miraculous and magical event. And while that's true for you, it's certainly not true for your employer. Many employers become downright hostile when you announce your news. They are looking down the road to when you are out on maternity leave or running home to tend to a sick child. But don't be discouraged because there are a growing number of companies and organisations that are prioritising family-friendliness and trying to create a work environment that supports the employee and her changing familial needs.

In the UK, the public sector performs well (the Crown Prosecution Service and the British Council in particular), and larger companies such as BT, Hewlett-Packard and Accenture have traditionally also had good packages for parents. Small companies can struggle more. As a small business owner herself, Kim can point to a number of times her 'mother guilt' has come not from missing a school play but rather by getting angry when an employee's family responsibilities affected productivity. Your pregnancy and impending motherhood are hard on an employer and you can't assume that just because your boss is female that you won't get a less than

7

positive reaction to your needs. As much as Kim is thrilled for you personally when you tell her you're pregnant, the manager in her unfortunately jumps to pregnancy brain, maternity leave, breast-feeding schedules and ultimately, reduced productivity. And Kim is a woman and a mother. Imagine how your male manager will take the news. Even in the most progressive company with the most progressive managers, the truth of family-friendliness emerges the second you announce your pregnancy.

We wish it were as simple as flexi-time and a softly-lit, private area to express milk. Corporate culture and politics are a fact of life for pregnant women and mothers. Workplaces become separated into the parents and non-parents (or pregnant women and non-pregnant ones). No one can deny that caregivers (and we're including parents as well as non-parents who are taking care of relatives) have more responsibilities vying for their time and attention than non-caregivers. Caregivers also have different priorities. The job is no longer the only thing in our lives. Websites and message boards are lit up with complaints on both sides of the issue. The employees, mostly women, who don't have children, feel unfairly saddled with assignments that require travel and late nights. Working women with children feel like they have been moved aside as the top performers because of their other responsibilities, which is probably the most obvious factual support for the sad truth that things in the workplace really haven't changed. But being aware of and sensitive to these issues will help you navigate the office politics and find ways to work more effectively with your colleagues who have a different reality at home.

Time to Break the News

There's one last piece of research to do before you share your news. Make sure you know your job performance status. More than a few women who have announced their pregnancy have been fired shortly after their announcement for an unrelated issue. Pull out the notes of your most recent review if you have one. Investigate

Is Your Workplace Family Friendly?

Is your office really working-parent friendly? Ask yourself these 10 questions. The answers will paint a clearer picture than your human resources manual ever could.

1. Are you the first woman in your organisation to become pregnant? Good luck, pioneer. You have an opportunity to create a positive precedent for those who follow.
2. When other women have shared their pregnancy news what has been the reaction? Have you noticed griping and gossiping behind her back?
3. Do you sense a feeling that they are happy for your/her news, but really more worried about decreased productivity, maternity leave and whether or not the women will return from maternity leave?
4. Did management encourage and support the pregnant woman to make a plan for her maternity leave?
5. Did management and/or colleagues show any interest in the pregnancy or act as if nothing had changed?
6. How did the pregnant woman's role in the organisation change when she returned from maternity leave?
7. Did the pregnant woman do all she could to prepare for a smooth exit and return?
8. Is your manager the type who doesn't want you

> taking sick days even when you're laid low with a stomach bug?
> 9. Are there qualified employees in your organisation or on your team who can assume some of your duties while you are gone?
> 10. Are there mothers in senior management positions?

how many sick and vacations days you have left. Review your current workload and what it will look like in six months.

Now you're ready. You've consulted the human resources manual. You've taken a good hard look at the culture and put the inevitable off for as long as possible. You are in your second trimester and its becoming impossible to hide behind loose fitting-clothes. If you don't break the news soon, it's going to get out without you controlling the message. And that is the last thing you want after all of your careful planning.

Schedule a private meeting with your boss and tell her in a professional way that you are indeed pregnant and due in six months. 'Your message needs to be, 'I care about this job, and I'm going to do everything I can to make sure things run smoothly while I'm not here," says DeAnne Rosenberg, a career consultant and author of *A Manager's Guide to Hiring the Best Person for Every Job*.

Let her know you would like to tell the team yourself and schedule another meeting to review your workload in a couple of weeks. Tell her that you will be formulating a plan and a recommendation for how the workload can be allocated while you are on maternity leave but don't make any recommendations until you have a constructed a thorough plan. The next section will guide you through how to do just that.

Help Them Help You

What do you do in a day? A week? A month? Write it all down. The goal is to create a written version of your office life that your manager and colleagues can consult while you are out. Include your job description, a calendar with daily, weekly and/or monthly duties. Some tasks will require step-by-step instructions. Include a list of helpful hints, client information and contact information for vendors, partners or any other people who could possibly be involved. Schedule training with the person covering for you well in advance of your planned departure. Pregnancy is a very unpredictable condition. One day you're fine and the next could find you getting early contractions and ordered on bed rest. We certainly hope that's not the case, but better safe than sorry. The career advisors on Monster.com suggest you create a workplace map where you write down (or draw) how someone else can easily navigate your workspace. Make sure regular clients or customers know that you'll be on leave and give instructions as to who they should contact while you're gone. And finally, set your email to automatically forward to the new temp, your home office, or your supervisor and leave a similar message on your voicemail.

It's best to start 'The Book of You' in your second trimester when your mind is still clear and your energy is at its peak. Most of this extra work will have to be done on your own time, and the last thing you want to be doing in your ninth month is staying late drawing a map of your desk!

Top Pregnancy Do's and Don'ts

1. **Don't share scans with your team.**
2. **Do keep photos on your desk.**
3. **Don't shop for baby furniture, plan the shower, interview nannies, or research baby names at work.**

4. **Do any personal errands at lunchtime.**
5. **Don't take on additional after-work responsibilities.**
6. **Do offer to take on planning, projects or meetings that are scheduled during work hours.**
7. **Don't talk about your excitement for your upcoming work break to colleagues.**
8. **Do plan your maternity leave carefully and document any conversations or e-mail exchanges with your boss about returning to work.**
9. **Don't fill everyone in on the directions from your doctor unless there's a potential emergency you need to alert people to.**
10. **Do eat and drink throughout the day.**

Pregnancy Brain and Other Side Effects of the Happiest Time of Your Life

Pregnant women fall into two camps: those who feel great during their pregnancy and those who don't. Their work lives can be very different. If you're feeling great, there's no reason not to make your work life as rich and full as it was before you were pregnant. And if you're feeling poorly, it's a good idea to try to fake it.

If you're not suffering from morning sickness, you're lucky. The statistics show that more than 50% of women do. You are also exhausted. Even though you want to behave as if nothing has changed, your body betrays you. It is changing every minute during your pregnancy. When Kim was pregnant, she fell asleep at 8:30 every night of her first trimester – and this from a girl who would normally have three or four work or social evening functions a week.

You also get this thing called 'Pregnancy Brain'. Information is going in, but processed thoughts aren't coming out. For years men and women have thought it was an excuse that pregnant women were using to cover up for their forgetfulness or odd behaviours. Fortunately, there is now proof from a 2008 study by two Australian researchers for the University of New South Wales. The study, published in *The Journal of Clinical and Experimental Neuropsychology*, found that the memory loss can extend up to a year after birth and was shown to effect new memories more than old. For example, a new phone number or person is really hard to remember when you are pregnant but information that you've had stored for a while is relatively accessible. Kim used to forget why she left the house and it took some real focus and a look at her electronic calendar to figure out where she was supposed to be. Caitlin's memory was pretty much shot for three years after having the twins so to help her work better, she started to take notes on what she agreed to or discussed. At one point she even carried a digital recorder. So if people start saying things like 'I already told you I was coming home late tonight,' or 'But you said that I had another week to finish the report,' believe them. You might have developed the Teflon memory that accompanies baby brain. The good news is that the condition doesn't seem to last more than one or two years. Pregnancy Brain can take quite a toll at work, especially as the Australian scientists have also shown that multi-tasking is one of the first functions to be disrupted.

You may not realise your brain is changing, but there's no missing the big changes in your body. Gaining weight, even from a growing baby, can be stressful and depressing for pregnant women. When we lose confidence in our appearance, it's easy to lose confidence on other fronts too. Make looking good a priority – even when you're feeling poorly. Dress for success. By all means investigate the increasing number of maternity-wear ranges but remember that you can be clever and resourceful with your pre-pregnancy wardrobe. For example, low-rise jeans are a great option in the beginning, because they sit under the little bump.

But you are going to need a few key new pieces for your working wardrobe. Be smart about your investment, though. A couple of great pieces (not shapeless shifts), supplemented with inexpensive t-shirts and yoga pants will go a long way. Kim survived her entire pregnancy on three form-fitting cashmere sweaters and three pairs of black pants in escalating sizes. She found trousers a better option because they could camouflage the sensible shoes that she had to wear, both for safety and ever-swelling ankles. These days so many maternity clothes are stylish, affordable and hard-wearing that you can pass them along to pregnant friends. Many familiar High Street names (such as Next and Dorothy Perkins) have maternity ranges, but specialist retailers include Blooming Marvellous (www.bloomingmarvellous.co.uk), From Here to Maternity (www.fromheretomaternity.co.uk) and Isabella Oliver (www.isabellaoliver.com), which stocks stylish wraparound dresses that expand with your bump. If you work in an industry where expensive suits are the norm, check out Crave Maternity (www.cravematernity.co.uk) or Push Maternity for some higher-priced but good quality pieces.

When Bad Things Happen to Good Women

The prevailing wisdom is that getting and staying pregnant is the easiest thing in the world. Unfortunately the reality is quite different. Sadly many women have difficulties in this regard and longer you wait, the harder it often is. So take care girls, you could be in for a rough road as these two stories (both with happy endings!) illustrate. We share these stories as a reminder that things don't (and won't) always go as planned, but you can see from these experiences that a positive attitude, clear-headedness and flexibility will help you navigate even the toughest waters.

The Word: What Doesn't Kill You Makes You Stronger

Even before she was married, US-based Katie Wainright knew she would have fertility problems. At 33, she got married and sought fertility treatment. After reviewing her history, the doctors skipped over all of the less invasive fertility options and went straight to IVF. In Vitro Fertilization is no picnic. When all other methods of assisted reproduction have failed (drugs, insemination, etc.) doctors resort to in vitro fertilisation or IVF. Simply put, a woman is given hormones by injection to stimulate egg production. Her hormone levels are monitored daily and when they hit the right level, the eggs are retrieved from the ovaries. Doctors will then fertilise them in a lab and monitor which ones look the most viable. Two to five of the most viable eggs are implanted in the woman's uterus with hopes one or more will attach and grow into a healthy foetus. It's painful and time-consuming.

For Katie, IVF meant that every morning she left her apartment at 6:30 a.m. to get to the hospital by 7:30 a.m. to get on the list for blood work so she could make it across town and be at her desk by 9:00 a.m. It should be noted that there were never fewer than 100 women at the hospital waiting for their blood work with her. And every evening she and her husband had to be home by 6:30 p.m. to administer her daily and painful shot of hormones. She wasn't telling anyone at work that she was going through fertility treatments, so getting to work on time was her number one priority. But it was by no means easy. The hormones made her feel crazy and stressed and she was desperate for it to work. And luckily it did. She got pregnant with her first child on the first try.

Then something went wrong. She had a bad reaction or a side effect (they never determined which) to the IVF and she became 'hyper stimulated' from the hormones. She blew up (literally; she started retaining fluid) and ended up in the hospital for 48 hours and away from work for 10 days. This is a dangerous condition and, although she was out of danger, she looked five months pregnant in her third week.

She told everyone at work that she had an allergic reaction to some medication and after 10 days went back to work as if nothing had happened. (It's important to note that Katie had a stressful job at the time, running a publicity department for a major publisher – you didn't just drop out of work for 10 days in her kind of job.)

She kept her pregnancy a secret for three months, except for the one colleague she had to tell because she was travelling on business and needed someone she could trust to administer her hormone shot (even after she was pregnant she continued to get the hormone shots).

Her first son Jack was born two weeks late after an emergency C-section and, all in all, after the fertility treatments, a severe bout of carpal tunnel from the pregnancy, and an emergency surgery, Katie had a healthy baby boy. After 12 weeks, she went back to work in great form. Her management welcomed her back and, although there was a bit of a tough transition because of the stress she had been under, she was back to 100% within a couple of weeks. She even earned a promotion to Associate Publisher. Things at work were operating very well. Her department was successful and her boss had promised her increased responsibilities and new challenges.

Katie and her husband had always wanted two children and so when Jack was a little over a year old they started the IVF process again. After 13 months and four failed attempts, Katie was despondent. During the fourth retrieval, they found a polyp, which can form when you have too many fertility treatments. It was removed surgically and Katie needed a month to recover before she could try again.

She was still keeping her secret, but it was taking a toll on her personally and professionally. Two weeks after an implantation, she would call from work for the result, only to hear yet again that she wasn't pregnant. Every time the IVF failed, she'd go through a hormone crash. As much as her mind (and body) wasn't on the job, Katie poured herself into work for two important reasons. First, she needed something to go well in her life and, secondly, she had exhausted her insurance and was using her savings to pay for the treatments at $7,000 a pop. [In the UK, roughly 25% of IVF is funded by the NHS, but in the private sector each round costs between £3,000 and £5,000.] She literally couldn't afford to lose her job.

After the third failed attempt, Katie told her boss what was going on. She was still doing her job, but was distracted and felt obligated to share the news. While her boss was personally sympathetic, she made it clear that it was Katie's problem and had better not impact her work.

On her sixth and final IVF (any more were just too dangerous) Katie got pregnant. She was panicked about the possibility of miscarriage, however, she had to tell her boss early in her pregnancy because they were going to a trade show where she couldn't do any heavy lifting. Her pregnancy proceeded as normal for the next few weeks and she was back to work in full form.

At her 30th week sonogram, everything looked great. Three days later she was spotting and headed to the hospital for monitoring. The baby's heartbeat was dipping slightly, so they admitted her for observation. She was worried about missing any more work time because she had been so distracted and wanted to go out on maternity leave with everything in good shape. And then six doctors rushed into her room because the baby was in distress. They moved her into a private room, put her on an IV to try and develop the baby's lungs and sent a team down from the NICU to explain the realities of a baby born at 30 weeks.

She heard what they were saying but didn't believe it. She had to get back to work. She wasn't delivering a baby that day. And then she felt a gush of liquid, which turned out to be blood, and by 1:00 p.m. on September 28, 55 days early and less than four hours after she had gotten to the hospital, she was rushed into emergency surgery and delivered a very sick, 2.8-pound baby girl.

Her husband called her boss and her NICU marathon began. After a couple of weeks of pumping, staying with her baby all day and going home to her son at night, Katie asked if she could come back to work part-time. She wanted to work then so she could take off when her baby was coming home from the NICU.

That was when she realised how badly the situation was for her at work. Apparently, things had been running so smoothly in her absence that she wasn't wanted back until she was ready to come back full-time. When she finally went back to work, eight weeks after her tiny daughter came home, she read the writing on the wall. She was not welcome in her job anymore and had better start looking for a new one. Three months later she began interviewing for a dream position that she landed.

We asked her why she didn't just give up working for a while and stay home with her babies and her answer struck a note with us: 'Before I came back from having Lucy, I loved my job. I like working and I am not cut out to be just at home to be doing the childcare thing. Plus, we need the income. My children are well-rounded and have a wonderful life. I love having a career, and I have worked for 18 years. I did not realise how much stress I was under at the time, but I was fortunate that it all worked out for my career and my family. I remind myself now, what doesn't kill me will make me stronger. I love my new job, and even if it is easily three times more responsibility and stress than the one I left, my children are doing well, and I am no longer distracted. I am very lucky.'

The Word: On the Job

Kara was a sports journalist for a national magazine married to another sports journalist and trying to start a family. She was about 10 weeks pregnant when she was assigned to cover a hockey tournament training camp. At the first practice, she sat in the stands and listened to a colleague talk about his newborn son. She kept quiet about her own baby news – as she was supposed to for another couple of weeks – and excused herself to use the ladies room.

At that time, she noticed a little spotting. It was not much and she wasn't even sure if she had seen correctly, so she went through the rest of her work at the arena for the next couple of hours then returned to the hotel. Once there, she was sure and called her obstetrician, who told her not to panic, to drink a lot, put her feet up, relax and wait to see what happened next. It could be nothing, the doctor told her. Try not to worry.

Easier said than done, but this is where work became a great escape. After researching the area hospitals to know exactly where she would go if needed, Kara did her best to put aside her situation and put work first.

She finished her current assignments then started planning ahead. If something was going wrong, she needed to have her work set up so she didn't leave any loose ends. At the time, her managing editor was not her biggest fan. She was already worried he would see her pregnancy as vulnerability and seek to exploit it. If somehow, the pregnancy left her unable to do her job for any period of time, for whatever reason, he would definitely use it to his advantage. She was not about to let that happen.

That night, Kara told one person at the office – a friend and colleague, who also happened to be pregnant. She was involved with Kara's assignments so now if something urgent happened and Kara somehow couldn't be contacted the next day without notice, somebody in the loop knew what was going on. They discussed not only the personal situation, but Kara updated her on the progress of the stories for that week's magazine and the future plans for covering the tournament.

The next day, after many hours in A&E confirming the miscarriage in progress, she returned to the hotel to pack and wait to leave for the airport. Again, she used organising work as a way to think about something else – and let anyone and everyone know her job was important to her and she would do it in a professional and responsible manner no matter the situation.

First she filed the stories she had finished the night before. She then emailed the public relations staff of the local team to tell them she wouldn't need her press box seat for the next night's game. She would have to deal with these people again and professional consideration was in order no matter what her situation. Again, she did not share the details of her story. Many women need and want to tell their tale, but work colleagues are not the people to share such serious and personal information. She sent an email to her pregnant friend in the office with the news, as well as some organisational stuff about the next week's stories.

Kara did not want her news to get out to everyone in the office, in particular her editor, so she called the editorial director – the big boss – a couple of times on his cell phone (it was the weekend). He did not answer so she left a message about a family emergency and left for home. (She would later tell him the truth and apologise – although not completely sincerely – for leaving the assignment without getting through to him first. It should be noted, he could not have been more supportive.)

Of course, there isn't always time to move down a professional checklist and, often, such things are the last thing on your mind. But it's not unimportant and it has multiple purposes.

First, it can take your mind off of whatever is happening – and seems to be happening in some kind of horrible, super-slow motion film reel.

Secondly, it shows that you value your work and your company.

Finally, you can return to work without anyone doubting your commitment or focus.

Girl Talk: Perfectionists and Pregnancy

Girl's Guide friend, publishing colleague, original member of our book group, former client and now working mum, Leigh Ann Ambrosi gave birth to a beautiful baby boy on February 20, 2008. As the Vice President for Marketing and Publicity for Sterling Publishing, she manages a department of 20 and is responsible for nine direct reports.

Leigh Ann is one of those girls who makes you feel less together. Gorgeous, with a killer body that she maintains with a rigorous exercise schedule, Leigh Ann always looks like she's walked out of the pages of a catalogue. In the 10 years we've known her, she's never been one minute late and is as organised as they get. You want to hate her but can't. She's as kind as she is perfect – never forgets a birthday, shows up to every event to lend support and is never more than a phone call away if you need her. She's also darn good at her job. Focused, driven and goal-oriented, she became a Vice President in her early 30s and is now in a senior leadership position at a growing company.

She has an hour and 45-minute commute to work. Before Max, she would get up every morning at 5:45, be at her desk by 8:30, work until 7 and get home just before 9. She hit the gym three nights a week and both days on the weekends. She attended at least one evening professional event per week, and she's never gone to bed with a dirty dish in the sink.

We spoke to Leigh Ann the day of Max's six month check-up on her last summer Friday in 2008. We wanted to know how a perfectionist made a smooth transition from pregnancy to working motherhood.

So, how is it?

It's been a million times harder than I've ever expected but the reward has been a million times greater than I expected too.

How do you mean?

You're going to laugh, but I saved Tina Constable's Maternity Leave Bible (a publisher at Random House and Leigh Ann's former boss and mentor) that she had given us when she went out on maternity leave. She did a great job preparing us for when she left, and I knew when I got pregnant I wanted to use this as a model.

That was 10 years ago!

It was eight years ago. You know I am a planner. I like to be prepared.

How did that plan go?

Well, not exactly as I hoped. First, getting pregnant was neither smooth nor easy for us. I got pregnant but it wasn't going great and I had to go to a number of doctor's appointments and started missing work. I was allowed to go to work, but then I had to go straight home and put my feet up. After a prior flawless attendance record, I was worried that my bosses would start to wonder about my absences, so I told them at six weeks I was pregnant. I miscarried that pregnancy in my tenth week. After two days at home, I wanted nothing more than to go back to work and be normal. No one on my staff knew and work went on as usual.

How was the next pregnancy?

Nine months later I got pregnant again. The doctors never

found out what happened to the first one. It was just one of those things. At the time I had no idea how common miscarriages were and I thought I was the only one, not one in three. So with this pregnancy, I was a nervous wreck. I was spotting in the beginning and they gave me an almost weekly ultra-sound.

When and how did you share the news about this pregnancy?
I told my bosses at 13 weeks. I had to use my vacation days because they were running out and the appointments weren't every week. I wanted to wait until it was 100% okay. By 13 weeks, I couldn't hide it anymore, I was starting to show. I told my staff individually. Everyone found out the same week and was thrilled for me. It really is a very family-friendly company. The members of the Executive Team are all young with young children at home and really want the work-balance equation to work for their employees.

How did things change at work when you were pregnant?
I still got to work on time every day, but other things had to give. Pregnant Leigh Ann was exhausted, barely making it home awake. I would be falling asleep at the dinner table. I was nauseous all the time. I'd get on the 7:20 a.m. train with a ginger ale and bag of saltines. I had to stop going to the gym during the week because I was just too tired!
Prior to my pregnancy, I used to go to every single evening author event, every corporate event, the awards dinners, you name it, anything publishing-wise, I was there to represent. That stopped. I wasn't in the mood. I didn't feel good. I was getting fat and just not feeling it. I started delegating more and it became a great opportunity for my staff to do the things that I was always doing. I'll admit it

took a little while, but I was so tired that I had to prioritise. Sooner or later I'd have to let go and this was my time. I was lucky. My staff really stepped up.

How did you prepare for your maternity leave?

My brilliant plan was to leave two full weeks before my due date on March 4. My last day of work was going to be February 15 and then I would go home and get everything ready. As I mentioned I had Tina's handy maternity pack as my guide and in January I started working on my own. Everyday I would make a note of everything that I had done and when I had down time or during lunch, I would flesh out each entry, explaining how to do everything in detail. It ended up being a 10-page document. I gave a copy to all of the department heads, my bosses and then each individual who was responsible for covering parts of my job. I had meetings with everyone, all my work was done, and they even threw me a baby shower on February 13. February 15 was my last day at work.

Why did you take two weeks off before your due date?

The commute was killing me and the doctor wanted me to take it easy. Also, I had planned to use the time to get everything ready: pack a bag, finish the room and try to remove myself from my work routine so I could prepare for the new mother thing. Five days later my water broke. My maternity leave officially began on February 20, 2008. So much for my two weeks off . . . I had two DAYS!

What is the company maternity policy and what did you do?

From the date your doctor pulled you out of work, the company pays in full until your due date. After that, in the United States you have six-weeks of full pay for a vaginal delivery and eight weeks full pay for a caesarean. My goal was to be gone from work for twelve to fourteen weeks, I was going to use some vacation time and take two weeks unpaid.

You're a Mum Now

Your little baby or babies are home from the hospital and you and she and your partner are trying to figure each other out. Does *that* cry mean I'm hungry or I'm tired? Is *that* cry belly pain? Is the baby latched onto the breast properly? Is it supposed to hurt? Am I supposed to be this tired? Doesn't this baby ever sleep somewhere other than my chest? Why can't his father calm him down? Why doesn't his father know where the extra wipes are? Why am I still fat?

Your career girl life as you knew it is completely forgotten. In those first few days, it's almost as if it never existed. Your maternity leave has begun in earnest and all those grandiose visions of resting and recuperating while the baby is sleeping have disappeared. This mummy thing is hard work and your maternity leave may be the only uninterrupted time you have with your child so make the most of every moment.

Even if you are lucky enough to have help, an experienced relative or maternity nurse, you are still trying to figure it all out. You are the mother and two weeks ago, considered yourself quite competent. How hard could mothering possibly be? Generations of other women have done it. Now you wonder, why can't you get your baby to sleep? Or eat? Or nurse?

Don't despair. Pretty soon you'll be a pro and your mind will start focusing on other concerns like what's happening at work. You may even worry: Are things running smoothly without me? More smoothly then when I was there? This chapter will arm you the strategies you need to enjoy your maternity leave and re-enter the workforce smoothly.

Hey Superwoman! The First Three Months Are Hard. Really Hard.

Your friends will tell you. Your colleagues will tell you. Your mother will tell you. But there's really no telling you until you've lived through the first three months of motherhood. How hard can it be with nothing to do all day but take care of a baby? Up until this point you've been managing projects, people, crazy bosses, busy partners and still finding a way to carve out time for yourself. Now you're feeding, changing, comforting, and in between, napping, doing some laundry and hanging out. There's no reason you can't check a few emails, join a few conference calls and, if you have a flexible partner or childcare lined up, venture out for a meeting or two. Right? Wrong.

Be realistic and be adaptable. The baby will not work on your schedule. As a matter of fact, you will be lucky to get into any schedule whatsoever if you are breastfeeding on demand. In the first few weeks, breastfeeding and/or pumping take over your life. Work is the last thing you will be thinking about, or able to focus on if someone should call with a question. Most new mums on maternity leave are, by and large, not contacted by their work – other than with congratulations, of course! – for some months, but if you run or work for a small business or are self-employed, you may have different arrangements in place. By all means let your boss know you've delivered, send a photo (not one of you in the hospital or the baby naked – nobody wants to see those) but set expectations and limits on your availability if it *is* likely that people will be contacting you.

If you want to become accessible – and again, this will depend very much on your own personal circumstances – make it a goal to check email once a day or keep your BlackBerry® by your side as Caitlin did. Instruct one person at the office to call you and leave a message in an emergency. You will respond within 24 hours. Otherwise, you are on baby time now. And baby time is 24/7. Don't beat yourself up for not getting anything done at home or at work. And don't ever turn down an offer for help. If your mother-in-law, who drives you absolutely mad, offers to come and watch the baby for a couple hours a week, accept the offer and give yourself a couple of options of how to spend the time excluding housework. Take a nap. Read a book. Get out of the house. Don't spend your precious couple of hours cleaning bottles and doing laundry. And be flexible: what sounded great two days ago might in fact not work at all today.

Does it suddenly seem that everyone you know has become a stay-at-home mum? Does it seem every time you turn on the television another celebrity mum has given birth and is already back to work in their size 0 jeans? Does it seem like you are the most disorganised, exhausted, fat new mother you've ever met? Did most things you did and thought before you gave birth seem a lifetime ago and completely irrelevant right now?

If you've answered yes to all of these questions, congratulations, you are now officially a new mother. Don't worry, these feelings too shall pass. But now is the time to review all of those plans you formulated during your pregnancy: personal, professional and financial.

How do you feel?

Your insides hurt. Your outsides hurt. Your uterus hurts. Your boobs hurt – if you're trying to breastfeed they are engorged and if you're not, they are engorged. In short, everything hurts. We were prepared for our maternity leave, but we weren't prepared for the pain. It's no wonder you need time off. It's more than figuring out what to do with this new baby, your body has to recover.

According to www.babycentre.co.uk, in the first few weeks post-partum you should expect: sore breasts, constipation, an uncomfortable episiotomy, haemorrhoids, hot and cold flashes, urinary or faecal incontinence, 'after pains' from uterine contractions, vaginal discharge and, of course, you still feel enormous (celebrity mums' overnight transformations not withstanding). Yikes.

'I was not prepared for how badly I felt physically,' recalls Leigh Ann Ambrosi. 'My episiotomy didn't heal correctly either, so I had to have two follow up procedures in my seventh week post-partum. I expected to at least be curious about what was happening at work but, in the beginning, I was so tired and hurting that I didn't even give it a second thought.'

But the pain is not limited to the physical; up to 80% of new mums experience irritability, sadness, crying, or anxiety, beginning within days or weeks postpartum. These "baby blues" are very common and may be related to physical changes (including hormonal changes, exhaustion, and unexpected birth experiences) and the emotional transition as you adjust to changing roles and your new baby.

If you've had a Caesarean, it's even harder. You will hear people talk about their C-sections as if they had a tooth filled. Don't believe them. A C-section is major surgery and includes a painful recovery.

More serious than the 'baby blues', post-natal depression (or post-partum depression; PPD) occurs in 10–25 percent of new mums. It can cause mood swings, anxiety, guilt, and persistent sadness. In her book, *Down Came the Rain: My Journey Through Post-*

Partum Depression, Brooke Shields writes, 'This was sadness of a shockingly different magnitude. It felt as if it would never go away.' She shares how she denied anything was wrong and only because of the persistence of friends and her husband was she persuaded to seek treatment through medication and therapy. She also admits to having suicidal thoughts.

Researchers aren't totally sure what's causes PPD, but they suspect that dropping hormones, along with environmental changes like exhaustion, being overwhelmed and feelings of stress and loss of identity, can combine to set it off. The 'baby blues' normally go away within a few days to a week. We didn't speak to one new mother who didn't break down in tears of frustration or exhaustion in the first weeks after the birth of her baby. Post-partum depression can happen anytime within the first year after childbirth and the symptoms are frighteningly similar to the baby blues. Keep track of the duration of the symptoms. Baby blues becomes postpartum depression when the feelings don't go away. If you or a loved one thinks you may be suffering from PPD, talk to your doctor as soon as possible.

Evaluating Your Options

Once you've been home with the baby for some time, you may be wondering if it's even realistic for you to go back to work. Is there ever going to be a childcare situation that you will be comfortable with? Can you afford going back or staying home? Are you even the stay-at-home type? There comes a point in every-one's maternity leave where you ask yourself, what if I don't go back? Now's the time to give that some real thought.

After reviewing your options, your finances might actually make some decisions for you. Your income and benefits may be necessary. Childcare is expensive, but so is not working. Track your monthly expenditures. How much do you need to earn to pay for the essentials? And do you really want to live on just the essen-tials? Be honest with yourself about the type of lifestyle you want.

As our favourite working mother, Linda Malkin, a risk management executive at a major hospital always tells us, 'A happy mother is a good mother'.

If you are going to be miserable because you are living on a tighter budget then that's probably not the best option for you. Remember, it's not an *all* or *nothing* proposition. You don't have to go straight back to work or give up work forever. Jennifer Heth, a working mum in Denver says, 'I haven't worked full-time since having kids. I worked for three years, part-time when Emma was little. After Charlie was born, I quit that job. I volunteered full-time (i.e. 40 hours/week) for about four years, but that certainly isn't the same as career-work. I am back at work again, but only three days a week. Working motherhood for me is definitely a balancing act.'

If you work for yourself or are in a position where if you don't work, you don't get paid, then cherish the first couple of weeks at home because that may be the only down time you get.

But keep in mind throughout your maternity leave, if you continue to feel like it will be impossible to jump back into a 40 hour work week, you *do* have options you can explore with your employer. For example, as of April 2009, in the UK parents of children under the age of 16 have the right to request flexible working arrangements (as long as they've worked for their employers for 26 weeks continuously before the request goes in). When you are ready to think about going back to work and if you would like to investigate this option, contact your employer to get the ball rolling.

Jayne Schmidt, a first-time mother of a six-month-old, works for the US Council on Accreditation (www.coa.org). She wrote the standards for 'Early Childcare and Development Services' for multi-social service providers which are facilities that provide more than childcare, such as community centres, so she knows a thing or two about childcare. Jayne recommends slowly transitioning into childcare and back to work, if at all possible. When a new babysitter first starts, she works from home for about three days, observing and training. When she first went back to work, her employer allowed her to begin first with half-days, working her way back a little more each week until she was fully on the new schedule after a couple of months. She's now works four, eight-hour days. 'Transitioning back into work over time really helped me both at home and at the office. I was able to give my full attention to wherever I was because I wasn't worrying about what was happening at the other place,' she says.

When a Girl's Just Gotta Get Back to Work

If you are in a job where if you don't work you don't get paid, maternity leave is generally shorter or blurred. Whether you own the business or are an hourly-wage worker or work for a small company, your time is literally your money, maternity leave fits in when you can afford it. But planning will most definitely help.

If you are running a business with an infrastructure and a team, then you can set up a system that will cover for you while you are gone. When Chris Colabella, owner and president of Construction Information Systems in New Jersey was pregnant with her first daughter in 1997, she was the Vice President in charge of operations and had a staff of eighteen – most of whom were in operations. To cover her maternity leave, she broke her group into separate departments and assigned 'team leaders' to each one who would oversee the work. It's a system that she still employs now. She was already removed from the daily tasks that needed to get done, so her presence wasn't needed day-to-day to keep the company running smoothly as long as her team leaders were in place.

Financially though was a different picture. The company was small enough not to be covered under federal legislation and they offered no paid maternity leave – even for an owner (very different from the UK) – so after she had her baby, she went on short-term disability from the state. She chose to keep her salary coming, and worked 12 days past her due date when she was finally induced. She stayed home for four weeks, stayed in touch, did a little work and even stopped in a few times. To many this would sound pretty skimpy, but the benefit of owning your own business, even if you can't afford to leave it unattended, is that if offers what many women describe as the key factor to successful working motherhood: flexibility.

Chris shared her story with us:

> I was so preoccupied with my first pregnancy with my daughter Kali that my work really suffered. I was aware of every single thing that was going on with my body. I was on a very strict diet. I made doctor appointments at very inconvenient times because I only wanted to see certain physicians in the practice. While at work, I was 'researching' baby-related info on the Web and running out to visit daycare centres and I was constantly worried about how I was going to balance it all because motherhood and my career were both a priority.
>
> When I returned from my maternity leave with Kali, I set up an elaborate schedule to maximise my time with her. I worked four days per week, one of which I brought her in to the office. Her father could telecommute (he worked for AT&T at the time) and took care of her at home twice a week and her grandmother watched her the fifth day. This went on for months but wasn't really working because of unexpected changes in all of our schedules. I finally put her into daycare when she was seven months old for four days while she continued to go her grandmother's for the fifth. Once she was in daycare, I left work early to pick her up at 3:30 p.m. so I could spend the afternoons with her. I only worked 35 hours per week until Kali turned one and did very little to further the growth or productivity of my

company. At work I maintained the status quo. At home I was trying to be supermum – cooking, cleaning, and spending quality time with my daughter and husband.

I remember it as very hectic and horrible with lots of running around and an added problem. Like most kids, daycare was making Kali sick. I had to take time off or would try to work from home (near impossible with a sick child) or I just gave up and brought her to the office with me. (I tried not to think about how she would infect the other people). She even contracted salmonella at daycare – which was a disaster. She was out of school for an entire month and although her grandmother helped, I missed even more work. Luckily by two years old she had built up a healthy immunity to those crazy daycare germs and I was finally on a schedule! Shortly thereafter I got pregnant with my second daughter and started the whole thing over again. Because I had a system that I perfected over two years, I just plugged my second daughter into it with a few important upgrades. When Myah started getting sick from daycare, I pulled her out and hired a nanny. I couldn't afford to miss months of work this time as I had been promoted and taken on more responsibilities.

As I added more value to the company (funny what happens when you can actually devote yourself to work) my compensation increased too. I was able to outsource more of the household work that would fill up my weekends and cause me to miss time with my children. I took control of my calendar and continue to be very organised and scheduled. I guess I've never really seen the work/mother balance as a problem to solve at work, but rather one to solve at home by lining up child care, household help, and a group of supportive people to step in when needed. As a business owner I had many options that an employee of any kind wouldn't have. I had already built up my staff to do everything that needed to be done, whether it was accounting, operations or sales. I just had to manage and oversee that process. My role at work was strategic development and my work decisions directly affected how we would grow our company. I weighed the options (work/mother balance again) and made a decision to grow more slowly. I also hired more people so that I didn't have any direct responsibility for the product or the sales which continues to give me flexibility and I've promoted people to be team leaders and managers so that I could be more autonomous. It's been a painfully slow and frustrating process, wasting a lot of time and money on incompetent people, but it's starting to come together now. I have a good staff, the company runs itself, I'm finally making decent money, I only work 35–40 hours per week and I never gave up the time with my kids.

Who's taking care of the children?

This is the most important section in the book. For women to be successful at work, they must have dependable childcare. End of story. Nanny or daycare, stay-at-home dad or in-home situation, it makes no difference. Quality and reliability are what you're looking for and finding quality childcare will be your first major parenting challenge. You're looking for a mummy or daddy substitute – someone who will nurture, love, cuddle, play with, and care for your child when you're at work. And boy, do you need to plan ahead. Reliable, affordable childcare takes time to find and competition for the best providers, whether it's a nanny or a daycare centre can be intense: this is very much the case in big cities, London especially. And it is, of course, expensive.

Investigate all of your options before you make any decisions. When you're pregnant, you might be convinced you can't live without a nanny only to walk by a daycare centre and fall in love with the warm, supportive environment you observe.

Not surprisingly, daycare is best when carer-to-child ratios are low. Look past the flashy set-ups. Pay special attention to how the caregivers interact with the children. Ask plenty of questions. And you can never start too early. It could take as long as six months to find an ideal situation for your family and your budget. These women (childcare providers are almost exclusively women) are going to be your surrogates during the day. You want them to treat your baby in the same manner you would. In the UK, the government agency SureStart is the place to go to for information on the regulation and licensing of childcare provision (www.surestart.gov.uk). Ofsted is another great source of information with its reports on childcare providers: visit www.ofsted.gov.uk/oxcare_providers/list for details.

Jayne Schmidt recommends you do a lot of research in advance and come to each daycare centre armed with a list of questions for the administrator, teachers and other parents you meet. She also recommends that you check the resources of your local community. For example, in Westchester County, New York, where she lives, the Childcare Council of Westchester provides a list of licensed childcare providers in Westchester, as well as provides resources to help choose the right placement for your child.

Some things you should consider: What is the ratio of carers or teachers to kids? How much time do the children spend outside? What is the curriculum? How often is the school closed for meetings and holidays? What is the carer or teacher turnover? How much parental participation is expected? What are the hours? Are they fully licensed, inspected and accredited? Are the kids actually learning or just playing? Are there art supplies, instruments, sports equipment and/or computers?

We spoke to a number of women who put their children in 'in-home' daycare: in the UK, this can encompass care by relatives (often grandparents), nannies (or nanny-shares), childminders (who must be registered with their local authority) and even au pairs. The advantages they reported included proximity to their homes, small 'group size' including sometimes even one-on-one care, as well as the low cost compared to other options. Personal recommendations can be a great help here, although it's essential that you take up references. The costs for childcare can vary dramatically across the country, with prices in London at the peak. There is help available, though; visit www.surestart.gov.uk/ surestartservices/support/helpwithchildcarecosts for information.

If you've never done any hiring in your professional life, you might want to read a few books. Alicia Rockmore's offers great advice a little later in this chapter. The goal when hiring a nanny is to find someone to care for your child with love, confidence and professionalism and someone who respects your authority. You are the parent and set the rules. As with all good employees, a nanny should show up on time everyday leaving her personal issues at home. In addition to her professionalism, look for someone who will be loving and extremely vigilant with your child.

Before you start interviewing nannies, create a list of job expectations. Consider: What are your office hours? How long is your commute? How long do you need to get ready in the morning? How soon could you realistically get home after work? Are there ever unavoidable late nights at the office? Are you looking for childcare only or do you need someone who will do housework when the children are napping? Set the parameters of the schedule and responsibilities then review your budget. Additional time and responsibilities cost money. Can you afford a nanny who can stay late three nights a week or must you simply leave work to relieve her? Ask your neighbours, friends and co-workers how much they pay their nannies. Rates and expectations vary from city to city.

If you're able to hire a good nanny then you have more than an employee, you have a partner in your home, helping you teach and guide your children as well as taking care of the more mundane domestic issues: laundry, cooking and cleaning. Unfortunately you can become absolutely dependent on the nanny and because there is only one of them (unlike a daycare centre) if she gets sick or has personal issues that keep her at home, you are in trouble.

Caitlin went through four nannies (four!) before deciding to put the twins into a preschool (fancy name for daycare centre) at age two. The first nanny turned out to be a racist. The second was excellent but only with them for a year because she decided to do missionary work in South America. The third nanny was unprofessional and heartless – after four months with the twins, she didn't even take a moment to call over a weekend after Caitlin's son had surgery on Friday. Later they were told by a neighbour that this same nanny would leave the kids strapped in a buggy while she made mobile phone calls in the courtyard. The fourth nanny, although highly recommended, showed up late almost every day, would often call in sick, and – here's the worst bit – was caught drinking sweet vermouth when babysitting late one night.

So, after the Friedmans' string of really bad luck with the nanny train, they decided to enrol the twins into what would be an excellent preschool around the corner.

What Caitlin learned about having a nanny care for your children is that she really needed someone who would show up on time, every day. She needed someone who cared for and about the kids. She needed someone who was open-minded, energetic and didn't drink (obviously!). The daycare (preschool, nursery) around the corner provided all of that, with its three teachers. And although slightly more expensive than a nanny because two kids are enrolled, it's worth every penny knowing that the school doors would be open at 8 a.m. and not shuttered because of migraine headaches.

If you have a relative willing to take care of your child for free, you may have hit the jackpot. But it's a difficult situation even if it seems like a dream come true. Even though it's a family member, you must treat it as a professional transaction. Be very clear about the work hours and your expectations for care. If your aunt is watching your baby and sticking her in front of the television for much of the day you need to address it. If your mother offers to help out a few days each week, but you know that she can't get anywhere before 10 a.m., before saying accepting her generous offer, be very clear about your expectations.

As a working mum you need to line up help that actually helps you. Amanda Dantico, a young woman we spoke to who was raised by a working mother advises us to 'find a childcare system that everyone is happy with', ideally 'one that is flexible supported by friends and family'. A good childcare system makes it easier for you to get to work with a clear head and relatively guilt-free. If the people or the circumstances are making it difficult for you to get back into work-mode then you may need to make some changes.

Galia Gichon, a personal financial planner and author of *My Money Matters*, recommends that when thinking about childcare you always overestimate the cost. She says, 'If you think you are getting a financial deal, it most likely will not work out. As a working parent, you need reliable childcare and that costs more than you think it will.'

Girl Talk: 'Alicia's Guide to Hiring and Keeping Great Nannies'

Alicia Rockmore, the founder of Buttoned Up! (www.getbuttonedup.com) calls herself an organisational maniac and she seamlessly juggles a fast-paced career and full home life. Prior to co-founding Buttoned Up, Inc., Alicia was a marketing executive at Unilever. Alicia was a career girl and had no plans to quit working once her daughter was born. She has an MBA from the University of Michigan and is a Certified Public Accountant, too. But she knew even before her daughter Lucy came unexpectedly into the world at 32 weeks that she was going to need more flexibility in her job. She was willing to put in the hours, but needed to be able to do them on her own schedule.

When she started looking for a new job, she realised that most of corporate America operated the same as Unilever – lots of travel, zero flexibility and minimal control over your options for growth. At that point, she decided to start her own business and conceived and launched Buttoned Up!

She now works more than she has ever before and maintains that the key to her success as a happy working mother has always been a great nanny. Because she's moved a number of times, Alicia is an expert at interviewing nannies. We spoke to her in mid-interview process and here are some of her techniques:

1. **Excellent nannies are hard to find. Expect to pay them well and treat them as part of the family.**
2. **I interview nannies the same way I would for any other job. I once called three agencies and had them send over ten candidates each. I can usually tell within five minutes which ones I want to interview further, because at first I have to like them. Then I ask them questions that get to their instincts. 'If you can't reach me and Lucy falls on the playground, what are you going to do?' I explain the job requirements and once I narrow down the list, say from 30 to three, Lucy becomes part of the process, too. I invite her to meet them and then watch how they interact with her. When**

she was a baby I had to rely on employment history and references.

3. When looking at employment history, I always look for consistency. I want to see long placements in homes because that ultimately says more than a reference. The two best nannies I've ever had worked with their last families for more than ten years.

4. I prefer nannies that have no other obligations in their life. No kids, no husband, or boyfriend. They are usually older. The hours are very flexible but generally between 7.00 a.m. and 6.00 p.m. They have to be willing to stay overnight even though my husband and I try not to travel at the same time.

5. And when you've got a good nanny, don't be afraid to give over tasks that it feels like a mum should do. When Lucy was a baby the nanny took her to music class and now the nanny packs Lucy's lunch. I choose to spend quality time with her and not do the routine stuff.

The Word

Susan Stein is a mum and the director of a preschool, The Children's Garden, in Manhattan. We spoke to her about working mother guilt, how to work best with your day care teachers and things to consider when you are interviewing schools:

We all know that dropping kids off at preschool is heartbreaking for the working mum. What would you like them to know to help them deal with their guilt or concerns about having other people take care of their children?

It's hard to describe just how seriously the teachers in our school take their job to care for the children in their charge during the day. Just about every one of our teachers is a working parent of necessity and has had to miss some occasion important to their child because of work commitments. They truly understand how difficult it is to leave their young child with someone else for long periods of the day, and they appreciate it when parents confide their own anxieties about childcare to them. The teachers really do want to 'fill in the blanks' of what goes on during the day or make a phone call to a parent to reassure them that their child is not merely being attended to, but that the teacher is really seeing their child. It goes a long way toward creating a relationship between the parents and teachers which is absolutely essential to the child making a great adjustment to school. What I never fail to be amazed by and I would want every mother (and father) to know is just how quickly the teachers come to know and love each child in their class and how quickly the children ease into the classroom routines and bond with the teachers. How do I know this? When I walk into a class sometimes it's the teachers, other times it's the children, but there is always someone ready to share an anecdote about the day. They can be funny stories, sometimes they're triumphs, and sometimes they're describing a disappointment, but there's never any mistaking the pride on the teachers' faces or the smiles on the children and there are infinitely many more smiles during a typical day than there are tears.

What should parents look for when interviewing preschools?
There is a definite intangible quality to the preschool visit; a certain gut feeling that, yes, I see my child here or no, I definitely don't. But there are a few things parents might also look for. What is the overall tone of the school? Do the carers greet you if you come into their classroom and then move back to the children? Look at the children and their interactions with each other and the teachers. Are they smiling, laughing, and maybe even singing?

Do the teachers and children appear to be relaxed as they move around the classroom? Depending upon the age of the children, are the teachers at the level of the children engaged in the children's activities or in conversation with them, or are they standing above the children, talking to one another. If a child is crying or children are squabbling, are you comfortable with how the teachers handle the situation? Regarding the art work, does it appear to be done by young children, who have their own varying abilities and ideas or can you see the hand of a teacher in the end product? Do the teachers use a variety of materials and can you get a sense of some of the things they've been exploring in the class? Are there areas for sand and water; a semblance of privacy, lots of books, a touch of nature? For lack of a better way to say it, is there anything cosy about the classroom that a young child can respond to or is everything exceedingly neat and precise? Are there things around the classroom that reflect the touch of the young children that spend a significant amount of time there, such as labelled family photographs, classroom photographs, birthday charts and so on. And of course, the subject that many prospective families mention to me: the importance of cleanliness. Things don't have to be in obsessive order, but the room, the toys, the general ambience should be one of cleanliness and good repair.

You were a working mum and you are the head of a preschool so tell us how new working mums can best work with preschool teachers?
Once your child has become comfortable with the classroom routines, at the beginning of the day, please come on time and greet the teachers. Show your children that you are comfortable with the idea that they will be spending the day at preschool. Settle your child in, give a kiss or hug goodbye and leave promptly so your child can make the transition to the school day. Please do not say, 'I wish I could stay here and do nothing but play all day.' Believe me, that does not endear a parent to very dedicated and hard-working teachers. Let the teachers know if there is anything

unique to your child that will comfort him or her if need be. Make sure your contact numbers are up-to-date. Have a back-up plan in the event your child gets sick, which you have to expect will happen. Teachers are uncomfortable turning sick children away and appreciate not being put on the spot. Try not to have your child be the last child to be picked up every evening. After a while, your child will notice it. From time to time incidents may crop up that will require you to meet with the teachers. Try to relax and remember that everyone in school really does have the best interests of your child at heart and just wants to make it as good as it can be for him or her. At the same time, though, remember, you are and will always be your child's best advocate, and misunderstandings between parents and teachers have been known to happen. If there's something you feel the teachers are missing or you want them to know, you must speak up and they will appreciate your candour.

Any suggestions for new mums that are preparing to put their children into preschool?
The one practical thing that immediately comes to mind is having your child on a schedule so that they come to school on time and rested, ready to have a great day. In addition, recognise that you and the teachers through your interactions, will be working together to create a warm and loving environment that will nurture and sustain your child during the day and at the same time, enable him or her to have a great time making new friends and learning new things.

The Unexpected

Kim loved every second of her pregnancy. Other than being a little tired in the first trimester, she felt fantastic. She worked for herself from home before she partnered with Caitlin and had only a few clients. She became obsessed with having an unassisted delivery and took natural childbirth classes. Soon this career girl started sounding like an earth mother. She wanted a drug-free birth and to be monitored as little as possible. She switched from an intervention-happy OB practice to a midwife in her seventh month. Four days before her due date, on December 30, 1999, she went into labour – although she didn't realise it until the next morning when those pains weren't stopping. Her son Thomas was born at 10:40 on the morning of December 31, 1999 at a hospital in Teaneck, New Jersey.

It seemed to go well. Thomas popped out looking healthy except for what his parents likened to a big, red grape stuck on the front of his eye. The midwife didn't appear worried, but they took Thomas off for some more tests. Apparently, there was something wrong with both of his eyes. The doctors couldn't be sure, but it looked to them like Thomas was blind. Blind?! How did that happen? Why hadn't anyone seen it on the scans? What was going on? Thomas was whisked off in an ambulance with his father to the Neonatal Intensive Care Unit at Columbia Presbyterian Hospital in New York City. They didn't know how to treat him in Teaneck. As one of the nurses told Kim after he was born, 'We don't get babies like that here.' So six hours later, Kim signed herself out and was on her way across the river to be with her son.

Why are we telling this story? Kim was self-employed and her husband had just quit his job to take care of the baby while she worked. In short, if she didn't work, she didn't get paid. But who could think about work when she had a blind child? On the other hand, if she didn't work, how was she going to take care of the blind child?

The good news is that after a couple weeks of testing, some crazy scares and a lot of intense observation, Kim and her family learned Thomas was not fully blind. He is legally blind and categorised visually impaired, but he's doing fantastically well in a mainstream public school.

Kim and her husband had prepared for maternity leave. She had told all of her clients she'd be taking two weeks off (which was great timing because of the holidays) and would be back to work the second week in January – except for one project which was due on January 5. She signed up for New Jersey's short-term disability insurance and had work lined up for the next three months.

And so in between trips to specialists (including an oncologist who had to rule out that Thomas didn't have retinal blastoma, a life-threatening cancer of the eye) and surgeons (Thomas had his first surgery at seven days old and his second at six months), Kim worked. She didn't have a choice and it probably saved her from losing her mind. Of course, she can't remember anything she worked on during that time, except for that one that was due on January 5. She still has perfect recall of every doctor visit with Thomas. But the point is, she made it through, with her business and sanity intact. She got extensions on most of the projects and has been blessed with a large and supportive family on both sides nearby.

Thomas's unexpected disability taught Kim a few important things that are worth passing along:

• Ask for help. Your friends and family (and in Kim's case, clients) will step up and be there for you. Her team of helpers were running errands, bringing food, changing diapers, and even editing press releases. Thomas's little village was born on the last day of the millennium, too.

- You can't plan for everything. When bad stuff happens, you'll just deal with it. Work may not be the priority at the moment of crisis, but as Kim's story illustrates, you can't just walk away from it either. Do the best you can. Be up front about what's happening and make every effort to get help.
- Stop trying to be perfect. We've noticed successful career women share some common traits and one of them is always striving for perfection. Prior to Thomas, Kim would spend two days labouring over a press release. After Thomas, she could suddenly knock one out in two hours. The end product wasn't much different – she just didn't have the time to strive for perfection anymore. As it turned out, good was more than good enough and, the funny thing is, it still is.

3

I'm Back

Here's the thing, girls . . . you are different after you have a baby, and we aren't just talking about the obvious. You likely won't even realise all the ways you've changed until you've gotten back into your old routine.

You might find that you're anxious to go to work in the morning but, once at your desk, you want nothing more than to go home. Or, you might be downright furious that your beloved suits no longer look right. Maybe you find yourself reluctant to take on any new work fearing you won't have the energy to get it done.

The reality is that you are a different kind of career woman now. You have huge new responsibilities and someone at home who doesn't care if you have a presentation the next morning. Your energy level, body, attention span and focus are most likely not as they were before you had the baby. Our boy Jim (see p. 143) wrote to us to say, 'The parent/child connection is the only one that can *never* be changed. Marriages, jobs, houses, they can come and go but you will always be a parent of that child. So don't pretend you can do it all – draw up new rules and boundaries and don't just hope it will all get back to normal.'

Things have radically changed. It does not have to be a negative, it is just the reality. Life is now different, not necessarily better or worse. Once you realise that – and how you have changed – we recommend you embrace it.

But It's Hard! We Can Say That, Right?

For everyone who is at the beginning stages of pregnancy or for whom it is something they have envisioned for their future, it is common to idealise the baby phase – never imagining that the baby just won't go to sleep at 8 all of the time, even if you have a presentation to write that night. And no, the baby won't respect your meeting-packed schedule enough not to be ill on a Tuesday. And even if the future dad is nurturing and dependable and insists he will do 50% of the childcare before you give birth, well, often it just doesn't work out that way. The fact is, being a completely honest and realistic – not bitter – working mum is profoundly difficult. You have not just the needs of your significant other, boss, colleagues and family to consider; now you have an infant. And your baby needs more from you than all of the above combined.

Before jumping into the solutions, tips and stories that will help you navigate this sometimes trying journey to get back into the work groove, we want you to know you are not alone. It isn't your imagination. Working motherhood is challenging. Even if you love being a mother and struggled to make it happen, even if you wanted it your whole life. You are still you, with dreams and ambitions, and setting those aside because of exhaustion or new responsibilities is difficult. It is also shocking to many of us who, during those first few weeks back at work, find ourselves surprisingly happy to be cranking out expense reports and worrying about what to order for lunch rather than being home unable to take a shower. That's normal and please don't beat yourself up. You love your baby, you love your home, you may also love your work. That's OK.

The biggest surprise to us is just how much of a toll the lack of sleep takes. Caitlin went back to work six weeks after her twins were born. And looking back on that foggy first three weeks back when all she wanted to do was curl up and sob under her desk (and she is NOT a crier), she can't believe she made it through. Yes, she had a supportive business partner, and a helpful spouse, but still after six weeks of being woken up every three hours, it was tough, really tough, to get back into the swing of things. So know that, again, it isn't just you. The toll that pregnancy takes on your body and hormones is significant but also, caring for an infant is infinitely more exhausting that anything you have ever or will ever do. So be realistic about how much to take on when you get back to work.

Here we're going to show you ways to work smarter not just harder and help you get your (back to work) groove back.

Am I Ruining My Child?

The first question you'll probably ask yourself on your first day leaving your child is, 'Am I ruining her?' Of course you're not ruining her. Have you, to the best of your ability set up safe and reliable childcare? Do you trust that in your absence your child's needs will be met? If you've answered yes to these questions, then without a doubt: You are absolutely not ruining your child by continuing to work. Read the studies. Children who are raised by people other than their parents have statistically the same chance of success as children who were raised by their parents.

The facts support working mums. The problem arises when all the facts in the world can't make your feelings of guilt go away. All you can do is make decisions that are right for you and your family based on needs, wants, goals and financial realities. If you are miserable working then you need to find a way to make a change, but if you're not miserable working then you should focus on the positives. We spoke to several people who were raised by a working mum. When asked how they felt about their mother working, almost everyone said they appreciated having such an inspirational role model.

Several responded that they learned 'independence' and 'self-reliance' at an early age, which helped instil confidence. Sharon Lowenheim shared this, 'I continued the same career for the first eight years of my post-motherhood life. I felt that it was important for my daughter to see that women worked, and that they could even be the primary bread-winner in their families (as I always was, even though my husband is a scientist).'

Supermum Doesn't Exist (Even in Comics)

After coming to terms with the fact that you are not ruining your child, the second most important thing you're going to have to realise is that you can't do it all at work and at home. Full stop. There is no supermum. In the post-feminist 70s, all working mums are supposed to aspire to this icon. Now that we have won the right to be at work, you can bring home the bacon, fry it up in a pan, bathe and feed the baby and never let your husband forget he's a man. The freedom to be everything somehow became the responsibility of doing everything. Because the only way you can be a super mum or super career girl – keeping everyone fed, loved and taken care of – is if you put yourself last. Maybe it can be done. But why would you want to and who would benefit from you killing yourself every day? Completely and totally neglecting yourself leads to burn out, nothing to give a partner and little to no energy for your baby. And think it through a little bit, if you continued to put yourself last, your dreams, goals and professional aspirations on the backburner, where will you be in 18 years? Working while raising children isn't for everyone, but for those of us who consider work an integral part of who they are, we just can't afford to chase some supermum ideal. So start by giving it up. Accept that you can do it all, just not all at the same time. Remind yourself that keeping *you* in the mix helps everyone in the long run and if your career is still a priority after having your baby, it is worth fighting for. With that said, you're mentally armed to be 'back'.

5 Ways to Say . . . I'm BACK!

If you love your job, it is essential to get those first few days, weeks and months back at the office after maternity leave right. It isn't easy. Your hormones are still completely off, you may be breast feeding, conflicted feelings about leaving your infant rise almost on the hour and you may feel a little paranoid about your job security. In part, you are right to feel paranoid because even if your job isn't at stake, your reputation as a valuable asset to the company just might be. It's difficult to feel completely confident that you can make the successful return after seeing colleagues throw in the career towel after having kids. So take a deep breath and vow to take control of this re-entry into work. Below we have outlined five actions to take within the first few months of your return that will shout out to your team and your boss . . . I AM BACK!

1. *Meet with the boss*

Schedule a meeting with your boss on your first day back. Go into this crucial get-together projecting enthusiasm for returning to work even if you are conflicted about it. If you need to, fake your energy and positive attitude, because this is business. Even if you are friendly with your boss, she is absolutely not your friend in this context. She may be happy for you, but she does not want you crying in the office about missing your baby. Often bosses have prepared themselves for you giving your notice or, at the very least, having lost your edge. If your job and career at this particular company is important to you then you must prove them wrong.

Be engaged, ask questions, demonstrate that you are up to speed and, if possible, have even moved a few things forward. Bring up the meetings you have scheduled with your team to review current issues or projects. Spend as little time as possible talking about the personal aspects of your maternity leave. Instead take the opportunity to bring up things you read or watched that are relevant to your company. Your boss wants nothing more than to take worrying about you and your workload off her plate so do it for her. And do it fast.

2. Meet with the team

If you have an assistant, a team or an entire division, focus on managing the minute you are back behind your desk. Pull in your senior team members individually to express your appreciation for what they accomplished in your absence. Get down to business by asking to be filled in on everything they may not have told you during your leave. If people have been dropping the ball or trying to undermine you, chances are you heard about it from someone when you were gone. Confront the colleagues and the issues head on as soon as possible. It will show the team that you are strong and you are back if you nip problems in the bud.

3. Get out there

Unfortunately people are going to assume that you are less relevant professionally now. Professional validation helps combat the invisibility issue many new mothers experience at work. So make it a priority, if you haven't already, to join high profile groups and professional organisations. Don't go overboard with the commitments, you do have a baby and about a million other things to worry about, but because most professional organisations cater to working people, the events are often at breakfast or lunch. Be strategic about what you take on, you are looking for high visibility and an opportunity to share what you've done or learned with your team.

4. Dress to kill

This is shallow (and more than a little bit annoying to many of us), but the truth is, we are often judged on our appearance. This especially holds true for the working mother. Many corporate cultures make it difficult for us to be heard, make an impact and be respected as a peer. It doesn't seem fair that we are combating the assumptions that we would rather be home by taking on more than our colleagues, but that's often what we have to do, at least in the beginning. So, yes it makes a difference if we return to work looking put together. How you present yourself says something to the outside world and, right now, you want to say . . . I'm back so listen to me, respect me and appreciate what I bring to this organisation.

5. Be confident

How you carry yourself those early days back at the office will set the tone for how you will be perceived moving forward. Contribute to the first team meeting by expressing your pleasure at being back. Don't be apologetic or tentative in any of those first meetings. You have no reason to be sorry. Maternity leave is your right and having a baby is your privilege and don't let anyone make you feel badly about taking time away from the office. Project to your boss, colleagues and staff that you belong back at the conference table.

Building Rapport with Your Boss

When you get back from maternity leave, it might take a little while to reconnect with your boss. You've been out for a while and work has been moving along without you. She or he may also be experiencing some unconscious and conscious emotional reactions related to your return including resentment you were gone, anxiety you will quit, concern that you have changed into another type of employee. You also want to remember that if you are having difficulties balancing everything, keep the personal stuff to yourself as working mum Felicia Watson does, 'If I'm going to miss a deadline , I don't use my family or children as an excuse.' Believe us, even if your ill child is the reason for being late on a project, don't bring them into it.

Here are some suggestions for how to build rapport with your boss:

Make their job easier

That's really why you were hired. A boss manages people who work on projects or aspects of the business they are responsible for. Your role as her employee is to make that go more smoothly. While you were out, her job was made a little more difficult. Now that you've returned, take back the work that was left on her plate and start making it known that you are back to make her life easier.

Share their concerns and priorities

Along the lines of 'mirroring', where you are adopting the behaviour of someone else in order to bond, we suggest that you tune into where your boss is coming from. If she is concerned about declining sales figures then you outline how you are going to contribute to fixing the problem. You will have opportunities to bond with your boss if your actions and deliverables reflect her priorities.

Show you care

Demonstrate you are invested in your job, the team and the company by being engaged in meetings, offering suggestions and solutions, asking questions and taking on new responsibilities.

Work hard but work smart

Since working mums have less time than they did before, you need to work just as hard but much more wisely. Efficiency and organisation are the key to finding that elusive work/life balance.

Working harder but smarter will also appeal to your boss, who most likely could do without the long lunches and random office chats.

Know the boss is not your friend
When you find yourself talking to your boss, don't waste her time by chatting about the baby. Yes, a good friend cares about your personal life and wants to hear details, but a good boss often doesn't. You also don't know how what you're sharing is being interpreted. The story you told her about your son smiling for the first time could be heard as a hint that you are going to quit to be a stay-at-home mum. So keep it all to yourself and focus the conversations on work.

Meet regularly
It is especially important in the first few weeks back to meet with your boss regularly. It's your chance to show him you are back in the swing of things. Be smart about what you discuss in the meetings and steer clear of sharing gossip or petty office issues.

Sell yourself and your accomplishments
Take opportunities to sell your accomplishments. In general, women don't do this enough, so much so that we dedicated huge sections in our *Kicking Your Career into Gear* book to the subject. It is most crucial for women just back from maternity leave to sell themselves, because we are often facing inherent sexism including the assumptions that we should – or would – rather be at home.

Notes on Breastfeeding from Lovers and Haters
One of the biggest challenges you may have as a mum is breast-feeding. When Nicole Lamborne, an obstetrician/gynaecologist and mother of three told us that they didn't teach her how to breastfeed in medical school, we weren't surprised. The prevailing

wisdom is that breastfeeding is the most natural thing in the world (why would anyone have to teach you?) – your baby pops out, latches on to the breast and you're off to the races.

The reality is that breastfeeding is difficult, at least in the beginning and it's especially difficult for working mothers because they have to express. And expressing isn't great (we're allowed to say that) – you have no connection to the baby, the machine is loud, there's nothing relaxing about sitting with your top down with two plastic bugles attached to your nipples, sucking away. We haven't spoken to a mother yet, working or not, who enjoys expressing breast milk.

We represent both ends of the spectrum of the breastfeeding experience. Kim delivered Thomas at term, and although he couldn't see, he managed to find the breast and latch on. Because he was only in the special care baby unit couple of days, and able to nurse, she only had to express a couple of times per day. When she got home from the hospital, with the help of a Boppy (a nursing pillow that helps with breastfeeding), inconceivable amounts of water, and her husband who kept pushing the baby's head in place, Kim was able to get into a groove. Since she worked from home for the first nine months, breastfeeding became an easy part of her routine after the second month. She had also purchased the Medela Pump n Style® like most new mothers do thinking that she'd be popping that out between errands to express like those new mothers you see in the breast pump advertisements. Ha! After the sterilising and two hours of reading the instructions, she gave the pump away and supplemented occasionally with formula.

Caitlin on the other hand was never able to get into a groove. First, she had two babies, both of whom were in the special care baby unit and unable to nurse. She had no option but pumping. She spent her days in the hospital pumping and her evenings at home pumping. She knew she was helping her babies by creating breast milk for them and that's what kept her going. She made it through six weeks of expressing and then she was relieved to turn off the pump.

Expressing at work is never easy, but here are few tips to make it easier:

- Breastfeeding is your right, so don't feel pressured to end it sooner than you're ready. And don't let others' discomfort deter you from doing what you think is right for you and your baby. Now is a great time to learn that to be a successful working mum you should be aware of your boss and colleagues' point-of-view, but don't let it push you into doing something that is in direct conflict with your beliefs.
- If you don't have an office with a door that shuts, make arrangements with your boss or human resources department to find a quiet private place for expressing. Also make sure there is a refrigerator available to you.
- Keep extra milk bags in your desk for the day you forget to bring in your portable bottles.
- Keep an extra shirt at work for the inevitable time that you will leak through your clothes.
- Make sure to keep your breastfeeding times clear on your schedule. Conference calls and meetings that delay your pumping session will get you off schedule and make the entire process even more difficult. Try to use those 30 minutes of pumping time to clear your head or get organised for the rest of the day. It's probably the only private time you'll have. Try to savour it.
- If it seems overwhelming and impossible to express at work, don't beat yourself up about supplementing with formula. Kim was obsessed with breastfeeding and really enjoyed it. She realised only after her son quit on her (he pushed her away at ten months old) that the reason he ate every three hours until he was six months, was because he was starving. He probably would have slept more, and she would have got more work

done if she had just supplemented with formula during the day.

Hello . . . I'm not JUST a Mum

Jennifer never thought that she would feel insecure after having her baby. Never one to notice if anyone was noticing her, she didn't consider how her role in the world would change once she became a mum. She can honestly say there wasn't even a fleeting thought about how she would feel about being treated differently. So, imagine her surprise when six months after having Adam she realised that the first question clients now asked, was about her son. People she had represented for years seemed surprised that she was more interested in discussing what was in the business section than the latest Super Nanny. Her younger staff now treated her differently, a little more distant and respectful, a little less peer-like. Gone was the Monday morning gossip over coffee, she was now a ma'am. And, embarrassingly, she missed the whistles she once ducked on the way to the office – they had dried up tout suite. It was like she aged 20 years in the three months she had been on bed rest. Once she began taking note of how people were interacting with her, she began to feel more like an unrelatable archetype and less like the fun career girl she once was.

Wait just a minute!

She liked that girl and she wanted her back. But the truth was that she was now a mum, who had to run out to relieve the nanny, who had to schedule appointments with the doctor, who couldn't ever join the team after work for drinks. The anger at becoming someone else turned into depression. And the erasing of her old self began. She began wearing the kinds of clothes she thought she should wear, the heels were put in the back of the closet, and her hair was now a warmer brown instead of the butter blond. Eventually, the paranoia about becoming invisible at work became reality.

Now this story may sound shallow, but even if you could care less about ever wearing that Missoni dress you saw in *Grazia*, you must have some version of Jennifer's story. Most of us go through a huge identity change – and crisis – when we become a mother. The way others treat you contributes to an already shaky self-esteem. Let's be honest, people have a lot of baggage when it comes to the concept of mum. At work, this could manifest itself in many ways. Your assistant, ten years younger than you, now sees a maternal figure and starts unloading her personal problems on you. Your boss, anxious about her own mothering skills, judges your priorities unfairly and pressures you to take on too much work. Your human resource director, with his history of female employees that don't return to work post-baby, constantly questions your commitment to the company.

We talk a lot in our books about the key to success being finding and projecting your authentic self. To navigate any big change, personal or professional, take time to reconnect with who you really are – now – not the girl you used to be.

The Word: Linda Brierty, Therapist

It seems like so many of us have a hard time, especially at the beginning, easing into our new identity as a mum. Do you have any thoughts about that to share with our readers?

The old version of motherhood was one of selfless martyrdom, sacrifice, the loss of self, and the complete devotion of life to the children and family. Obviously, this could create resentment and limit a woman's potential. The new paradigm of motherhood is seen as an expansion of the sense of self, not a negation of the original identity. Nothing has to be lost! There is much to be gained - greater depths of love, compassion and empathy, and selflessness in the best possible sense of the word - seeing the world beyond the limitations of the individual ego. Motherhood can facilitate opening our hearts to all beings. We can find strengths and potentials we never knew we had in our role as mother. We can also learn to mother ourselves every step of the way, and avoid the common pitfall of self-neglect. We can remember to nurture all of our relationships simultaneously to maintain a support network while raising a child. Keep your interests and passions alive to the extent that you can. In fact, you may find that motherhood makes you more effective; you may even manage your time better than before – because there will be less of it! You may also find that your child inspires you to be your best self, emotionally, professionally, in terms of health and personal development. Parenthood can also be a deeply spiritual and transformational event, if we see it as a gift and are grateful. Not only will you be raising your child, your child will be raising you.

15 Working Mum Mantras

1. I can't control everything.
2. I am doing my best.
3. I love my family and I love myself.
4. I can't care what others think.
5. I am relevant and important at work and at home.
6. I don't have to do everything.
7. Nothing is perfect.
8. I deserve time for myself.
9. When I take care of myself, I'm taking care of my family.
10. I am not ruining my child because I go to work.
11. It's OK to love working.
12. I can ask for help.
13. Other people can do things as well as I can.

> 14. My career is as important as my husband's.
> 15. My child does not love the nanny more than me.

Are You in High Gear Already?

Now that you're back in action, opportunities for advancement and big projects are going to come your way. And projects that you would have campaigned for before you had a baby, need to be careful considered now before you accept. Your priorities have changed. You can make different choices and still be a great career girl. What if you're asked to fly to New York for three days to pitch a new client? What if you need to work over a weekend to finish a presentation? You have a baby who needs every second of your spare time, so the answer is always 'no', right? WRONG. The answer is actually 'maybe'.

Before accepting or declining, find out how high-profile the assignment is, how much your boss and, more importantly, your company is invested in it, ask yourself if you are the best person for the job and try to figure out how much of an impact a success would have on your career in the short and long term. Most importantly, talk to your significant other about the opportunity to see if it's even possible for you to commit any additional time. And don't forget to do a gut-check as Mompreneur Felicia Watson advises, 'I would say that if there's a project that I'm stressing about because of the deadline and I have some inner turmoil that's carried over to my family time, I would pass on it. My children are only young once and I don't want to miss it or be preoccupied during that precious time with them.'

Is It Working at Home?

Family stresses are going to arise the day you go back to work because many of you are one of *two* working parents who are trying to share responsibility. In fact, this is such a challenge that we devote an entire chapter to it later in the book. But here's a little preview. When you have children, everything gets dirtier, the laundry triples (or even quadruples), the quick trips to the supermarket become major – sometimes multi-trolley – excursions and new appointments and obligations begin to fill the family calendar. With both parents working, there isn't that much time you are physically home to do what needs to get done. There are now many more things to discuss, coordinate, agree on, plan for and delegate but less quiet time together to do that. And who can deal with talking about anything while getting breakfast together at the same time as dressing for an important client meeting? The vision of a family rushing out the door in the morning is a cliché that is exploited by every cereal bar and frozen waffle maker in the country but it happens in millions of households every day and reflects our harried reality. And when it comes to keeping everything running smoothly at home, do you feel like you're always doing more than your partner? (Single mums, we know you put in 110% everyday). You are not crazy. Chances are good that if you have a husband, you are doing more work than he is.

Just look at the stats and you'll see it is not your imagination. A recent study from the University of Wisconsin's National Survey of Families and Households found that in households where the wife and the husband have full-time jobs, the woman does 28 hours of housework and the man only 16. We suspect the situation is true pretty much around the world. And this doesn't count childcare, where it has been demonstrated in multiple studies that the mother does triple the work. Why? Because we're women and we're often better at multi-tasking, organising, being patient, thinking ahead, putting ourselves last. We absolutely hate to generalise about gender issues, but this is really true: Women are better at running a house while also working than men. It could be just the way we're wired that way or it could be that all of us have set the bar too low for men. Why is it OK for them to do less housework when we work the same hours?

Because women are naturally care-takers, we are too often the solution to making an unworkable situation tolerable. We take too much on. We agree to pick up prescriptions during our lunch hour, drop the dog off at the vet before work, cancel our business trip because of a scheduling conflict and find ourselves doing the third load of laundry even though we did the first two.

The trick to making it all work – without resenting, or worse, hating each other – is a combination of systems and constant communication. You're a professional woman, bring some of that organisational spirit home and post a family calendar. Put everything on there from doctor's appointments and vacations to business trips and veterinary check-ups. Go over the calendar together so you both can prioritise the responsibilities and have a conversation about what is really important to each of you.

Make a list of household chores – and we mean all of them. The big, small, daily, monthly and yearly: walking the dog, changing the sheets, going to the tip, making dinner, packing lunch, buying the seasonal clothing, vacuuming the house. Everything you can think of should go on there. Then pull out the calendar and start splitting things up. If it's too overwhelming to look at five months from now then start with this month. When it starts looking like 50/50 then you're getting better. Keep going. Make a list of all the people who you give household responsibilities to – that could be a plumber, lawnmower, babysitter, the daycare, nanny or relative that cares for your baby while you're at work, a housecleaner, even the local teenager who cleans out your garage – and split up who is the point person for each.

We were taught growing up that we can have it all. Sure you can, but maybe not all of it today. What you can aspire to rather than the unattainable perfection is a work/home situation that goes smoothly *most* of the time.

Girl Talk: Single Mum Trials and Triumphs

Hillary McCarthy did not intend to be a single mother. But when her son's father backed out of the relationship and the parenting responsibilities within just a few months of the birth, she had to reconfigure not just her life but her definition of family. We wanted to include her in this book because she inspires us. Through a lot of hard work she has embraced her role as sole provider for her son and created a support system that works.

What kind of help do you have (hopefully lots)?
It was critically important for me to have a presence at Luke's pre-school and get to know the other families, so I take him to school three times a week at 8:30 a.m. before work. I have hired a nanny who picks Luke up in the afternoon, does our laundry and stays until I get home at 5:30. She keeps the house neat but because she is taking care of Luke, doesn't do any real cleaning.

Did you know right away what kind of help you needed?
It took me a while to figure it all out. Initially, I worked out of my home as a consultant and had lots of time to devote to my son. It meant I caught up at night while he was sleeping but it was worth it to me both financially and emotionally. I will say, though, those first two years took a toll on me. I lost myself in the mix – completely giving up working out, I didn't sleep enough and became depressed. I was trying to take care of everything in our home and lives by myself and allowing no time for me to do the things I

loved. I am in a much better place now that I make that time to work out and socialise.

Since you are doing much of this alone, do you have a few systems that you could share with mums just trying to figure this out?

Our nightly ritual now begins in the kitchen. Luke 'helps' me while I prepare our dinner. It's a great time for us to reconnect and I get to hear about his day. When you work full-time, every second counts. As for school mornings? Those are tough. I allow Luke to watch TV while I shower and get dressed. Then it's breakfast and racing to get him ready.

How do you fit in the household stuff (paying bills, cleaning) without a second set of hands?

Hmmm. I clean the bathroom when Luke is bathing! It keeps him company and allows me to multi-task. I make our beds as soon as we get up; my eyes probably aren't even open. I handle the kitchen while I'm prepping meals. So, if something's on the stove, I'm cleaning out the fridge. Multi-tasking all the time. I pay bills online, either from my office during lunch or in the evenings.

What is the biggest surprise you've had since becoming a working mother?

How much I can accomplish in a single day! I never gave myself credit for this until very recently, but now I'm becoming proud of what I've accomplished for me and Luke.

Anything else you want to share?

I am a different person than who I was before Luke, but I

think I veered too far away. It is so incredibly important to maintain who you are, at your core. I've only recently seen glimpses of my old self, and I'm working hard to bring her back. Also, let go of the ideals of family and embrace what it really is. What I have with my son is beautiful and I cherish it.

4

Centre Yourself for Success

When writing this chapter we reviewed long lists of what working mums could do to set themselves up for a successful go at their new role. We had notes about hiring housecleaners and dog walkers, skipping bake sales and saying no to volunteer work. We realised we were encouraging you to pursue a work/life balance that would be both expensive (defeating the purpose of why many of us work in the first place) and unsatisfying. Back to square one we went and used this chapter to offer you methods of centering yourself as a working mum. After all, you have much, much more on your plate now and the best way to deal with that is to nurture yourself and your spirit and learn to deal with the emotional hurdles of your new dual roles.

The Painful Compromises: Missing Moments

The bummer is that children go through huge changes over the first few years and it is inevitable that working mums will miss a milestone or two. While you are working on the annual budget, your child could have just taken his first step or said her first word. Health Insurance agent and mum Lorraine Nellis shares this, 'The truth is that if you work, someone else will share some of the milestone moments, but know that you will still have your own great memories.'

What you have to tell yourself is this: The first time you see your baby take a step is your first time. And there will be developments that you will witness over their lifetime that are just as amazing compared to every other debut you may have missed.

And get rid of the guilt! (Guilt is such a pervasive problem for working mums that we devote a whole section to it in chapter eight.)

We spoke to working mother Maria Morris who struggled with guilt for the first years of working and parenting. Maria said, 'I have always said that being raised Catholic removed the blood from my veins and replaced it with guilt. Being a working mother solidified that! So it's hard for me to admit this, but the moment I drop the kids off and get back into the car, I get a chance to breathe. I feel free! I feel like what I was before kids. I change the satellite radio from Disney to [controversial American DJ] Howard Stern (yeah, I listen to him) and drink my coffee. I look down at myself to see how much snot or food-remnants I have on me. I fix my hair and head off. Yeah, it's a tough, tough choice, but the fact is I also can't wait to pick them up at the end of the day.'

That isn't to say it isn't painful or doesn't make you regret – hopefully briefly – the decision to go back to work. It hurts to miss the signs of your baby growing up, but that is at the heart of the compromise to be a working mum. You have to make peace with the fact that there will be things you miss but your relationship with your child transcends any one step. Maria recommends cutting back on how much time and energy you put into chores because she found that, 'by simplifying the world around me I don't miss as many of those little moments and there are so many of them.'

Thoughts from Allison Taylor, a Working Mum

When I was 18 and pregnant, I began college. Thanks to the support of my mother, who looked after my son while I attended classes, I completed my BA by the time he was two.

I went to work as soon as I graduated, which was a difficult and exhilarating transition. Work demands your attention but so do your baby and home. I had to learn to become mindful in the role I was playing at any given time and give my all in every area. The thing to accept is that your life is always evolving and changing. You are growing as you cycle through whatever career or family expansion you take on. Before you try to schedule your life, you must prioritise.

The only way to organise and manage is to first decide your centre. For every woman this is different. What is important to you? What do you need to see, do, achieve, teach or discover to feel you are fulfilling your purpose? When your life reflects your highest priorities, your children learn to manage their goals, their talents, and they become competent and dignified individuals. That is what I learned from my mother, who made my education a priority for both of us before she passed away.

I have been through many changes in my home life and my career, but there's always more to learn. There lives a spirit in each of us, the spirit of a unique woman. The only way to honour yourself is to listen to your passions and to love the life you are creating. It is hard to get up so early, to pack the lunches, to concentrate on the presentation, to keep it all together. Only you can define your goals based on your personal mission. Take time to be your own company and remember what you bring to each and every relationship.

It's hard to be a working mum. It's hard to separate from your child when you go to work and it's hard to turn off the office when you come home to the baby. When I was younger, I completely underestimated the importance of doing things for myself that were healthy for my mind, spirit and body. If you neglect yourself, you'll be trying to run your family on empty. Be gentle as you grapple with the tough stuff. If it all seems too much, accept a helping hand. As women, we sometimes think if we are not working like dogs to shine in our career while raising stellar children while doing laundry and cooking gourmet dinner while making dentist appointments as we have the oil changed and balance our chequebooks while spinning plates on our heads . . . we aren't doing anything special. You do not have to prove your stamina to anyone. If we could wear one less hat, let it be the one that is self-critical.

I have found recently in my life, meeting women in all types of careers with all different families, sometimes the best thing we can do for ourselves is to recognise and compliment another woman. See her strength and empathise with her struggles. There is nothing more heartbreaking or detrimental to our success than cutting each other down. Surround yourself with positive and humorous women who are also working mums. We need to celebrate each other.

You Can't Afford to Run Yourself Ragged

Even if your partner is an excellent co-parent, as the mother of the household, you are its centre. You are the touchstone, the constant, the heart of the home. We know how corny that sounds, and believe us, we are cynical urban girls and we don't throw around words like 'touchstone' lightly. But we have found even when we don't want to be the one that knows where everything is, when the parent-teacher meeting is scheduled, or who we hire for babysitting on Thursday nights, we are. In addition to being the head of household, emotionally and/or otherwise, you have your career to take care of. As a working mother, you are being judged by your colleagues, many of whom expected you to bag it all for life at home. Some of them may have been counting on it.

As unfair as it may seem, especially when you are running on empty, you have to work harder, better and smarter in the early days of returning to the office. You need to demonstrate that you haven't lost your ambition, edge and guts.

How are you going to do all of that – kick butt at work, run your household, be there for your child – if you are rundown? The answer quite simply is you can't. It is essential that you take care of yourself both physically and mentally right now. You absolutely must take time for yourself to recharge. Don't think of going to get a massage or taking a few hours on the weekend to see a movie as shirking your responsibilities. Think of those moments alone, and time away from your duties, as doctor's orders. With everything you are doing, you can't afford to get sick or burnt out. When you are depleted, you start losing focus, you have a harder time making decisions and getting things done. And let's not forget how quickly you lose your patience and temper when you're tired. On the flipside, when you are well-rested after spending a few hours or, even a day, alone you can be fully present at work and home.

And it's really all about being fully present and engaged, isn't it? Be home when you are home and at work when you are at work.

The only way to have that focus is by making sure you are not running on empty. So here are your orders from us: Take a break. You, the family and the employer deserve to have your best.

Asking for What You Need

When we interviewed women for our second book, *The Girl's Guide to Being a Boss*, about their management challenges, most of them included their reluctance to delegate. Some of the women felt they could do tasks quicker, if not better than, their employees. Or they felt uncomfortable telling people what to do. Many felt like the only way to guarantee it was done right was to do it themselves.

We think this unwillingness to take anything off our plates effects us at home just as much as the office. And as with work, if we don't ask for help or delegate tasks, at home we find our list longer at the end of each day. Even if you do a better job cleaning the house, and you don't put the reds in with the whites when you do the laundry, and you cook things that the kids actually eat . . . let your partner take on some of the work. And don't wait for them to ask either, because it might not happen. Just start handing off some tasks then leave them to it without chiming in with your suggestions, advice or criticism.

Working mum-raised Amanda Dantico shares this, 'My sister and I, and even my father, were all assigned chores when we were old enough. All of us cleaned the bathrooms, did the dishes, laundry, yard work, vacuuming and dusting. My mother didn't want us growing up on fast food, which I thank her for now, but we all had to help cook dinner. My mum keeps a very clean house, but she learned fast that she had to just let it go and know that not all the chores were going to get done.'

The key to your success both at work and at home is asking and delegating because everyone might not be noticing what you are doing. And they, for sure, are not reading your mind. So if you need time or a change in the schedule to accommodate your professional responsibilities then ask for it. If you need a cleaner to come in once a month or once a week to help, and you can afford it, then ask for it. If you need your partner to take on more responsibility, then ask for it. Of course this is the hardest ask of all, so be sure to read about delegating to your partner in chapter seven.

Working Mums Online

Where these women get the time, we will never know but they are out there. And there are a lot of them. Working women everywhere are blogging or chatting about their experiences, challenges, tips, solutions to everyday problems, healthy foods, favourite celebrities, TV shows and, of course, partners. Most of them have ways for you to contribute your own stories or tips to share, as well as find a community of women going through some of the same things you are experiencing every day. Some of the better blogs and forums can be found on bigger sites that include much more than one woman's personal musings. If you are looking to connect, know you're not alone or share your own stories, struggles or triumphs, maybe you can find what you're looking for online in those few free moments for yourself. Mumsnet (www.mumsnet.com) is probably the biggest and highest-profile in the UK, but you can also visit BabyCentre (www.babycentre.co.uk), Bounty (www.bounty.com), NetMums (www.netmums.com), UKParentsLounge (www.ukparentslounge.com) or Help for Busy Mums (www.helpforbusymums.com) to name just a few.

And of course you can always visit our favourite blog, www.girlsguidetobusiness.com.

The Right to Change Your Mind

We have the power to make choices that will affect how we work, how we parent, and how we want to live. We do it all the time. Too often we forget we're allowed to change our minds. If there's one thing we've learned from writing this book, it's that you really don't know anything until you know. You think you will want to stay home after you've had your baby only to realise you can't wait to get back to work. You think you will love breastfeeding, only to discover that you keep getting clogged milk ducts and you hate it. These scenarios point to the larger issues. We're all just trying to figure it out and even with the most thorough planning and advance research, the solutions you've come up with often just don't work.

Don't feel bad about it. Just try something else. Do more research, ask friends and colleagues for their ideas. You have the power to change your situation, just know that the changes could take years to happen. It took Eileen seven years to get her family an international posting (see The Word, this chapter) and Nicole is still trying to find the work situation that will make her happiest at home (see Girl Talk, this chapter). None of this is easy, but here are some things to keep in mind:

- If you know something is not working, don't wait for it to fix itself. It won't. Kim's son was having problems in school and instead of dealing with it right away, as she would any problem at work, she trusted the teachers knew more than she did. They didn't. Once she intervened and put new systems in place, her son began to flourish.
- Be willing to adapt the system you've created. As your kids grow up, and as your responsibilities change at work, you will need a new schedule and a new way to distribute the responsibilities.
- You have the power to make radical change. If you hate your job because it doesn't allow you to be flexible, start looking for

a new job. Be willing to take less money if it offers more flexibility. Time is worth money to working mothers.

Just Say 'NO'

Many of us say yes to whatever is asked of us. Whether we are conditioned to be people pleasers or it's just in our nature, the consequences are the same – we do too much. Before agreeing to anything, look at what's already on your plate. Then look at the timing of the favour, assignment, task, chore that is being asked of you.

Because you have so little time now you have to become highly selective about what you take on and sometimes you are going to have to say no, which is very difficult for most of us. We interviewed Jane Miller, a single mother of two children and the editor at a major publishing house. When we asked her how she manages to get everything done at work she shared this, 'Sometimes I just have to stay a little later to work on a major project but the key for me is that I am extremely efficient at the office. I don't do unnecessary lunch dates and try to make smart benefit/cost choices, where the cost side of the equation is my time and the benefit side is the revenue I'll bring in. Knowing that I have to leave at 5:30 has made me focus hard on what I choose to take on. It has also taught me how to say no to various things, not always easy. In fact, the other day someone got annoyed with me when he asked a favour that I couldn't do. OK, he was annoyed but then he has a stay-at-home wife to look after his house and kids.'

10 signs that things need readjusting in your life

1. **You never have a second to yourself.**
2. **You are angry much of the time.**

---

3. **You constantly fight with your partner over the chores.**
4. **You micromanage your employees and your spouse.**
5. **You resent your kids for needing attention from you.**
6. **You agree to unnecessary business trips just to get away.**
7. **Around Sunday evening, you begin to dread going to work.**
8. **On Friday afternoon, you begin to dread the weekend with the family.**
9. **You are exhausted most of the time.**
10. **Social time with friends is a distant memory.**

---

10 Things to Do for Yourself

We do not make or take enough time for ourselves. In fact, a study conducted by the Families and Work Institute on the changing workforce found that modern dads spend 1.3 hours each workday on themselves while mums only take 0.9 hours. Depressingly this number is obviously shrinking because back in 1977 a similar study found that mums had 1.6 hours for themselves. The thing is, we need downtime to recharge so we can not only enjoy life more but we will have more to give. Here are 10 things you can try doing for yourself, ideally by yourself.

- Read an escapist novel. You want something entertaining that will take your mind off of everything you have on your to-do list. Caitlin's secret is young adult novels, because there isn't anything more relaxing than reading about heroines stressing about proms, boys or getting into college. Ahh . . . those were the days.
- Watch all of the television shows you can't seem to find time

for on DVD. Make sure Mad Men and Spooks are on your list. Such good television.

- Lunch with old friends. We are talking about getting together with people who knew you before, during and after your new life as a working mother. It is fun to talk and laugh about the days that you now realise were in retrospect, really easy.
- Stretch, take up yoga or get to the gym. Getting physically active can take your mind off things while boosting your confidence and energy and reducing stress. Nothing bad about that.
- Schedule a weekly breakfast with your significant other. OK we know this is all about you time, but it's nice to reconnect and nothing kills a relationship faster than only spending time talking about errands, chores and bills. Boooorrring.
- Negotiate to sleep late on a weekend day. Hey, you're exhausted and knowing you won't have to get up at the crack of down on Saturday or Sunday can get you through a tough week.
- Start walking at lunch. Sounds silly, but with your iPod filled with your personalised playlist, it can be beyond relaxing and rejuvenating to get some fresh air.
- Get up a little earlier and spend an hour alone. Read a book, the paper, or just tune out over that first cup of delicious coffee. A quiet house is a nice way to enter the day.
- While most of us don't have the time or money for a spa day, an hour with a masseuse feels pretty great.
- Start planning a weekend away, either with your spouse, alone or with your best friend. Just having a personal trip on the calendar – even if it is six months away can be a reminder that downtime is coming up.

Knowing How You Work Best

Time to be honest. How many of us, pre- or post-pregnancy, work eight, ten or twelve hours straight? Many of us put in a solid three, and then take a lunch break, getting back to work half speed for a few hours, then full speed again after a coffee break. Others work through lunch, crashing around four and being pretty useless until the end of the day. At our office, we've noticed that the staff is a little slow to start but really focused from eleven until seven. In fact, we have one employee who can only work well if she comes in around ten in the morning, so we've switched her hours to accommodate her.

Whatever your rhythm is, after you have a baby it will change, so start paying attention to the times of day that you are most productive and see if you can work your job around it. It's not always easy if you find yourself wide awake and focused at 3 a.m. but hopefully your good hours will intersect with your on-the-clock hours. If you have the kind of job and company that offers flexibility then you may want to consider shifting your schedule around to maximise your most productive self. If not, then at least tackle the tough assignments when you are at your best. We had a boss who encouraged us to work through our to-do lists in the morning, crossing off the most challenging tasks first. Leave the brainless work on your list to do when you are, in fact, brainless.

Girl Talk: Jen Groover, Inventor

We met Jen Groover (www.jengroover.com) at the Pennsylvania's Governor's Conference for Women and were not only impressed by her success (she's invented about a zillion products!) but her attitude. She may well be the most positive person we've ever met. It turns out she wasn't always this way. She started out as a fitness expert. Right out of college she opened a gym and was training clients, teaching aerobics and competing nationally in aerobics competitions. After two national competitions in 2000, Jen returned home physically and mentally exhausted – which was typical for her after a big event. She figured she'd recover in a couple of weeks like she'd done every time before but it didn't happen. As a matter of fact, she proceeded to get worse and worse. She dragged herself (literally) from doctor to doctor who kept telling her she was fine. She knew she wasn't fine and began doing her own research. She finally found a doctor who was willing to consider that this 27-year old woman in peak physical condition was suffering from Chronic Fatigue Syndrome. Her tests were conclusive and her doctor was declarative. If she didn't change her life immediately, she wouldn't ever heal.

For the first time in her life, Jen was terrified. She was used to relying on herself as she'd been on her own since her late teens. She had opened and run a successful business and constantly giving her woman clients advice about how to start businesses for themselves. She knew she was an ideas person, but had no idea how to turn her ideas into money, even though she watched her clients do exactly that. She sold her gym to her partner and began studying intellectual property. At the same time, she went on a journey of self-exploration to help repair her damaged body.

She credits yoga, massage therapy and reiki with the repair to her body, and her new positive attitude came from working diligently to change her thought processes. She makes a conscious decision every day to be a positive thinker. Now she's the mother of four and a-half year old twins and we spoke to Jen about her hard-fought battle to get healthy and centered in her life.

We heard your story, however it doesn't sound as if you're going any slower than you did before you got sick. What has changed?

I still do as much as I did before, maybe more, with the kids involved, but I do everything differently. I've learned to say no after too many years of saying yes because I didn't want to disappoint people. Or because I thought they wouldn't like me if I said No. What I learned is that if I didn't prioritise my health and take care of myself, I would be of no use to anyone – not my employees, my husband or my children.

How do you take care of yourself?

For starters, I eat healthy, am active – no more gym, lots of running after kids – take vitamins and drink acai berry juice for the antioxidants. I have also learned how to change my thought process away from negative thinking (how am I ever going to get this all done?) to positive thinking (I can get this all done if I do x, y and z.) Although for me it's more important sometimes to NOT do x, y or z. I've learned that my body has limits and if I need to take a day off after a big, adrenaline-charged event, then I not only will, but I better had because otherwise it will negatively impact whatever comes after it. I am much smarter about setting boundaries now.

But how did you get to this new place?

It was a total spiritual journey for me and it was extremely difficult. I poured myself into it 1000% and tried to rid myself of layers of negative thinking and baggage from my childhood. It wasn't easy, but it worked. I made a conscious decision to vibrate on the highest, most positive level every single day.

How has motherhood changed you?
I have a completely different vision of perfection then I used to have. When I was younger, I strove to be perfect in every single thing. Now I am striving to be successful and honour the commitments that I make to my family and business relationships to the best of my ability.

5

It's Never Quiet on the Home Front

Now that you're centered, you need some real, practical tips because frankly, life is a little insane now. And it isn't going to slow down anytime soon. Sure the diapers will go away, but they will be replaced by accidents (gross but true). Kindergarten begins but so does conjunctivitis. Unless you develop at least something resembling a 'go with the flow' attitude, you will absolutely lose your mind. In this chapter we talk about the typical schedule of a working family including the new significance of breakfast and dinner. We share tips from busy mums on how to make life a little easier, and we'll touch on how your responsibilities at home could impact your job. As two working mums with two companies between us, we know how the lines blur between work and home these days, but there are strategies that will help all parties – your family, your boss, your employees and yourself – can have their needs met. At least most of the time.

Is a Smooth Morning Possible?

All of those images you see in TV adverts and films – the harried working mums, half-dressed for work, running around feeding the family and jumping out of the way of flying oatmeal – are inspired by truth. Most of us only have two hours in the morning, if that, to get ourselves showered and dressed, the children up dressed and fed, daycare bags or lunches packed and household chores taken care of. It's a lot to cram into a little window and even if we wake up with the best of intentions, stress can lead to arguments and tension. Suddenly, everyone is heading off into the world without the support they need.

Is it possible to do things differently? Of course. But let's start with your attitude about the morning. First things first: Don't hold onto the hope that you will have any time, space or peace to focus on your own needs once everyone is awake. Your children are going to need and want your full attention and don't care if you are anxious about an forthcoming review. Instead of waking up at the first cry or tug at your bedcovers, set the alarm earlier. Half an hour, an hour, whatever you need to take care of your needs whether that is showering, ironing, running, meditating or gathering your thoughts for the workday ahead. Any little bit of time that you carve out for yourself makes a huge difference in everyone's day. If you are collected while the chaos whirls around you then you won't easily be thrown off your game in the likely event something goes wrong.

Here are a few additional tips – gathered from talking to working women like you – that may help you ease into the day:

- After you are showered don't put on your work clothes. Change into casual clothes to buzz through breakfast and the morning list. Not having to worry about spilled orange juice on your suit or creases in the shirt you just ironed can reduce unnecessary stress.
- Pack lunch or snacks the night before and have everything

ready to pop into a backpack. When you do the shopping, pick up things like juice boxes and small bottles of water in bulk ahead of time so they will always be on hand to send off with your kids.

- Get an automatic coffee maker so you can have that first cup seconds after opening your eyes. OK, this one was from Caitlin who is admittedly a caffeine addict.
- Feed your kids while they are still in their pyjamas so you don't care if (when) they spill their breakfast.
- Take five minutes each morning to review the running household list before you leave for work. It is helpful to know what errands you each have to take care of at lunch or on the way home.
- Eat something healthy with your kids. Too many of us grab something to eat while driving. It isn't good for you and you're missing quality time with your family.
- Don't expect anything to go smoothly and then be grateful when something does.
- Spend a few minutes every morning focused exclusively on your kids. No multi-tasking, putting away dishes while you are hurrying them along. If you give them your attention before they head off into the world, it will do wonders for their confidence and self-esteem.

Now, the kids are with their caretakers, and it's back to just you. Take a huge breath and clear your head. If there has been some tension between you and your partner, let it go, because in just a little while your office is going to need your full attention. To make the transition, many of the mothers we spoke to stop at their favourite morning spot to pick up a fresh cup of coffee, a few meet a colleague to catch up before going into the office or walk rather than take a cab from the train station. Whatever it is, try and find something, a pre-work ritual, that signals the end of your mum self and the beginning of your work self.

10 things you should do at home to make your life easier

1. Don't do laundry every day.
2. Try giving the kids a bath every other day.
3. Plan meals in advance.
4. Use leftovers for snacks or lunches.
5. Multi-task the chores (clean the bathrooms when your kids are in the bath, scrub the kitchen while the pasta water is boiling)
6. Have weekly meetings with your spouse to evenly delegate the chores, appointments, errands and other household responsibilities.
7. Pay your bills online.
8. Get help whenever you can.
9. Prep for morning at night and for night in the morning.
10. Don't over schedule yourself with obligations (know your limitations).

Preparing Your Family for Business Travel

Business trips are a necessity for many of us and although our families would rather we stay home, it often isn't possible to opt out. When your children are still infants your first business trip can be a heart-wrenching experience or a welcomed break depending on the support you have on the home front.

Preparing everyone for a forthcoming trip starts with coordinating the schedule with all of the caregivers, most importantly your partner. If your child is old enough to understand, start telling them a few days before you leave that you are taking a trip but will be back. Gerri Cristantiello tells her husband first, and then as it gets closer to the date she begins to tell her young son.

Gerri writes, 'I tell him how many nights I will be away and that daddy will take care of him, that I will come back and, most importantly, that he can call me any time he wants to. So if he misses me or wants to talk to me, he can call me on my mobile phone. I tell him how many times he will go to sleep before he sees me.'

Expect your partner to push back a little or a lot when you have a business trip on the calendar. As annoying as that may be, most spouses would just rather not do the home stuff solo. Some of our readers suggested that their husbands were anxious about the childcare responsibility. Others just felt like their spouses gave them grief because they just didn't want to work as hard as we do. But some maybe just feel ill-equipped to juggle it all without you. Even if you have a completely supportive and confident partner, you might be feeling emotional – sad, anxious, nervous, excited – about leaving. The first trip is always the hardest, but once you return and see that your family is healthy and happy, the house still standing, everyone still loves you and your spouse hasn't lost his or her mind, you'll be better prepared for the next one.

Business trips are complicated aspects of our job responsibilities because they demand huge sacrifices of your personal time. And, as we know, that personal time isn't just yours to give up anymore. If your job requires you to spend a lot of time on the road and your partner just can't make up for it due to their own careers then it might be a sign that things need to change. Most jobs however don't have you living out of a suitcase, so don't beat yourself up when you do need to take a trip on behalf of the company. And remind a resentful spouse that your job and your salary are important too.

How and Why to Make the Most of a Business Trip

We have confessed in a few *Girl's Guide* books – including this one – how much we love a business trip. It helps that we actually like what we do most of the time so that even the business part of the trip isn't painful and can even be unexpected fun. We also have identified two pieces of planning that make just about every trip comfortable and relaxing. We make reservations at the best-reviewed restaurants specialising in local fare and we stay at boutique hotels. These are two, sometimes inexpensive, ways that we've discovered make being away from home more pleasant.

Whatever makes a trip more fun for you, add it into the mix as you are planning. Can you sneak in that movie you've been dying to see? Pick up the novel at the airport bookshop that has been getting rave reviews? Are there friends that live locally you could see? If you have any control over your schedule try to book meetings in such a way that you end up with either a morning or an afternoon to enjoy guilt-free you time.

If you just dread business trips and can't get your head around enjoying them then know this, business trips offer both professional and personal opportunities. They are good for business because if you do a good job – contribute at an important meeting, learn something crucial that you can share with the team back at the office, meet a potential client, land new business – you are making a statement to your boss that you are an asset. Trips away from the office can also help your career in the bigger picture. When you travel, you are expanding your network of contacts and that can help you far beyond your current position at your current company. Make the most of being out there by setting up meetings, drinks, meals with people in your field. Do research ahead of time. Are there people you want to know in that city? Are there people in your network that could make an introduction before you get to town? Having contacts around the country in your industry can be a huge resource for you down the road when you need advice, job opportunities, connections, guidance or recommendations. Make the most of each trip by thinking bigger about your career. So get enough sleep, stay in places you love, carve out a little time for yourself to recharge and appreciate the time you have been given to expand your career.

Business trips also offer opportunities for personal growth as well because at no other time will you have a chunk of time alone. You don't know how great that is until you find yourself sitting on the edge of your bed in a quiet hotel room deciding between watching a movie or taking a hot shower. We mothers are so conditioned to the constant interruptions that to have the mental and emotional space to reflect on anything is a gift. So when you are on a business trip, take some time to think about your career and ask yourself some questions. What's working and what isn't? How can you contribute more or pull back a little? Are you still inspired by what you do or is it time for a change? Draft an action plan for how to take charge of the direction of your career a little. Our third book, *The Girl's Guide to Kicking Your Career into Gear,* was inspired by women who were looking for ways to take charge of their professional lives. If you find yourself with some space to start thinking about it . . . take advantage of it.

Family Holidays Aren't Always a Holiday

When Caitlin and Andrew took their kids on their first vacation, she came back needing one. It wasn't that she didn't enjoy the twins or being away, it was that she made the mistake of trying to do it all. She tried to juggle 'relaxing' with her family, while keeping track at things at work and finishing up a book proposal. Don't make the mistake of going into a family trip thinking it's going to be filled with hours of free time. Afternoons when everyone else kicks back and lets you work on the laptop is a pipedream. Debbie Shandel concurs, 'Unfortunately there is no such thing as a true vacation. The BlackBerry® beckons at every turn. I try to answer the quick questions on the go but reserve the longer and more research-laden responses for at night after the kids are asleep. I must admit I am not that great with boundaries between work and vacation and that is something that I need to work on. You know it's bad when your 5-year-old says, 'Put down the BlackBerry®, mummy, and come on the water slide!!!"

We should all make more of an effort to log-off. Kids want and deserve our full attention because they most likely only get it in bits and pieces most of the time. If you don't give them what they need, they will jump up and down, start an argument or send some other signal that what they need is *you*. It's no one's fault, it's just the way it is for working families. So when you are with them 24/7, they are excited and most likely won't be leaving you alone to work.

Plan to check out from work – at least the majority of the time – when you are on vacation by preparing everyone from your assistant to your clients. Wrap up loose ends, finish projects and schedule meetings with your reports to go over to-do lists, provide your boss with an overview of where things stand and what is going to be done while you are away. If possible, try to check in with the team once a day and tell everyone that you'll be occasionally checking email. Even if a day goes by where you are incommunicado, knowing that you are making an effort will ease even the most anxious team member. So you don't come back completely stressed out, set reasonable expectations for yourself as well. Know that your job when on a trip with your family is to be the mum and it will be very difficult to do more than that.

Truth: Kids Get Sick

They all get sick, especially if your kids are at daycare. In the winter, there might be months when someone is out once or twice a week with something. There is the ridiculously contagious conjunctivitis that seems to go round and round the classroom and the lingering cough that makes a brutal return just as you're leaving for the office. There are the weird diseases (slapped cheek syndrome – have you heard of it?) and the seemingly endless winter sniffles. Sometimes it may seem that, literally, there is always something.

Cold and flu season is especially difficult for us. In 2007 *Working Mother* magazine conducted a survey on this very issue. It was discovered that nearly 50% of the respondents agreed that the work/life balance is jeopardised during this time because although 33% of us have sent our children to school sick, 70% of us are wracked with guilt about doing it. With the most common reason being mums can't afford to take the day off thanks to unpaid sick days, most families face an impossible decision.

And, yes it is no surprise this affects working mums more than dads. In fact, in a 2003 study, the Kaiser Family Foundation found that 49% of mums miss work when taking care of a sick child compared to only 30% of dads.

We asked several of the women we interviewed about this issue and most of them agreed that in their households they were the ones who either stayed home with a sick child or was responsible for arranging the coverage. When pressed for details, a few of them owned up to the fact that they felt strongly that children needed their mothers when they were sick. Others said that they were the ones who knew how best to navigate the doctor's surgery and the chemist. And most of the women took on the responsibility of a sick child without a single discussion with their spouse about that being fair.

For those of you who take this on without thought, know this . . . the choice to always be the one staying home could be having an impact on your career. If it's your choice then that's great, but if you are the one missing an important meeting or the third day of work because you don't feel comfortable having anyone else take care of your child or worse, you buy that your spouse's career is more important, then wait a minute. Days home with a sick child are something to be negotiated. When it looks like things are heading in that direction, compare diaries and see who has the more flexible morning, day or week ahead of them? Can you split the day with one of you taking the morning shift at home while the other does the afternoon? If both of you are maxed out, do you have another set of hands to call in?

The point is, the challenge of having a sick child who needs to be home during the work week is one to be shared. It really isn't up to you to solve the problem, and it is wrong that this too often falls into the mother's lap. So you don't leave the discussion to the last minute when you have a sniffling child and a spouse halfway out the door, have a contingency plan in place for emergencies. Do you have a trustworthy neighbour, best friend, a relative, a babysitter with a flexible schedule that can jump in at the last minute? If not, let the negotiations begin.

Caitlin Shares Her Absolutely Worst Week Ever

I am sharing this story because I want you to know the truth that even if you use all of the useful strategies we offer things can still go awry. You have no control over most things that happen in life, especially when you have children. To set the scene of this Worst Week Ever, my twins were almost four. For those of you who haven't been around four-year-olds, they are walking, talking, and intentionally not-listening little bundles of non-stop energy. It started on a Saturday morning when my daughter Taylor woke up with the early signs of conjunctivitis in her left eye (a very contagious condition that can require antibiotic drops). Knowing that unless she was on the drops for 24 hours she couldn't go to school on Monday, we rushed her to the hospital for a prescription. After a two-hour wait, the A&E doctor confirmed the diagnosis and gave me the drops, telling me to only put them in the affected eye. I begged her for an extra prescription for my son Declan just in case (since, as I said, this is a very contagious condition) but she refused (I guess she didn't want to lose her medical licence).

We started the antibiotics that afternoon and because the infection was very mild, it looked clear by Sunday afternoon. This was a huge relief because I was scheduled for jury duty on Monday, Tuesday and Wednesday and Andrew had a book deadline which meant the kids absolutely had to go to school.

On Monday morning, Taylor cries from the bedroom 'My eye!' and we rush in to see that sure enough her right eye was now infected. To make this all just a little better, moments later Declan shouts 'My eye!' He had contracted conjunctivitis too. So I help get the kids dressed while Andrew is close to crying at the kitchen table knowing that his writing day has gone out the window, only to be replaced by taking care of two four-year-olds too contagious to leave the house. He takes them to the doctor's office to get Declan's prescription and I leave for jury duty. While trying to get out of sitting for a four-week trial, I get an email from Andrew telling me that when coming back from the doctor's office, the kids were fighting to open a door and Taylor's toe got jammed underneath it, pulling part of the nail off.

I was released a little early that day and rushed home to look at the eye, toe, other eye and to see if Andrew was still alive. He had done an excellent job cleaning and wrapping Taylor's toe so we thought it would be ok until about 7p.m. when it looked much worse and we decided a trip to A&E was in order. So Andrew takes her and is there until 2 a.m. And no one wants to be in A&E in New York City (or really, anywhere) at 2 a.m.

Monday: Zero work got done.

By Tuesday morning, Declan's eye was cleared and I took him to school before going down to serve my second day of jury duty. While Andrew was taking care of Taylor and Declan was playing at school, I was actually selected for a trial. Even though I thought for sure that I would be released once I told all of the lawyers that I had found someone guilty the last time I served. I guess that made me even more appealing because I was among the first selected. We all got let go for lunch, and when I told Andrew that I was on a jury he just about broke down on the phone after having spent five hours trying to convince Taylor that staying inside was loads more fun than going to the park with the other kids. After a rollercoaster of an afternoon, the jurors were miraculously dismissed, thanks to a little game of chicken between the lawyers that ended in a settlement. I was beyond relieved.

Tuesday: Zero work got done, panic sets in and Andrew and I start fighting.

So, now we're at Wednesday morning. Andrew brings Declan to school and I bring Taylor to the doctor's for a follow up visit on the toe. The nurse looks at it and says it's in great shape but when the doctor takes a peek she sees an infection under the nail and recommends that we go to a plastic surgeon as soon as possible. What?! A plastic surgeon? So I bring Taylor home, while we wait for the appointment and Andrew starts getting ready to take her. Thankfully, he does the tough doctor's visits with the kids because frankly I just can't handle it. So he brings her to the plastic surgeon, who takes off most of the nail on her big toe and I pick Declan up from school.

Wednesday: Zero work got done, full-blown anxiety attacks and lots of arguing.

Taylor is still home on Thursday, Declan is off to school. I bring her into the office so that I can finish up a few proposals and answer some of the hundreds of emails that I couldn't deal with reading on my BlackBerry®.

Thursday: Some work gets done. Thank God.

On Friday, I take Taylor for a follow-up visit at the plastic surgeon and, thankfully, we're in the clear. She's on the way to being healed and can now take a bath and return to school on Monday. One would think that, maybe, for a few hours during nap I could get work done but no, the pre-school scheduled a training for the teachers that afternoon wouldn't you know it, so we had to pick Declan up. Both kids back at home.

Friday: A tiny little bit of work gets done.

And I'm counting down the hours until Monday morning at 8:01 when I turn the kids over to the very capable teachers at The Children's Garden.

Lessons Learned: Don't panic when things start going south because there is really nothing you can do about it most of the time. Do what you can to make things better for the people in your life and at work. Don't beat yourself up over things out of your control and, most importantly, the key to dealing with any crises personal or professional is good communication. Be clear about what you need and what you can do and stick to what you promise.

8 things to do when you are left without help

1. Don't panic.
2. Have a sit down conversation with your co-parent on how to realistically split up the day. Prioritise who has what scheduled or due.
3. Communicate with your boss without giving too many details. She doesn't want to hear it. She just wants to know how you are covering things and how things are not going to slip off your plate and land on to hers.
4. Set up a schedule for yourself so you don't lose your mind. Can you get a few hours of work done while your child is sleeping, watching television, or working on an art project?
5. If possible, tire your child out. Seriously, the more physical activity they do in the morning, the less energy they will have in the afternoon and they might just take an extra-long nap.
6. If you have a BlackBerry®, use it. If you have conference calls scheduled, see if you can move them because nothing screams unprofessional more than a screaming baby.
7. Don't let anything drop but try to communicate

> with as many people as possible, delegate what
> needs delegating and don't neglect your child.
>
> 8. See if you can get a babysitter that night so you can
>   have some extra hours to work.

Working with Your Child's School

You've worked so hard to balance the schedules between your office and your home. Now there's the oft-forgotten factor – school. How much of your time is the school expecting? What is a must and what can be missed?

Let's start with the basics. They expect you to help your children with homework, be engaged with the lessons, appreciate the job of the teachers, drop off and pick up on time and respect the rules of the school. They will want you to come to parent–teacher meetings. Beyond that, they could expect you to help raise funds, go to Parent Teacher Association meetings, make costumes for the spring play or help build the new jungle gym over the weekend. Every school has the spoken and unspoken expectations for parental participation. The trick is to figure them out, do what you can and not take on anymore than you can handle.

Ask the head teacher of the school what events they are planning over the course of the year that they would expect parents to attend or help with. See how far in advance you can schedule a parent-teacher meeting, so you can secure a lunchtime slot. Ask what activities they would ideally like parents to participate in or contribute to (this would be the originally unsaid expectations). Ask if there are family barbeques, bake sales or fundraising events in the works. Preschool director Susan Stein advises parents to 'Try to participate in at least one classroom activity over the year. Kids are so proud when it's their parents who are reading a story, going on a trip with the class or doing a cooking project with their friends. If the school has fundraisers or regularly scheduled meetings, try to participate in some way and if you can't be there, at the very least acknowledge your regret that you won't be attending.'

You want to know everything that might require more time from you because, only then can you be firm about what you can take on and what you can't. If you are cornered by the teacher one day after school and asked if you are coming in over the weekend to help paint the classroom, chances are that you will say yes without taking the time to figure out if you have the childcare at home that would even make it possible. Susan says her teachers 'know how busy parents are, so responding to the basics of classroom administration are much appreciated: parents should read all notices that are sent home the first time and respond to any requests promptly, whether it's returning permission slips, sign-up sheets, labelling/checking/updating extra clothing, etc.'

The teachers are, in many ways your partner, and their influence is significant, so don't take them for granted. Susan says, 'Just acknowledging the work around the classroom, or relating an anecdote from the weekend about some school-related matter tells the teachers you appreciate their efforts. And of course, a spontaneous gift of flowers for the classroom or cookies is always nice too.'

Is a Smooth Evening Possible?

Some people refer to evening with small children as the witching hour. Either the kids are so excited to see their parents that the adrenaline is making them nuts or their hunger and exhaustion is making them impossibly cranky. And let's be honest, it isn't always easy to shake off our own workday stress and we might be tired, hungry and cranky ourselves. We've heard a bunch of tips from working mums on how to make the transition from day to evening a bonding experience for everyone.

- **Feed them and you** Snacks on the way home can be a lifesaver. Kids tend to calm down when they're not ravenous,

99

so if you pick up your kids from daycare bring something, or if they are at home with the childminder or nanny then make sure they give them something to keep them going. And don't forget to eat a little protein yourself, a piece of cheese, yogurt anything that will give you energy going into dinnertime.

- **Set up a 'transition space'** A pile of pillows in their room, a chair, anywhere you can spend 10 minutes decompressing with your kids. Remember you are shaking off the day too, so turn off the mobile phone and pull out Dr. Seuss.

- **Eat dinner together** It's not always possible, and let's face it, it's rarely easy to eat early, but it's a nice way to wind down and reconnect. It's also a time to focus exclusively on the kids, who need some attention from you. So have wine with your spouse later and pasta with your kids now.

- **Have a nightly ritual** We've always heard kids respond well to having a schedule, what is surprising is how quickly a busy working mum will start relying on one too. Knowing exactly what needs to get done helps all of us exhausted parents get through the long list that includes making dinner, eating dinner, cleaning up after dinner, giving a bath, changing into pyjamas, reading stories, getting everyone to bed and wrapping up whatever work you had left.

- **Be firm about bedtime** Stick to a bedtime and a system for keeping the kids in bed. There are whole books on the subject so all we'll say is this – the sooner they learn to put themselves to sleep, the better it will be for you.

- **Be aware of bath time** Some children relax after a soak in the tub and some get ramped up. Schedule the bath time around your child's temperament. It took Caitlin and Andrew months to realise that their kids would run around in circles after their lavender-scented bubble bath.

- **Read to your children** At least one book a night. In just 15 minutes each night, you can teach you kids to appreciate reading, help develop and nurture their imagination and rediscover books you loved.

- **Turn off** Turn off the office until your children go down. If you let yourself, you can begin to enjoy the rhythm of bedtime. It's a time to calm down, refocus and reconnect with your family and disconnect from the demands of clients, employees and employers. After the kids are down, then dive back in. Most of the women we interviewed reminded us to give the children your attention when you get home from work and turn off the BlackBerry® for a few hours. Our friend Stacy Maddox shared this, 'When my 'berry is on, the urge to check in has become too compelling. I know it's a problem when my toddler daughter tells me I need to stop doing my emails.'

BlackBerry®: Is It Really a Mum's Best Friend?

We can't live without our BlackBerrys. We check them first thing in the morning and lastly before we go to bed. They are never more than an arm's length way. Our rationale is that if we're on top of things at work then we can be more flexible in how we spend our time. In theory that makes sense. The reality often looks more like working all of the time – especially to our children. Kim's son has asked her to stop looking at the BlackBerry® when he's with her, and Caitlin's husband has instituted a no BlackBerry® peek during the movies and dinner.

How did it go so wrong so fast? We thought the BlackBerry® was the best thing in the world when we first got them. Caitlin's always looking for good news, and Kim is trying to stay one step ahead of the to-do list. Through excessive use, we've created a monster that our families resent and our clients now expect that we are continuously available. Will Schwalbe, a friend to Girl's Guide and author of *Send: Why People Email So Badly and How to Do It Better* (Canongate, 2007) recommends the following tips to cut down on BlackBerry® and email use:

- If you send an email and don't need or want a reply, end it with, 'thanks, no reply necessary'.
- If an email volley seems as if it will never end, schedule a phone call to wrap up the issue.
- If you don't want emails at all hours of the day and night, don't send or reply to them on those hours. You can actually write up all the replies in advance, just don't send them until an appropriate time.
- When trying to figure out if it's an appropriate time to pull out the BlackBerry®, ask yourself if would be an appropriate time to pull out a crossword puzzle. If the answer is no, leave the 'berry in the bag.

Girl Talk

We interviewed Kelly Winston, a working mum with two daughters, who is one of those people who impresses you with how together she always appears. While we really wanted to ask her how on earth she seems so perfect, we decided that might make her uncomfortable, so we stuck with these questions.

Do you think it is ever possible to strike a perfect balance between being a great mum and great employee?
My generation was taught by our pioneering mothers that we could be anything we wanted to be. But what they forgot to teach us was that we cannot be everything to everyone at the same time. That is our dilemma and the balance left to be discovered by today's women.

Recently, I had a girls' weekend with two friends from college. I work full-time in communications. My friend in

California works three days a week for a management consulting firm, and my friend in Texas just left her public interest job and is now home full-time and expecting her third. The amazing thing was that none of us were exactly sure we were doing the right thing. My California friend has now passed up the opportunity for promotion twice to preserve her wonderful schedule, and while, as a mother, she knows it is the right thing for her and her family, the Type-A side of her still longs to prove herself.

Lately, I've been thinking a lot about choosing what I *should* do vs. what I *can* do. I can take on more responsibility, create grand plans and strategies and execute the heck out of them. But that isn't necessarily what I should do. I'm not living or working just for myself, and expending all my energy and emotional reserves between 8:00–6:00 isn't fair to those I committed to long before I committed to this job. So, for me, it isn't a matter of striking a balance between being a great mum and a great employee. It's about remembering to balance what I can do and what I should do.

We look at the coverage of celebrity mums with their entourages of nannies and wonder if there are any realistic role models in the media today?

I tend to think of celebrity mothering the same way I think of celebrity weight loss. Magazines splash the headlines 'Diet Secrets of the Stars' across the cover, but nowhere in the article does it say that to achieve the same effects you need to hire a personal chef who specialises in Mediterranean fare and a personal trainer who will kick your butt four hours per day. In my opinion, even the 'down-to-earth' media stars – Reese Witherspoon, for example, who is one of the few who admits how hard it actually is – live a life so far removed from my own that there is no sense in drawing a comparison.

I know many women who look to their own mothers for inspiration. My neighbour said to me once, 'My mum and I fought a lot when I was growing up, but her working was never the reason.' My mother was a homemaker and a volunteer, but she has always encouraged me to be true to myself.

I also look to the President of my local liberal arts university, who is a great inspiration to me. When I was a freelancer, we used to be in the same yoga class at 5:00 on Wednesdays. Since returning to the corporate setting full-time, I haven't been once. Recently we exchanged emails, and she wrote, 'Find time for yoga. Young mums need it the most!'

Any tips you can share for those mums looking for a smoother morning?
When I chose to go back into the corporate workplace, my greatest fear was that my two least favourite times of the day – morning routine and late afternoon – was all I would have left with my own children. It still isn't easy. At times I want to pull out my hair (or theirs). But since it is all I have, I find that I love those hours no matter what.

That being said, here are my tips . . .

Make yourself get up and finish your own routine before your preschool children awake. As hard as it is when that alarm goes off, I am always glad to have time to focus on them exclusively without trying to remember if I put mascara on both eyes or only one. (By the way, I am terrible at actually following my advice on this one. I love and crave sleep too much to be rational before the sun is up!)

What about a smoother bedtime?

My older daughter (age 6) has a responsibility chart in her room that her nanny created. It allows her to check off every step required for going to bed, e.g., go to potty, wash hands, brush teeth, put clothes in laundry basket. It is such a relief to be able to say simply, 'Go and do your chart,' rather than give a separate instruction for each item. We use a kitchen timer and if she gets it all done in 20 minutes, she gets an extra chapter or song at bedtime. I cannot wait for my younger daughter to get to that point!

Do you and your husband have time alone?

We do. I have a triple life - that is employee, mother and wife. Wife is the one that gets neglected most often. Admittedly, I pour out a lot of myself at work. When I get home, I rally and do the same for the kids. But by the time it's just the two of us, I'm spent! Fall is the best season for us, because we have two season tickets to our local NFL [American football] games. Most Sundays we have four hours to sit together in the afternoon – when we're both wide awake – and cheer.

We also make it a point not to discuss household business at 9 p.m. When we're both drained, a simple question, 'Did you call the tree guy?' can sound like an accusation. And the response often because something like this: 'No, I didn't call the tree guy. Don't you think, after you've asked me three times that if I DID call the tree guy, you'd be the first to know?' We try to have breakfast or lunch on neutral territory every other week. We each bring our list of questions and to-dos. Not romantic, but effective!

What do you think the biggest challenges are that first year of working and mothering?

Aside from everything I wrote about above . . . I still haven't figured out how to feed everyone dinner. I know that sounds ridiculous because there are a lot of solutions out there. One friend cooks after her kids go to bed for herself and her husband. Then the next night, she reheats leftovers for the kids and starts over. I've just never been able to get into that kind of groove. Feeding the children is actually easy. Cut up fruit, steam some veggies, add fish sticks or Bagel Bites and voila! But that precludes any sort of family meal time, which is important to me. It also means Nick and I stand at the fridge scratching our heads at 8:30, and my father-in-law (who prefers to eat before 6) is left to his own devices.

Sometimes I remember to order from Weekday Gourmet so that I have easy meals in the freezer, but then I forget to thaw them out and/or ask my nanny to put it in the oven. My manager thinks I'm a very organised person. He's never been to my house for dinner.

Do you find yourself doing more at home than your husband? If so, any advice for women who are faced with a similar challenge?

YES. To his credit, he offers and, I believe, legitimately wants to do more. However, he doesn't see what needs to be done as easily as I do or often at all. When I see something, I do it, even if that means picking up after him. It's easier and faster than delegating. (Funny, that's something I constantly work on at the office as well.) I laugh that the work that needs to be done at home is like one court's definition of pornography – I can't define it, but I know it when I see it! Sometimes I'll try to start a list for him, and to his credit he will often make one for himself for the weekends. But his list usually involves projects like install intercom system or blow leaves off roof. My mental list is created and checked off minute-by-minute – bring items left downstairs (including his coat and tie) upstairs, check washer (to make sure the load of washing he started was moved to the dryer), clean jam off countertop (from when he made the kids' sandwiches).

6

Work at Home and Home at Work

Harried working mothers often forget that many of the skills that make them great employees and bosses could also help them at home. At the same time, aspects of your home life can be carried over and used effectively at the office. We are so busy trying to maintain the boundaries between our professional and personal lives that we may be missing opportunities to make our lives easier.

Nothing, absolutely nothing, will test and hone your patience like having children. We read somewhere that the average child says 'Mum' 200-plus times a day. That alone will drive you round the bend. And how about the numerous times you are interrupted at home? Doesn't it always seem like that the time your child is suddenly dying for a snack is when you are trying to finish a paragraph or clean the kitchen? Your children want as much of your attention as they can get and when you're not exhausted it's the greatest feeling in the world. Unfortunately, for the first couple of years after your baby is born you are exhausted. All of the time.

The good news is that these same factors: the neediness, the lack of control and requisite selflessness can make you a more patient, understanding and compassionate boss.

There are myriad opportunities to grow alongside your child. Your career is important to you, so take a broad perspective about the challenges you are overcoming at home. Do a little self examination. If you are fighting for equal housework at home, do you take that spirit into your boss' office when asking for a pay rise? If you are taking on the bulk of childcare on the weekends and declining offers of help from the people around you, are you also stretching yourself too thin at the office? If your spouse has told you that you are too critical of his parenting style, are you micromanaging your team as well?

Beyond the business skills you are developing while parenting, if you step back and look at the dynamics of parenting, you can also see the more philosophical truths that you can bring into work – you can't control everything, you should appreciate the downtime when it comes and realise nothing stays the same. Life is a series of moments.

While the Mum Hat and the Work Hat are different, you are still wearing both – and you are not two people. How can you seamlessly merge your two selves to be a more successful career girl and more fulfilled mother? How can you take what you learn in each world and make a stronger, smarter, happier you? The key is to be engaged in all aspects of your life, giving full focus to what's in front of you at that moment. Don't rush past the challenges or tough conversations, because every one of them is an opportunity for you to get better or become clearer about something. And all of this learning can be applied to all aspects of your life.

In this chapter, you'll find suggestions for how to bring that business-self home to get things a little more streamlined, to delegate effectively and to apply some of that hard-earned workplace savvy to negotiations for time off over the breakfast table. And you'll also see where some of those things you are learning at home can actually help you at the office.

Be an Office Manager at Home

For those of you who are or have a reliable, smart, organised office manager then consider yourself lucky. Office managers clean up the mess and implement the systems you need to do your job. They make it easier for you to buzz through your to-do list because they have taken away the clutter and distractions. Now we all know that nothing brings clutter and distraction like children. Even those who maintain the most pristine households find themselves picking up Lego® and cream crackers embedded in the sofa.

Setting up a system for organising your family will go a long way to helping your life run more smoothly. The systems will be different for everyone but here are some helpful fundamentals to guide you.

The weekday system

The key to a smooth week is a reasonable and realistic schedule. All too often we high-achieving women think we can do everything in half the time that it actually takes. Start by writing down the entire family schedule (it doesn't matter how well you think you know it, to create an effective system it needs to be on paper.) Start with the times that everyone has to be at their first location. For example, you need to be at work at 9:00 a.m., the kids need to be at the bus stop by 8.15 a.m. and your partner needs to catch a 7.45 a.m. train.

Next, list all of the tasks that need to be accomplished to get everyone out the door on time. No task is too small to include, then keep track of the time these tasks take for a week. You might be surprised by how much time it actually takes to get the kids cleaned, dressed, fed, and packed. And don't forget that you also have to get yourself cleaned and dressed and out the door. To calculate your ideal wakeup time, tally the minutes for each task. Add 10 minutes for a cushion and then subtract it from the wakeup times. This will give you your optimum wake up time.

Once you've got the morning in check, tackle the afternoon. Apply the same process to the 'Back in the Door' activities and schedule. Write down everyone's schedules (and this can be tricky as they frequently change from week to week) and make a plan for coverage. Pick-ups, play dates, practices and not to mention after-work responsibilities and family time are really tough to cover adequately, but seeing it all on paper will help it feel more manageable.

Assign responsibilities to each member of the family – don't forget the children can (and should) be responsible for appropriate tasks.

Next, consider your priorities and don't be afraid to think out of the box to stay in line with them. Sitting down together for a family meal is one of Chris Colabella's biggest priorities. But with two daughters who have a daily schedule of sports games, practices and more than an hour of homework each, sitting down to a formal dinner became an impossible and unpleasant event. Food was rushed, the girls were tired, and the time they shared was neither pleasant nor productive. The mum in Chris became sad and frustrated. The manager in her went to work. How could she re-arrange the schedule so she and the girls spent positive time around the table? Breakfast time for her was the obvious choice. They are all early risers and now every morning before school they sit down to 'dinner'. She cooks the family meals on Sunday because that's the only time she has free, and at night they grab something light – could be soup or fruit and yogurt – and don't put a lot of pressure around the evening schedule. By 9:00 p.m., everyone, including Chris is exhausted and ready for bed. 5:30 a.m. comes pretty quickly.

Of course Chris's solution may not work for you, but the lessons are critical. Stay focused on your priorities and keep adjusting the system (and perhaps the schedule) until you find a solution that works for your family.

You have all the information you need now to create the family schedule and accompanying list of individual responsibilities. We recommend you use the same system you use at work. Or if you are separated and sharing custody of your child, consider an online calendar so you can both be on top of the schedule and aware of any changes.

By the time the weekend rolls around we are exhausted. Fight the urge to lay around the house (would it were possible) and get a few things checked off your list so you can start the week relaxed on Monday.

The weekend systems

- Review the week ahead of you with your spouse and make a weekly to-do list.
- Think about the forthcoming weekend plans and add confirm play dates to the weekly to-do list. You don't want to be waking up on a rainy Saturday with nothing planned for rambunctious kids.
- Stick to the school's nap, lunch and snack schedule whenever possible. It makes it much easier for your preschooler to transition between home and school when the schedule is the same.
- Pay the bills.
- Commit to giving yourselves some time together (date night?) and some time alone (yoga studio?) and fit that into the schedule of every weekend.

Shopping

- Plan meals ahead of time. It really helps to know what your dinner options are when you are exhausted.

- Include a few frozen meals in there and these days there are loads of guilt-free options.
- When shopping, there are certain things you will always need. Buy the following items in bulk to avoid last minute trips to the store: nappies, plasters, nappy rash cream, baby shampoo, baby wipes, t-shirts, socks (because they disappear, even in your own washer/dryer), juice boxes and every snack known to woman. Caitlin and Andrew can't believe how much their kids can eat.

It might seem overwhelming at first to have to create and follow any system when you are already feeling like every day is crunch time but, believe us, just like a well-run office when you remove the clutter, you can just focus on enjoying your children.

Negotiating Tactics That Might Just Work at Home

We'll deal with this more in Chapter Seven (because never is negotiation more important than with dealing with one's partner), but negotiating is one of the key work skills that you can bring home. You've realised by now that you can't do it all, that work responsibilities are nipping at your heels as you run out the door to pick up your kid from day care. That this time you absolutely can't avoid the business trip. That you need to start exercising before you leave for work. Whatever it is you need today, you will also need something tomorrow, next week and six months from now. Because of the inflexibility of time in your child's schedule, you and your partner are the ones who need to adjust. The only wiggle room you have is what the other gives you, so get your negotiation face on.

The good news is that you are Ms. Career woman, and you have likely gotten a raise, promotion or a coveted project utilising the very skills that are going to make your life easier at home. And remember, we as women are more likely to say yes without putting our partner through the same hoops so make sure you are walking away with something - even if it's a morning to sleep in - if you are asked to do significantly more on the home front. Now, in an ideal world, all of us would just do whatever our partner needed without fuss, but let's get real. We are tired and burnt out and neither of us have a lot of extra energy to give. So let's start with having some compassion for each other's situation, but don't let it get in the way of asking for what you need.

The Word: A Couple of Thoughts from the Top of the Ladder

Lisa M. Weber is the president of Individual Business at MetLife, Inc and the mother of two children. We have always maintained that the view is much different from the highest rungs of the ladder, and in an interview for the Forte Foundation website Lisa shares two important pieces of advice that can help us all:

High-ranking executive women should *not* try to achieve work-life balance. According to Lisa, 'People struggle so much with the word balance. Give it up. There is no such thing as balance. It is about prioritisation. If you want balance, you cannot be in these jobs. I know that's very disappointing for some, but you cannot be the president of a business and work from home three days a week when you have 20,000 people running around the country.'

With two school-age children, Lisa rises at 4 a.m. on the week-ends so that she can work before her children wake up. She clears her calendar for special or one-time events, like the installation of her son's braces, the first day of school, their departure to summer camp and extended family vacations, but she prioritises her work to ensure that high-level matters are addressed and completed as well.

When your life is in 'family mode', be a good role model. When

Lisa gave birth to her first child, a son, she stayed home for five weeks. 'He was a preemie and in the hospital for three of the five weeks,' she recalls. 'And going back to work so fast was a huge mistake . . . not only from the standpoint of me not being able to spend that time and bond with my son, but also in not being the role model that I believe I am for other women.' After the birth of her daughter, Lisa stayed home for three months (again, this is much more common in the US than it is in the UK and other countries). She offers unsolicited advice to others urging them to do what is right for their situation.

Running an Effective Meeting for Your Staff and Your Family

Put on your office hat for a second. Meetings are effective when the parties come prepared and fully-focused. We dread most meetings because they are a waste of time. Usually, the only thing actually agreed to is when to have the next meeting. If the manager comes to the meeting with a specific list of items to address, delegates tasks, is provided with updates and recaps next steps then it's a successful meeting.

Think about how many details you are juggling at home. During any given month you could be planning a birthday party or buying gifts for someone else's, scheduling a business trip, buying new clothes because your baby had a growth spurt, trying to accommodate your nanny's request for a week off, taking the dog to the vet, negotiating for night-time coverage thanks to a big project at work, trying to get a run in at least a few times a week, finding a painter for the house, taking the car in for a tune up, researching local daycare centres. Wow. That is a whole lot of stuff and we're guessing your list for next month is even longer. It seems like it's in your family's best interest for you to set up a family meeting to start delegating and figure out if maybe you need another set of hands for some of it.

As we know, the best way to handle a meeting is to come

prepared. So write down everything that needs to get done this month – both the household jobs and everything about your work that could be impacting your personal time. That includes any commitments that will require skipping a morning or evening with your child. Write down any scheduling issues your school or nanny has brought up. Remember to include any doctor's appointments, car and pet care. Now, factor in any personal time you want to get in there and need to discuss.

Ideally, you each will come to the meeting with your list because your partner will have his job responsibilities and requests for personal time to add to the mix. He may also be aware of household tasks that you forgot (yes, it's true . . . you don't know everything) to include.

To keep the meeting focused, try to schedule it at a time when you are conscious. That would mean Friday night is most likely out, as is the crack of dawn on Monday. We spoke to several women who find time during the week for a breakfast or lunch with their spouses to get through the to-do list outside of the chaos of the household.

Respectfully Delegating Childcare
Delegation, of course, is another area to put your brilliant professional skills to work at home. When you are a working mum you will find yourself telling a nanny, preschool teacher, or teenage babysitter what to do and how to do it. So put on your boss hat and delegate with respect. Be clear about your expectations when you tell someone what to do. Give them the tools they need to get the job done and set them up for success. If you hire a babysitter for the night, make sure he has your contact numbers and emergency information. Give him a tour of the house and show him where all of the supplies are stored. Walk him through the evening's schedule and fill him in on the temperament of your child. The more information you give the people jumping into care for your child, the better.

If the providers are not doing things the way you would like – too little time outside, feeding them too many sweets – instead of blowing up, double check to see if you have given them what they need to do the job the way you expect. If the nanny isn't taking your child out enough during the day, find out if she is at a loss for where to go or if she is concerned about the temperature outside. If she is feeding them sweets, is there a shortage of healthy snacks in the fridge? Good delegating, like anything else, relies on good communication. So before yelling at your childcare providers, apply your professional problem solving skills and figure out the root of the problem.

And accept the fact that you can't do everything yourself. Working mother and Internet professional Lori Greene reminds us that, 'Working mothers need to delegate, delegate, delegate. Your children should do chores and work around the house. You should share the load with your husband – because if you take it all on yourself, you only have yourself to blame when you're doing 85% of everything. Try to start off on the right foot about sharing responsibilities and LET GO OF CONTROL. Nobody will do it exactly like you and you need to accept that.'

Drawing Boundaries

Drawing that boundary between work and home is impossible these days, especially for working mums who are tethered to their BlackBerry®. Working mother Maria Morris agrees, 'I'm always accessible and can work anytime but I have learned to turn off the computer once the kids are home as I'm not good to anyone when doing both. If I want to clear some emails, I'll wait until they're in bed because it will only take a half hour and I won't be screaming at anyone!'

Not screaming is always good and, in reality, if you are trying to work while parenting you aren't doing a great job in either camp. It's also a fast track to total burnout if you can't ever focus on one thing. That headache you get after putting your kids down could be due in part to the fact that you were emailing, while boiling pasta water and answering to both 'Mummy!' and 'Honey!' Kim Parrish, creator and founder of the Kim Parrish Collection shares this, 'I used to live by the philosophy, 'Work Hard, Play Hard.' But after Chase was born we realised we would need to alter our definition of playing to include blocks, toy cars and pop-up books. Finding balance has been quite a challenge. Craig and I both enjoy the hurdles associated with achieving goals, growing businesses, launching product lines and networking our resources. We've had to become creative in finding the hours in a day needed to finish projects without pulling time or attention away from Chase. It's not unusual that we'll leave the office at 5 p.m. only to return to 'work-mode' at 8 p.m. once Chase is tucked into bed so we can finish a project.'

No one should feel like they have to put away the ambition once they become a mother. We have all worked too hard on ourselves and our careers to toss either away. But there is a way to structure the day so you are not killing yourself trying to do everything at the same time. Burnout is real. It makes you tired, irritable, unable to concentrate and motivate. It leads to short tempers, late projects and a seriously compromised quality of life. What you need to do now as a working mum is prioritise everything and everyone. That includes your children, friendships, relationships with family members, travel, business projects, holidays, goals and, not least of all, your romantic life. The upshot of every major change in your life is as something goes away, another takes its place. You have a new kind of emotionally rich life when you become a parent and, along with that, your free time and wiggle room has gone out the window.

Enter each day knowing you are going to do your best and give what you can give. Since people (your boss, child, spouse) won't be setting boundaries for you, it's up to you.

On the work front decide how available you want to be to your employer and/or employees and clients when you are not in the office. Think carefully about the projects you take on, the business travel you commit to. On the home front make sure the household tasks are assigned evenly, and don't volunteer for too much. Maria Morris adds, 'Keep the activities that add to your entire family's well-being not just your child's. If your entire family is paying the price for the activity, is it worth it? My favourite activity is soccer practice as I get to sit down with a cold drink and chat with the other mums while my kid is running around. I get to chill for an hour – pure bliss!'

Be Open to Advice (Some of It May Just Work)

You routinely collaborate with colleagues and seek the suggestions and support of your boss and mentor at work, use the same tools in your home life. Seek out advice and be open to even the unsolicited sort. Your abrasive mother-in-law, the busy body on line in front of you at the supermarket, your best friend with triplets or your client who happens to be a single mother – all of these women could have advice that helps you figure out this working mum thing. We know, it's hard to hear advice from people you may find annoying or have complicated relationships with, but when you are both mothers, things change. Seriously, they do. You now have something profound in common. The responsibility for another human being. And for those of us who have that responsibility plus are still ambitious and engaged in our careers, we have even more in common. Be open to advice from the working mothers around you and don't be afraid to ask them questions.

A few helpful questions to ask other working mums:

- What is your morning schedule?

- How do you deal with the guilt of seeing your child crying when you drop them off at nursery or the childminder?
- How do you find time for yourself?
- What do you do if you find yourself doing all of the housework and most of the childcare?
- How late do your kids stay up and what is the night-time routine?
- What do you do if your kids just don't stay in bed?
- When do you think it would be ok for me to go on a business trip?
- Do you feel like your boss is unsupportive of your role as working mother?
- Did you feel as though your colleagues made assumptions about you and your work when you got back from maternity leave?
- Do you feel like you constantly have to prove yourself at work now that you are a working mum?

Don't Micromanage Your Team or Your Partner

If you want your partner more engaged in taking care of the kids or the housework then please, let them do it their way. Nothing is more debilitating and annoying than having someone over your shoulder telling you how to fill the dishwasher the 'right' way. Over the summer, Kim was staying with friends who have a 4-year-old daughter. One afternoon the husband took the daughter for a stroll into town to the library. It was a short trip, but instead of spending the 30 minutes relaxing, the wife complained to Kim about how she was sure he forgot to pack a snack 'because he always does' and how he never changes her into sneakers. And, most of all how frustrated she was that he didn't do more. Didn't do more?! Would you?

Kim Parrish says, 'Of course I micromanaged at first! Luckily, my husband is a strong, loving, kind man who realises his wife has the best interest of the family in mind. When we first had Chase I barked out orders better than any drill sergeant. I've since learned to realise I need to relax, and trust in Craig's parenting skills. He may do things differently, but there are no set rules to proper parenting and Chase benefits from the variety.'

When we wrote our second book, *The Girl's Guide to Being a Boss without Being a Bitch* we interviewed 150 women on various aspects of leadership. We asked a few of the very well-respected managers how they got the best work from their employees. They said, most of all, let them do their job. If you micromanage, they will eventually give up and leave everything for you to do. It's true, when you constantly correct someone on the job they are doing, you are undermining their self-confidence. And only self-confident people take on more. So if you want your partner to do more, start with appreciating the bit he does now. Believe us; you don't want to become Kim's friend who is heading for zero help from her husband.

Your chance to get this started on the right foot at the beginning is to let your partner spend time with your baby solo. There is a myth that women are born all the answers when it comes to how to take care of an infant. We are so committed to this untruth that we are often hesitant to ask for advice and are offended if people step in to guide us. But why should we know everything about babies? Most of us are learning on the job, so let your partner figure things out too. If you let him find his way into parenting on his own, then he will have the confidence to take care of the baby without you (a gift six months down the road when you have a work crisis or just need a break). If, however you are criticising his methods of childcare, won't leave him alone with the baby, jump in to take over the minute there is a cry, then you are setting patterns that will bite you down the road when you are ready for more autonomy.

The Word: Advice from One Working Mother

Caitlin was working with Amy Shanler from Staples on a few projects. It turned out they both had twins, and lucky for Caitlin, Amy's were six months older. Over the course of the next several months, Amy was kind enough to share her tips for transitioning from cribs to toddler beds, ideas about meal planning and morning schedules. She was so generous with her time and experience that it actually made those early years of parenting twins easier for Caitlin. Here were some of the questions she asked Amy:

What was it like for you coming back to work after having the twins?
I feel like I had two back-to-work transitions. Actually, three. When the kids were born, I had plans of returning to my previous job at a PR agency. However, the more time I spent with them and balancing the demands of my role and the cost to keep both babies in day care full-time, I knew something had to give. So my first return back after maternity leave was a visit to my current employer to give my notice. That went a lot better than I thought. People were happy to see me and the babies, and understood the economics of my situation. All was good, but I felt a sense of sadness as I cleaned out my office. I still consider that *my* office even though someone else had moved in.

Then I had the start of my job as executive director of the Publicity Club. For my first professional meeting, I brought the babies. There's nothing like taking notes on your assignments, roles, and responsibilities while feeding two babies bottles. This job brought the joys of working out of the house, with a few events per month where I would leave the kids with a sitter. It was a good balance. However, the taste of working and responsibility left me wanting more (and truthfully, I was a little bored with Mother Goose and Pat the Bunny). Plus, I was working so hard, taking care

123

of kids during the day and on the laptop until quite late. Frankly, I didn't have a lot of time for my husband and figured I could achieve greater balance if I went back to work full-time.

So onto my first full-time position after the babies were born. Honestly, I had the easiest transition, in part because my kids were 15-months-old, and in part because my boss is one of the greatest, most understanding souls in the world. He is a father of four, values my work (he was my client while I was at the PR agency), and saw me working so hard and delivering results that he understood when I needed to pick up the kids and run them to the doctor.

The biggest surprise was that I was happy. This happiness spread beyond work into my home life. I was glad to see my kids because I missed them. We had fun when we were together. I was able to leave work at work, or tend to anything I had to put on hold after the kids were in bed. I saw my husband and we were able to catch up on life. Work for me is good.

What were you going through emotionally those first few months? Were you questioning your choices?
My kids got so much more out of daycare in the first week than I could have given them in a month. On day two, the teacher said, 'You don't paint with them at home, do you?' Um, paint? 'No.' 'Yeah, we could tell.' I thought to myself: are you going to come to my house to clean it up? All kidding aside, the talented caregivers at our daycare have much more creativity and experience stimulating children than I do. I recognised this early on and this helped increase my comfort level in their situation.

Do you wish you had handled things differently in any way?
I really overcompensated when I had to be out of the office for my kids – on the BlackBerry® in the doctor's waiting room or conducting conference calls on the way to CVS. I eventually learned the work will still be there. If my kids really need me, I really need to

be there for them – fully there, not half in my email. I did figure this out and no real harm done, but it's something I wish I learned earlier.

What did you learn from the working mums around you?
It all comes down to priorities and perspective. At the end of the day, what is the most important thing? And what is the worst that can happen if . . . The answers to those questions keep things real. They also had support and were not afraid to use it. My teammate has her mum living with her; the boss' boss has a nanny. And that is OK. Just because you have help doesn't stop you from being the mum.

Did you feel at any point that you were being judged by your co-workers or treated differently?
I am not sure if anything I felt overtly – it was more the internal angst I felt when I walked in at 9:10 and imagined I felt people hush. Or when I needed to leave at 5 and asked a teammate to do the 5–5:30 meeting for me. She never said anything about it, but I imagine there were comments made. I overcompensate, though – and feel like I need to clean my inbox before work the next day. If I can't work a 'normal' work day, I'll show them I can still keep up my work and even do better.

Girl Talk: Susan Bursk

Susan Bursk is a third-generation working mother. Her grandparents owned several restaurants together and her parents opened a hardware store and worked together six days a week. She shares with us what it was like to have a working mother at a time when it was highly unusual.

Tell us what it was like for you to be one of the only kids with a mum at work?

My mum approached everything with such a positive attitude. She made me feel as though I was very special and lucky to be the only child in grammar school that went to an after school day camp. I remember I would always volunteer my mother to do things at school . . . i.e. bake cakes for the May Festival. Sometimes she would say, 'Aren't there any other mothers to bake a cake?' But she never let me down. She was always there for me whenever I asked her to do something for my school. I think it was my way of knowing that when I needed her, she could be counted on . . . and she never made me feel guilty about it.

Were you jealous of the other kids?

While other mums wore dresses, mine wore pants. For me, growing up with a working mum and grandmother was the way it was. I asked one of my closest friends if I ever said anything to her about my mum always working. She said, 'Everyone knew your parents had a business and worked. It was just the way it was.'

What changes did you make when you became a working mum based on how you were raised?

My mum was always available for me and I wanted to be sure my son knew I was always available for him. However, what I came to realise was what I needed from my mum, my son did not necessarily need from me. I spoke to my mum every day on the phone. Literally every day until the day she died. Although my son and I have a close relationship, we don't have that same need for daily contact. We are different people, with different needs and expectations. While I recognise our similarities, more importantly, I recognise our differences and embrace them.

Do you have any advice for women in that first tough year of being a working mum?
In general, I believe women tend to do it all – taking care of the house, the bills, the marketing, making meals for the family and working full/part-time on top of all that. I think it's important to recognise that we are not superhuman and that's ok. Paying attention to what is considered realistic expectations is the first step to alleviating guilt. Asking for help is the second step. And the third step is getting help, whether it's from family, friends, or hiring a nanny or housekeeper. Whatever you need to do to make it work and lessen the feeling of 'I need to do it all.'

7

A Partnership That Works

Ask any working mother who does more at home and the answer will be the mother. Can all of us working mothers possibly be martyrs, or worse, delusional? Unfortunately, not. The sad truth is that women shoulder the majority of responsibilities on the home front even if they also contribute to the family financially. Most families need two working parents to survive, so how come every time I come home from work, my children ask me what's for dinner even though my husband has been home for two hours?

We think it's time for a change and unfortunately, change takes time. Don't be discouraged when you try out our recommendations on your partner and you are met with nothing resembling enthusiasm. Don't give in because 'it's just easier to do it yourself.' This chapter will arm you with the tools you need to create a better working family partnership. Your children will be happier if you and your partner are working as a team. You will be happier if you and your partner are working as a team.

Read this chapter and follow its advice. This may be the most important chapter in the book because if your partnership is solid then your children can thrive and you two can love and respect each other and maybe even have a little fun together facing the challenges that raising kids in this century brings.

Just Because You *Can*, Doesn't Mean You Should

We keep hearing the same frustration voiced in our interviews. 'Why can't my partner do as much as I can?' We don't need studies to show us that working mothers shoulder significantly more of the responsibilities at home (although there are many to cite). Men wouldn't even argue the point. We then ask the question, 'Why aren't you demanding more support from your partners?' The answers have been either 'I am the mother so it's my responsibility', or 'It's just easier if I do it myself.'

Just because you gave birth to the child does not mean it's solely your responsibility to take care of him. It takes a village to raise a child and, in absence of one, you had better force your partner to share in the responsibility. Standing up for yourself is not just a matter of trying to achieve fairness and equality. Standing up for yourself will save you hours of anger and frustration. Women who feel overburdened for too long report feelings of anger and resentment toward their other halves. The spouses report they are taken by surprise by the level and intensity of their partner's anger. You can see how resentment, anger and surprise can cause problems for a marriage. And when there are problems in a marriage, you suffer, your spouse suffers, your child suffers and your job suffers.

Of course it is easier to just do it yourself – and you *can* probably do it better too. But you need to delegate (just like your boss explained in your last review). You have too many things on your plate and if you don't get them off, you will be crushed. If your spouse is already maxed out, then try and find a way to get help from a relative or if you can afford it, hire someone to walk the dog, mow the lawn, clean the house, or any task that you and your spouse continually argue about.

The Word: The Right Partner Makes All the Difference

Eileen Moore Andersen earned her MBA from Emory University in Atlanta and is a Regional Controller working for General Mills in a joint venture with Nestlé. She's the mother of two girls and her husband is a stay-at-home dad named Dave.

Eileen and Dave's passion is travel. They met while they were studying abroad in Austria during college and got married shortly after they graduated. Eileen followed Dave to Atlanta where he was doing graduate work at Emory. To pay the bills she got a temporary clerical job at Coca-Cola. She was ultimately hired full-time and she and Dave decided that international travel was their goal and getting there through her job was the easiest route.

While Dave was working on his PhD, Eileen was accepted into Emory's evening MBA program. It was a total grind and they rarely saw each other, but they were in no rush to have children and an MBA would open the doors they needed to get overseas.

After Eileen graduated, she got accepted into the MBA Enterprise Corp which is an NGO that sends MBAs to developing countries where they work in different companies creating business plans and helping them grow. Eileen and Dave were off to Ukraine in 1997 for a 15-month assignment including a 10-week home study learning the local language. This was not a big bucks job. Eileen was paid $900 a month and lodging for her and her husband.

During the Ukraine placement Eileen worked for small and medium enterprises including a glass factory and a fish farm where she helped them write business plans. She ended up staying for two years. During that time, Dave did all sorts of little jobs. He taught undergraduate literature courses at an English language university and he was editing an online news daily translating Ukrainian into English.

When she returned to the States in the summer of 2000, the economy was booming, so Eileen was able to be patient and look for a multinational that would be in line with their longer-term goals. They chose to settle in Minneapolis as it was Dave's hometown and there were a number of multinational companies for Eileen to apply to. That summer they lived off credit cards and Dave's tips from his barista job at Caribou Coffee.

Three months after being back, Eileen landed a job at Pillsbury (Pillsbury was acquired by General Mills in 2001) and Dave started teaching at the University of Wisconsin-River Falls. Their daughter Rosie was born in July 2002. Bridget was born in 2004 and when she was four months old they were transferred to Albuquerque (a means to the end of getting overseas) and started a family. In June 2007, Eileen and her family finally got their overseas placement. They were off to Chile on a three-year contract.

Their hope is to get one more three-year overseas contract and then return to the States. Her girls will be ready to put down roots and Dave and Eileen's parents will be in their 80s. Dave and Eileen want their girls to experience the world and she is very proud that they've accomplished it. The girls are fluent in Spanish and already understand that when it's winter in Chile, it's summer in the United States. Eileen's not sure she understood that until she was an adult.

Eileen credits her family's success to Dave (and we would guess he would say the same about her). Their priorities and goals have always been aligned (travel and adventure) and they've always acted as a team. He's been a stay-at-home dad since the girls were born.

Eileen shares some thoughts about juggling work and family and working internationally:

- If you want to work internationally, you need to have patience and be true to your mission. It took me seven years to get us to Chile and during those seven years I just kept telling anyone who would listen that I wanted to work internationally. It is very expensive for a company to send an employee overseas and they need to be sure it will work out. Our experience in the Ukraine really helped to give my company the confidence that I would be able to handle the challenges and stresses unique to life abroad. Be wary, sometimes your company will offer you things that won't quite fit with the long-term goal. It's tempting to take these jobs out of company loyalty and it's hard to say no (or in other words, tempting to say yes – the path of least resistance). The challenge comes in working with your company to fill their needs while at the same time tapping into your talents and passions.

- To solve the work-balance mystery I say this: Choose your spouse carefully and find a company that pays more than just lip service to 'work life balance.' I put a barrier between my work life and my private life. I may be here until 8:00 p.m. but I never work on weekends.

- When I was trying to balance work and graduate school, I thought I would be constantly juggling the balls between them. What I learned is that there weren't three balls in the air. There was only the ball that I was holding. When I put down the work ball, I can pick up the family ball.

- The big factor that allows me to have one ball at a time is Dave. Having his support, and knowing that he is home holding the family ball allows me to be fully in the moment. We choose quality time over quantity time and lifestyle over money. We've made these decisions together and we're a team. I just want to add, although I know I'm lucky to have met David, pure luck hasn't gotten me where I am. Choices, clarity of mission and perseverance are the defining factors. When I tell people that I backpacked through Central America for five months, sometimes they say 'oh, you're so lucky to have done that'. My response is always 'What's stopping you?' I will admit to being lucky that I grew up in a developed country where women are equals (more or less–in the global sense!) and I had parents who loved me and valued education and had the means and willingness to educate me. But the fact that I was in Central America for five months meant I took a risk, rejected stability, quit a job, and sacrificed a 'climb up the ladder' to pursue what gave me joy. I'm proud of the choices I've made but they haven't come without sacrifice.

Stay-at-Home Dads: Are They the Answer?

A Stay-At-Home Dad sounds like an ideal situation if you can afford it. Who doesn't want a wife? Who wouldn't be thrilled to have someone at home taking care of the children, the house and you? Be careful what you wish for. Stay-at-home dads are not wives and women are reluctant to give them the carte blanche at home the way men typically do with their wives. 'My husband has been a stay-at-home dad since our daughters were born. I guess I feel like I am cheating because I don't have the stresses that other working mums do. But I admit that I probably do more that most at-work fathers do too,' said Eileen.

Even though their numbers are on the rise, however you look at the figures, stay-at-home dads are still a significant minority and they face challenges and stresses that stay-at-home mothers don't. The biggest one may be the attitudes of their wives. Both Kim and Penelope Trunk (see The Word) believe that their marriages failed in part because their husbands chose to stay at home with their children. 'I don't think many of these guys are actually choosing to stay-at-home. Their careers had either stalled or never gotten going, and they figured why not stay home with kids and work on some other projects,' said Penelope Trunk. Kim said that she was constantly frustrated by how her husband managed the family. Her house was spotless and her son was loved and well attended to, but that wasn't enough for her. She wanted her husband to be Super mum replacing her: scheduling play dates, volunteering at the school, and doing it exactly the way she would have done it if she chose to stay home instead. Not only is that unrealistic, it's unfair and a trap that many women fall into.

The stress on the stay-at-home dad is taking a toll on more than their marriages. Researchers conducting a study for the National Institutes for Health in Framingham, Massachusetts, found men who have been stay-at-home dads most of their adult lives have an 82 percent higher risk of death from heart disease than men who work outside the home. An 82 percent higher risk of dying because they chose to stay home! Worse, the inverse is also true: the study also found women in high-demand jobs – compared with women in low-authority jobs – have a three times greater risk of heart disease.

Researchers speculate that the role reversal is actually behind the statistics. Bucking society's conventions is stressful, so if you are going to try this route, you need to be very supportive of each other. Apparently it's a matter of life and death.

Ways to make a stay-at-home dad situation work

- Set expectations together for how the household will run. Your husband is not your employee and needs to be a partner in all decision-making. He is running the household now, once you agree to a plan, you need to let him be in charge.

- Make sure that staying home with the kids is more than a default position. He has to want to take care of the children and home. This is no easy job, not only because childcare is exhausting, but the role reversal can take its toll, too.
- Stay involved with what's going on but don't micromanage. If you want to be part of the meetings with the teacher, then let him know to check your calendar before scheduling any meetings. Don't be the scheduler because it's just easier than communicating your schedule.
- Set a system for communicating what's going on at home and for you at work. Make time for each other outside the family.
- Give him lots of positive reinforcement and keep your criticisms to yourself.
- Just because you earn it, doesn't make it *your* money. This is a family decision and therefore all assets belong to the family.
- Whenever you're frustrated, and there will be numerous times, do a role reversal in your head. If you were the stay-at-home, how would you want to be treated?

The Word

Miles Hill, a writer and stay-at-home dad talks to us about parenting, balance and offers a few suggestions for making it work when you are taking the unconventional route:

Did you leave a career to raise your children?
I was an ink-stained wretch slaving away at home before and after the stork arrived; although post-stork my slaving time took a major hit. In our case, my wife, a chef, usually works afternoons and nights, which means I've been the one to make dinner, read, get everybody off to bed. The exceptions to this were the first four months of our son's life, when my wife was often up breast-feeding. Many couples can trade off when the working parent gets home. In our case that's almost never been feasible.

How was it decided that it was going to be you at home?
Sometimes who stays home is decided *for* rather than *by* you. We couldn't afford for my wife to stay home. A couple of months after our son was born my wife was offered a position as chef of a popular upmarket restaurant. The bacon she was bringing home would increase by 50 percent. Oh sure, we'll turn it down. In retrospect, I can't believe we didn't talk more about this. On the other hand, my wife's career might not be what it is today if we had.

What about your writing career?
As each of our kids has grown, they've required less hands-on time, which meant that I had time to write. We still needed a parent at home, but that dovetailed with my desire to always be working on something. Our kids have benefited, but I've also benefited. When we made the decision for me to stay home we didn't know that my wife would remain the primary breadwinner for most of our family life. That hasn't always been easy. When people make assumptions about what my life has been like they assume I've made a sacrifice. I don't see it that way. From my perspective it's my wife who's made the sacrifice. At times both of have wished that we could switch roles without an incredible financial penalty. The hero of this story isn't the dad who gives up everything to stay at home. The hero is my wife who gave up a lot of family life to support us.

You have taken the unconventional path and people are often uncomfortable (and closed-minded) with that. Has socialising been awkward at any point?

There have been a few times when people found out I was the guy on home watch and after following it up with 'So, are you getting anything done?' (Yeah, actually, I'm raising my kids) then mysteriously sighted someone across the room they needed to see RIGHT NOW, afraid I was going to start blathering about nappies or the benefits of the Montessori method, I suppose. Thank God most of our friends have been unconventional – artists or restaurant people or independent operators of one stripe or another. The really unexpected thing was how many women wanted to chat me up whenever I was out walking around with my two-year-old in a backpack. On weekend visits to parks and playgrounds with my wife, all of these mums and nannies would look up and say 'Hi, how's it going?' and my wife would give me one of her raised-eyebrow *and-who's-that?* looks.

Have you enjoyed this time in your life?

I'm the kind of ham who was born to read aloud to his kids – creating character voices, imitating sound effects, the whole tootling calliope. And my kids ate it up. I loved that intimacy of being inside a story together. Most dads barely get to kiss their young kids goodnight. And now that our older one has left for college I'm even more appreciative of my good fortune. I don't suppose there's any way to empirically parse this, but I also have a sense that our kids are more evenly ballasted because they had a dad at home. They'll throw a line to either me or their mum.

Okay, a few other realities. I've had moments when I looked in the mirror and saw a mad person staring back–*What could I have been thinking!* My mind's turning to mush! If I don't start talking to more adults I'm going to go insane. My wife's career has eclipsed my own, such as it is. During my time at home, I've ghosted several books, written a cookbook with her, and just finished the draft of a novel. But does it put us on a career par? Let's just say that [popular US TV station] the Food Network isn't likely to call anytime soon for my recipe for Shrimp Risotto. On the other hand, she's missed out on some of the pleasures of walking alongside Will and Lyra in *The Golden Compass* or the satisfactions of building a Lego 'setup' on the living room carpet. I think missing those moments is harder on women than on men. (Okay, if that's sexist, so be it.) Men seem to paper over ordinary reality with a kind of noise to remind them that they're there and only wake up to what they missed years later. My father, a sales manager, was frequently on the road, leaving my brothers and me alone with our mother in rural Michigan for a week at a time. He once confessed how much seeing me interact with our son and daughter pained him, made him realise how much he'd missed.

Slightly off topic. I think I've been a better dad than a writer. Whether that's good or bad I can't say, but I wouldn't trade one for the other.

What would you say to couples who are considering this route but may be apprehensive?
I would encourage them to ask themselves why are you nervous about this option? If saying the phrase *My husband's at home with the kids,* makes you see lights floating at the edge of your vision or your stomach do a tarantella then maybe you ought to reconsider. Nothing's more effective at revealing a partiality to traditional gender roles than trying to mess with them. Not everybody has to be a pioneer. Talk about it and keep talking. (I wish I'd done more of this.) Talk about who will handle what, and when. Nothing has to be set in stone, but believe me, if you both have different expectations about how the operation will work it's better to find out now instead of trying to negotiate your way out of a 4:30 a.m. conflict. Talk about the future. How long do you envision the arrangement lasting? Until the kids are in school? Longer? Does your spouse have the kind of career that can be put on hold and

then picked up in three, five, 10 years? How will you feel about being the primary breadwinner? How does your spouse feel about that? Any arrangement is going to chafe at some time or another and if you don't talk about it you're dead. I can't say it enough: Talk.

Plenty of Sunshine and Water Daily: How to Cultivate a Good Partner

In the words of Aretha Franklin, R-E-S-P-E-C-T., respect, and more than just a little bit. Good partnerships come from shared values and great communication and an underlying respect for the other person's contribution to the parenting. Wow. That sounds simple. And it is on paper. In the real world of sleep deprivation, money stresses, sick children and cranky employers, finding time for great communication seems like a pipedream. You need to make it a priority.

The only way to juggle the schedules, handle the unexpected, and otherwise get along is to be flexible, supportive of each other, occasionally selfless and find time to talk things over. Working mothers never feel like their partners understand their challenges. Working fathers all too often think that earning money for their family covers off their contribution. Sorry. It's 2009 now. We're on an equal playing field and working fathers need to share in the childcare in the same way that working mothers do. Here's a couple of tips that can help you open the lines of communication:

- Schedule and keep a weekly meeting where you review schedules, problems, successes and new ideas for how the family can operate more efficiently.
- Don't assume because your partner does it differently than you would, that you would do it better. Different is not a value judgment. It's just different.
- Praise each other for a job well done. (Management 101)

- Address problems immediately. Don't grit your teeth and bear it. You will just react inappropriately when the straw breaks the camel's back and do great damage to your cause of equality.
- Set goals together – financial goals are key. Are you savers or spenders? Do you want to try and earn more money or just spend less to cover the additional expense of the children? Fighting over money is very common. And take it from Kim, once you start it's very difficult to stop!
- Give each other a break. You're both learning at this. Isn't it more fun to learn together?

Negotiating with Your Partner

You've been working really hard to cultivate a strong partnership, but you still feel like there is an inequality in the workload and you need to find a way to approach the problem fairly. Once again, your business girl training kicks in. Why not just negotiate? Give a little to get a little. We've included a little primer on negotiation:

You can't always get what you want . . . but you can negotiate.

- The key to any successful negotiation is that both parties walk away feeling like they won something. So make sure when you begin the discussion you are ready to listen to what they want and give something back too.
- Walk into a negotiation with a plan. Know what you want and be specific. If you want your partner to cover Tuesday and Thursday nights, so you can take a class then ask for that. If you want every other Saturday morning to play tennis then that's the 'ask.'
- Do your research. In this arena it would be: How much do you do today? What have they asked for recently? If you 'win' this negotiation then are things out-of-balance at home? What would you need to do to get it back?
- Think and ask big. If you have already sold yourself out at the

beginning of the negotiation then you have no wiggle room. So, make sure you go in high and be willing to come down.

- Make a commitment to yourself to hold your ground. You will not believe what some people will sink to in order to not take on more at home. The guilt-trips, the sulking, the attempt to change the agreement. Stand strong. Just like at the office, you have to be your own advocate. If you know what you want, that you deserve it or need it, then ASK for it.

- Be willing to give something. You can always begin the discussion with your offer and then tackle your ask. That sets a positive tone and your partner might be more receptive to what you are asking for.

The Word: Linda Brierty, Therapist

Can you share some tips with our readers on how to negotiate more help at home since so many of us do too much on that front?

Finding balance and a sense of equality on the domestic side of things is a major challenge for most families. The primary breadwinner often feels overwhelmed by financial responsibility, and the partner more in charge of the home front often feels isolated, abandoned, and alone. Obviously in single parent households, this is exacerbated. In families with two breadwinners, it would be nice if domestic duties were divided evenly, but how often does this happen? There is usually a primary parent, largely responsible for the day-to-day running of the home. To avoid resentment, it is helpful to break down responsibilities and agree about who is responsible for what. Be careful not to enable, and 'pick up the slack' if one partner is not meeting their end of the bargain. Divide responsibilities by identifying each other's strengths, and make sure you agree with each other and feel that it is equitable. Then, the agreement must be maintained. Have a weekly 'check-in' about how things are going. Try to avoid a victim mentality – if your needs are not being met, it is up to you to communicate and address the situation. Remember to appreciate all the things that your partner is doing. No one wants to feel taken for granted. Learn to ask for what you want and need in a positive, productive way, rather than through complaining, accusing or fighting. End the conversation with what you see as the solution.

'Girl' Talk: Let's hear from our boy Jim

We wanted to include Jim in this book because as someone raised by two working parents and now a working dad himself, he offers a unique point-of-view on these issues. From what we can see, he is also someone who has his priorities straight (giving enough to work to have significant responsibilities while spending quality time with a son who adores him).

So you were a latch-key kid. We don't hear that phrase used that often anymore.
When I was older, in 5th grade, I became a latch-key kid. We had some babysitters for nights my parents might be away, but we always came home from school ourselves and it was not unusual for us to be alone in the afternoon.

What was the good, bad and ugly about being a latch-key kid?
It was a real mix bag that I think led to us being very independent. We had to be responsible for our afternoon activities, schoolwork, taking care of the house, feeding the cat, making sure our parents knew where we were, not

fighting too much with my brother. That was all good for us in the long run. It was NOT easy resisting my dad's stash of cookies, but we tried. The bad? What else? I loved my mum and wished she was home. You fall and get hurt, you are alone. But you know what? It made us appreciate them more.

Did your parents miss a lot of your events, games and other school activities?
Sure, on weekdays, especially my dad. But they always tried (and usually did make) evening games and weekends for sure.

How do you do things differently than your parents?
I play with my kid more for sure, especially sports. I think the value of play at a young age cannot be overstated. I avoid too strict a curriculum; I want my kid to have fun! I try and do what he wants to do at least a few days a week, not what I want.

What should working mums do to make their children feel loved and taken care of even if they miss activities because they are working?
Just take an interest in the activities and engage them. Make them talk about it and never break a promise. I see how heartbroken my kid is at age five when I promise to be there and can't make it. I think the mum and all parents should try and find time to be at one game, one event a season and not be afraid to tell the boss that's what you are doing.

How do you prioritise work and parenting?
It is so hard, isn't it? Basically, I work my tail off at work,

do a little personal work and draw lines. I know the idea is 24/7, but I log off when I'm at home. I turn off my phone, IM and 'berry because I know I need to. My parents lived in a 9–5 world and there is something to be said for that. I think we have become slaves to work and really many of us don't have to be, we just think we do. Home is for family first and you need to draw those lines for your children.

8

Traps We Fall Into

All of us reading, contributing and writing this book have something in common. We are ambitious, perfection-seeking women who want to stand out at everything we attempt. We're not saying we want to have it all. We're saying we want, more than want, we *expect* to excel at everything we do. We've done well in school and in our careers. Now we're having babies so we're going to be great mothers. And great partners to our significant others, too. The sad fact is we just can't do it all well all of the time. Sometimes something has to give – work, motherhood, marriage – choose one. And that's what this chapter is all about – successfully navigating the negative traps to help us make better choices. Choices that will help us be better wives, mothers and career girls. None of this is easy, and much of it is downright unpleasant. But forewarned is forearmed – and so we go ably forward and we offer some ways to avoid the five most common traps we fall into.

Trap #1: Vilifying and/or Romanticising Stay-at-Home Mums

Sadly, there remains a lot of tension between stay-at-home mums and stay-working mums. For the working mums, the ones at home appear to be quickly going brain-dead, more interested in *The Backyardigans* than Baghdad. For the mums at home, the ones heading into offices each morning seem selfish and shallow, more interested in their careers and mani/pedis than their children.

Sigh.

Why the passing of all this judgment? Could be because none of us are 100% satisfied with our decision and secretly wonder whether we got it wrong? Could it be because some of us wish we could have a little more choice in the matter because we work because we need the money, and many of us stay home because it's cheaper than childcare?

Does jealousy contribute to the great divide? The stay-at-home mum longing for what she thinks is a more stimulating environment, while the working mum longs for more quality time with her children? There is also a whole lot of projecting going on. We had one interviewee tell us that she has been 'envious of stay-at-home mums because they seem to build in more socialisation time for themselves and their children, have time for exercising and hobbies and have done a good job of building support systems and staying connected.'

When we first read this answer we immediately thought of a handful of women who have, in fact, figured out how to have it all while on the clock at home, but then we remembered the other 95% who were just as confused about the choice to opt out. You see there is no one-size-fits-all solution to getting what you want out of life, while being a great parent, spouse, friend, daughter, colleague, employer and employee.

Whatever the reasons for the rift that keeps on growing, we simply don't appreciate how difficult it is for all of us. We all know how hard it is to be at home with children. They take an enormous amount of energy, time and attention. It's exhausting and depleting in a way that work just isn't. On the other hand, working while parenting is as challenging but in a different way. When you work and parent you are managing two different lives, each with relationships and responsibilities. You can't let anyone down because the stakes are so high.

What we have in common is this: both of our jobs (don't kid yourself that running a household and parenting full-time is anything but a job) require us to put others first. So rather than beat each other up about what we're not and what we should be, let's support one another. It may take all of our lives a little easier because the truth is we're actually not that different. It's time we appreciated that and united.

Relationships with other parents are important, whether they work or stay at home. Other mothers could have the answers you are looking for when it comes to how to get your child to sleep before midnight, or how to get them to eat carrots. Why do you want to rule out a huge chunk of the population as a potential resource or friend just because they made a different personal choice than you? Not only can meet lifelong friends on the playground but one working mum we spoke to told us that she relies on stay-at-home mums, because they 'are so helpful with school and practise drop offs or pick ups if you can't get off of work in time.' Although, don't take too much advantage, this is exactly the kind of scenario that leads to resentment. Lorraine Nellis tells us that 'Maintaining friendships with other parents is a great way to know what your kids are doing at all times.'

Like politics and religion, working mums versus stay-at-home mums is a topic often best left out of discussion at a dinner party. Unfortunately, each side has clung to their distinct and divergent view, leaving little room for any grey area or respectful discourse. We'd like to try and change that; we'd like all mums to start focusing on our similarities and not our differences. Maybe there won't ever be a truce (though we can hope), but can there be a little more understanding? Civility and consideration can go a long way in this world. There is no one way to parent a child. In other words – in case we haven't driven the point home yet – all stay-at-home mums are not the same and all working mothers are not the same. The choices do not define the woman and they shouldn't pigeon hole others' opinions of them. But it often does and the debate gets heated and women end up skewering each other instead of supporting one another. In the end, does it make you feel more confident as a mother, better about your working situation, superior to the woman who has the different life?

No. So what's the point?

For a little light on the situation, we go to Oprah. On the show, women took part in a heated and often nasty debate about the choices they and those around them had made. But the results of an Oprah.com poll, in which more than 15,000 women (working mothers and stay-at-home mothers) responded, show the divide might not be as great as we think.

From stay-at-home mums:
Do stay-at-home mums get the respect they deserve?
  5% – Yes   85% – No

Do you wish you worked?
36% – Yes   64% – No

Overall are you satisfied with the job you are doing as a parent?
80% – Yes   20% – No

Would you describe your children as happy?
97% – Yes   3% – No

Is it possible to give 100 percent to motherhood and a career?
71% – Yes   29% – No

From working mums:
Do stay-at-home mums get the respect they deserve?
17% – Yes   83% – No

Would you quit to stay home if you could?
66% – Yes   34% – No

Overall, are you satisfied with the job you are doing as a parent?
71% – Yes   29% – No

Would you describe your children as happy?
93% – Yes   7% – No

Is it possible to give 100 percent to motherhood and a career?
61% – Yes   39% – No

The Word: It's More Than Bring and Buy Sales and Lift-sharing

Stay-at-home mums work hard, too. They may not be career girls like us, but many of them contribute to their communities in ways that we could only imagine and that benefit all of us. Their stories are as inspiring as those of women juggling work and family. Jennifer Heth should be the poster girl for a mother who has this job.

Service and volunteerism have been an intrinsic part of Jen's life since she was a young girl. She volunteered during high school and college and armed with a journalism degree, was accepted into the Peace Corps after college. She was stationed in the Dominican Republic and responsible for establishing a Parent–Teacher Association and convincing the community to become involved with the local school and their children's education. She's also a girl who operates best with a full plate and thrives on being busy.

After the Peace Corps, Jen moved home to Colorado and got married. She and her husband moved to a nice area in downtown Denver and decided to start a family. Jen was working as the Marketing Director of the non-profit Denver Children's Museum. In that job, Jen worked 12-hour days and many nights and week-ends. She knew that she wouldn't be able to create the kind of family she wanted without making a change.

When she was pregnant with Emma, she decided not to return to her job. She gave her employer ample notice and even helped find and train her replacement. As a manager she had more than a few bad experiences with women who went out on maternity leave planning to come back, only to tell her two weeks before they were expected back that they weren't returning.

She planned to stay home with Emma for six to 12 months and then start looking for a new job. Shortly after Emma was born, Jen's mother was diagnosed with terminal cancer. Jen spent the next year raising her daughter and taking care of her ailing mother. Eighteen months after Emma was born, Jen's mother died.

'I needed the time with Emma, and I needed to grieve for my mother,' Jen said when recalling this time. 'My mother and I were very close. I think after she died, it reinforced the mother-daugh-ter bond I was creating with Emma.'

Six months later, Jen landed a job where she could work from home. As the Marketing Manager for a non-profit, Denver Telecomm, she organised meetings, members and conferences. It worked out great until Charlie was born. While Emma had been a great sleeper, Charlie never slept. He didn't nap, he never wanted to be put down, and he constantly needed attention. She put Emma in preschool three days a week, quit her job and poured herself into her kids.

Sending her kids to public school was a priority for Jen and her husband. As their local school district was populated with affluent families, many of them chose to send their children to private school. To increase enrolment, the local school became a magnet school for the deaf and hard-of-hearing as well as offering a traditional curriculum and a program for the gifted. Many of the students were bussed in from other parts of the city. It led to an interesting and diverse student population but little parental involvement in the school.

A combination of Jen's professional training and her personal convictions led her to become very active in the school almost immediately after Emma enrolled. She spent Emma's kindergarten year volunteering and assessing what was needed. When Emma started school, she had a plan to present to the principal. Her year of observation and research led her to a couple of conclusions: the school needed a PTA and an enrichment program that wasn't just available to the gifted-and-talented, but one that was available to all of the student body.

Jen got to work. She became the President of the PTA and began recruiting parents and running fundraising activities. She also began to formulate the enrichment program. Throughout this her goal was to create programs and systems that other parents could be trained for and take over. When the PTA was up and running, she tackled the enrichment program which presented a number of unique challenges.

The goals for the program were to include all of the students from K-5; to mix them up so they could meet other children in the school of other ages and backgrounds, and to offer a wide range of activities that the students could choose for themselves. To do this required energy, principal buy-in and funding.

Jen wrote and won a grant from the city of Denver, got the PTA to match it (because her fundraising efforts had been so successful there was a surplus of money) and set about to create the programs. During this, we should mention that she was a full-time mother of two kids, and handled all of the responsibilities at home while also carving out time for herself. Her husband's job requires a lot of travel and his schedule was very unpredictable. We should also remind our readers that she wasn't being paid to do any of this.

The program was finally ready. Armed with $4500 and a cadre of volunteer instructors from the community who she had recruited, the first session of the Enrichment Program was launched with 25 classes offered every Friday afternoon in four week sessions. The classes were all taught by professionals in the community, were available to 350 students and included: cooking, yoga, architecture, martial arts, cultural studies, animal care, fire fighting and various sports. They ran three sessions throughout the year.

The program was so successful, that the agency that awarded Jen the original grant, Community Resources, has adopted it and is marketing it to other school districts in Colorado. They also did a very smart thing. They offered Jen a part-time job running one of their other programs. She is now working part-time for Community Resources, raising her family, running the enrich-ment program for the school that Charlie now attends (this will be her last year as she's got a new team almost trained and ready to go) and is setting her sights on the middle school.

We think she should run for office. Seriously.

Trap #2: Hiding Out at Work

Work is our safe place. We can control it and most days have a really good time when we are there. We use our brains to solve problems, work under deadline pressure and get paid for what we do. We believe we're good mothers because we work and we'll admit it: many days we'd rather be at work then at home, chang-ing nappies, running after toddlers or arguing with our partners about who's going to get up in the middle of the night.

When we searched 'hiding at work' on www.workitmom.com, one of our favourite working mum blog sites (check out the sidebar later in this chapter for more) we found this one from Diane who works at home, 'I shut myself in the bedroom to get a project finished. Well, I want to share my little secret: I'm done, but I'm hiding in here just enjoying the relative silence, the pit-pat of rain on the roof, and surfing the Web. Every now and then a hoard of dogs, cats, and a toddler can be heard clamouring outside the door wanting in. Hee hee, I wonder how long I can stay in here . . . ??'

Diane's hiding is perfectly harmless. It's when hiding evolves to avoiding that problems can occur. Kim knows this all too well. As a business owner and primary earner for her family, she could always rationalise the extra hours at night in the office, or the time on the weekend. Her son wasn't suffering. He was with his father or grandmothers. Her marriage however was a different story.

Here are some ways to stop hiding:
- Ruth Klein in her book, *Time Management Secrets for Working Women: Getting Organized to Get the Most Out of Each Day* (Sourcebooks Inc, 2005) recommends 'The Three-Ds Filing System' which we like. The D's stand for 'Do it this morning.' 'Do it this afternoon.' And 'Do it Now.' We can apply it easily to our email Inbox which has become our *de facto* to-do list. When you get to work, open your email and organise the Three-Ds. Be realistic about what you can get done in one day and don't forget to factor in time-sucking meetings and conference calls. When you've got all of those things done, go home to your family (or run to the gym – as we keep reminding you, one of the secrets to happy working motherhood is for your life to include more than just work and mothering).
- Schedule the nights you need to work late in advance. If your child or spouse knows that one night a week, you need to work late or attend evening work functions then you are no longer hiding. You've set the expectation for your schedule. Now stick to it. Nothing upsets children (and spouses for that matter) more than constantly changing the schedule.

- Keep your promises. If you've told your family you will be home for dinner, go home and eat – even if you have heaps of work to do. You can always work remotely after the kids go to bed or get up early the next morning.
- Make sure you include a little down time in your day, even if it's just to read a magazine, listen to the radio or sit quietly on your commute. A little break from work and mothering and the needs of others may be all the recharge you require.

Trap #3: Buckling Under the Weight of Guilt

Oh, the mother guilt. Blogs, websites and psychologists' couches are filled with mothers describing their daily feelings of guilt. Every single working mum we interviewed for this book mentioned the guilt they feel about any number of aspects of their lives. And the guilt begins before your baby is even born. Linda Barnes Gray, a college librarian and mother of two tells us, 'After reading a number of books, I thought about going without any drugs to deliver my first and then my husband said people no longer bite a bullet for surgery, why should I go without pain medication? He made sense, but so many women (and so many books!) are so adamant about the effects of medication on the baby. In the end, my baby was in distress and I had to have a C-section so all my guilt was for nothing. And then I picked up a book that had a chapter on breastfeeding with the following chapter about bottle feeding which was laden with guilt trips about not breastfeeding. It made me pretty angry, since breast-feeding is not for everyone. I believe if it is not good for mum, it is not good for baby, since they can feel our stress.'

All mother's feel guilt occasionally but ample evidence sugges-tions that working mums face an inordinate amount of guilt, especially from outside sources and most heart wrenchingly, when it comes from children themselves in the form of that dreaded question, 'Mummy, why do you have to go to work?' Mother guilt will always exist whether we put it on ourselves or not. Our goal isn't to eradicate it, but to manage it better. Based on the recommendations of the experts, our interviews and personal experience, we've created a 'Five-Step Program for Managing Mother Guilt'.

1. **Assess whether the guilt is deserved.** Before you make a ruling, remember, by definition, guilt is an emotional experience that occurs when a person realises or believes – whether justified or not – that she has violated a moral standard. A moral standard is pretty strong litmus test, but if you can't be objective ask your partner or working mother friend to make the ruling. Most mother guilt is unwarranted. Chris Colabella expressed how many of us feel: 'After my daughter Kali was born, I felt very guilty all of the time. I felt like I wasn't being a good mother, but I also felt like I wasn't working as hard as I should.' For the record, Chris changed her entire work schedule to spend more time with her daughter, hired extra people to cover the missing time at work and reduced her pay to offset the additional headcount. Kim feels guilty that she can't be the room mother for her son's class, even though she knows she not only would hate it, but would be terrible in the role. Caitlin gets the 'guilts' when she spends one-on-one time with her daughter – even though it means that her son is spending the equivalent time with his father. If the guilt is unwarranted, then let it go. Just like that. If the guilt is warranted, make amends. A heartfelt apology is an easy place to start.

2. **Assess your priorities, create your boundaries and stick to them.** If you've set up a four-day work week to spend more time with your child, then don't work on your child's time. And vice versa. If you are telecommuting, don't play with your child during work time. If it's important that you take your child to the doctor then take her. Make up the time

you missed from work on your own time. Breaking promises and commitments leads to guilt, so stick to your word.

3. If the guilt is coming from an external source, then stop it as quickly as possible. Don't apologise (remember you didn't do anything wrong). Explain why the guilt-trip that is being laid on you is inappropriate and move on. If you are dealing with habitual guilters (such as Kim's grandmother who has done post-doctorate work in guilt-tripping) then minimise your contact with them.

4. Just say no. Much of our guilt stems from the feeling of letting others down. If we don't make the commitments in the first place, we can't let anyone down, and we don't feel guilty.

5. Forgive yourself. You will make mistakes. You will be overextended, overscheduled and overwhelmed. It's okay. We've all been there. Go back to step one. Make amends and try to learn from your error.

Trap #4: Not Appreciating Ourselves

After interviewing the hundreds of women for all of our books we realised that we all suffer from the same thing: we don't appreciate ourselves. We discount and down-play how much we accomplish in a day and minimise how hard it really is. We can all find someone who is doing more or juggling more than we are. It doesn't mean we're not juggling a lot. And all of a sudden before you know it you are piling more and more on your plate and eventually something gives, and for many of the women we've talked to, it's their health. Stress related illnesses are real and prevalent. IBS, TMJ, migraines, take your pick.

Laurice, a mother of four boys (three of whom are triplets) and owner of a cleaning business, has been suffering from debilitating migraines for the past year and doctors can't find a cause. None of the migraine medications are working. She describes her situation, 'The doctor did mention that it would certainly help to eliminate as much stress as possible, caffeine and to get a good night's sleep. How interesting . . . I get woken many nights, I drink Diet Coke and tea daily and I've spent almost every waking moment this entire summer with three 7-year olds and a 5-year old while running a business. I think a weekly root canal may be less stressful!'

We couldn't agree more, but she continues, 'I'm being funny and my husband is fantastic! My business does not take that much of my time and the kids are pretty good, and my husband is very hands on. I have to start taking better care of myself. I need to drink more water, lay off the caffeine, etc. Things I know to do, I just don't always actually do.'

Laurice is not unusual. Most of the women we talk to minimise the challenges they handle on a daily basis and take too much blame for what doesn't go right. Would Laurice's headaches go away if she drank more water and slept more? Maybe. But is that really the point? Isn't the point that she's managing a ton every day, which she discounts and then when something suffers (her health), she blames herself because really it's no big deal to take care of a business, four kids and a house all on your own because she has a supportive husband.

In 2000, Naomi G. Swanson, published an article in the *Journal of the American Women's Medical Association* that found that, 'high-strain jobs have been linked with psychological distress, pain, and reduced physical functioning among nurses; increased sickness absenteeism and depressive symptoms among female workers in a wide variety of occupations; significant increases in blood pressure among more highly educated female white-collar workers; an increased risk of myocardial infarction; and more than twice the risk for short (24 days or less) menstrual cycles.'

But the answer isn't to stop work. The article also showed that, 'overall employment has many benefits for women, including increased financial resources, a sense of achievement, and reduced social isolation, all of which can benefit health. Additionally, some research has indicated that women who occupy multiple roles (mother, worker, spouse) experience better mental and physical health than women who occupy few roles, perhaps because with multiple roles, the stresses of one role may be offset by the rewards of another.'

The kicker apparently though is when one of the role's negative offsets the other's positives. For example if you lose your childcare due to a sick child, more often than not mothers leave work, therefore increasing stress. It's more of what we know – this job is really hard and when it gets off track it can make us sick. Swanson's article offers recommendations for how organisations can reduce stress for working mothers that include: '... expanding promotion and career ladders, introducing such family support programs as flexible schedules and dependent care programs and introducing clear, accessible, and enforced policies against sex discrimination and sexual harassment.'

We would add that working mothers can reduce their own stress by asking for more help – especially when their health is being affected.

Trap #5: Seeking Perfection

Oh for over-achieving women, good is just *not* good enough. We need to be perfect – at work, at home, in bed with our partners. When we asked working mums if they thought they were good mothers, they all answered, 'they could be better if ... .' We know most of these women who we polled. And they are great mothers. Why aren't they satisfied? Nicki's story will shed a little light on the topic.

Girl Talk: Nicki's Relentless, Exhausting and Wholly Unnecessary Pursuit of Perfection

Nicki Dugan is the Senior Director of Corporate Communications at Yahoo!. Unlike most of us, Nicki Dugan started worrying about the age-old balancing act of being a good mother with a dynamic career when she was seventeen years old. She even spoke to her high school guidance counsellor about it. She couldn't see a way to do everything well. In her recollection, she had the perfect mother – stay-at-home and always available to her – just the kind of mother Nicki wanted to be herself someday. And yet she also wanted a career.

Unable to reconcile this conundrum, she chased her work ambitions full-throttle. She started working at a magazine in New York City and, like all perfectionists, poured everything she had into it. Twelve hour days were the norm – she was often the first one in, the last one to leave and got promoted quickly. At 25, she married her college sweetheart and followed him to Hawaii, where he was stationed in the Marine Corps. She took a job in public relations and continued to excel. She was driven by a fear of mediocrity and gave 100 percent in everything she took on.

Having a family was always in the plan for her and her husband but they kept putting it off – in part because of Nicki's 'can't do it all' fear. She and her husband eventually moved to San Francisco and became part of the dot-com revolution. She landed a job at Yahoo!, where she remains. But work was only one part of Nicki's life. She was a devoted wife, avid gardener, creative cook, jewellery maker, and social organiser. She also became obsessed with running marathons.

At 34 and after nine years of marriage, she opted for motherhood. In fact, she found out later that she ran her tenth marathon three weeks pregnant. And, as we learned from Nicki, being a perfect career girl, wife, friend, and mother was harder than she had ever imagined at seventeen. She shares her hard-learned lessons with the rest of us.

How did your work life change after you had Max [Nicki's first child]?

I had been at Yahoo! for two years by the time I got pregnant, working 60 hours weeks right up until my due date. When I came back after maternity leave, I felt like I had lost in musical chairs but I didn't do anything to reclaim my seat. For the first time in my life, I voluntarily took a backseat in my job. I was afraid of putting my neck out the way I had always done before because I just didn't think I would be able to pull it off. I stopped going for high-profile projects because I knew I had to be home to relieve the nanny. I skulked out at 5:00 p.m. knowing that the others would be there long into the night, as I always had. It really set me back.

But we thought Yahoo! was a family-friendly place?

The irony is that it actually is family-friendly – I mean as family-friendly as a Web company can be. But there weren't many Yahoo! mothers at the time. And I put the pressure, the unrealistic expectations and the paranoia squarely on myself. My colleagues later told me that, as I snuck home at night, they thought, 'Hey, she's a good mother.' Meanwhile, I beat myself up as 'one of those slackers.'

I tried to compartmentalise my life unnecessarily. I rarely spoke about Max in the office, not wanting to draw attention to my new 'career handicap', and I was constantly feeling both guilty about my parenting and frustrated that my career had stalled. There were days when I'd cry in the mother's room, full of guilt about having to take time out to express milk as my peers raced around. But when I walked in and found our very accomplished CFO's gear in there one day (she was on her third kid), it gave me new perspective on these conflicting emotions. It helped me stop feeling like a horrible mother and I stopped beating myself up about work, but it didn't really improve until after my second son was born.

We're listening to your story and asking ourselves where was your husband in all of this? Why did you have to get home to relieve the nanny? Why did you have to take a backseat at work? Why weren't you making him more responsible for co-parenting?

When Max was born, my husband was in a consulting position that required him to be out of town Monday through Friday, so the nanny (and she was extraordinary) and I did everything. He would return home on Friday night, full of questions about how to take care of his own son. I resented him but felt like caring for Max was more my responsibility because I was the mother. 'I am the one who can breastfeed and I am the one who can get it done, so I will.' Aside from changing nappies, there were so few things I ever really asked him to do. Something had to give, so my husband hired a cleaning lady. Instead of thinking it was a great thing, all I could think was that if I didn't do it myself, I was a failure.

How did you get back in the groove?

I think what changed all of that for me was getting some really tough feedback in a review. The first bad review I had ever had. I think some of it was unfair, but she basically made me realise I was putting this baggage on myself, and because of this baggage I wasn't contributing anymore and something had to change. I could have quit then, but I didn't want to. As hard as it was to hear, my boss was right. I had changed. I had to prove to myself that my old self was there – I just needed to find her again.

In addition to the bad review, she also gave me an opportunity to birth a big project for the company. It was an awesome challenge and mine to own from start to finish. I am really glad that I stuck it out because through it all I found a way to ask for more help at home so I could get the project done. I also finally regained my confidence.

Any words of advice?

My biggest regret in some ways was that I didn't have the confidence to jump back into work with both feet after Max was born. It would have made those years so much easier. I let 'working mother' become the oxymoron I'd always feared it would be. I expected far too much of myself and created a self-fulfilling prophecy that left me living in constant turmoil. As I pureed homemade organic baby food at midnight (after all, I had to be perfect), I felt the creeping anxiety of all the work I should be doing instead. And vice versa.

Now I try to apply the deathbed test as I pick my battles. Isn't this Halloween parade more important in the long run than going to the office? Isn't this work project better for our family than chaperoning that field trip? I've finally realised that the world won't stop if I take a time out from either work or family. The theme of my life has been a constant pursuit of perfection and the fact that I couldn't be near the same person I was before I had my children was hard to accept. But what I realised is that good enough sometimes just has to be good enough. And I finally give myself credit for all the things I accomplish in a day. But it's a process getting to a new place. I still don't delegate enough to my husband and I occasionally beat myself up when I think I could've done a better job. And I still haven't made it to surf camp. But it's on my list – I promise.

Keeping Your Career

ng a mother offers a
e opportunity to take
back and decide what
you want f   be in it for the money
or you cou   h Ann did during her
maternity leave, your career is an essential part of your identity.
The key is to have a work situation that supports and offers you
what you need from a job as a working mum: money, security,
inspiration, motivation and flexibility. Once you have taken a
moment to look in the mirror at the new professional you, taken
stock of the time and energy now required of you at home and
reviewed your new financial landscape you can begin your list of
job requirements. These are the qualities – pay, benefits, hours,
opportunities – that will help you plan your next steps whether
that is asking for a chance in your schedule or looking for a new
career altogether. Whichever way you want to go, this chapter
will help you figure out if you need to reconfigure your current

job or look for something new all together, where to start and who to turn to for help.

Your Crystal Ball

If you could look into the crystal ball and see the future, would you be surprised with what you see? If you've set clear goals for yourself the answer should be No. Of course unexpected things always come up (see Girl Talk: Nicole Lamborne) but your life (and especially your work life) shouldn't be a total surprise.

If you can't predict the future, it's probably because like us, you've been trying to do so much for so long and at such a fast speed that you have lost sight of what you want. If anything, working on this book has really taught us the power of choice. Most of the working mums who shared their stories with us, even though they struggle and have made mistakes, are optimistic about the future and the potential their careers still hold.

It's important to review your goals now so the crystal ball won't reveal too many surprises.

Girls Guide Tips for Effective Goal-Setting

1. You've got to want it. When setting goals for yourself and your family make sure you focus on things that you really want and not just what 'you're supposed' to want. Do you really want to be the boss in five years or is being the right hand to the boss a better role for you? If you don't really want it, it won't happen. Sometimes, though, you don't find out until you give it a chance. Ever since we published our first book, people have been telling us we should get a television show. Producers, agents, friends, you name it, they've told us we need a reality show. Well, after five years of not making any progress (and it's the only thing we've ever set our minds to that hasn't happened), we realised we didn't really want to star in a television show. Caitlin wants to produce one, so she is working to make

that happen instead and we have no doubt that it will happen.

2. One goal can't get in the way of another – which is actually the trap that many working women fall into. Our prime working years coincide with our prime baby-making years and you need to plan around it. Physically, mentally and emotionally, you just can't give that much energy to your career and baby. Take a longer view, know that you'll be a little slower when the kids are young, but have ample opportunity to make up the time.

3. Be positive when setting goals. We have fallen into this trap for years. Our thinking focused on what we didn't want to do – take on a new client or hire a new person, for example – versus what we did want, which was to grow both businesses slowly and steadily so that we could work less.

4. Write your goals down on paper and be as specific as possible. 'I want a promotion and payrise' is not an effective goal statement. You need to be spell out the terms. 'I want to be the Marketing Director running a department of 20 and making $150,000 in three years.'

5. Aim high. You haven't come this far in your career and life to start thinking small now. You are a working mother, you're already a superstar.

The Word: How to Succeed in Business When I Should Be Out Freezing My Eggs

Elissa Ellis Sangster is the Executive Director for the Forté Foundation, an organisation dedicated to inspiring women business leaders. Prior to her position with Forté, Elissa served as the Assistant Dean and Director of the MBA Program at the

McCombs School of Business at the University of Texas at Austin and saw first-hand the issues affecting women's abilities to seek, prepare for and attain business leadership positions.

Elissa has an MBA herself and believes that MBA's are important for women because to really succeed in business you need to be bold and confident when you walk through the doors of big business (or a big bank when you need money for your start-up business!). According to Elissa, 'An MBA is extremely empowering. It provides a set of skills and a way of thinking that is really valued in the marketplace. Its broad curriculum teaches you to be a critical thinker, a problem-solver and entrepreneurial in all things. And most importantly, you will create a network for life of friends and colleagues who you can count on and connect with for your entire careers. It's also a lot of fun.'

The median age for students in an MBA program is 28 and your prime career years begin the second you graduate – once again coinciding with your prime family years. This fact is not lost on the women in the programs. Most of women MBAs want to know when they should plan to have their kids. Elissa shared, 'At one conference, an attendee asked a panellist if she should consider freezing her eggs since she was already 35. The panellist told her she should have frozen her eggs at 27. The women in the room looked as if they were going to get up en masse to run out and get their eggs frozen.'

Elissa recently got married for the first time and at 40 is trying to create a family of her own. Her work with the Forté Foundation has given her the opportunity to travel all over the country meeting business women. Elissa offers some thoughts about successful woman business leaders:

- Find the right partner. Don't marry somebody until you have conversations about how you want your life to look after having babies. Don't accept a partner who's not going to be supportive of your decision to keep working.

- Even with the most enlightened partners, the burden of responsibility lands on women. Be prepared for it.
- The hard part is changing the business culture that has made a focus on 'face time' and being in the office. Gen X wants more flexibility and as they move into senior leadership positions, the culture will change. Women are going to be a big part of this change. But it's going to take time.

Girl Talk: There's No Such Thing As a Part-Time Doctor

Dr. Nicole Lamborne is the mother of three children and an obstetrician/gynaecologist in a private practice and clinic. She is married to a paediatrician who she met in her first year of medical school.

Nicole is an extraordinary woman, so it's no surprise to us that her working motherhood journey has been an extraordinary one as well. Nicole got pregnant in her third year of residency – quite by accident. Yes, you read that correctly, a third year resident in obstetrics married to a third year resident in paediatrics had an unplanned pregnancy. Nicole forgot to take her birth control pill one day and because of their crazy schedules she and her husband only had sex one time that month!

She never imagined she could be pregnant when she started feeling sick at work. No one in their right mind would get pregnant during their residency. The shifts are 36-hours long. But since she was in training to be a doctor, she decided to treat herself as one of her patients and took a home pregnancy test (during her shift at work). She also had some light spotting so to rule out a miscarriage, had a friend from her residency sneak into an examining room after their shifts ended to do an ultrasound. They saw a heartbeat. Nicole was indeed pregnant.

She did not have the kind of job where you call in sick to work. At her hospital, if you were sick, you came to work, strapped yourself to an I.V. for 30 minutes and then got back on the job. She was in a competitive program too. The last thing she wanted anyone to know was that she was pregnant. She was able to keep her pregnancy a secret for five months, even though she frequently had to scrub out of a surgery and throw up.

At five months she went to her program director with a plan to complete her residency on-time. She would work right through her pregnancy and take maternity leave instead of doing the four weeks of service work that she had planned to do in Bolivia. Even though Nicole and her husband had always planned on having a family, this was not the timing she envisioned so she just worked through her pregnancy as if nothing was different. She ignored all the signs that she needed to take it easy (doctors do make the worst patients!) and went into pre-term labour. After a serious talk with her chief resident, she agreed to take it easy. Her daughter was delivered healthy at full term. She went back to work four weeks later but it was much harder than she expected. She wanted to quit her residency and stay home with her daughter. After a lot of soul-searching and discussions with her husband, she decided to finish her residency, get her board certification and then quit working to stay home with her baby. That didn't happen.

As of this writing, Nicole has three children – eight, five and three – and is a practising obstetrician and gynaecologist. Ideally she would work less, but she shares with us the trade-offs she's made in search of solutions to create the life that she wants with her family and work. Her journey hasn't been easy, and it's not even complete, but we applaud and admire her effort. She inspires us because if she can make it work and maintain the hope of achieving her ultimate schedule and balance then there is hope for us all.

We're shocked that you wanted to quit working to raise your children. You are a doctor – and have ostensibly worked toward that goal your entire life.

I know. It doesn't make that much sense. I never thought I could feel about a child the way I felt about Gabriella when she was born. When I was with her I was so incredibly happy, nothing else mattered. I was in a dilemma. I loved being with Gabriella and I had worked my entire life to be a doctor (not to mention the amount of debt that I had built up in the effort.) If I didn't finish my residency and get board certified then I was giving up ever becoming a doctor.

I often think that intense jobs attract intense people who just can't figure out how to do anything halfway. You want to throw yourself into it 100 percent. If I am a doctor then I want to be the best doctor and simultaneously, I also want to be the best mother I can be. I just didn't know how to do it. So I organised my priorities and took all the perks that being a Chief Resident would offer and went back to work.

Chief Residents can do things that third years couldn't. My attending physician liked me and I had been an exemplary resident up until that point. So I figured, if I had to leave to pick up Gabriella, I had to leave.

I was on call from 6 a.m. to 6 p.m. and Gabriella was in a home daycare. We had my mum as a back up, so if Harry (Nicole's husband) or I got caught in surgery then my mother would pick her up.

My other priority was breastfeeding. No other new mothers had ever been in the program, so there was no model to follow. I would tell people I was going to express and nobody said a word. The hardest part was when I was stuck in a surgery or an emergency C-section then I would miss my window. But I had dedicated myself to it so I stuck with it.

I looked at work the same way. I had dedicated myself to it and was now going to see it through to board certification. I went through the checklist: pass the written test at the end of the residency, complete a big research project, find a part-time private practice job where I could get enough experience to sit for my oral boards, get board certified and quit to stay home with Gabriella.

But you're still working?

I know. When I started looking for a job, I was clear that I didn't want to be a high powered doctor who wanted to see a million patients. I wanted to have time to be with my family. My ideal was a part-time role but no one would take someone on part-time because the cost of malpractice is so high. And in OB you had to be willing to take call.

When you first come out of residency, you are a salary paid physician either by a group health system or a private practice. I found a private physician who needed help and was willing to let me work less if I took less pay. I planned on joining his practice when my fourth year finished. During the time I was finishing school, he took on another partner so by the time I started, I had two bosses instead of one and the new partner demanded that I do equal work. It was a little less than twice what I was doing and they would pay me more. I agreed to come up to full-time with them, because I was the youngest in the group, I wanted to prove my worth and pull my weight and then go part-time.

So it sounds like this part-time doctor thing really isn't an option.

It's funny, I just kept thinking, if I just do this one more thing, then I will get a part-time situation. That first year was really tough, on me and Harry. His job was particularly demanding with long hours and lots of weekends. We tried to coordinate our weekend schedules so that wouldn't both be on call because we'd have to ship Gabriella off with her grandparents. That year we had to leave her with Harry's parents Christmas Day because we were both on call the day after Christmas.

It didn't feel right and we didn't want to continue long term but couldn't come up with any solutions yet. I was happy in my job at this point and I felt rewarded. One of my partners then got pregnant and offered me a bonus if I would cover her maternity leave. We needed the money (we both had so much school debt) and since I was building a practice, it seemed to make sense.

Harry, on the other hand, was miserable in his job and decided to go back to the hospital where he had set hours. Set hours were great, but the 90 minute drive to work, each way, that he took on wasn't. It was very stressful and if our daughter was sick, it was on me, and our practice just kept getting busier.

Right before my partner went out on maternity leave, I got pregnant with Michaela. I know you must think I am crazy with everything else that we were juggling, but Gabriela was almost two and I didn't want only one child and I didn't want them to be too spaced apart. I needed to do it now or it wasn't going to happen. I tell my patients all the time, there's no good time to have a baby.

I thought if I could just get a little more help, I could handle it and it's almost time to take my oral boards and once I am board certified I can finally work part-time.

So how did it go with Michaela?

I felt physically very well with Michaela, ate well, and slept more but I have a heart problem so I was being careful.

Did you just say you had a heart problem?

Oh sorry, yes. They found the hole in my heart during my pregnancy with Gabriella. There's nothing they can really do until you have a problem, like a stroke. Basically it would just make me tired and I have a low heart rate because my heart is working much harder.

But I was feeling good and work was going well. The only challenge was without the help of my extended family or Harry, I was going to have to make a change when Michaela was born.

I was offered a partnership in May and decided not to take it. I felt that for the health of our family, it made more sense to make a change and move closer to my job. My plan had always been to cut back and if I signed on as full partner I would never cut back.

I called my mentor from medical school to help me figure out a job where I could balance my family life and my career. She called me back a day later and offered me a job working in her practice with a group of five.

I was moving toward a better life, more regular hours, less stress, more doctors, and when I was covering labour and delivery, I didn't have to do patient hours in the office too, so that would leave me more energy. With OB work, it's not just the hours that you put in, it's the intensity of them.

In January 2004, just after Michaela turned one, I passed my oral boards and started my new job. The change was huge. We were closer to Harry's job which required no evenings or weekends, and I had a much better schedule Between those factors and being closer to my mum, I was feeling really good.

I didn't feel like I was done having children after Michaela and realised I wanted one more. And when we got married Harry always wanted three. When Michaela was 18-months-old I got pregnant with Nicholas.

Okay, what happened next?
It's a long story, but the short story is that I had a stroke and had to get my heart repaired. Nicholas' delivery was really difficult but he was fine, and after I recovered, I realised I was back to the way I felt with Gabriella. I didn't get the bonding time in the beginning and I was two months back at work then I had a really difficult case where a woman had lost her baby. It emotionally destroyed me and I didn't want to be a doctor anymore.

Please tell us there's a happy ending.
Actually there is. Although the opportunity for part-time work hasn't happened, I have found a great job with the Our Lady of Lourdes health system. They offered me a job working at a clinic in Camden, N.J. with set hours. I resigned from my practice and accepted. A couple of my patients wanted to follow me, so Our Lady of Lourdes set me up with an office to see patients privately one day a week.

It started out as a small little extra thing that I did and it just grew and grew. After a month, we realised I needed to make it a real practice. It's been working so far. The clinic work really rejuvenated me. I always wanted to do service work and with my small practice and the clinic, practising medicine is making me happy again.

I still struggle with wanting to be a mum and be present more but I haven't added evening or weekend hours. My plan is to build this private practice over three or four years and add other doctors. As the original member of the group, I will get a bigger draw. By the time it's all up and running my school loans and the bulk of our mortgage will be paid off. I like delivering babies but I am happiest with my children. With the new job, I've requested Gabriella's swim meets off and I've made a bunch of Michaela's soccer games, too.

I remind my kids that I am not the only parent who works or has a demanding job. I think Gabriella is starting to get it. She loves telling her friends that her mum delivers babies, and her daddy takes care of them.

Time for a Change

It's pretty impossible for an obstetrician to work part time or from home, but that's certainly not the case for most positions. The corporate world is changing dramatically right now. As we become a global workforce and communication technology continues to improve, the need to be in an office every day has diminished significantly in the last ten years. Many jobs still require face time to get ahead, but more often than not, management is interested in results and if you can prove that you will be more productive in a less traditional working arrangement (part-time, flex-time, job sharing or telecommuting) then you should make a business case for it. You need to demonstrate that your productivity will actually increase if you have the flexibility to make your own schedule.

Of course it's a scary change but if your current situation isn't working then you really have nothing to lose by asking. Consider the following list.

It might be time to speak to your boss about a flexible schedule if you . . .
- Still enjoy the essence of your job
- Like your colleagues
- Have a supportive boss
- Feel that if you just had more flexible time then you could better juggle work and family responsibilities
- You can see yourself going back to full-time in a few years
- Don't see yourself as a stay-at-home mum
- Have the financial flexibility to work at a reduced salary

Thinking About (and Pitching) Your Options

In a perfect world, we would have more flexibility in our schedules. There are a few options for you to explore if changing when and how you work is a priority for you. Before you consider any of the options we outline below you need to do a little research. Work with your spouse to determine the ideal work schedule, how much you need to make to see if there is any wiggle room on the salary, and if you are thinking of spending any time working at home, do you have the space to set up a home office? Then, look at your job responsibilities to see if you could honestly make the case for telecommuting, job sharing or compressing your schedule. For those who manage a big staff, it is unlikely you could sell your boss on you working from home, even for a day. But if you are part of a creative team somewhere and you already spend a chunk of the day working solo then it might be easier to transition to telecommuting.

Look around the office to see if there is anyone else that has negotiated for a change in her schedule. It's always easier to get something if precedent has been set. If you want to go to part-time, be prepared for a significant pay cut. Asking for a part-time position could either be a huge relief for your boss because it does save money or it could be a huge burden for them if it means a pile of work that they would need to delegate. So know that asking for that radical shift in your job could go either way and you might end up looking elsewhere for the job solution.

If you have done your research both at home and at work then go to your boss with a fully thought out and detailed proposal. Be ready to make the case for how you are going to get your job done as efficiently as you do now. Illustrate how this would not make more work for you boss. That is what bosses care about at the end of the day. Demonstrate how you are set up to make a smooth transition by showing how you would manage delegating or working from home on existing projects. Before asking, employer and working mum Sarah Rubenstein advises, 'Approach the issue as a proposal that you have given a lot of careful consideration to and come to the discussion with a few suggestions as to how you can make it work for both parties.'

Going in confident, with your facts at your fingertips will make it more difficult for your boss not to at least consider your request. You may want to proactively offer to try out the new situation before asking for any commitment from the company.

Some of Flexible Working Options

Flexi-time

This is an option that appeals to many of us. In fact, a 2000 study by the Radcliff Public Policy Center with Harris Interactive found that for women in their 20s, 30s and 40s having a work schedule that allows them to spend more time with their families was *the* most important job characteristic. A flexi-time schedule could be a range of different arrangements including working at the office for a partial day and working late at night to finish, compressing the work week so you spend four long days but have that fifth day off.

Job Sharing

Rarer than flexi-time, job sharing is literally splitting your job with another employee. We have known a few people who have done this and its success is often contingent upon excellent communication between the colleagues. If you decide to share your job then you are essentially going down to part-time so you will be taking a pay cut and your benefits may be impacted.

Part-time

Part-time employees work less hours or fewer days than full-time employees. They might be working 3 full days a week or five half days. They also might only work during certain parts of the year or have heavier schedules only during high-seasons. Your salary as a part-time employee is reduced and it is more difficult to hold on to your benefits but if you can swing it, then balancing everything at home can be significantly easier.

Telecommuting

Telecommuting is working from home for someone else. It can be pretty amazing if all parties are comfortable with it and is an increasingly popular option for many people. We have an interview at the end of this chapter with a woman that worked this arrangement out with her company so make sure you read it if this set up appeals to you. Also read Pros and Cons of Telecommuting later in this chapter.

If you decide to pursue changing your work schedule with your current employer then please go into the negotiation prepared. Timing is also essential so make the 'ask' when your standing at the company is at a peak. You are in a better position to get what you want when you can confidently demonstrate your experience and contribution to your boss. Being a great employee with a proven track record and knowing that you are an asset to the company makes any request more likely to be granted.

The Word: Pounds and Pence

We asked personal finance expert Galia Gichon (www.down-toearthfinance.com) to share some of her top financial steps to take to prepare for going to part-time.

1. Women don't take into account their time off. It isn't uncommon to take a break from the work world or go part-time, but if you do, be sure to invest in yourself. Continue to network in your industry, take consulting projects, keep up on business reading and attend industry conferences. When you are ready to go back to work full-time or have more time to work, you will find that the time you had invested in yourself pays off.

2. Once you decide to go part-time, create a separate savings account just for the possibility of staying at home or increased expenses. If it is separate from your other savings, it will have more meaning. Also, make your savings automatic to an online savings account – you will end up saving more – I see it over and over.

3. Focus on the big money picture of how much you should be saving. Of course you know how much you need to cover your mortgage or rent, but do you know how much to save annually for your child's tertiary education or to retire successfully? Schedule an appointment with an independent financial advisor (visit www.unbiased.co.uk to find one in your area) or take advantage of online financial calculators at ThisIsMoney (www.thisismoney.co.uk/calculators). For information on school fees planning in particular, visit the SFIA website at www.sfia.co.uk. Whether you save those calculations or not, it takes the guesswork out of the equation.

4. Bring positive money habits into your life on a weekly basis. See if any of your friends have great money habits that you want to learn and start practising yourself. Start weekly coffee sessions to motivate each other how you can support each other (i.e. savings contest). Read a personal finance blog of someone that is trying to change their financial habits or bookmark a site that will help you focus on your money more regularly such as Moneysavingexpert.co.uk.

Pros and Cons of Telecommuting

Working from home sounds ideal, doesn't it? You get the salary and benefits while having the freedom to work in your pyjamas. Just like with every work situation, there are pros and cons to moving the office into your home.

The upsides of telecommuting
- There is more flexibility during the day to work when you work best.
- More work gets done without the endless interruptions, meetings and socialising that goes on in most offices.
- You are free to create an office environment that inspires you.
- It's nice to be home near your children and you can take advantage of that by having lunch or a snack with them during the day.
- No commuting time.
- You can have a freelance lifestyle without the financial concerns.

The downsides of telecommuting
- Your freedom is somewhat of an illusion.
- If you get a new boss or the company restructures you could be back in the office within days because not everyone is OK with it.

- It is difficult to turn off the job when it's just a few doors (or feet) away.
- You may find yourself with a bigger workload as your ability to turn around work increases.
- With your children nearby, it can be hard to stay away and you may end up resenting having to close that office door.

A Note from the Authors About Working from Home

We both spent two years or so working out of our home offices. This was years ago and before we merged to launch YC Media (www.ycmedia.com). The office set-ups were similar in that we both had desks in the corners of our tiny apartments. Hey, they don't call them bedroom businesses for nothing. The first few months of working from home are often a dream – get up whenever you wake up, take a break when you feel like it, work out when you're in the mood, make yourself a delicious lunch, play with the kids or let them interrupt you whenever they want a little mum-time. It's all pretty great as you get a taste of freedom during the work week. Then you reach a fork in the road. You can either let your productivity continue to diminish or you can start treating your workday like you did when you were steps away from your boss, not miles.

Obviously, we recommend taking control of your workday because if you give into the potential slothfulness you might lose your cushy gig. Start with the childcare situation. To work efficiently and effectively, you absolutely must have some kind of childcare because most jobs can't be squeezed in during nap and after bedtime. Set up a home office that offers private space and get a separate phone line. Get up early, take a shower, put on real clothes and get to your desk when everyone else does. Commit to putting in a full day with a few benefits thrown in like lunch with your kids, a trip to the gym or something else that lets you enjoy your situation.

We've now reviewed the flexi-time options and maybe you decided those wouldn't work for you or your employer has turned you down. Is it time to go? Read through the statements below and gage the emotional ramifications and practical aspects of staying at your job.

It might be time to go if you . . .

- Dread going to work
- Can't give your best because of family obligations
- Have a boss who is far from supportive of working mothers
- See no working mums in senior positions
- No longer are passionate or even energised by the job
- Can't pay the new layer of bills with your salary and were turned down for a payrise.
- Feel like you can't be the kind of mum you want to be while working

Beginning the Job Hunt

Now that you are a mum as well as a professional, your requirements for your next position may have changed, so before you start looking take stock of yourself, the situation and your finances.

What do you have to give?
Ask yourself how much you want and can give to your next job. Consider how your personal life has impacted your energy level, focus, biorhythms and passion for your career and work with those facts. The new you just might be looking for something else these days, and it's important that you know what that is before you look for and take another gig.

How much money do you need now?
Now that your situation has changed you may also need a bigger salary than you originally thought. Before calling headhunters, do

a household budget to see how much you need for monthly expenses. Add to that number how much you would like to add to savings plans in an ideal world. After looking at these household numbers you may feel really differently about what your next job should pay.

Your schedule

Before starting to look for a new job consider your schedule. Is your childcare situation flexible or do you absolutely need to get home at a certain time? Could you save significant money on childcare if you changed your work schedule? What is the ideal balance of work and home? Now, you may not find the perfect solution but going into a job search with some clarity of your best situation may help you negotiate for something better.

Build the network

There are so many ways to build your network these days. Many of us use LinkedIn to maintain and grow our virtual little black book. And although social networking sites are mostly used for socialising, the friends, former classmates and acquaintances you may find there are worth contacting when you start looking for a job. There are professional organisations to join, former and current mentors to meet with. Don't think small when planning your next move. That holds especially true when it comes to tapping into your resources.

Be clear about what you want

To maximise any and all contacts and opportunities have a clear vision for what you are looking for from your next job. As the founders of Girl's Guide (www.girlsguidetobusiness.com), we have received hundreds of emails from women asking for career advice or networking help. If the cold call email includes a clear ask from us such as someone is looking for an informational interview with someone in the public relations field or someone needs a few tips for how to start their own business, we can offer advice. So help your network help you by being direct and clear about what you want.

Selling Yourself in an Interview

See above for our line about being clear with your network when you are looking for a job because the same holds true during an interview. Many new working mums (and those re-entering the workforce) are unsure if and how to bring their personal situation into an interview. Reluctant to turn off a potential employer who might assume a working mum will be running out at 5 p.m. every night, most of us keep mum. Jamie Pennington, founder of Flexible Executives (www.flexibleexecutives.com), doesn't recommend this tactic. 'Don't hesitate to say that you are the mother of young children – that is a huge part of your identity and any attempts to cover that up or overpromise on expectations will leave you running ragged trying to please other people. You will undoubtedly feel like you can never let your guard down.'

A job interview is a job interview whether you have children or not. In a single conversation you have to convince someone that your personality, experience and skills are the best for the job. So do your homework by researching the company and ideally the interviewer. Practise, come in with a copy of your CV and references and be ready to sell yourself. Jamie reminds us, 'Companies want people who bring energy and edge, and your experiences as a mother can bring a unique perspective to many corporate circles. The corporate world has made great strides over the last 10 years in this area and as women start more companies and assume more responsibilities in corporate life, we expect those strides to continue.'

The Realities of Starting Your Own Business

If you are feeling ready to start your own business then congratulations! As many of you know by now we love being entrepreneurs and wrote our first book in this series about it, *The Girl's Guide to Starting Your Own Business*. Being an entrepreneur includes everything good and everything bad about business. There are challenges to keep you engaged, conflicts to keep you on your toes, opportunities to keep you passionate and successes to keep you confident. And while you may find yourself frustrated, anxious and exhausted you will never be bored. Ever. The absolute best thing about starting a business? It's all yours. You can create a company and culture that is a true reflection of you. Oh, and you have more control of your income, growth and future which is really amazing.

Ask yourself if this is the best time to step out on your own. Follow the steps we outlined in our first book starting with asking yourself if you have the desire, money, focus, time and endurance to be an entrepreneur. Not everyone wants to be the one wearing all of the hats and that's fine. Just know that before you quit your job. Check in with your family to see if they're on board with you taking this major step. A new business is a lot like a newborn in that it requires lots of love and attention that may call for sacrifices in other areas of your life. And you don't want to have to make the choice between your two babies. You also want to be clear about what type of business suits your skills, budget, and lifestyle. If you have a one-year-old at home and your spouse is on the road a lot then opening a retail store which will require your physical presence is a bad idea. If you have preschoolers who need to be picked up at 5 pm each night then you might want to consider a consulting business rather than a restaurant.

Look closely at your personal budget before doing anything. If you have debt as well as a big monthly nut then think about starting your business on the side for additional income. If you are financially healthy then figure out how much buffer you have to start your business and get it up and running before taking a salary. And what about that start up money? Now that you know how much you need to make in the first year now figure out how much your business needs to get off the ground. Make decisions about when to launch and what to launch once you know the financial landscape because it will impact your next steps. If you have no capital then what about a consulting or other service based business that doesn't require huge overhead? If that's the direction you want to go then do you have the contacts and reputation for that type of business which is mostly driven by word-of-mouth. If you are committed to doing a business that requires a significant investment upfront then how are you at fundraising? Remember, even if you are asking your best friend for money, they will most likely want and need a business plan to review so that should be what you do before any ask.

As you can see starting a business is complicated. There are a million questions to ask yourself and professionals but don't let that stop you from pursuing your dreams. For working mums the question often comes down to not 'Can I do this?' but 'Can I do this right now?' Just know that it is extremely hard work with a potentially bigger pay off down the road emotionally, professionally and financially.

A Few Words from Mumpreneur Sarah Rubenstein:

Before Sarah Rubenstein went out on her own and to found ModernTots (www.moderntots.com) she found herself a working mum trying to make her career still work in a working mum-unfriendly corporate environment. We spoke to her about the signs it was time to go and how becoming a mother gave her the confidence to launch her own business.

You are the mother of a 6- year-old and the founder of ModernTots. How did that business come about?
My decision to start my own company was absolutely influenced by becoming a mother. The unique, modern, children's products I

was looking for to use in my home with my son just weren't readily available. So I set out to find them and then to create a resource to make them available for other parents.

What about the emotional changes that impacted your decision to become an entrepreneur?

There was something about becoming a mother that made me stronger, braver, and gave me the tenacity to be able to start and run a company of my own.

You were in advertising when you got pregnant. What was it like for you?

While I was pregnant I was not treated any differently than any other staff member. I was expected to travel, stay on my feet for hours, and work until late at night just as I did before. Always an aggressive corporate climber, once I had my son, I was no longer considered to be as capable as my single counterparts. People who left before 8 p.m. received dirty looks and comments in the board room the next day. It was not permissible to be out of the office due to a sick child.

Did it get worse?

It came to a point where I did not display photographs of my son in my office because it was not only a reminder to me of who I wished I was with, but it was in effect a demotion. This seemed only to be true for the women in the office because the fathers proudly displayed their family photos around their offices and on their desks.

How have you decided to do things differently now that you run a business?

I'm proud to employ working mothers and strongly believe it is the individual choice to be dedicated to their job and has nothing to do with being a mother or not. The culture here is different from other companies in that we support them as much as we can, including welcoming children into the office.

The Word: A Job-sharing Story from Linda Connolly, Co-owner of Dahlia Site Selection & Events

When we first met Linda she was job sharing a promotions position at a national magazine. She and her job-share partner Mendy Brannon had such a great rapport that they eventually decided to quit the magazine and open a business together.

Why did you decide to look for a job-share position?
My job-share partner and I were both looking for new careers, a career that gave us flexibility in our personal lives. As you get older, your priorities change. It was important for me to be able to spend time with my son and family, and have time for myself–that's the reason we decided on a job share. We see a job share as two people working in one position giving more to a company, not less: more experience, more work and more ideas. And having the free time to pursue other opportunities while we work in a position that we both really liked was an ideal situation.

When does a job share work well for all parties?
The secret to a successful job share is finding the right partner. Mendy and I worked together at two different magazines. We developed camaraderie and a partnership. We worked in two different positions but sought advice and ideas from one another on our projects. We each have different strengths and personalities that we would bring to the job share.

What challenges did you encounter while job sharing?

The most difficult aspect of the job share situation is relaying information. From the beginning, we were very conscious of not having our colleagues have to repeat anything. We had to develop a system that would keep us updated and informed of each other's work. This took extra time and work, and frequently we would speak to one another on our days off but the luxury of having the flexibility was worth it.

Things to Know If You Decide to Opt Out

If you have decided that you want to be a stay-at-home mum, we congratulate you for following your heart and making a decision that is right for you. Before closing your office door, there are a few things you should prepare yourself for. If you think there is any chance that you will return to the workforce in a year, five years or ten years, then while you are home protect and nurture your career. If you find after a year that you want to or have to go back to work but have haven't picked up a phone to anyone from your professional life during that time, you're starting from scratch. If you haven't kept on top of changes in your industry or technology then even if you left a senior position, you're at a disadvantage when going up against other candidates for a job.

Too many of the women we interviewed that had transitioned from home back to work struggled with major confidence issues. Tragically we were told by women who had given their all to their children and communities that they felt that they hadn't done anything worth bringing up in an interview. One woman had raised thousands of dollars for her children's school during her time out of the rat race but still she told us that she didn't know what to put on her CV. We recently interviewed someone for a job as our office manager who had taken a year off to deal with her son's medical issues. She spent much of the time focused on her earlier jobs and skimmed over the twelve months that she was organising doctor appointments, scheduling tutors, researching specialists. It was only when she started talking about those aspects of her year where she began to make sense as a new recruit for us.

Don't undervalue or undersell what you do as you are raising your children. Being paid is nice but volunteering can be just as stressful and requires to use and hone the skills you had developed while in the workforce. So while you are away, keep track of your accomplishments just as you do now. On a final note, when you are ready to start looking and interviewing put your activities and contributions into 'work-speak'.

A few ways to nurture your career while you are at home:

- Maintain your network
- Keep on top of cultural trends that have an impact on your industry
- Keep up with current events
- Read trade magazines and websites
- If possible put your skills to work in your community
- Keep in touch with your mentor
- Train yourself on new technology

Advice from Someone Who Has Been on Both Sides

Gail Mangurian, was a teacher for many years before deciding to become a stay-at-home mum to raise her children. As someone who has worked both inside and outside of the house she wanted to share this advice with all of us.

'These days my twenty-three year old daughter is very involved in her marketing career. She is working hard and enjoying her achievements. I am proud of her and what she is doing, and I encourage her to pursue her dreams. My advice to her and all the young women who are entering the workplace or changing career paths would be to ... follow your heart. Try to get in touch with what your intuition is telling you, is right for you. Keep in mind that the heart can lead in different directions for different people. It is my fervent hope that my daughter and other young women will have a legitimate choice between working outside the home versus staying at home to raise a family. It seems more difficult than ever to resist the societal pressures placed on women to have full-time careers outside the home. What is politically correct is often not what is right for the individual. How wonderful that there is such a wide spectrum of opportunities for young women nowadays. I hope that they will support each other's differing choices and encourage each other to listen to what the heart is saying.'

Girl Talk: Lynn Abrams

Our friend Lynn Abrams is one of the smartest, most ambitious women we know, a go-getter with a top job at a national magazine. When she had her second child we were all prepared for her to happily jump back into the professional pool but a series of situations made her look at her decisions and choices a little differently.

So you have two children and recently had your third. Around the time your first two were 3 and 1, you made a major decision about the structure of your job. Can you tell us about that?

When my family and I moved out of New York City to a nearby suburb last year, I started commuting to work five days a week, an hour and a half each way. The commute quickly became a grind: I was leaving the house at 8 a.m. and returning at 8 p.m. By the time I got home at night, our full-time nanny had already put the baby down, and my 3-year-old was ready for bed. I wasn't seeing my children, and I was missing out on those (mostly) precious toddler years. To complicate matters, I didn't love the childcare my kids were getting. I felt that if I was at least working from home, a nanny would be more on her toes, and less likely to, say, plop my kids in front of the TV for hours at a time. I thought the best decision for me would be to work from home full time. Working from home full time wasn't something I thought my boss would ever go for. In fact, before I accepted my current position as a magazine editor, I had requested to work from home one day a week, and my boss shot me down. So it's surprising that I eventually got what I wanted – and more.

Were you concerned about how working from home would impact the growth of your career?

Yes. In fact, just moving out of the city made me feel like less of a player. Instead of going out for drinks with colleagues or business associates, I was running for the train. Once I stopped going into the city all together, it meant giving up a lot of chances to attend movie premieres, have spontaneous lunches with high powered publicists, editors and writers. I told myself that, for now, my career was just going to move along in a straight line. For the next few years while the kids were young, I would not be making any professional advances. It was definitely a trade-off.

Was it a difficult decision to make?

In the end, no. The commute was exhausting, and I was missing my kids. By working from home, I got to keep my career (more or less) *and* be an at-home mum. It was the perfect place to be at this point in my life.

How did you approach asking your boss?

After four months of commuting, I set up a meeting with my boss and told her I was quitting. That I needed to be around more to watch my kids grow up and make sure they were ok. My plan was that I would pursue a career as a full-time freelance editor and work from home. That's when my boss completely shocked me and made me an offer I couldn't refuse. She told me I could keep my job and benefits and work full-time from home. It was like winning the lottery. I wouldn't have to chase down work as a freelancer, and I could be around enough to see my kids.

What compromises did you have to make for this to work?

Even if it was her idea, she put plenty of safeguards into place to make sure the arrangement worked for her. I had to pay out of my own pocket to set up a home office, complete with all the software that would be compatible with my work office. I had to be at my desk and available from 9–6, in case she ever wanted to do an impromptu phone conference. And she had me become a member of a free video conference service, so that when we did have conference calls, she could actually see me at my desk (and, I suspect, make sure I wasn't working in my pyjamas). There were times where it felt like Big Brother was watching me, which was disconcerting, to say the least.

How was transitioning to working from home?

It took me a good three months to get used to working from home. It was crucial that I had a separate office, where I could shut the door and not hear the goings-on of the household. (I also put up a baby gate, so the kids couldn't come flying into my office during, say, a phone meeting with my boss). The challenge was creating an environment in my home where I could focus on my work. Creating the right environment helped me make the mental shift into work mode, even if I wasn't exactly making the physical shift into a corporate office. It was a challenging transition for my kids too. They needed to learn that even though mummy was home, I wasn't available to them (unless, of course, it was an emergency). So just like I did when I would leave for the train, I would tell my kids at 9 a.m., 'Mummy is going to work now.' And then at noon I'd pop out and have lunch with them. They quickly grasped that mummy had work time, while they had play time with the nanny. But the good news was that at 6, when the work day was over, I had a one-minute commute to the playroom upstairs, and I got to be with my kids.

Do you miss the office environment?

There are times when I go into the city once a week, for an important lunch or meeting. That gives me my fix of office gossip, and getting dressed up, which I *really* miss. Believe it or not, it's not always fun wearing shorts and tee shirts to work five days a week. Sometimes putting on a suit or Jimmy Choos helps shift you into work mode and gives you a level of confidence that you don't get by wearing slippers. That said, I actually find that I get more work done at home than in an office environment. When a co-worker isn't spontaneously dropping by your office for an hour-long gossip session, you actually work.

Is there anything you would have done differently?

Sometimes I wonder if going freelance would have been the best overall solution. Even though this arrangement has allowed me to see my kids a few more hours a day, and to basically know what's going on inside the house with our nanny, etc., I am still beholden to my office between the hours of 9 and 6. It's not like I can take my daughter to a play date and not work for a couple of hours in the afternoon. I have to be available, just like I would be in an office. And that can be extremely stressful. If I were freelance, I could set my own schedule a little bit more and carve out even more time for my children. Sounds ideal, but the money and benefits wouldn't be nearly as steady as they are now.

Do you have any advice for readers thinking about approaching their boss with the request to work from home?
If working from home or part-time is something you really feel strongly about, you ultimately need to be prepared to leave your full-time position if your boss won't allow you to make a shift. But the key is helping your boss understand that a work from home situation is achievable (for most jobs, not all, of course). As long as you're willing to come into your office for key meetings, lunches, etc., there's little reason why someone can't make phone calls and do computer work from a satellite location. You just need to be able to layout your work-from-home plan so your employer understands you can accomplish all the work you do now . . . and maybe more. You can also offer to do it on a trial basis. See if they'll let you work from home for three months before they have to sign up for the idea. If you make a seamless transition to the home office, they'll have little reason not to allow you to make a full-time change. Finding precedence within your company also helps. Do a little research. Who in your corporation is successfully working from home? Give those names to your boss, with their superiors' contact information. Your boss

may feel more comfortable giving you the green light if he or she doesn't have to break new ground within the company.

10

The New You

Now that you have the tools and inspiration to be the best mum *you* can be and now that the United States has a President and First Lady committed to family issues, it's also a good time to consider how you can help other working mums. We have never been so proud and inspired as when we read that Harvard-educated, powerful attorney and hospital administrator, Michelle Obama was taking time out during her husband's historic presidency to be 'Mom in Chief'. She plans to dedicate their time in office to raising her children and helping working women get the resources they need for their children to thrive. She is choosing to stay home so the rest of us have an opportunity to work. Please don't waste this historic opportunity. If there was ever a time for mothers (working and stay-at-home) to band together then it's now.

Our New Feminism

In the introduction to her book, *Mothers on the Fast Track* (Oxford, 2007) Mary Ann Mason writes: 'We know more about why women don't succeed than about how they do. Arlie Hochschild in *The Second Shift* shows that, in spite of woman's massive entry into full-time employment, they still bear the burden of family care at home. Ann Crittenden, in *The Wages of Motherhood*, argues that working mothers lose out on economic fronts in large part because our society doesn't value motherhood. And Joan Williams in *Unbending Gender* observes that the inflexible 'ideal worker' model of the American workplace discriminates against mothers, undermining the purpose of Title VII.'

In the face of all of this irrefutable evidence that women have it much harder, what are we supposed to do? Do we just give up? Can any of us afford to 'Opt-Out'? And do we want to? We love working and we shouldn't have to give it up. Men don't. While we've always considered ourselves feminists, our feminism was of the decidedly dormant variety. To be honest, we were more concerned with gay rights then we ever were with women's rights. Unlike our gay friends, we never felt discriminated against *until* we had children.

Becoming working mothers and writing this book has awakened our political fervour. We work because it's our right to work and be mothers. After you have children, it becomes all too obvious that women are pressured to make sacrifices and choices – and judged by society for them – that men don't. And the more we think about it, the more stridently feminist we become.

In her revolutionary 100-page book, *Get to Work: A Manifesto for Women of the World* (Viking, 2006) philosopher, feminist and retired professor Linda Hirshman calls all women into the workplace – because that's where the power is. She offers a 'Strategic Plan to Get to Work' that's a bit extreme but gets us thinking. Here it is:

- Don't study art. Use your education to prepare for a lifetime of work.
- Never quit a job until you have another one. Take work seriously.
- Never know when you're out of milk. Bargain relentlessly for a just household.
- Consider a reproductive strike.
- Get the government you deserve. Stop electing governments that punish women's work.

We're all in, except for the reproductive strike. If women don't stand up and ask for a fair deal on the home front, they will never get one. Until men are forced to make the same choices and sacrifices we do, things will never change. Author's Note: We promise that we won't return to the soapbox until our next book.

The Word: Catherine Wolfram and the Opt-Out Option

Catherine Wolfram is an Associate Professor of Economics at the University of California, Berkeley, Haas School of Business. She earned her PhD in Economics from MIT and did her undergraduate work at Harvard. As a tenured professor in a highly competitive university, she is on 'the fast track', as defined by her colleague and author, Mary Ann Mason in her book, *Mothers on the Fast Track* (Oxford, 2007).

Like many fast track women, she is married to a PhD who she met in graduate school. She is also the mother of two children. Like top corporate jobs, coveted tenured positions at universities are mainly populated by men. Academia is not widely considered a family-friendly environment although you can create a flexible schedule. A colleague of Catherine's is fond of saying, 'Academia gives you the flexibility to work whichever 16 hours of the day you'd like.'

To understand Catherine's story, we need to take a moment to explain tenure. Achieving tenure is the Holy Grail in academia because it guarantees a scholar the right to research and publish any interest, whether or not it conflicts with the university's policies. Without tenure, academics would focus on keeping their jobs not discovery. Achieving tenure is a rigorous and political process. You are literally on the clock. In the United States, a 'tenure track' professor (a university lecturer on academic probation) has six years to gain a national reputation with publication while teaching classes and winning research grants to fund studies.

Once again, studies have shown (including one authored by Mason) that it's much more difficult for women to achieve tenure than men. Unfortunately, the biological and tenure clocks are ticking on the same schedule. In the US, the average professor achieves tenure at 40. On average, you have as many as six years to earn it. The more prestigious the university, the more competitive the tenure process is and usually requires the entire six years to complete. You don't have to be a math whiz like Catherine to figure this one out. If you finish your PhD in your early 30s, the six years you are working toward tenure are the six years you've got left to create a family.

As a matter of fact, the percentage of tenured women professors are so disturbingly low versus the PhDs awarded to women, that in 2005, nine top universities, including Berkeley, adopted policies to make tenure more family-friendly including: offering extensions of the tenure clock in the event of childbirth or adoption, and generous leave or relief from teaching.

When Catherine got pregnant in her sixth year, she opted to stop her tenure clock during her maternity leave even though she had finished most of the required work. While she was out, she received a tenure offer from another university. As Berkeley was her first choice, she gave them an opportunity to make her a counteroffer. However, technically she wasn't qualified to sit for the tenure at Berkeley because she had chosen to delay the clock for her maternity leave. She wasn't asking for special allowances, she was just asking to be evaluated on her regular schedule. The University refused. With the full support of the business school, she spent two months fighting the system and was eventually awarded her tenure.

Remember the great thing about tenure is that you can study anything that interests you. Normally Catherine's research focuses on energy markets. One day while flipping through her Harvard alumni newsletter, she noticed a high number of women graduates who had opted-out of the workforce force to bring up a family. So she decided to study it. Now as important as her energy studies are, the public took little interest when they were published. Not so with the publication of 'Opt-Out Patterns Across Careers: Labour Force Participation Among Highly Educated Mothers' co-authored with Jane Leber Herr.

Catherine and Jane followed the career paths of nearly 1,000 women who graduated from Harvard between 1988 and 1991, using a rich set of biographical data culled from 10th and 15th anniversary reunion surveys. Their work showed that by the time the graduates are 15 years out of college, 28% of the Harvard women who went on to get their MBAs were stay-at-home mums, compared to only 6% of women who got medical degrees. The study also looked at the career paths of Harvard women who became lawyers and found 21% chose to stay home with their children.

The reasons why more MBAs opt out may speak to the differences in the family-friendliness of the fields. Catherine and Jane's statistics show these women have the financial ability to opt-out but also they are in careers with very little flexibility in a culture that is still male-dominated and would never be confused with being family-friendly. For these women to spend any time with their families, opting-out may seem like the only choice. Doctors, on the other hand, are doing 'good' work and can eventually set a more flexible schedule and the lawyers often have too much loan-debt to have a choice at all.

So the rich and successful choose to stay home to raise their children? Big deal. They can afford it. Harvard women tend to marry highly-educated and well-paid men, giving these women the *option* to stay home which many women in the population don't have. Also, many Harvard women have accrued their own wealth (through family or prior earnings) again, offering them the *option* to opt-out when other women wouldn't.

Why should the rest of us care? We can't afford to leave our jobs (and we really don't want to anyway.) We must care because these 'fast track' women are exactly the ones we need to keep in the workforce. They are the ones most likely to rise to a level in business where they can make decisions that can help other working women and make the necessary changes that include: paid maternity leave, flexible schedules, and affordable healthcare.

One final disturbing thought from the press release about Catherine and Jane's study:

'Another consideration is that many of these women are married to men who are just as ambitious as they are', said Joan Williams, director of the Center for WorkLife Law at the University of California and an expert on work and family life issues.

Williams said she believes that what has been termed the 'opt-out revolution', the notion that working women choose parenting over building their careers, is more complicated than meets the eye. Men who are in the upper ranks of their profession with stay-at-home-wives earn 30% more than men who are married to women who work, she said. Those men who want to reach the highest rungs of their career and earn the most money often need a stay-at-home wife to take care of all other aspects of their life, including raising a family, Williams said. 'And since many women in business school marry those men, they end up being stay-at-home wives, regardless of their own vision of what they wanted from their careers.'

The Word: Work–Life Balance Takes Work

Kingsley Shannon is a Senior Manager of Brand Services for Calphalon and lives in Atlanta with her husband and two children, one- and five-years old. Her five-year-old son was born while she was a Brand Manager at Maytag in Iowa. Kingsley had an excellent employment record at Maytag. She had developed a reputation as a conscientious employee and strong leader. Her managers and team liked and respected her.

Prior to getting pregnant, Kingsley had watched how a number of other women handled their pregnancies and maternity leave. She had a good pregnancy, but suffered from high blood pressure which required her to go to a number of extra doctor's appointments. Her managers subscribed to a philosophy that she employs today: 'We're all responsible adults. If you have a doctor's appointment go and take care of it. We're not watching your hours. Getting the work done is what matters.' It wasn't a corporate policy, but rather an unwritten agreement between manager and staff member.

Kingsley loved her job, but like most American families, she needed it to help support her family. So for her, the question of work life balance came up the second she found out she was pregnant. As with everything else she had done before professionally, she decided to make a plan and stick to it.

It began with preparing for her maternity leave. As the team leader, she found it relatively easy to set the strategy in advance and created a detailed project list that outlined where and how everything was running. She set it up so that from an executional stand-point it could run without her. She had a strong number two and a great outside agency partner who she empowered to make decisions in her absence. She cleared the budgets with her senior management, downloaded a complete project status and made it clear that she would not be checking in during her maternity leave.

She planned to be out for twelve weeks. Maytag paid in full for eight because she had a caesarean, and she used vacation for two weeks and took two weeks unpaid. Kingsley went back to work but missed her son more than she even anticipated. Her son was in an in-home daycare from 7:30 in the morning until 5:30 in the evening. And she missed him and started looking for ways to maximise her time with him. She either worked through lunch or went to visit him, and except in the extreme case, walked out the door at 5:00 p.m. She was still unsatisfied. She wanted more time.

Maytag had no corporate policy for flexi-time although over the years she had heard whispers that it was happening. When Jack was nine months old, she asked her manager if she could work four ten-hour days and take Fridays off. Her commitment to them (and what ultimately got it approved) was that if there was ever a time that they felt she was out of the office then she would come back. It wasn't a program that went through HR, it was a privilege that she was granted from her management because of her strong track record and their desire to keep her as an employee.

It went very well. She worked four ten-hour days for a little more than two years when she was promoted to a different division. The new manager was willing give it a trial (even though as she puts it, 'he wasn't normally an active work–life balance guy') and then evaluate. She made the same commitment, if there was ever time that they felt her missing, then she would come back. She never had to go back.

As a manager, she was able to set up the workflow so that her team was working on things that didn't require her input on Fridays. She scheduled all of her meetings between Monday and Thursday. She checked in from home during nap time on Fridays.

She had been at Maytag for eight years and earned their trust. They knew she was an asset and a responsible employee. In her first year with Jack, she learned what her work-balance threshold was and set her boundaries accordingly. And she stuck to them with no guilt. Kingsley noted, 'Many women I talk to feel like they can't say no, and are always feeling guilty. I don't.'

Now Kingsley is at Calphalon back to working five days a week albeit on flexi-hours. It's not her ideal, but she gets in at 7a.m. and tries to leave at 4p.m. to beat the traffic. She's still firm in her boundaries and only travels or stays late when she absolutely must. She'd still love to be home with her kids, but she also loves her job and the new challenges and opportunities it has presented her. And she feels proud that she can support her family.

In the beginning, everyone was sceptical, but by the end they all had the same question, 'How did you do it?'

Kingsley shares some tips for how to do it:

- Create a work balance ideal and work toward it. Be very clear about what your desires are. Set boundaries and do not apologise. And don't feel guilty. You need to take your daughter to the doctor, and you need to get work done. They shouldn't be mutually exclusive. In most cases, over-delivering on the work front awards you more freedom. And experience breeds success. If you're able to run out for a couple of errands and still get all of your work done, your manager knows it and you both gain confidence and build trust from that interaction. But if the work suffers, then it's a completely different story. You win a work-life balance only if you give enough on the work front.
- Both your employer *and* your family need to feel like you are trying to balance. You have to be reasonable with your employer. Don't expect them to bend over backwards to accommodate your personal life. Pick and choose your spots. Make a decision and don't ask for everything.

- Assess your priorities and work out what you want to spend your money on. I decided when I had Jack to hire a cleaning lady once a week, and it was the best money I ever spent. For me, it was more important to get home and have quality time with my kids, then to have a night out with another couple. We are willing to pay for convenience so I can have more time with our kids.

- Don't be available to your employer 24/7. BlackBerry® is great for me. I leave at 4:00 p.m. and check e-mail up till close of business and tie up any loose ends. After business hours and on weekends, I *choose* if I want to look at it and catch up before getting into the office. (Sometimes I make the mental decision that it is family time and I am not looking at it until after the kids are in bed or Saturday afternoon.) I typically make it a practice not to respond after business hours unless it is an absolute emergency. If I do respond it is because I know I am going to have a busy day and won't have time in the morning *or* because I am managing my workload on my time outside of the hours I am in the office. People know I do not conduct business on Saturday because I have set the expectation of not responding to their weekend queries. I read a lot that comes through but wait until I am at work, during business hours to respond.

Role Models, not Catwalk Models

Every day we read about the celebrity supermums featured in those trashy (but delicious) magazines. And you know what we see? Beautiful and accomplished women, back to their pre-baby – actually, pre-*puberty* weight – three weeks after giving birth. We see them storming through airport security, with guards and nannies in tow. We see £100,000 baby room renovations, and cashmere-themed baby showers hosted by the Victoria Beckhams of the world. Sure it's fun to take a sneak peek inside an assistant-supported world but that isn't our life. And it isn't the life of almost everyone we know. Working mum Arianne Weeks agrees, 'I do feel the media creates unrealistic role models – celebrities and otherwise. But that goes along with a perfectionist attitude that is rampant in our culture. So many of us experience a constant feeling that there is a right and wrong way to be doing everything and motherhood is a part of that.'

The realistic role models for working mums might be sitting in the conference room during your weekly meeting. Their lives may not be as glamorous, and they may still be carrying a few baby pounds and have decided to live with their wrinkles instead of booting them away, but anyone managing to be a great mother while taking care of herself and her career is now your role model. Believe us, these women have invaluable systems for running their lives learned through trial and error and real-life experience. Rather than look to the 'Just Like Us!' pages, ask the real women around you how they get their kids off to school in the morning.

The American Academy of Pediatrics states on its website: 'A mother who successfully manages both an outside job and parenthood provides a role model for her child. In most families with working mothers, each person plays a more active role in the household. The children tend to look after one another and help in other ways. The father is more likely to help with household chores and child rearing as well as breadwinning. These positive outcomes are most likely when the working mother feels valued and supported by family, friends, and co-workers.'

You may not like it, or have ever planned for it, but as a working mother you are a role model not just for your children, but for other women in your organisation. How you manage your work and family will be carefully watched by the women coming up the ladder behind you. When surveyed, the number one question young career women ask is, 'When is the best time to have a baby?' Of course we know now the answer is there is a never a good time to have a baby. You just work it out as you go along – hopefully with the help of this book.

As a working mother role model we encourage you to be honest about the challenges that you face. If asked, be honest with women about the challenges of working motherhood. Help them navigate their pregnancy and maternity leaves professionally and pro-actively. Welcome them back and be supportive when they have a hard time – because you know they will have a hard time.

Also, you can work within your organisation to change policies that negatively affect working women. If they don't offer flexi-time as a corporate policy, then do it within your own department and share the successful results with management.

Get Active and Political

If the US presidential election of 2008 proved anything, it's that change is possible if we become part of the democratic process – wherever you live. Big business will not change until the government requires it to, so we have to actively lobby government to support issues that affect working mothers and their families. Write to your MP to show your support for legislative improvements that have been proposed at local or national level. Work with your human resources departments to make changes in policy. As the country's upcoming leaders, you have a responsibility to speak up and try to effect change. Go online and research the working mother advocacy organisations (there are lots of them now) and volunteer. You can make a difference if you want to. Betty's story certainly shows that.

Girl Talk: The More Things Change . . .

Betty Holcomb was a 35-year-old successful freelance writer when she became pregnant with her first child in 1984. As she expected, becoming a mother was the life-changing event that everybody warned her it would be. What she didn't expect was that her professional life was going to change dramatically too.

In theory, she had a great set-up. As a freelance writer, she could maintain a flexible schedule. She would still need childcare (her salary was a necessity to her family, and as a freelancer, if you don't work, you don't get paid) and she set about to find some.

It's important to set the stage for working mothers in the 80s. It may be clichéd now, but in 1984 the image of the woman wearing the power suit holding a briefcase in one hand and the baby in the other was the reality. In 1984, pregnancy discrimination was all too real. Most employers expected women to stay at home after they gave birth and so summarily firing them when they announced their pregnancies was not uncommon. Remember, the US Pregnancy Discrimination Act was not passed until 1986!

Working motherhood was becoming a national issue in the 80s and not only had Betty just joined the ranks of working mums, she was being assigned high-profile magazine pieces about the subject, including a cover story for *New York* magazine. Huge debates about national funding for childcare began and there was a lot of romance about how women entering the workplace could balance work and family and actually have it all. (Sound familiar?)

Like other women who began working in the wake of the women's movement of the 70s, Betty believed the hype. She thought women could have it all without sacrificing their careers. She believed that her husband would contribute 50% to the parenting and domestic issues. She believed that safe, affordable, childcare would be easy to find, so she could continue the career that she had already invested 15 years in and that the workplace welcomed women back after maternity leave.

So it was nothing short of stunning to her, when on assignment for *Savvy* magazine about women returning from maternity leave, she began calling women in management at major corporations and had them sobbing to her about their experiences. She was the first person who many of these women had shared their stories with and their stories were all the same. They felt isolated and pushed aside at work. They were forced to pretend their children didn't exist, fearing plum assignments would be taken away and they would be passed over for promotion. They were marginalised in the workplace and, worse, they felt like they were bad mothers because they chose to return to working and allowed others to care for their children.

That story led to writing regularly for *Working Mother* (a revolutionary publication at the time) and when someone went on maternity leave, she took a staff position. *Working Mother* became the right place at the right time to partner with advocacy groups around the issues of women in the workplace. She spent her days researching the companies that were truly 'family friendly' and working on the first ever Working Mother '100 Best' list.

The combination of being a working mother and her work on the subject turned Betty into a born-again feminist. She enrolled in a graduate programme in women's history at Sarah Lawrence University and began writing newsletters for various child advocacy organisations.

Betty has since written two books, *Not Guilty! The Good News for Working Mothers* (Simon & Schuster, 1998) and *The Best Friend's Guide to Maternity Leave* (Perseus, 2001) for which we owe her a debt of gratitude as we've referred to them both liberally in the writing of this book. She's currently the Policy Director for Child Care, Inc. (CCI), a non-profit organisation that works to expand and improve early care and education across New York State.

Betty's experience, as well as the experience of the hundreds of women she's interviewed, sounds frighteningly familiar. We spoke to her about what has changed in the last 20 years and what we can all do to make the workplace a friendlier place for working women and families.

Your experience in 1984 sounds way too much like our experience in 2009. What has really changed?
It would be really silly to say nothing has changed. I think most Americans today would never say, unequivocally, women shouldn't work. Up until 1986, it was just expected that women would quit their jobs when they got pregnant–no matter if they needed the money. The biggest difference now though is that laws protect women from discrimination. You can't understate how important the sexual and pregnancy discrimination laws and the Family Medical Leave Act are for women in the United States. You can just point to the issues in the Presidential Election in 2008. Women and family issues are significant parts of the platforms of both parties.

Also, the quality and attitude toward early education has completely changed since I had Rachel. The federal childcare block grant passed in 1990 supports early education in every US state. Study after study has proven that children benefit from early education, so daycare centres are no longer stigmatised. When I told people that I had Rachel in an amazing and supportive daycare centre, I was treated like I was committing child abuse. Now more than 75% of preschool age children are in some form of early development program.

Has anything become worse?

I wrote an article in 2000 in *Ms* magazine called 'Friendly for Whose Family?' that looked at the distribution for family friendly benefits and found that the people who need them the least, management, generally, are the ones who receive the lion's share of the benefits. If anything that divide has got worse. I have done some research for an update to the story and it looks like we're going to have to accomplish parity through public policy because employers are more stubborn now that there is a labour surplus.

In times of labour shortages – or in times of labour shortages in emerging industries (high-tech, communications, pharmaceuticals), companies are actively engaged in trying to recruit and retain workers and therefore very bullish on work family balance issues. In times of labour surplus, simply put, not so much. When there's no motivation, it's easier to slide back into old grooves and habits, which are employment practices and attitudes that are fundamentally biased toward active parenting.

And, if you look at the statistics, men's engagement in childcare and housework has changed the least. Domestic issues are still largely a women's problem.

What can we do to make a change?

For the first time in the major political arena, presidential candidates are talking about early childhood education, and not as an after-thought. It's high up there in the conversation.

And you can continue to help change the attitudes toward working women. When I had Rachel, everything about my life was determined by the fact that I was a mother. Why are we still making mothers feel guilty about choosing work *and* family?

If there was a romance when I was young, it was about women going into the workplace. The new romance is around women going home and being the perfect mother and homemaker. There is not much at all in the data to indicate that it is actually happening, but it's being romanticised. If anything once you have children, you feel more need for the additional income and that's where women are really challenged.

Discrimination is harder for younger women to see. The fact that a woman could be fired for becoming pregnant is an outrage now. But discrimination now is not as black and white. Are you being discriminated against because you are no longer in the running for the big job after becoming a mother?

A Final Note

The amazing thing about becoming a mother is you just don't know how it is going to affect you. We had a similar experience writing this book. We thought we had all of the answers – we were very, very in touch with both our frustrations and our failures, and thought we had created systems to work smarter. We also demanded support on the home front.

But the more interviews we did and the more studies we read, the more we realised that we're still very much a work in progress, too. The women's stories that we share in this book all taught us important lessons about time management and the importance of planning ahead but what really struck us was that the women who were really flourishing in both roles had two things in common: 1) they settled for good enough and 2) they had a supportive partner *or* hired a supportive infrastructure to share the load. Good partners or nannies seem to be the key to success because they mitigate the mother guilt. Penelope Trunk said it best, 'women can't be good at their jobs if they don't trust that their children are being cared for properly.' And that's the secret.

If you can go to work trusting (and that is a loaded word on purpose) that your children are safe and loved, then you miss only a couple of beats at work when you return from maternity leave. If you have ongoing stresses and pressures about the kids' well-being, then it's really hard to do a good job.

And after hearing more times than we can count during the writing of this book statements like: 'I'm trying to juggle my work and family' and 'I'm looking to achieve a work/life balance', we're going to go out on a limb and recommend you give up on both of those goals. Right now.

You're not a circus performer. The art of juggling takes years to perfect and, frankly, you don't have the time. Look at it another way: even the most accomplished jugglers drop the ball some-times. Do you really want to choose what hits the ground – your career or your family? You don't control enough factors in your work or your family life to keep the balance. One sick kid and there it goes. We're visual thinkers. We don't like to think about our balls hitting the ground or our butts slamming down when the seesaw goes out of balance.

So instead of juggling, try aiming for harmony instead. The goal is to get all part of your life into agreement and that requires communication and negotiation at home and at work. And remember your life isn't written in stone. The most professionally identified woman we know has decided to become a stay-at-home mum while another who swore to us she would *never* put their child in daycare decided to do just that three weeks into her mater-nity leave. If you find yourself going back to work and loving it, you may still desire to change your schedule, gravitate towards different projects or make a career change.

So the lesson is keep an open mind, and start training yourself to cut down and cut back – you can't do it all. We know, easier said than done, but start taking steps. Choose one hour of your day and focus on one thing only. If you choose work, pick a task and immerse yourself in it completely. Don't check email. Don't answer the phone. Don't chat with someone. Just complete the task with full focus. We guarantee you will be amazed by two things: 1) the speed with which the task gets completed and 2) how happy you are with the final product. Little by little start applying it to all aspects of your life. But start slowly. It's very difficult to make a paradigm shift all at once. Your goal is to stop juggling everything by the end of three months.

Motherhood is one of the most profound experiences you can have and it will change you in infinite ways. As with any major life upheaval, it will inspire you to take stock of what you want and what you value. Take the opportunity to evaluate your goals and priorities. Get to know yourself and the job you're in a little better. Are you comfortable blurring the lines between work and home or do you need to establish stricter boundaries? How important is your job? What do you want out of your professional life now? Do you want to pull back from your career or put in more energy?

As you are getting used to working while parenting, you want to keep open all options available to you. You also want to maintain a solid relationship and great reputation so you can negotiate from a position of strength should you decide to make a professional change.

Ultimately, we hope this book gave you the tools and inspiration you need to be the most capable, confident and fulfilled working mother you can be.

Good luck. We're rooting for you.

Resources

RESEARCH

- *Not Guilty! The Good News for Working Mothers* by Betty Holcomb
- *The Best Friend's Guide to Maternity Leave* by Betty Holcomb
- *Down Came the Rain: My Journey Through Post-Partum Depression* by Brooke Shields
- The U.S. Equal Employment Opportunity Commission, the government agency in charge of administering and enforcing the Pregnancy Discrimination Act: www.eeoc.gov/facts/fs-preg.html
- Americans with Disabilities Act: www.ada.gov/
- U.S. Department of Labor/Family Medical Leave Act: www.dol.gov/esa/whd/fmla/
- www.babycenter.com
- www.wikipedia.com
- *Working Mother*: www.workingmother.com
- MumsRising: www.mumsrising.org
- Center for Work and The Family: www.centerforworkandfamily.com
- Kaiser Family Foundation: www.kff.org
- Sloan Work and Family Research Network: wfnetwork.bc.edu/
- U.S. Office of Personnel Management: www.opm.gov
- Council on Accreditation: www.coa.org
- Child Care Inc.: www.childcareinc.org

- www.kidshealth.org
- National Association for the Education of Young Children: www.naeyc.org

CAREER ADVICE

- *A Manager's Guide to Hiring the Best Person for Every Job* by DeAnne Rosenberg
- *The Girl's Guide to Starting Your Own Business* By Caitlin Friedman and Kimberly Yorio
- *The Girl's Guide to Being a Boss without Being a Bitch* By Caitlin Friedman and Kimberly Yorio
- *The Girl's Guide to Kicking Your Career into Gear* By Caitlin Friedman and Kimberly Yorio
- www.monster.com
- www.ycmedia.com
- www.girlsguidetobusiness.com
- www.flexibleexecutives.com

FINANCIAL ADVICE

- www.moneysupermarket.com
- www.thisismoney.co.uk
- http://moneycentral.msn.com
- www.moneysavingexpert.com

UK RESEARCH

- Office of Public Sector Information for the Employment Rights Act:
  www.opsi.gov.uk/acts/acts1996/ukpga_19960018_en_1 and the Sex Discrimination Act:
  www.opsi.gov.uk/si/si2008/uksi_20080656_en_1
- www.direct.gov.uk
- Mumsnet: www.mumsnet.com

Index